# OUTCAST
## ~1883~

*FLATS JUNCTION SERIES*
BOOK 3

# SARA DAHMEN

OUTCAST 1883

Copyright ©2022 by Sara Dahmen

Promontory Press
www.promontorypress.com

ISBN: 978-1-77374-102-4

Cover designed by Edge of Water Design
Typeset by Spica Book Design
Interior Artwork Copyright © 2022 Sara Dahmen
Printed in Canada

0 9 8 7 6 5 4 3 2 1

*To my three children*
*and to John, moja miłość*
*for without you, where would I belong?*

CHAPTER ONE

# Marie

*January 24, 1883*

The thin line of bronze glimmers like a golden vein between the battered copper of the old kettle and the black of a thousand fires, but it's the holes in between the chopped teeth of the copper seam that worry me.

If the seam splits, I won't be able to hide the repair. *Piekło! Oh hell!*

Even though I'm the only copper and tin smith for near one hundred miles around, Kate Davies, owner of the General Store, has never entrusted me with any of her repair work.

Until now.

Kate prefers to use her inherited wealth to order new kettles or cups when hers start to leak. Whether it's spite or simply a preference for city-made, pressed tin goods . . .

Well. I've never asked.

But this. This copper heirloom piece her father left her? Brought by his grandmother from her native Wales?

This Kate refused to ship East to fix.

I shuddered when I first looked inside, but my pride didn't let me speak. It's not an easy repair. And Kate is not an easy woman.

Then again, neither am I, as my husband has long reminded me.

After staring for another moment at the seam, I add more coal to the large tin brazier to raise the furnace temperature higher. The winter wind tears around the corner of the shop, and I shiver in spite of the heat and raise my puckered, scar-crossed fingers to the small flames growing around the fuel. In the deep corners of shadow, fresh tin cups sparkle on sanded shelves. More tinkle from strings on the low blackened beams of the ceiling. There is a new chink in the wall next to the shelves. The mid-afternoon sunlight jolts through it.

The whine of the wind in the crack becomes a scream. I should clog it.

I turn from Kate's repair, unwilling—or perhaps unable—to tackle it. What do they call this? Hysteria? Refusal? Laziness?

Taking up the latest broadsheet on my counter, I glance at the headline again:

**Local Posse? Or Lawmen?**

Ah! A good distraction. Who should the town pay for protection?

At the bottom is a large ad paid jointly by Lara O'Donnell and Sadie Fawcett, looking for a seamstress able to create the latest fashions. Shaking my head at the frivolousness, I

2

crinkle the paper and stuff it in the chinking's hole, putting an end to the wind's intrusion.

I turn to check on the coals and peer at the kettle once more. The bottom and sides both are put together with the handmade seams that a woodworker would call dovetail. Sometimes I make new pots with such cramp seams, when the jagged, tooth-like shapes are carefully fit together, overlapping slightly, and then heated and hammered into one thickness before I braze the cracks with high heat and tin, creating bronze and making the vessel watertight. This I do with new copper, in the next room using Thaddeus's forge at high heat, with his blacksmithing tongs and anvil. One of our old apprentices, Jeremiah, kept the bellows running so the fire was hot enough. Now I think on it, I haven't done any cramp seams since Jeremiah left for the far West. Thaddeus vowed to find more help, but that was two years ago.

I stare at Kate's kettle.

The copper will gleam when it's clean.

I think of that while I heat where the side seam meets the bottom of the kettle, where the metal is most frail and the leak is the worst. My hope is to heat it enough to spread the copper out a little, though that will make it thinner, and then clean and braze the remaining spaces shut with more bronze.

That is, if I don't create a bigger hole with too hot a fire or hammer the wrong place and force the brittle copper to break further.

I wish this were all more precise! Even after decades as a full smith, I am always reminded of my strangeness.

One wrong repair could ruin me.

My position is always fragile, no matter how many tea kettles I repair or pots I fix.

Frowning at the muck crusted under the rolled top and at the heavy globs of old tin leaking through the widening cracks in the seam, I wonder if I will be able to balance the fragile copper and the heat. It's possible I could melt a hole in it. Or create more leaks instead of less.

If I fail …

If I fail, and it all splits or burns, I will have to admit to the failure. Will I lose business? Perhaps. Will Kate turn against me? Of course. She already considers me suspect. Less than a woman.

Could I make another? Maybe. Except it would not be her great-grandmother's, and the beauty of the heirloom is because it is just that.

Would Kate hold it against our family?

She wouldn't keep us from our credit at the General, would she?

She wouldn't starve my children …

*Stop!* I won't fail. I have been over this how many times?

I am a smith. I have proven it.

I've been one since 1865, and even after my father and brothers died, when there was no one left to keep the business alive!

The heat of the tin furnace inches through the sheep wool I use to hold the kettle over the coals. Finally, the copper starts to discolor with warmth, the metal rolling with red and yellow, blue and green. Quickly, I slide Kate's precious family treasure over the long beakhorn stake and raise the worn rawhide hammer. One fast, hard tap, and I should know if it works.

"MAMA!"

4

My arm crashes with utter loss of precision on the weakest point of the teakettle's bottom side seam, splitting it open and cracking the copper so deeply it spiders up the side and through the base.

The hammer slips along the copper's side, and the kettle spins on the edge of the tinner's anvil, gouging the bottom with a deep dent. Ruined further!

"*Cholera! Shit!*"

I fling the hammer on the damp, cold earth of the shop floor and swing my palm across Urszula's soft cheek. The hit is flat and thin.

"What the hell are you doing in here?"

She sucks in her breath at the reprimand, and her tears mirror the ones clawing up my throat. She spins around and runs into the house, and I deflate at once. My gentle, youngest daughter who rarely disobeys. She would only come in if she truly needed me. The thought sticks.

What could she possibly need?

I pause, torn between the needs of the tin shop and the distress of my daughter. I dislike leaving the tools in disarray and the coals fuzzy with red-orange glow. I never leave the tin shop without tidying the fat wooden counters at least. And my heavy book with my fanciful sketches and horrible attempt at bookkeeping sits out for any visitor to see.

Damnation.

I march through Thaddeus's forge, realizing belatedly that he's not at his fire. As I reach the thick oak door separating the house from the metal shops, the door behind me yanks open.

"Marie!"

I turn, and my lungs frost over with the cold air blasting in and the vision of my husband storming through, Doctor Patrick Kinney a step behind. Following the doc is Jane Weber – Jane Kinney, I remind myself.

"What is it?" My voice rises with shock.

My husband slams his thick palm into the door. It bangs open and I hurry with him, the small hairs on my neck aware of Doc Kinney's harried breathing.

In the kitchen, the air is stifling with heaviness. Thaddeus shoves past the glossy stove and open hearth, where soup pops overloudly.

Doc Kinney overtakes me, matching Thaddeus's stride. Our four children cluster around the bed brought near the fire, none jerking back as the deep wheeze and startling choke of their grandfather cuts through the room.

Thaddeus pushes Kaspar and Natan over without ceremony, and Helena moves to sit on the edge of the bedding next to Berit, my queenly mother-in-law. She clutches Walter's gnarled, quivering fingers as he attempts to take another breath, but it only sounds like a gasp. His skin looks pale and blue, as if he is cold and not burning with a fever.

Doc Kinney takes one look at Walter, and immediately opens his bag.

"Water. Hot!" he barks, and Jane jumps, taking over my kitchen as if it is her own, pulling a pot and a pitcher from a sideboard. My hands feel thick and clay-like, clenching and unclenching.

It must be dire, for Thaddeus to have gone for the doc.

No one moves as Doc Kinney opens Walter's mouth and prods his neck. He grimaces. Behind us, Jane's tinkling in the cupboards sounds riotous.

The instruments Doctor Kinney lifts from his old worn bag shine, a silver gleam with an edge of deadliness. I do not like the saws, the knives. Ice pours into my blood, and my own breathing feels tight.

But Walter's breathing is worse. Each inhale sounds shorter and smothered and stale. Doctor Kinney puts an instrument to Walter's chest, and Berit grips him tighter.

"He's far gone," Doc Kinney says. Perhaps he speaks to Thaddeus, Berit, me, or all of us together. "I'm not sure anythin' I can do will save him."

He picks up a small knife, and Thaddeus goes still next to me. His fingers fumble at my wrist, pinching the fabric and the edge of my skin.

"You're a doc, aren't you?" I ask, unable to mask the fear and sarcasm. "You're supposed to be better than the last one."

Doctor Kinney's blue eyes glance up, but they are clouded and he seems beyond the reality of our hot kitchen and chilly winter day. Jane bustles up, a small copper kettle filled with steaming water. The doctor takes a moment to dip his shiny tools into the boiling liquid.

Walter's next inhale stops halfway, and the world shifts under my feet.

"No!"

The cry is Helena, and I do not know if it is because Walter is not breathing or because the doctor turns and at once slides a knife along the loose skin of Walter's throat.

Thaddeus jerks as the instrument slices into his father's neck, and I grip his bicep as the muscles turn to rock.

"Let him try," I mutter, for his ears only, but Kaspar is hanging over my shoulder and hears every word. "You brought him here."

Thaddeus shoots me a black look. Next to him, Natan turns white, then green as he stares at the doctor's deft stroke and probe, as blood spurts on the damp flannel of Walter's shoulders.

The moment stretches, and Walter doesn't breathe again.

The doctor sits back and sighs, wiping the blood on a rag Jane hands him. She finds my eyes as she plays the nurse, and I fear I look wild and shaken, because she turns away from me almost at once.

"Well?" Thaddeus demands. "What is it?"

Doctor Kinney shakes his head and puts the glinting knife back into the steaming kettle.

"It's too late."

"Too late!" My voice rises. "Too late for what?"

"He was too sick, too long." The doctor takes back his instruments and stands, placing them back in his bag with careful speed. His shoulders sink slightly, and Jane hands him his Stetson. He meets my eyes, then Thaddeus's. "No fee. I'm very sorry."

The couple departs, and no one turns to walk them out.

We are stuck, staring at the body in the bed. It was so instant. So fast.

Walter is dead.

It's a cold, sudden jolt to see him without the constant shaking and twitches and jerks. It's eerie and shocking in a way I cannot grasp at first. It's only when Berit folds her slim fingers over Walter's thick, snarled ones that I pull in a breath.

Try as I might to ignore the dread, his death feels like a harbinger in my entire reality, and my body protests against it with every fiber. Another death. Less than a year after I last miscarried. It cannot all be happening again ... so much loss.

I wipe my sticky, flux covered fingers on the frayed edge of my leather apron and reach to squeeze Berit's shoulders with my scarred hands. When I bend my dark head so our cheeks whisper together, the line-feathered skin of her jaw is soft. A waft of potatoes and sage and faintly sour milk surrounds me, and in the next intake of her air, a shudder jerks through her, hard and deep and crackling.

Kaspar sniffs loudly. He's already twelve, but tears drip off his long dark lashes and glide through the grime of his cheeks, tracing spidery paths along the circles of his cheekbones. I'd like to smile at him, give him some sign that it is alright to be sad, but Thaddeus won't approve if I encourage sentiment in the boys.

Helena, our eldest, frowns at Kaspar as he grinds his palm into his face, her smooth black hair barely in place and her body stiff. She pokes him in the side. He only shifts away from his big sister, and the tears continue. Natan has not moved, taking it all in, a copy of Thaddeus in all ways.

"Is *Babcia grandmother* going to be alright?" Urszula whispers, tugging at my skirt.

I kneel next to her and notice how white and round her eyes are as she watches Berit smooth out Walter's cooling brow.

"She'll be fine, in time," I whisper back, and offer a one-armed embrace before standing.

My own grief rises up and chokes any further words. It's an iron ball, a black and screaming weight, and is as familiar today as it was when I first felt the bite of it.

9

Walter's bulk takes up most of the sheets; his withered limbs still oddly great, boasting of a long-lost strength. We all stare at Berit's hunched shoulders as a silent sob shakes the entire bed.

I have wept like that before, and I might when the heavy dirt of Walter's grave cuts the earth. Or I will let tears fall when I trace the copper marker for his tombstone, and the slice of the snips carves out the finishing touch of his life.

What can I put on his marker? There are so many things. *Father. Beloved Father-In-Law ... Grandfather.* A good man, a strong one. Kind and accepting and calm. And always there to bolster me even when I had lost all my blood kin.

My husband's arms twine tightly across his wide chest as he frowns down at the collapsed, quiet form of his father.

"So then, Marya. We won't be able to bury him with the frozen ground. He'll have to go to the old livery building with the others," Thaddeus says curtly.

I am disconcerted briefly by his brusqueness. "I know, Tadeusz, but let it be for a moment."

"Mm." He chews on his mouth and tugs on his beard hard, but the softness touches his eyes when I use his given Polish name, and it is enough to quiet him. The grey in his black hair seems whiter, tickling the edges of his ears, and a worry snakes through me as familiar as grief. I'm sure there is grey in my own dark crown, mirroring Thaddeus's. We are not as young as we were when we married back in '67, when Flats Junction was only known on the maps as Flats Town.

Walter's death reminds me of how quickly life disappears in the Dakota Territory.

What has Thaddeus always said to me? *Death is the way of it.*

But that does not take away its bite.

I try to keep a steady eye on everyone and think what I must do to keep some semblance of calm around the sorrow, even though I want to disappear into the tin shop and ignore the sadness pouring through everyone.

They'll all be looking to me to make something edible for dinner, what with Berit beside herself. What should I cook? Can I even remember how to do it? I grasp at these tangible things, clouding my ears to the fidgeting of my children, the clamor of the damn chickens outside, and the heavy silence of my husband. My mind races with thoughts: the small farm to manage, the work in the shop—both mine and Thaddeus's—the food to finish. Should I send Helena or Natan to run for Father Jonathon? We hadn't even had time for last rites.

Damn the incompetence of the doctor!

Or is it us to blame? Were we wrong to believe that it was only a cough and a cold and old age and a fever?

It's been long since I've had to wrestle with a death that belongs to me—my parents and brothers and unborn babes. I've made a new family with children and in-laws of my own. And while Thaddeus and I have watched friends lose life, limb, and livelihood, we ourselves have been fortunate.

I cannot help but believe, deep in my soul, that Walter's death begins the corrosion of my latest attempt to cobble a family together. It's all so delicate, this lineage of ours.

Will Berit be next? One of the children? My husband? Me?

As I think of Thaddeus, the air shifts. Smoke and coal and sweat surround me when he comes near and intertwines his ridged, scarred fingers with mine. It is a habitual gesture, built on history and comfort and memory, and when I look up into his height, the grey eyes glitter once, briefly. Leaning into him, shifting a step back, our bodies melt as the fabric between us slides and rasps. It's as if we were forged separately and then placed together as a well-cut fit.

"Mama, are you sad too?" Urszula asks, still whispering. Her question ends in a heavy clearing of her throat, her own eyes trickling.

"Of course I am," I say softly, and pat her black plaits again with a heavy hand. She leans into me, slim arms curling around her father's waist as well.

Thaddeus looks down at the whorl of her soft cowlick, as if surprised to find her there.

"So now what happens?" Helena asks briskly, harshly, her rough hands on the worn blue calico of her skirts, and twitching along the fine stitching and embroidery she adds to all her clothes. "Do we just wait for the doc to come back and do a laying out?"

Thaddeus suddenly comes to life. "No," he booms. "And I wouldn't have Doc Kinney do anything more anyway."

I frown up at him. "You just brought him here!"

"A last resort."

"Asking the doc to undertake your father is hardly—"

"I'm not the only one in Flats Junction to think he's *niebezpieczny dangerous*. And now we've proof!"

"We haven't any proof other than you were too stubborn to get him sooner!"

"The doc slit his throat! The sawbones! I—"

"He was dead before that—you know it!"

Thaddeus presses his mouth together hard and folds his arms tight.

Damnation. I clench my scarred hands into the heavy flannel of my dress, fingering the edges of my leather apron as I do. So much to consider! Walter's funeral without a laying out, winter's coldness … Kate's damaged kettle! My legs sway under me suddenly, and Thaddeus absently grips my elbow with thumb and forefinger, regardless of our argument.

Slowly, I join Helena by the hearth and check the bread in the side oven built into the stone fireplace. It's not quite ready yet, so I push it back in on the wooden paddle and glance over Helena's shoulder. I watch her skeptically as she pokes a spoon in and stirs with tentative strokes.

"Do you think we should get some of the dried herbs from the barn?" I ask her, wanting her sour attitude away from the hearth. If I must play the cook, I want it my own way. Anything to move, to ignore the body in the bed and my husband's anger.

My daughter's eyebrows knit together. "How much, Mother?"

"Just guess. Cooking's mostly guessing," I say, pushing her out of the way with a hip. "You know it's just that."

She sweeps out, her black braids flying and her shoulders pulled back against the cold. She has forgotten a shawl. I hear her cuss at the chickens as she goes out the back door. I'd reprimand her if I could, but likely she's heard those cusses from my own lips when I maneuver around the damn birds.

"I'm to the shop. Then wood for the coffin." Thaddeus tromps past. Kaspar and Natan follow.

I glance up at him, surprised, but he continues past into the blacksmith's forge without another word.

I think of my own tin and copper projects and wish I'd have the chance to dive into them myself. How I need

13

the metal and the numbers and the mechanics to escape in times like these! Well, damn. Bellies must be fed; food must be heated; plates set out; and water pulled from the joint well out back.

Well. There's no time for grief. There's work to be done, just not the type of work I'd prefer. Sighing, I stir the stew half-heartedly and push at the chunks of tomato and rabbit.

"Eggs. And the herbs," Helena announces, coming in from the late, cold sunshine. The dust from our little farm swirls around her. She forgets the door with her full arms and, beyond the yard, the empty shell of the Svendsen barn stretches across the earth, reaching for me in reproach. The line of our land ends abruptly at the doorstep of the building, and the wind sometimes whispers through the cracks in the boards just loud enough for me to hear it in the house. It sounds like the ghosts of my brothers and father, reminding me to remember them, to never forget the years spent living in there … I cannot remember my mother's voice. And beyond that is the prairie, rolling and undulating, the grasses bumping along the curves of the land. It is not like the Lake Michigan beach in Chicago, which I barely recall. But that was a rhythmic drift of waves. Here the wind kisses the grasses with an unending, muted roar in the fury of winter storms when the ice slices like the edge of newly cut tin. Or it dances across the tops of the flowers, bobbing them against one another through the heat of summer. It's never a quiet breeze.

Shutting the door, I take the herbs from Helena and pulverize them within my palms, watching the frosty green of the fronds slip into the slurry of flour and tomato and onion with some trepidation.

14

"Back into the tin shop later?" Helena asks briskly, moving around me to take down a whole stake of crockery, so matter-of-fact in the face of her grandfather's death it's a slap.

I glance up at her. "So clear to get me out of the kitchen?"

"Yes."

Her candor is jarring and yet not surprising. It seems Walter's death will loosen more things than the fabric of my carefully constructed family unit. Helena's tongue is the first thing to slip, and it is both a relief and ugly.

"Where are the boys?" she asks, glancing around the kitchen, her glance purposefully missing her grandmother and the body of her grandfather.

"Your father took them into the forge." As I mention it, the ring of hammers pounds through the heavy oak door between the shop and kitchen. I can tell which hammer strike is Thaddeus and which is Kaspar's based on the rhythm and ring of each. Thaddeus's is extra hard-and-fast today against his grief, and I flinch with the first few smashes.

"Lucky *skurwysyn bastards*," Helena mutters. "At least they can hit something when they're upset."

She turns to the bread oven with the paddle in hand. It's not a moment too soon, as the first tendrils of overdone crust curl around us. The bread is scorched on the very edges, but the smell propels Berit from her immobile seat by Walter's side.

"Oh dear, I've left the food!" she says, her blue eyes barely focused. "How long have I been sitting?"

"Not long, Mother," I say, soft as I might, using the rusty title for her.

She falters, looking once more at Walter's prone form. The bedding is yellowed and sodden with his old sweat, the rancid blooms an echo of his slow descent into the final days of life. No matter how many sprigs of fresh mint Berit tucked under his pillow all this past fall, she could not stop the smell of death.

"Oh. Well, then."

The words are a reminder of Walter's speech, and suddenly the sorrow screams inside my chest. I shove it down, focusing as best I can on Berit. "It's all not too ruined," I tell her. She gazes at the bread on the paddle Helena takes to the table, but she does not seem to actually see it.

"Mother," I repeat. "Why don't you take a seat? Urszula? Come here," I beckon my younger daughter closer.

Urszula sidles away from Walter's side, where she's been staring at her grandfather's melted, slack face.

"Set the table, will you? Then tell your Father that you and Natan will go to the O'Donnell's for the lumber."

"Yes, mama."

We'll make our own casket. We can afford the store-bought coffins if we skimped on some sugar and molasses for a month, but I don't like to use Kate's store more than necessary.

"I'll go to the lumber yard." Helena jumps into the conversation. "Urszula can stay and comfort Grandmother." She says the last bit almost belatedly, as if offering an excuse.

"You're going to run errands?" I lift my eyebrows. Her hands clench slightly, once, and then relax as she gazes straight at me. Our dark eyes meet and clash, bouncing uncertainty and misunderstanding back and forth. I would like to know more of my daughter's mind so many times. Instead, I'm often confounded by her choices.

16

"I can manage this," she says stoutly, already marching out the door. "I'm almost fifteen, Mother."

She's gone into the waning sunlight before I can open my mouth again.

Urszula stares at me, her coffee-colored eyes wide, and I gesture wordlessly to the place beside Berit on the long bench at the kitchen table.

As my daughter sits, she coughs twice, the second louder than the first.

The harshness of it reminds me of Walter's croup. Worry skitters through me again as I stir the soup and slice the bread. I want to run from it all. I want to be back in the shop.

I have so carefully created a family and a life and a trade. I don't wish to deal with death, with illness, with the recognition of the loss sure to come this winter, when sickness can wash over the town in a ravenous hunger.

My attention jerks back to Urszula as my daughter coughs once more. Disruption such as this can pull on my deep weakness. Any unknown threatens my mind's strength every time, no matter how hard I try to ignore the yank of the darkness. It is always lurking inside.

*She will be fine.*

I squeeze my eyes shut and push into the thought. *We all will be safe.*

It cannot all collapse, or I will be lost.

## CHAPTER TWO

# Kate

*January 27, 1883*

No one is in the store today except Horeb and Gil. The snap of Horeb's suspenders is twice as twangy in the silence. The floors go on creaking of their own accord.

Outside, another blizzard gasps across the wide prairie and undulates into and over my town in gusts and gales.

The warmth of the big stove has yet to kick its heat into the far corners of the room, and I wonder whether Patrick will have to go out into the storm.

*Stop.*

It's not my place to think of the doctor anymore. It's a habit I must break.

The wind smashes itself across the panes, and pounds arrows of snow against the General's brittle walls. I narrow my eyes at the clouds, and push pins deeper into the thick, slippery strands of hair at my nape.

Days like this, I wish for anyone to walk in, just to keep me from my own thoughts.

Finally, the warmth of the stove curls around my ankles.

"Cheat, is it?" Horeb screeches.

I jump in my seat, though the accusation is one I'm used to hearing near every day.

"Ain't," Gil says.

"Sure is, I seen you move backwards! With my own eyes, don't I?"

"Nope."

I sigh loudly, and set to tapping a pencil against the fat wood of the counter. It shuts their mouths, the tapping.

But it sounds too like a fancy wind-up clock, reminding me of time past and time ahead. Things I must do if I am to keep everyone on their toes, everyone needing my store. Needing me.

So I can be good for something. Needed for everything.

Then again, if everyone in Flats Junction goes on so sickly and dies ...

As I think it, Bern Masson swirls in, a dark mass spinning in from the cold. His black eyes meet mine through the oily lamplight and grey gloom and a shiver runs up and down my back, quick-like. I never know if it's fear or resignation or excitement.

"Braved the weather, boy?" Horeb cackles.

Bern ignores him and stalks toward me, all long muscle and clean-shaven. When he comes up to the counter, he's still close enough that I can smell him—the cattle, the bunkhouse sweat, the horses.

"Didn't expect anyone here," he says to me in a near whisper.

I glance over his shoulder at Horeb and Gil, and give him a small shake of my head.

"Danny give you boys a day off?" I ask, my voice at normal sound. "For the weather?"

"The Svendsen ranch hands will never have a day off," he says, taking my hint and slouching a bit under his hat with what I take to be disappointment. "We're short as it is."

"How many more?"

Chairs go off creaking as Horeb and Gil lean in, no pretense.

Bern folds his arms, clad in worn leather and wool, over the smooth wood next to the register. "Four."

"Dead?"

"Not yet."

"They're going to run out of room in the old livery, what with all the coffins stacking up," I say, trying not to visualize the rows of rough coffins with the frozen bodies of old and young waiting for burial come spring.

"It'll stink to all edges of the world come March," he says grimly.

Bile rises in my throat at the thought of it. Bern glances at me and seems to reconsider his grisly chatter. I don't know why he bothers. We've more history between us than either of us wishes to say—will ever say.

"Have you heard yet what it is?" I ask.

"You know I hold no mind for the doc no more," he reminds, his tone rough and harsh. "Nor his ... wife."

Our eyes meet. The memories of Bern courting Jane and of the doctor courting me swarm through my mind, first gold and then broken. So many promises, broken. Jane and her declarations of friendship, which had to be hollow, as what friend steals the man a'courting another? And every-thing Patrick and I had shared … all dust, now.

Lies.

I should not be surprised. But, fool of me, I still am.

"Well, he's not stupid. Someone has to know what ails everyone—it's flying from home to home with no stopping it, neither." I stand up straighter and run my hands down my skirts. Bern watches, his face a mask of disinterest.

"I just come by to get some tea," he finally says, pulling the excuse out of thin air. "For the sickly ones what are stuck abed in the bunkhouse."

I ring him up a few blocks of it, and he tips his hat at me before walking out. It's not regret in his eyes—I'm think-ing it's disappointment. Well, he made a gamble coming out to the General, and I won't say I'm sorry to see him go. Not after thinking on Patrick as long as I have today. No one else need be crowding my head.

Horeb and Gil stand together and stretch in their own ways—Horeb like a skeletal cat, undulating with bones and sinew and Gil scratching his chest and arms.

"Best be off to get a hot meal afore it gets dark, eh Kitty?" Horeb says, by way of goodbye. He and Gil swing open the door and a scream of wind bounces in, toppling the straw hats dangling from the rafters.

I sigh again when the General is silent again.

It gets so quiet. Too quiet. I need more, or I'll spend the next decades of my life clattering around in my own head. Likely I'll go insane before then, what with all the quiet.

Just as I go to turn the latch on the door, three figures appear at the bottom of the steps and struggle up toward the porch. I squint against the shadows, and in the moment the storm blows in the objects of my musings and I can't stop my heart from thudding hard, once.

And if maybe my breathing hitches, it's probably just the cold as it takes another bite out of the stove's warmth.

"Kate!" Patrick greets me with a hesitant sparkle in his eyes and his gaze heats me up for all the work I've tried to do to forget him. My hand goes up to touch his face, only remembering right at the end that he's no longer mine and I cannot go 'round fondling other people's husbands. The vows make such a thing improper. And heaven knows he's married a proper woman. Clearly it's what he wanted—a dried-up, damaged widow—

"Just talking about you," I say, and then close my fists. "That is, we've been talking about the deaths. Any more?"

The question takes the wind out of him, and he deflates. It near gives me pleasure to see it, to watch him think back on who has died over the past week.

"Too many," Jane interjects, and I frown at her. "Even if it was one, it'd be too many."

I snort and retreat back behind the counter, crossing my arms. Behind the newlyweds, Widow Hawks pokes a finger into the flour sacks and it takes me all my will to bite my tongue on the corner and hush myself.

"Figured it out, yet?"

Patrick nods, and peers up at the bottles I've got behind me, stacked in glittery rows of brown and green and blue. "How much iodine do you have?"

"How much credit do you have?" I ask, and he flinches.

"It's not about money, Kitty, not now."

I want to strike him for daring to call me Kitty. I want to tell him to leave my store and never come back. I want to tell Jane that he's not hers, that I was supposed to marry him, that he was supposed to make my standing in Flats Junction higher. A married woman. A bigger force to be reckoned with. An immoveable pillar of the community.

Necessary.

"It's about money if I'm running a competent and fair business, Pat. I'm building something here, and it doesn't survive if I'm giving out credit to all who ask."

He stares at me for a moment, and I recognize the set of his jaw. My heels dig into the lasts of my boots. Let him try talking 'round me, now.

"It's life and death. I've a need for rubbin' alcohol, the biggest bottle of iodine you can get, and bleached cotton, nothin' else there, and have you any lime? And I'll need—"

"Stop!"

The doctor, Jane, and Widow Hawks all pause at my command, and there's a strange niggle of delight at seeing them listen so quick.

"I haven't got some of what you want, or most of the supplies in, Pat. You know the rail's not working half the time in these storms, and I'm not holding your supplies in the hopes you'll come buying once or twice a year. Not anymore. Put in an order and I'll see what I can do."

"We need a department store," Jane muses. Her eyes flash to mine, and I grind my teeth against the implication.

"Out west here doesn't need anything so fancy," I retort, feeling the jab as well as saying it. "Fancy things don't make it."

"The railroad can get the town to grow if there's enough here for people to stay," she argues, and I hate that her point is valid. "And then things like … like the …" she glances at Patrick. "The glycerine and iodine. Those things and … oysters and fine china … people will buy those things if they can."

I shake my head, but feel it spinning inside, just the same.

"I've the alcohol and the cotton, but you'll have to wait for the rest, whenever I can get an order in through the telegrams and hope it's filled in coming months," I say resolutely. "In the meantime, order what you need from your own contacts."

"I thought we could depend on you, Kate," Widow Hawks suddenly says. "I thought you'd want to play a part in saving the people of Flats Junction."

My jaw sets. "Are so many sick?"

"It's diphtheria," Jane says quietly, and at the name of the thing, an iron band seems to wind around my lungs.

Widow Hawks stares at me, her eyes a challenge and liquid with the remembering. I want to shut my own against it, and huff out through my nose to block the past.

"And why should *you* care," I hiss at her. "I have no family and no children to lose, and you left your family at Fort Randall when we brought you back from the ragged tents of … of your people. Neither of us has anything else to lose with this … disease."

"Why should I want to see more death? I would heal many if they took my herbs."

"If they'd even listen to you," Patrick counters, a touch of something in his tone. I raise my eyebrows at him. Is that jealousy? Disbelief?

He's right in that, at least. No one in Flats Junction would go running to my mother for a remedy. And yet … I

24

stare at him as if seeing him anew. Yet half of Flats Junction won't come running to him, neither. The things some say on him. The words they call him.

Perhaps it's better, in the end, that I didn't wed him. Maybe he wouldn't have been a powerful enough husband. Heaven knows the coloring of my hair and skin needs a man with some strength and backbone.

I inhale to ask them if that'll be all, as I always do when I want someone to get fast from my store before I forget to say nice things aloud, but multiple pairs of booted, heavy feet pound on the outside stairs and the porch.

"Now who is it?" I ask, testy. I'd resigned myself to the peace and quiet of the store, hadn't I, not five minutes ago! Now everyone's coming in, as if they think I'm hosting a fancy parlor meeting, or in charge of the Prime Inn, putting out those oysters Jane mentions.

For a brief moment, I imagine silks on my arms and my hair curled the way they do East, and I'm walking through town and seeing all the buildings, and I know the deeds of them are mine. The General, a real mercantile, the Prime Inn …

The door yawns open, and dark figures stream in, one after the other, all lead by Yves Gardnier, the man who styles himself important to Flats Junction ever since riding through earlier this Fall.

For a moment, I allow the buried panic to boil up, hot and fast and angry. Then it's gone, and I have the presence of mind to touch my hair, checking the pins again, and looking as if I've no care in the world.

Arnold, his skin like midnight under the brim of his wide hat and teeth flashing whiter than fresh snow, pushes in first. He grins, as if putting everyone at ease, but it only serves to make my fingers grip the counter.

Jane takes a step behind Patrick, and I realize Widow Hawks is now nothing but two bright eyes in the darker shadows behind the rusty plow.

I eye up the guns and long knives bristling on each shoulder and belt walking through my doorway. The paths between my goods, meager though they are, feel clogged with the smell of horse dung and stale clothes and black powder.

They are like a beehive. Safe from a distance but deadly when angered.

Yves's eyes are like bullets, drilling into me, as the members of his posse float around the store, touching and fondling all the items. My eyes cannot be in more than one place at once, and the tingling is back in my spine. This time, I know it's fear.

Arnold bends down, spurs singing, and admires the game left by Horeb and Gilroy.

"Checkaas?" he scoffs in a long, Tennessee drawl mixed with African twang. "A chyl's game. It's chess for men lahke me."

"Stop with zee chattering, yes." Yves shoulders past Arnold as his blue, red-rimmed eyes sweep over the board before he finds my face. Gently tugging his hat off to reveal his non-existent hair, he gives me an attempted apologetic grin. "Arnold's only proud of zee fact he did not ever be beaten in zee chess. It ees his favorite story."

He marches up to the counter with a tight swagger, and I bite my lips hard so that I do not smile at the wrong time when his small height is matched by the height of the boards. I lean over, and allow him to take my hand and brush it with his chapped lips while muttering some nonsense in French.

My eyes drift over the others as they finger the rusty plough, the jugs of horehound and tins of allspice. The room feels tense, unpredictable.

Patrick and Jane stand to the side, uncertain but unable to go—the door is near blocked and I never got him his items. Well, let them see what I can do—how I can hold my own!

I didn't need him before, not really. And I don't now, neither.

The posse has not visited Flats Junction often 'til recently. They sometimes passed through in pursuit of criminals—real or simply a rival, I never knew—or to stop for a night's rest. They always eat at the food hall Matthew Winters set up. My earliest memory is how old Harry let them fill up their saddlebags without paying. He'd said it was the price paid to have the General left in one piece.

Natty Martin sidles past Yves, the grease on his hair leaving slime marks along his buckskin-covered shoulders. His wild, hungry eyes slip on everything as his skinny thumbs rub along the edges of his pistols. If anyone will try to steal more than what will go in the saddlebags, I expect it to be Natty. I recall the stories of his ill-gotten horse and how he once shot a woman and her five children when she wouldn't give him a hot meal. If I ever caught him stealing from me …

"Matt Winters should have dinner ready at the mess," I say, hoping to distract half the group into leaving the building. "Or you might want to try The Golden Nail. Toot's cooking can't be beat, as you know."

"We are already eating there, and the food is very good tonight, yes." Yves shrugs and glances around. "You seem to be down on zee supplies. Forget how to order more as Flats Junction grows?"

My lips tighten and I breathe in once through my nose. I glance at Patrick—just out of habit, I'm thinking, because when has a man ever come to my rescue?

"I ordered well enough, but there's no train for two weeks. Weather, as it is every year." I hide my defensiveness by tossing my head. Pins slip and one skitters down near Yves boots.

There's a swoop of an overly-wide body diving for the twist of metal, and one of the men comes up for air with the pin trapped gingerly between his dusty fingers. Matthias Hummel has never spoken, so far as I've heard tell, though now he stares at me from under pale lashes as I snatch the hair piece away and shove it into my hair. If anyone speaks of Yves and his men, they mention Matthias's strength. He's a giant—blond and green-eyed—and his silence is unnerving and spooky.

Once, Sadie Fawcett whispered to me that she'd heard he'd taken an Indian lover who'd died in childbirth. I don't know if that is true, or if Sadie just wanted to pass speculation. She may have done it to make me feel as though my own life is not so very unusual. Or perhaps she wanted to see if I would react to such a tale, so similar to my own. All it does is make me unwilling to smile at Matthias.

Evan Banks, a large man with a long, matted brown hair and full beard that hides most of his squat face follows Matthias everywhere. He leans to stare at me from a moment, grunts, and then runs his eyes over the shelves before plodding to the candy counter with heavy flat-footed steps, his cracked boots spitting old leather as he goes.

28

Two others squeeze by Yves and Matthias to take the last open spots along the counter. Harry used to tell me stories about Patty Hunter and Victoria Mateman, when he wanted to remind me of what can happen to women in the west. Both Sadie and Alice Brinkley re-tell the same tale of how the two women used to entice men into their room and then slice …

They lean forward and stare dead eyes into me. Gooseflesh rips through my chest. I can't tell if they want me as a trophy, an Indian slave, or as target practice. Although I return their silent, unnerving stares, I wonder if only Yves can save me from them … for a price I'm not willing to pay. Suppose I was married? Would he bother me so, then?

Yves elbows the girls. "Enough, my sweetlings. Give me room."

The women transform into giggling girls. Patty flounces directly over to the spools of novelties strung from wooden pegs 'and along a low shelf at the side of my big counter. Tiny, child-like Victoria sticks to her side, brown eyes fixed on Patty's swaying waist.

"This one's nice," Patty prods a pink grosgrain ribbon.

"It's a lovely pink," Jane murmurs, watching them.

What is she doing? They'll notice her! I shake my head as a warning, but it's too late.

Patty's already rounding on Jane. She throws her black leather coat open and reveals a short double-barrel shotgun—the barrels and butt stock hacked off—hanging by a leather lanyard between her ample, swaying bosom.

"Pink!" she screeches. "What's wrong with pink?"

Patty steps toward Jane as every man and Victoria stare at her bouncing chest, but I'm mostly stuck on the clinking guns.

How can my evening be any worse? This. A gunfight in the General!

And then Patrick slides between Patty and his wife, a move that surprises me. So the man can speak in the face of danger, then? "I'm certain Mrs. Kinney only thinks it's goin' to be a very fine color on you."

She grabs his head and pulls it to within an inch of the black barrels. "I *know* it is!" A whirling growl leaps out of Patty's throat as she turns a deep shade of red.

Her fellow posse members step back. Evan Banks knocks over the stacked cans of peaches. The crash sends a jolt through the store. Patrick jerks backward and topples the checkerboard. The pieces clatter to the ground and roll under barrels and bins, hidden by the dust and grime. Numbly, I wonder how long it will take to find them all.

Patty pulls out a gun. "The Powdered Rose girls wear pink, yeah?" she bellows.

My mind screams for me to duck behind the counter, but I'm stunned. Glued. My toes are too heavy to shift.

"*Whores*! You mean *whores*!?" Her arm swings wide, the gun facing off every person in the store. None of Yves's men flinch, but I think my legs are frozen. "And what the fuck does that mean? Are you saying I'm a whore? The fucking whores! Goddamn. I hate every fucking whore who walks this earth, and they all should die of their own filth. Whores. As if I ever would take a man in my bed again!"

Yves takes a step forward. "That ees enough, eh? We 'ave zee business here, no need for the bullets, sweetling."

Victoria steps close and slides a hand up and down the taller Patty's back and buttock and Patty just lets the puff leave her. The gun goes back inside its holder, and Patty rolls her eyes at everyone. "Cowards," she sniffs, one veiled eye on Yves. She returns to the ribbons as if nothing has happened while Victoria pulls last year's Harper's Bazaar catalogue over and starts to page through the plates of the latest fashions.

When Yves steps back, a silver flash catches the light. He places the knife back in his belt, and notices me staring. *What in all?!* The realization hits me so hard I almost forget to school my face. Would he have stabbed his own posse member to keep her from going on a rampage? I suppose. The chills return. Damn it all … and now he wants to do dealings with me? My breath comes faster, unstoppable.

I find my tongue, try to ignore my heartbeat, and focus back on Yves, who is watching me blatantly. "I haven't seen you in Flats Junction in several months."

"Yes," Yves agrees. "But we have been busy."

"Places needed checkin'," Arnold adds, as he steps close and runs a long dark finger along the edge of my counter. "A few stores helped us stay working dee fine life." His eyes measure the state of my General in one swoop. "They're more stocked up now, thank ee to us."

"Train's late, that's all," I say again.

"Yep, broken rail," Arnold mentions. "We seen it."

Natty grunts out a laugh. "And dat engineer sure is dead! Ha. Ha."

Goddamn it! My head tips back and I exhale a bitter breath of defeat and I wish Patrick, Jane, and Widow Hawks weren't hearing me beg, because surely that's what Yves has in mind or he wouldn't come so far in the winter winds. My goods, broken track, murdered repair crew, delayed train, winter—I rock my head forward and find Yves staring back with a baleful smile cutting across his face. Without flinching, I smile back slowly, which checks his gloating. His grin falters. I have to hold this … I have to play.

"Mmm. Zat ees too bad about zee train, Kate," Yves says, his tone casual, and strolls behind the counter into my space.

My knees go tight, but I hold my ground and cross my arms. My winter supplies! I wonder how many other stores along the line have suffered and are now ripe for blackmail. *What would Father do?* The thought comes hot and fast and I turn from it. I will be more than he was. But then … he was a good blackmailer, too …

"We take zee tobacco, all of—"

"I'm out!" My patience suddenly snaps. Of course they'd want exactly what I cannot give them! I'll show them what it means to cut off a store. They won't have anything to buy!

Yves's face pinches and lips twist. "Oh?" His eyes dart across my remaining goods; the glittering case of dully gold and brass watches, the soft pile of old boots in the corner, scattered peach cans, and stop on the yellowing edges of my ledger. He wipes a hand slowly along his baldness and sighs. "Zen we will be needing other things to last us."

My belly twists, but I stiffen my back and stare straight. "You can see I don't have much because … *the train's late!*" I slap the ledger closed. "Better go to Yankton."

Arnold chokes out a wry laugh, and even Victoria grins a little. Good. Let them see my fire! I'm not as easy as Harry was.

Yves clicks his tongue in disappointment. "My dear, we are not een Yankton! We are here … now … wiz you." His voice softens. "It ees my favorite of zee prairie." He claps his hands once and loud. "We need zee supplies to protect you from zee terrible criminals. So, *mon cherie*, we'll have zee rest of your coffee, zee big box of rifle cartridges and zee shotgun shells. For zee ladies."

Patty clears her throat and taps her shotgun.

Victoria looks up from the catalogues. "Peaches, you promised!"

Yves threw his hands. "Ah yes! We'll take all of zee shotgun shells and as many of zee cans of zee peaches, yes?" He nods.

"*All* the shotgun shells?" If I'm short of dry supplies, people will have to hunt more. They'll need that ammunition. I've never been out before ... *What is happening? How can I stop this bleeding of my very world?*

"Boss," Arnold calls out as he points down at the flour and sugar sacks. "We needin' this too." He bends over the sacks. "There is some cah-fee!"

Yves waves his hand. "Take it, take it all."

As the dark man takes my remaining stock of sugar, both white and brown, flour, and coffee, I write it all down in the back page, where Harry showed me the past items he gave to Yves. He'd said it was for safety. It could be held over their heads someday. Maybe. Arnold, his arms full of different sacks, shuffles toward the door and bumps into unsteady and simple Evan, who falls back against the plow.

He yelps, as shrill and high as a wounded puppy and jerks away, stuffing a fat finger into his mouth.

Matthias moves to Evan's side, steady and calm, and takes the hand, inspecting it. After a few seconds, he shrugs.

The air ripples. Widow Hawks suddenly bends over Evan's cut, her steely head bound in the long braid along her back. I want to shout at her to go away, so they don't see us together. I don't want them to compare our faces, but they're all watching her every move.

When she steps away, the wound is bound. Evan looks at his finger, as if surprised by the dressing. Arnold loads him up with two huge sacks of flour and he tromps out the door.

Yves's shiny head swings back and forth between Patrick and Jane, and then Widow Hawks. His eyes narrow and he slips toward them.

"Mrs ... Kinney, you are saying?" he asks, his lilt a sing-song. "So this is zee doctor I am hearing so much in zee mess hall tonight? Zee one who brings back ..." His eyes turn to Widow Hawks. "Zee problem."

"Problem?" I chortle, then clamp my lips together.

Too late. Yves turns to me, eyebrows ever higher. "Yes. They is saying maybe it is her fault, you see. Or, the fault of zee doctor and his brand new wife."

"Yves, speak straight. It's how we do it here," I snap, my nerves finally nearing their worst. I just want them out of my store, out of Flats Junction, and for the train to come soon. Most of all, I want my store back under my complete control. "What is said?"

"Zee sickness what is killing. Zee sickness you brought back, when you are bringing back zee ..." Yves trails off, his eyes hazy as he stares at Widow Hawks. "Zee *savage*!" He finds the word with glee, saliva glistening in the corners of his mouth.

Patrick and Jane are immoveable statues, and Widow Hawks slinks backward, deeper into the store. Maybe it will swallow her. Maybe she'll disappear.

Maybe then all my troubles will turn to triumphs, if only she would leave me alone.

"Yves!" I say loudly at his back just before he grabs the door handle. "You aren't thinking of leaving without paying me?"

He turns, smiles thinly and shakes his head. "Of course we will be paying zee bill. Next time, maybe, when we have zee money."

"What?" I storm around the counter. "You took more than Harry—more than usual! And you've left no coffee and no ammunition! And it's winter!"

Natty places himself between me and the door, grinning. His teeth are black along the edges, and there's a piece of chewed bread sticking to the edge of his mouth.

I stare at it, repulsed, and my fists open and close. I clear my throat. "Damn it, you owe me, Yves. For this and for the damn train."

"*Oui.* Next time." He leaves without looking back, Natty following, and the entire posse disappears into the swirl of white and darkening afternoon.

I slap my hands over my face. I just gave away my goods to the very ones who sabotage the train to keep supplies from arriving in the first place!

And—worse—I have witnesses.

I glare at Jane and Patrick and Widow Hawks. "Well, you heard the man. Get out, before you spread that sickness to me!"

"Kate—the supplies ..." Patrick's mouth trembles, and a piece inside of me breaks at the small tell. He cares too much for his patients to be afraid of the posse and is definitely not of me.

I fling the rubbing alcohol and the bleached cotton at him. "It's all you're getting, what with your poor credit. All I can *afford* to give you!"

Let him see how much he needs me, let him wish he'd treated me well! Let Jane bemoan how unfortunate it is that they cannot get what they need, not without me!

My heart bangs in my chest as I think of what I have just lost. How will I tell everyone there is no more easy ammunition? How will I manage their glares when they want coffee? How can I still be ... what I want to be? Who I *must* be?

"Take it, and go, before anyone thinks I've sickness in the store!"

"Kate, you know it's not true—" Patrick pauses when Jane puts a hand on his arm. His immediate yield to her grates on me further.

"I'm closing. Now!"

I march to the door and fling it open. The doctor and Jane leave at once, stepping back out into the swirls and holding onto the rope that will take them along home in the dark. Widow Hawks will go with them—she chose, in the end, to stay with them.

Her head is high as she passes me, and she stops. I want to shove her out, and my hand twists on the door. "You know how the diphtheria spreads. How it kills. Daughter—"

"I haven't forgotten. You won't let me forget. Go."

She floats out, following Jane and Patrick, and I slam and bolt the door. For a long moment, long enough that a candle snuffs, I stand with my back to the oak and let the shaking slide out of me. I won't sink to the floor and cry. I'm not a fool and I'm not weak. I'm not!

Slowly, I step back up to the counter and even more slowly do I close the ledger showing my lost supplies and my—Yves's—debt. Patrick's list of hopeful supplies catches my eye. I crumple it.

Then I trail my hand on the board under the counter, where a large bottle of iodine clinks alone on the shelf.

CHAPTER THREE

# $\mathcal{J}ane$

*January 29, 1883*

Patrick devours his dinner of flapjacks, tucking them into his stomach before the rising steam can reach the ceiling.

I wonder whether he will have to go out today, to count the dead, to hear the rattle in the chest, to convince parents it's not just the croup but something worse. I'd rather he stay in, and perhaps regale me with more stories about his apprenticeship in Boston, or why he studied animal husbandry before focusing on people and their ailments. Or perhaps we could sit side by side at his office desk, under the ochre light from the lamp and try to organize his messy files and books. Although this is my second marriage, it is nothing like my first, and I am still adjusting.

"Will you want some more tea?" I ask him, cupping my chin in my hand and meeting his blue eyes with my brown ones. "Or do you need to go on any patient rounds?"

He glances outside. "I have no need to be anywhere for now."

"Paperwork, then?" I ask him.

He smiles at me, the corners of his eyes bunching into true mirth lines. "Jane, we've a lifetime to manage my office. Do you have things you must do?" He waves his hand, encompassing the whole kitchen. "Other than the dishes, that is."

I shrug. Of course I have things I must do. But I have Widow Hawks—*Esther!*—to help with the chores around the house. And even then, a woman's work is never done—planting and cooking, washing and cleaning, preserving and managing the costs of the household expenses.

She comes in now through the back kitchen door, cat-like and smooth, in her mix of hides and calico, the steel braid swinging. With one fluid movement she drops the firewood next to the stove. My eyes rake over the rest of the kitchen, then land on the pantry.

"We're out of eggs," I mention. "So I'll run to the General for some. Maybe … maybe we can bring in pullets in a few months?"

"Do you have someone who can get you chicks?" Patrick asks.

I hesitate, choked on the answer. Yes. And no.

"I'm … sure I can find someone."

"Marie Kotlarczyk hates chickens—she'd probably be glad to give you some to keep her flock down," he tells me, always able to supply gossip, given his rounds with patients, to the finest detail.

"She's a whole family of growing children to feed!" I protest.

"Well, they're all down now—the younger two, anyway—with the diphtheria," Patrick says. "No one is eating much, I'd guess."

"Well, I'll see if she's in, too, then," I say, resigning myself to facing two women who treat me frosty instead of just one.

"I'll clean the dishes if you wish to go to the General," Esther says gently. "I am sure Katherine would prefer you do the shopping, Jane."

I glance at her, my eyebrows rising. She shrugs one shoulder. I suppose she's correct—I'm the lesser of the two evils, perhaps, in Kate's eyes. Then again, who can understand the mercurial moods undulating inside of that woman. Perhaps today she'd prefer to see her mother, instead of the woman who stole her beau.

My reflex is first to brush off the offer, but I must stop thinking of myself as a housekeeper. I'm not one, anymore, just like I'm not a widow, either. I'm a wife again.

It's very strange and disconcerting to realize I no longer will be paid to clean the floors, wash clothes, cook meals, or even blacken the stove. It is all mine, just as the good doctor is mine.

"Pick up some lime for me, too, will you?" Patrick asks from the table. The question is casual and simple, but Esther and I exchange a glance, lightning fast. Has he already forgotten Kate's anger?

Rising, I head to the hallway for my wraps against the January ice and wind, which creeps through the floorboards and walls no matter how heavy I dress.

Esther meets me there as I wind the scarf around my face.

"This is leaking," she says, handing me our big tin washpan. "And you might ask for the copper ladle to be repaired, too." She places it inside the washpan.

"I suppose I can ask for those chicks while I'm at it." I work to keep the resignation out of my voice, but Esther hears it, and her eyes pull in more light, growing brighter as she searches my face.

"You worry too much, Jane."

"You always say that."

"I'm right, in your case."

I want to tell her she's wrong—that just because I'm a white woman doesn't mean my task at fitting in in Flats Junction is any easier. That my status as a Boston woman, an Easterner, an outsider, is one that I don't believe I will ever shake. Look at Patrick—here for nearing ten years, and only half accepted! How will I ever find those woman friends to whom I can quickly run over for a cup of flour, or ask for chickens? Had I moved to Flats Junction when it was still small, still Flats Town, still run and operated by Percy Davies and Esther herself, I might have had a chance to slide into existence without sidelong glances and huffs from the town folk.

And it doesn't help that I left and then came back. I know they all think I am foolish and fickle. I suppose I look so, from their view.

What I don't know is how to change their minds.

As I turn to the door with the repairs for Marie under my arm, a rapid knocking rattles through the house, and I nearly drop the washbin.

"Who's out in this?" I wonder.

Patrick appears in the hallway at once, his shadow bouncing against the duskiness of the walls and lantern light in the hall, his step quick and spry. "Comin'!" he bellows.

The screen shrieks, and the heavy door scrapes inward across several floorboards. The damp wind barrels down the length of the house as Patrick flings open the door and screen beyond.

"Reverend Painter, what brings you out in this weather?" Patrick reaches for his heavy old frock coat as he asks, already preparing to go out.

The Reverend's voice is low by nature, raspy from long lectures every Sunday at the Lutheran church, but it's quieter than usual.

"You've got to come, doc—they're all sick with the cough. My Sally is praying her heart out, but that's not going to save my children."

"How many?" Patrick's voice fills with that strange combination of clinical interest and genuine concern.

"All of them!"

Patrick throws on his overcoat and lifts his creased leather medical bag from under the coat pegs. Without a glance at me, he's off with Reverend Painter, heading off in the scouring wind to where the Painter house leans against St. Diana's Lutheran Church on the far west side of town, just north of the tannery. I wonder if he will be home in time for dinner, or if it will be an all-night vigil.

With a strange start, I realize this will now be part of my life, possibly every day. I will constantly be worrying over him in the weather, or darkness; probably both. I'd worried of him before, but this is different, deeper. He's my husband. I'm not sure how I like it.

I stand in the open door, bracing against glacial wind, not knowing what I want from him, but only that it's more than this. He's half-way across the snow-powdered yard before it hits me. I'd hoped for a kiss.

How ridiculous to expect something so sentimental from him when he's in his doctoring element, and certainly not in front of the Reverend! It would be incredibly improper.

Behind me, Esther tinkers in the kitchen. I almost envy her dishwashing, and how the hot water will flow off the glossy surface of the pancake iron, and the bright silver of the forks will sit perfectly when all is done and finished. To stay home, away from the vitriol of Kate and Marie, without having to mince on my feet to test their moods or if they will decide to warm to my presence finally …

I step out against the frosty breeze as it twists my scarf, and stub my toe against a knot in the wood of the porch. Wincing, I stomp my heel down on the offending knot, which only serves to jar the back of my leg. I step back as I buckle, catching my skirt on a heel and crashing down hard on my knee. The washpan and ladle fly out across the small front yard. Crying out as the other knee follows, I close my eyes and slap my palms into the dirty porch planks. Grime grinds into the soft flesh of my thumb and wrist, and pokes my fingers, combined with the ice and snow of the Reverend's boots.

It reminds me of how all I've done since my first husband died is stumble around and fall—always unable to find my footing!

Frustration wells in me. I wish I could … I should smash something. Rip a …. Had I been unmarried, I might destroy a pair of gloves … slash the seams … break a glass!

43

But no. Mrs. Molhurst next door would certainly spy on me. And Esther doesn't need a madwoman wrecking everything in the house—things we have precious little coin to replace.

I gingerly stand, pick up the items, and head off down the road. No one is out, as it will be in the other seasons—now it's a matter of errands only when the weather is without a blizzard, and then only when needed.

As my boots crunch on the old snow and I dodge piles of horse dung, I burrow deeper into my scarf against the wind. Returning to Flats Junction from my softer life as a cook in a fine Gloucester house was not easy. It meant saying farewell yet again to the comforts of Eastern living. It was another good-bye to my dear Aunt Mary and my parents. I had found shallow but comfortable solace in the regularity of my job as a cook in a fine house and in the courtship of a proper farmer for the past year. And to return and take the wagon trip to Fort Randall in early November was deeply trying, both emotionally and physically. And why? To bring back Widow Hawks—*Esther!*—because the West didn't feel like home without her.

And now ... now people say we brought the diphtheria back! That she is the reason children are dying, and elderly perish!

It cannot be so! It makes no sense. She has been nowhere but our own home, ever since her own burned to the ground in a hateful act of anonymous arson.

There must be answers—scientific, medical answers. Surely Patrick knows!

I pass the cooper's, sitting empty since before I've been in Flats Junction. Ever since Franklin lost his arm, Kate orders buckets and barrels from out East, which are brought in on the train. Franklin himself now runs the train depot. I wonder how it feels to manage the unloading of goods he used to be able to make himself.

Entering the tinshop by the side door, avoiding the blacksmith's forge and the press of bodies and fire in there, I wait for my eyes to adjust from the white brilliance of the sun's snow glare.

"Well?"

I blink a few more times, then focus on Marie. She stands on the far side of her bench, with tools and hammers littered across it. Black-oiled machines stand sentinel on the corners and along benches, looking otherworldly and complicated.

"I—I have washbins. A wash bin. That leaks," I say, placing the item on the wide, pitted counter. It's worn dark brown where sleeves have rubbed it smooth and discolored over the years. "And a ladle that's loose."

She sighs and sets down her tools, one that looks wickedly sharp on the end. The metal she held clatters loudly as she tosses it on the workbench.

My blood feels filled with steel as she marches closer and grabs the washbin. Frowning, she flips it over and around, her scarred fingers tracing the seams and nails catching on invisible problems. I discover I'm holding my breath.

"I've always a backlog, but these are easy enough," she finally declares, not meeting my eyes. "Come back tomorrow."

"So fast?" The words escape without my realization, and I bite the inside of my cheek, appalled. How can I forget my manners so quickly?

OUTCAST ~1883~

She looks up, and her dark brown eyes are unreadable. "Of course. Why would I not manage my trade as I have always done?"

"I … I wasn't—" *I wasn't implying anything*, I want to say. *I am sorry for the loss of your father-in-law. I worry for your children, too. I wonder if you like me.*

"Did you think I will do wrong by you, simply because your husband cut open Walter's throat?" There's still veiled anger in her voice, but it's buried so deep I'm not sure if it's sorrow or blame or resentment.

After a moment, her shoulders slump. "Well, then. We don't know one another well, do we?"

"You … you'd offered me tea, once," I remind her. My voice sounds thinner, and I clear it. "I'd … I'd like that, still."

She glances toward the door where her shop is connected to the forge. "Well, the children are ill—perhaps another time."

"Of course!" I leap at the second offer. "I—yes!"

I'm desperate. It fills my bones and makes me sweat under my arms and down my back, despite the chill of the day. I so wish for acceptance, for a friend. To replace Kate. I cannot lean on my husband for such a thing, no matter how much I might wish to do so. He is a man, and a woman's way is different. Women hold together the foundation of our society—we cannot help it, it is a biological urge. We weave the fabric of the culture with our bonds as we bear the children and bring them up in our preference. We are the creators of the community. And if I fail to join it, to carve a place for myself within it, then I am lost.

Marie offers another faint smile, brief and cursory. It is my dismissal. Nodding to her, I head to the door. Her skirts rustle as she moves back to work, and I gulp before turning.

46

"I—I am so sorry—about Walter."

She freezes, and her hand trembles slightly as she grips the black iron box of the machine nearest her.

For a moment, I think I have overstepped. Perhaps I ought to say that Patrick meant well, that the operation is the only way to save someone so far gone. I want to say that they should have called for the doctor a day sooner. That I wish she wouldn't dislike me always.

But when she looks at me, her face is softer than I've ever seen.

"Thank you. He ... he was a good man."

I want to say so much more now that she has opened the conversation, but the door yanks wide and tall. Anette Zalenski barges in in a swirl of blue and pink, holding a massive basket and surrounded by six of her eight children.

"Mar—oh! Mrs. Weber!" She pulls up fast, and the wicker of the basket crackles. She shakes her head. "I mean, Mrs. Kinney! How goes it?"

Her children scamper through the tinshop and the forge and a second later the heavy door bangs shut.

Anette offers a grin. "They wanted to see how the children are doing—and it will keep Mother entertained."

"Oh, but—!" Anette and Marie both pause, waiting. I gulp and finish. "But—Marie's children are ill—with the diphtheria."

They stare at me longer.

My eyes close, and suddenly I have an acute empathy for Patrick, and the small battles he fights each time he attempts to explain the science behind his reasons and actions, even knowing the science itself will be questioned. And I only have the words I've absorbed from him, his books, and the other books I've read long ago. I doubt they will be enough.

And they will only further remind these women how desperately different I am.

But to not speak will be a disservice as well.

I open my eyes and look straight at them both. "Anette's children have been safe and healthy on the farm all these weeks—away from the illness. To spend time with Urszula and Natan now will surely infect them."

"Are you saying my children will make Anette's sick?" Marie's eyes narrow.

"I am."

"But how do you know this?" Anette presses, her smooth forehead gathering in wrinkles. "Did the doctor say so?"

"I—" He has, but will his knowledge carry weight, or will they scoff at it? Patrick's precarious position is never known—people's opinions sway so wildly where he is concerned. My tongue feels thick and heavy.

"It doesn't matter what the doctor says," Marie finally decides. "Your mother needs the distraction from Walter's death, and the children could do with some cheer. And you won't stay long."

"No, I can't—it's getting late enough in the winter and I've seeds to sort," Anette says. She follows Marie out of the shop, her long arms still hugging the basket to her chest. As they exit, her blue eyes cut sideways to me, and I cannot tell if it is with worry or contemplation.

Now empty-handed, I cross Second Street and head down the path past the coopers again and onto Davies Avenue toward the General. The sky is a mix of powder blue and pale slate, and the sign above the old Main Inn swings on its hinges with a creak and rusty groaning. Patrons inside the Golden Nail Saloon babble so loudly I can hear it on the wind as if everyone shouted out the windows. Snippets of "Don'tcha know?" and "That's what they all say!" zip through the air so fast I barely have a moment to truly hear them before those words, too, are gone.

And then I'm at the General, climbing the steps even as my feet feel filled with clay and the backs of my eyes ache.

I don't wish to speak with Kate today. Or for a long time.

Perhaps she feels the same.

I did, after all, somehow make the doctor fall in love with me instead.

When the door opens and the bell jingles, I feel as though all eyes land on me, and I want to shrink inside my coat and wraps at it. But all turn back to their tasks, voices muted and low—a strange change from the usual boisterous chatter.

Marta Brinkley, in from the Brinkley farm for the day, riffles through the odds-and-ends bin of cloth with her widowed and unmarried sisters—Kjersti and Else Henderssen, respectively. Their heads group together, with red and blonde hairs gleaming in the lamplights, and their gazes slip back and forth, as if daring anyone to listen in on their muttering. The dark looks are unlike Marta, and she turns from me as I smile at her. The cold doesn't seem to leave my fingers even as I step further into the General.

Tate and Thunder, two of Danny Svendsen's ranch hands, argue in the darkest corner, arms flailing. Sadie Fawcett wanders with dreamy eyes, both hands clasped over her newest bump. Isaac and Hannah Horowitz discuss the price of different shoelaces to buy in bulk from one of Kate's catalogues.

And Kate? Kate flies around with an air of … glee, I suppose. She's in her element—answering questions, taking orders, measuring cloth. She is a coil, a spring, a whiplash.

"'Scuse," Lara O'Donnell pushes past, squeezing me into the rusty plow. "I need to speak to Kate about this delay with Mikey's specialty mahogany wood—" She runs straight into Elaine Warren. That is to say, their bosoms run into each other, and the women glare. Behind us, Horeb cackles with delight, and both women turn their beady gazes on him.

"Aw, can't be fussing on a little bumping and bouncing, can we?" he chuckles, rubbing his long fingers together. "Store's busy, ain't it?"

He speaks directly to each woman's chest, while Gil moves two checkers without Horeb noticing. Elaine's fists curl.

"Watch your eyes—else I'll tell Toot to serve you piss beer for a month!"

"And the Lord will send you straight to hell!" Lara adds, fingering the cross around her neck. The movement does nothing to distract Horeb, who makes a valiant, if brief, effort to be gentlemanly. Lara opens her mouth, likely to deliver her special Irish-Catholic curses, when Kate appears at our shoulder.

"Who's next?"

"I am!" Lara says imperiously, and marches behind Kate to the counter. Her voice, so famous in the choir at St. Aloysius, booms through the store. "This delay in the trains is unbearable! And the lack of stock! No ammunition! No coffee! How could you miscalculate, Kate? You've been running the General for what? Six years? Seven? This is not to be borne!"

Kate meets my eyes in the gloom, and her jaw tightens so hard I can see the tendons pop. After holding my stare a fraction longer than I like, she turns to Lara and begins to placate her with soft words.

"Terrible thing, isn't it?" A new voice, low and with a deep drawl, speaks so close to my ear it tickles the small hairs around it. "So many things unavailable, and at this time of year, too."

The ice that has not left my fingers crawls up to my neck. I press my lips together and turn around slowly.

Bern Masson, another of Danny's cowboys and my old beau, stands within inches of me, the heat of his body pushing into mine like unwanted feelers.

"Yes … yes," I find my voice quickly. "Yes—it's a terrible thing."

He stares at me, the long planes of his face both familiar and yet jarring. After a moment, his lips pull up into a half-smile. It's an odd thing to see on him, I realize, for in all the months of his courting, I cannot remember a moment he smiled.

"Yes. Terrible."

His tone implies more, and I glance at him even sharper. Does he know? Did the posse brag about their outright stealing? Will Kate be a laughingstock for being so weak?

"But not so terrible for you, has it been, Jane?" He uses my front name with defiant familiarity, and I want to tell him he has no right—that he must call me Mrs. Kinney now that I am remarried. "You've broken our understanding, and Kate's prospects, and landed yourself your previous employer as Widow Hawks doesn't have a home for you to live in anymore. Worked out right grand from where I see it."

"We never had an understanding!" I say, hard and low.

His eyebrows go up. "It was implied, I think."

"Implied intent is not an understanding in the least," I sling back, knowing I'm fooling no one. He walked me home every night for uncounted weeks, danced with me at the harvest festival, and spoke to me of the future. What else was there to describe his dedication?

He snorts. "You must have little sense for life, Jane, if you think that's true. But I suppose being an Eastern woman, you don't have the way of it in the West."

His lips curl and his eyes burn into me before he saunters off to sling an arm around Tate and Thunder in the back.

I let out the breath I'd buried deep inside my lungs and then make my way to the counter, to wait for Kate's attention, as much as it chafes me.

When it is my turn, Kate looks at me with an expression that is flat and without a sparkle. I expect the rancor and the masked pain writing itself briefly across her cheekbones, as if it is the only way she can force herself to look at me square. But it's the boiling fury that comes next, fleeting though it may be, that strikes me with a thousand pricks. Kate is—*was*—my first friend in Flats Junction, and admittedly I still have some small hope that we can repair our relationship. What will I need to do? How can I make it better? I have no idea. The loss of her friendship cuts and dampens some of the joy I feel being back in Flats Junction. And I must, for the sake of my sanity, fight against the deep worry I've harbored from the first: Kate wants Patrick. She could try to change his mind yet, and the rules are different here. A man leaves a woman much easier.

Will she ever forgive me for hooking the man she preferred over all others?

"Patrick has asked for lime, for one of the diphtheria treatments," I say. "And we need eggs, too, please."

Her mouth goes thin. "The lime is dear. And I don't know when I'll get more, what with the trains so ..." She seems to remember who she is talking to—and how I was witness to it all. Her cheeks flare with a plum-red flush, and she shoves pins deep inside her thick hair with quick, hard jabs. "That is ... I might have one bottle. But it will have to go on your account. And there's not much more leeway—I cannot keep just ..."

"Giving things away," I finish, my voice a hair above a whisper.

Kate hesitates, then spins to the rambling cubbies behind her register. After a moment, as the dark brown and blue bottles jostle with her brisk search, she lifts up one.

"So this will help all the sick?"

"I ... I don't know. He didn't explain it." I wish he had, though. I want to know as much as I can, if only to never be caught unaware about health questions as I have been offered today.

Kate seems triumphant at my statement, switching from cold to smug in a breath. My words seem to affect her in ways I cannot fathom, as if I can worm inside her and make her flip on half a sentence, but I do not know which words are magic and which cause ill will.

53

I exit before Bern has a chance to corner me again, but I am sure I feel his eyes in the crease of my neck and shoulders as I go.

What can I do, to forget how friendless I feel? Where to put my restless mind and twitching hands? I refuse to give in and do any damage in my frustrations—no more reasons to rip a dress to shreds or pound a skillet into a bag of flour.

My mind hitches to the sickness spreading and killing. Before I'd married Patrick, back when I was married to Henry and he was wasting away from his illness, I'd spent far too much time over medical journals and whatever books were in the Boston library than was proper for a businessman's wife. Henry had forbidden me to speak to the doctors who treated him, worried my audacity to speak in medical terms would sour them and make him look an idiot husband. But Patrick is different, I remind myself. He has always said I might allow my curiosity to grow, to read his books and sit in his office chair as I do.

Perhaps now is the time to see if he truly meant it.

Besides, I need a deep distraction to rid myself of mourning how Kate and I have lost what little relationship we'd had. But then—it seems that some friendships are spun like glass and will spider with pressure, irreparable. Or like eggshells, others might say, fragile, crystal, careful. Untried. But I must believe other friendships are different. Made of salt and earth and water. Things that existed before man and will after. A muddy friendship. That, I think I should like.

CHAPTER FOUR

# Marie

*January 30, 1883*

The snow slashing our one bedroom window finishes well before morning and will vanish from every crack and crevasse in the house by midday. By the time the early pearl-grey of daybreak touches the yard, everything will be wet in the creases of the woodwork. There's shifts and mutterings in the room adjoining the main bedroom, and I cringe, waiting for the strange, barking cough wracking Urszula's thin frame. It doesn't come now, and I breathe out carefully, afraid to stir the air with my hope. Please God she is getting well.

I need to check on the hearth and start boiling the overnight oats. Berit has done her chores in a trance since Walter passed, so I want to keep helping more than I usually do. Still, my irritation at the list of growing repairs and orders in the tinshop claws up my spine. I shake it off. There's no time to do much other than worry and act, and as much as I try, the two are constantly twined in my mind.

Good God, I am so tired.

I sit up in bed, pushing down my chemise from my hips and reach for my skirts. Chores won't wait.

"Stay." Thaddeus's deep voice is low with morning muddle, half smothered by the pillow.

The light is still soft and blue. It feels mightily fanciful and frivolous to leave the chores even five minutes longer, but I can't ignore the ache in my bones or my womb.

"Sleep well?" I ask him, falling into the bedding.

His bare arm circles my shoulder and pulls me closer. "No."

"What are you worrying on?"

"Shouldn't it be the other way around?"

"You're the one who says he didn't sleep."

He's quiet for a long moment, one scarred finger tracing lines and patterns along my skin. "Flats Junction is growing. Have you noticed? The new greenhorns Danny Svendsen brings in, and the small shops springing up along the edges. We should order more stock."

"Can we afford it?"

He pauses a fraction too long, then changes the subject. "You get up with Urszula?"

"A few times." Eight, but what does it matter? She's not coughing now. Perhaps the onion compresses helped. Even as I think the words, the dread throttles the hope. Walter's death was the start of the unraveling. It is impossible not to think it. To believe it.

"You're fretting on her too fierce," Thaddeus says, reading the tense lines of my shoulders for what they are.

"We're both worrying on things we have no way to fix," I say.

56

He snorts, but shrugs.

"Think we should have Doc Kinney come check on her?" I ask, knowing the answer already.

"Why do you even bring it up, Marya?"

"To see if we are still of the same mind."

"Are we?"

"Well, then, so we are."

But we aren't. For all I still do not understand what Doc Kinney had hoped to do with Walter, or whether the operation would have succeeded, it is not important now. I cannot help but hope he will be able to aid Urszula should we need it—if we decide to call him … It was the doc before him, Doc Gunnarsen, who was the real quack. "Berit and I will take care of Urszula the best we can. I think it's been good for Berit anyway, to keep her busy."

Thaddeus rolls onto his forearms and lifts his great body above mine. "I've a notion to keep busy before the sun rises, and the chickens wake."

"The damn *kurczaki chickens*—"

He smothers my mouth with his, and I'm surrounded by the echo of the soot and fire always in his beard and along his skin. The ache in my blood is no match for my desire for him, no matter the years we've been wed. My legs lock about his hips, and we fold into one another with the naturalness of time and the speed of a pair who knows the other's preferences and the tick of a morning clock. He is a weight at the last, resting and inhaling great gulps of air as he recovers.

I sigh into his neck and think about the results of our prolific turns in the sheets. I suppose I will have to speak to him again, but there is no rush. Death is often the way of it, here. Did I not just remind myself of that? Best to enjoy the pleasure where it comes.

"That—" A hard cough from the children's room next door slices through the walls snuffing out my scrabbling for romantic phrases.

Thaddeus snaps his head toward a second string of coughs. "That's not Urszula."

"No!" I peel myself from under him, pull on the white flannel chemise and yank on my underskirts, and fly from our room with my stays untied.

I tear from our room to the next, a narrow room, which Thaddeus built as part of the home's addition several years ago. The wide, hand-cut planks creak with each step. I stop. Who is it? Urszula, in the right lower bunk, is quiet in her bedding, huddled against her fever but asleep. Thank God—then I hear it. Kaspar!

I slap at the curtain over the small window for some light. Kaspar's cough repeats, lifting his upper body off the lower-bunk mattress. I lean close, smoothing back his dark hair. His face is mottled as he fights to find a full breath. I caress his warm forehead, feeling the heat of the fever lift off his skin, leaving my palm slick with his sweat.

"Hush. It will be all right." Fear careens into my throat as a scream, but I bite it back.

Natan watches me from his bedding, looking the best of all the children, and Urszula keeps sleeping, her frame thinner than ever and her lips chapped.

Helena's bunk above Natan is empty. Did the coughing force her from bed? Maybe she started the chores on her own.

"Stay in bed," I tell Natan. He nods and throws his blanket over his head.

58

I pull the covers up over Kaspar. "I'll get you some broth. Stay abed."

"But Father—" he rasps, before falling back to tight, short coughs.

"Your father managed the forge all alone for many years," I remind him. And while Thaddeus has come to depend on both his sons and their young arms, he can do without a short time. We are not so needy.

I turn and check on Urszula. She's silent and still and peaceful for now, so I let her sleep and creep out and into the short hallway. When I close the door and turn, I collide with Thaddeus's chest.

He throws a shawl over my shoulders with haphazard care. "Who?"

"Kaspar."

His whole body tenses with the news, then I can feel him bury the emotion. "Well then. Natan must be near healed soon enough."

He means he will work double to keep up with orders. That he cannot keep on without help, or an apprentice. Shaking his head, he turns back into our bedroom, his bare feet thudding loudly.

Berit is already bending across the fieldstone fireplace, her long, slim feet planted widely on the blackened hearthstone and her honey hair all white in the single lantern light. "I heard more coughing," she says, straightening as we march in.

I glance around briefly for Helena, but she's absent here, too. "Kaspar now," I tell her, hiding my fear behind a layer of resignation so she doesn't hear the panic underlying every move I make, but the attempt is fruitless. To hide my fears further, I smile briefly at Berit. The ghost of her old grin flutters across her lips and brushes into her blue eyes.

Thaddeus thumps in, his boots already on and his vest done up tightly under his soot-stained leather apron. He's jammed his cap over his peppery hair and frowns around the room. "Breakfast?"

His stoic manner is enough to put me at ease for all I'm churned up inside with nerves.

"It's ready. But Helena's out in the barn."

Thaddeus grumbles as he heads out into the cold to call for her, then comes in a few moments later. "She's not there."

"What?" I look at Berit. She shrugs and pulls the oats from the fire. "Where could she possibly be at this hour?"

"I'll switch her bottom," Thaddeus growls into his bowl.

"She's a bit old for that."

He spares me an incredulous flick of a glance. "Lives under my roof and eats my food, I'll say who's too old for a thrashing."

I don't bother to argue more, and instead put my dish in the wash bin before checking on the sick children once more. Urszula seems incredibly sleepy and weak, and I press my hands to her throat, which is swelling for all I'm willing it to stay slim and soft.

Natan growls through the soreness in his mouth, protesting my insistence that he stay in bed. "Father needs my help!" he says hoarsely. "Kaspar's too sick."

"And you've still a fever and can barely sit up," I tell him firmly. "*Babcia* will manage you, and I'll check in when I can."

Without a means to ease their suffering, I block it out, dress fully, and head to the tinshop, wondering how

I will concentrate with the swirling in my mind. I twirl a sharp awl and trace out a pattern while Thaddeus forms hinges in the forge nearby, his hammer strikes short and quick and high.

I try not to think of the children, though Helena's whereabouts grate on my nerves. Fool girl! There are chores and errands!

My repairs on Jane's washbin do not take near as long as I expect, and I place it to the side to return in a day or so if she does not come in before then.

"Marya. Let's go to the General."

"For metal?"

Thaddeus nods, and I grab my wrap, swinging it over my hair and around my mouth and nose as we walk south toward the store.

When we arrive, Thaddeus marches twenty paces across the creaking, complaining planks of the General Store. He skirts around the pile of tumbling flour sacks, nudging rolling cans of canned peaches and powdered milk with his booted toe.

"You ordering or me?" he grouses.

I shake my head at him. I know enough how Kate feels about me, and she knows what I think of her. No need to make this transaction troublesome.

He sighs heavily, walks up to where Kate is waiting with an annoyed smile plastered to the corners of her mouth and holds up his thick fingers at her. "I'll need pig iron and coal, and hope it can make it in before the storms come in worse this winter."

Kate flips to our ear-marked page. "Well … for once you're paid up."

Thaddeus glowers, and continues with his list, his deep voice echoing through the space, bouncing off the barrels of last spring's seed and the clutter of secondhand shoes in the near pile.

The shop ceiling is taller than other buildings, and soars above us fifteen feet, lost in fat wood beams and half-rusted pressed tin tiles. Thaddeus is so tall he could reach and swing from the thick beams supporting the stretched walls, though the idea of him doing such a frivolous thing makes me smile inwardly.

He notices my small grin and turns his glower on me. He ticks off the rest and finishes. "And the usual order of tinplate and copper sheet for my wife."

Kate shoots me a bland look, then lifts her chin at Thaddeus. "I'll put the order through on the next train. You might get it yet before spring, depending."

"I need it before then."

"I can't control the weather."

"Hm. How much?"

"It'll all come to well over thirty dollars. The price per pound of tinplate alone keeps going up," she says.

Thaddeus sighs loudly before he pulls out our cash, combined particularly for this shopping trip. Counting it quickly into his dry, soot-stained palm, I watch as he comes up short. When he looks up at me, the embarrassment and frustration across his eyes keeps my tart tongue more civil than usual.

"I can cut back the order of tin," I say.

He shakes his great shaggy head. "Can't. It'll put you behind in spring."

"Well, has Marie finished my father's teakettle repairs?" Kate asks.

My stomach jolts. The damn copper kettle! Kate's heirloom. It still sits—worse off than before—since the day Walter died.

"I'm sure she's nearly done," Thaddeus says slowly, his eyes raking me.

"I'll have to see it soon, then, won't I? And then we can re-open your line of credit at the very least."

Why is she asking such. She knows the push and pull of sales, of a business—and that the winter is inherently slow! What is the purpose, other than her abiding dislike for me, for my role as a woman in a man's trade?

"What with Walter's death—and now the children so sick …" I swallow the lump of bile in my throat. Thaddeus watches me carefully, and I'm painfully aware of my tells. But Kate does not know me well enough to understand how discomfited I am by this discussion. "It will be done, and soon, as soon as the children are well."

"Mm." Kate's response only reminds me how little she knows, being without children herself.

Thaddeus strides fast on the way back home, and I have to trot to keep up with him until I yank on his arm. "Slow down for me, will you?" There is another reason for my slowness, but one I am loathe to admit to him—or even to myself.

He pauses long enough for me to settle my arm in the crick of his elbow. As we go through the dirty snow and frozen mud ruts, nodding at Alan Lampton as he hauls a bale of hay toward his pigsty, Thaddeus finally huffs.

"So—you didn't wish to finish Kate's copper kettle?"

"It's true I was working on it the day your father passed!" I retort.

"You've had time since. We need credit if we're going to put in that metal order and stay on track to keep orders flowing in and out of both our shops. And she's not handing out credit anymore, for whatever reason."

"It'll get done," I promise, though a shiver snakes and spiders down my back as I do. I haven't even looked at the kettle since that fateful day. I know the damage is worse. I know it'll be harder to fix. But I'm quite sure it's manageable.

"Well, then. Finish it fast."

"So you're telling me how to run my business?"

"I'm telling you what you already know. We need the stock, the credit."

"If it takes another month or two, it'll keep. It hasn't been used in several years—I don't think she's missing her tea. It's an heirloom for looks only."

"Then you'd best not ruin it."

My throat closes. We near the house and he pushes on the door.

"Else things'll get tight," he reminds, unnecessarily.

"They always are," I say, as we enter the back door into our family kitchen.

"What is?" Helena's dark head looks up from the hearth as we enter, shaking muck from our boots at the threshold.

"Where were you?" Thaddeus booms.

Helena freezes for only a moment, then smoothly smiles, even as her eyes glance back and forth. "I went for a walk."

Thaddeus quivers. I want to believe her. He does, too. And we've no proof she's done anything but.

"How is dinner?" I ask instead, breaking the moment.

"It'll be soon. But what is it, Mother?"

I force her out of the way to check the soup over the fire myself. She snorts behind me as I do, but I must be allowed some pretenses to pretend I know what I'm doing in the kitchen, even if I gave up the womanly arts long ago.

"Just business. Don't worry yourself."

"How can I not?" she asks. "It's all you and Father discuss—metal, business, numbers, debt. Was it this romantic when you were courting?"

I shoot her a glance. "We didn't court."

"Why not?"

Why is she asking this now, when the supper needs tending while Berit does chores and the children cough in the back bedroom, and my skin crawls with worry about so many things I cannot keep them straight in my mind?

"What is this interest in the past?" I ask her. "You've never bothered before."

"I'm old enough to learn the wiles of men and how it works."

"So you can experience it?"

"So I can avoid it, Mother. I'd like to know how to spot and stop the advances from those I don't like." She walks from me and picks up the sewing she's left strewn on the table, piling pieces in an orderly fashion. Where I am precise on my tinplate seams, Helena has exacting stitches and an uncanny knack for understanding the geometry of cloth.

I stir the soup more vigorously than I intend, and some sloshes out onto the fire below, sizzling and hissing and burning. Someday, I hope we get a real stove. It would be a luxury, to be sure. Maybe I will take up more cooking, then.

"Do you think you'll have so many suitors?" I ask, keeping my tone even and near disinterested. Is she trying to tell me something? Have I missed a hint these past days? "Is someone bothering you?"

She tosses her head. "Certainly not! I simply want to know how it all works."

It's an odd thing for a girl to request, though when I peek at her, I realize she's far from a girl—she's blossoming, and I've been too busy with the damn business to notice.

My arm twitches, a gentle agony. I want to put my arm around her, to hold her down so she is short and small and unknowledgeable. If I can squeeze her, perhaps she will be a little girl again, not this young woman with a stubborn tilt to her chin full of defiant expectations.

But it's too late. And I've gone too long without offering her physical comfort to start now. She will think it strange.

Helena stares into my eyes, as if daring me to question her, daring me to answer.

"You're too young to know." I shake my own head. "You'll learn soon enough."

"I'm nearly the age you were, when you married Father and had your own shop!" she suddenly bursts. "I'm only a few years from that! Yet you treat me like a child!"

"You are a child."

"I am not!"

"What do you want?" I smash my fists into my apron. "Would you like to learn the trade? You've never had such an inclination before."

"I've no desire to make things with metal," she says. "I don't want your business."

"It's a good way of life," I say, knowing I sound defensive. "And I'm laying the bricks of a road. For you. You can be a tinsmith. It's not so odd a thing to see a woman doing it here in Flats Junction."

It's a half-truth, and both Helena and I know it. She rolls her eyes slowly.

While I've spent near twenty years as the tinsmith, I'm still a woman in a man's role. I always will be. It is a contrast no one will ever see past. There will never come a time when a newcomer walks into my shop and does not start and flinch at the sight of me wielding the tools and hammers and machines. I am always outside the trade, looking in, no matter if I am a master at it or no.

A woman in my place will always sit just outside the circles.

"I want to create other things. Prettier things," Helena says quietly, but with the immoveable edge to her voice that reminds me so much of Thaddeus.

It's impossible to stop the flare of indignant heat that rushes across my chest and flows into my hands, where they are gnarled with years of burns and old scars. "You don't think the things I build in the shop are pretty?"

She half-rolls her eyes again, fluttering them behind half-closed eyelids. It takes all my willpower not to slap her for the barely contained lack of respect she shows me now.

"They are. They shine, and such. But … well, they're … I want to have more choices."

"A woman has less choices than you think," I remind her.

"Well, I'm not interested, Mother. I see what you fret on, I see what you and Father argue about—and it's no secret the trade is changing faster than you can manage."

My blood feels cold, suddenly. "What do you mean?"

She shakes her head. "If you aren't keeping up with what the newspapers say, even with your own work, then why should I wish for a business that is already dying?"

"Helena!"

"What? Do you think I don't read when I visit the General? Do you think just because you and Father don't bother to pay for the papers from the city, that the latest inventions and ideas just don't exist?"

"The trade doesn't change that much."

"Well, there's some truth to that," she says, her voice rising with argument. "But one thing doesn't—and it's that a woman still isn't welcome in it! I have no reason to want to fight the rest of my life."

"I'm not fighting for my place, *córka*."

Helena turns away, uninterested in disagreeing what we both know. I have been fortunate, despite all the losses of family and babes, to have had so many choices—in a husband, a trade, and even in growing my business to where it sits now. I want to offer that to her—if not, to what purpose has my life been?

Well, then. I suppose I can always give the business to Natan or Kaspar, if they choose it. But they will likely follow Thaddeus, and take up the blacksmithing, given the choice. Then again, there is Urszula.

As I think her name, the deep cough from the back room jolts me, and I ignore the new clutch of pain in my chest.

They must get well! They must! And—both my youngest are strong and healthy. They will recover. It has only been a few days with this illness. Walter was old. Walter was weak.

Berit enters, her arms full of eggs and a pail of milk. As she strides in, her head still tall and queenly, her blonde hair now gone completely to pale honey-white, I find myself counting the wrinkles along her brow and mouth. Has she aged much? Have I not noticed another change?

But she looks much the same that she always has—she is Anette's mother, the surrogate mother I had even before she married Walter and I married Thaddeus. She seems unchanged by the years, and relief trembles through my veins.

"It didn't burn!" I announce as she comes toward the hearth.

"Ah, good, *honning dear*," she says, as she always has. I feel nineteen again, and for a moment, I bask in it. But the moment is short, and Helena sighs loudly behind us as she marches toward the back rooms.

"What is it?" I swing to face her.

"I just don't want to have to listen to their coughing all night," she complains, jerking her eyes and head toward the bedrooms. Natan's deep, thick cough seems to shake the boards around the door as she does.

"We all listen to them," I tell her. "You think the boards between your bedroom and ours are so thick? Your grandmother can even hear it when she sleeps out in kitchen bed."

Berit studiously tastes the soup as Helena and I round each other. I cannot remember the last time I spoke with my daughter without us circling like fighting cocks. She is my eldest, but she is also my firstborn. I am hardest on her while I love her the fiercest.

She tosses her head in a faintly familiar way, and turns away, letting the door bang shut behind her.

69

I sigh. "Well, then. I don't think I was so much trouble to my mother."

"Children are always trouble," Berit says. "But they seem to always be worth it. It's a mother's curse."

"Ha!" I look around the kitchen. "Do you want more help?"

Her eyes glint at me. "You've time to work in the shop for a bit yet, Marie."

When I enter the tinshop and light the lamps, I first remind myself to block out the worry about the lack of credit, the chance that Thaddeus and I will not get the metal stock we need to build more wares and make the money we need to survive, and—most importantly—that the children will get better.

I pull out Kate's kettle and examine the damage—both the original and what I did when Urszula surprised me—and wonder how I'll fix it without her knowing that it was worse before it got better.

She'd spoken more words to me the time she dropped it off than she ever had in her life. Kate has always made a point of avoiding me. I'm not sure if it's because I'd reneged on handshake promises made to her late father, Percy Davies, or if she simply thinks we are competitive. Perhaps she doesn't like how I speak, or thinks I am too successful. Perhaps she does not like anyone, or other women.

All I know is she does not give me the time of day, lifting her nose when we pass and offering only cursory service when I shop at the General Store.

But early January, she'd arrived and stepped into my tinshop for the first time in her life. I near dropped a hammer in surprise when she announced herself.

And then she'd unwrapped this copper kettle, in all its rose and gold glory, and spoke of its past.

"Only Father polished this, as he didn't trust … Widow Hawks … with the proper care of it," she'd said, her words staccato and careful. "He'd tell stories about his mother, how she'd make a quick soup, and how she'd give over to bare but fancy teas in the Carolina hills."

"It's fine work," I'd told her honestly, my hands itching to touch the smooth sides.

"It's from Wales."

Brought on some ill-tempered ship well before the Dakotas were a wisp of possibility, I wager, brought by Percy's grandmother to the States and preserved with love and tenderness.

The sentimentality of the whole thing surprised me. Kate is not one to discuss her past or her feelings, instead broadcasting her state of mind by how she answers questions over the counter.

Yet she's given it to me to repair, trusting—*needing*—to keep it close instead of hoping it will make a journey east, to a more experienced shop. Does she not trust the trains? Does she think it will be ruined further in the journey there and back, or perhaps not even make it back to the Dakotas? Are the trains so unreliable these days? I'm loathe to think on it, and what that might mean for me, even if I can find the funds for the coming months' supplies.

I turn the copper kettle in my hands, imagining all the food that has been prepared over the decades in the cave of its belly.

Placing it back on the bottoming stake, I reach for the rawhide, to smooth out the jagged edges of the cracks. I try not to think too hard on what I must do to repair this—it is difficult. Not impossible, not yet, but difficult to be sure now that I have made it worse.

"*Mother*!"

Helena's tone is wild, untamed with attitude. Her voice frays the last of my resolute forgetfulness, and fear slashes through me. I drop the hammer as the kettle spins unevenly on the stake. "What?"

"It's Urszula!"

Skirts yank at my ankles as I dash out, stubbing my toe on the threshold from the forge to the house, and slamming my hands on the door between kitchen and bedroom hallway.

When I reach the children's bedrooms, Natan is out of bed, looking pale and weak. On her mattress, Urszula shudders as she pulls in a ragged, torn breath. Her cheeks blotch white and purple, and her eyes pop open and then squeeze shut in between each breath.

Thaddeus pounds in, his chest heaving with the run.

I round on him. "She cannot breathe!"

Please let her take the next breath! Let her be well! Even as I pray, throaty coughs echo through the house, each one squeezing harder on my heart. The fear throttles me as if I, too, am gasping for breath with blue fingers and an impossible windpipe. I sit on the edge of the bed. The next question comes unbidden, but it slips across my lips, almost like a reflex. "Tadeusz. We must ask Doc—"

"*Psiakrew, nie! Hell, no.* We both agreed! Not hours ago!"

Urszula's next bout of hacking seems to shake the bronze grains of the wood between bedrooms. I cringe.

72

His eyes round out, full of fear and yet he must know we cannot do more than we have done, and still she's failing.

"If she's not better tonight, we'll discuss it," I say.

The next hours I sit near her, only getting up to make more onion compresses. As I listen to the ragged breathing of the boys, I watch her lips for the tinge of blue that Walter's had at the very end. I see her ribs ride up and down with the shallow gasps that serve as her breathing. I pray. And I distract myself by thinking about how I might fix Kate's kettle, so that I am not completely overtaken by fear and worry of things that have not yet come to pass.

Thaddeus enters slowly with a candle lantern. The pinpricks of light dance merrily around the room. "How are they?"

"The boys seem well enough. But she's ..." I have no words for the pain in my head and heart when I think of Urszula. "Can you sit with her a moment?"

He nods and takes my place, and I quickly duck out to the outhouse and back, moving as fast as I might before the weather puts a long chill in my fingers and toes.

Damnation and hell. What have my children done to deserve this illness? I'm powerless to stop this sickness from rampaging through their young bodies.

When I tiptoe back in, I see that Helena is sleeping with her grandmother to avoid the coughing in the children's room. Berit seems to welcome the warmth of another body after the loss of Walter's heat. They curl around each other in the big bed in the main room, letting the deep orange and yellow of the dying hearth fire wash over their limbs. As I put an extra blanket on their sleeping shoulders, I am struck by the papery softness of Berit's spidery skin matched against the round, curving limbs of Helena's youth.

When I walk back into the children's rooms, Urszula's cough rattles against the wood planks between bedroom, hall, and kitchen. I am torn between my children who are sick and the need to find some solid comfort in Thaddeus's arms. He settles my need by curling his great, massive body around mine and pulling me to Helena's cold mattress.

"You'll get sick yourself if you don't sleep," he says lowly into my ear. "And stop fretting. They're strong, hearty children. They'll get well."

I want to believe him, and every fiber of my heart stretches toward his conviction, but my head and logic war with the emotions. "What if they don't? Is anyone else in town still sick?"

Thaddeus's hesitation is all I need for confirmation, but I wait, knowing the heavy silence will force him to confess what he has heard from customers waiting at the forge.

He sighs and presses his strong cheekbones into the crown of my head. "The Painter children. And ..."

The tension pulls through my arms. "And what?"

"Anette's. Two of the little ones. Coughing up bad."

"Did the Painters see the doc? Did Jacob and Anette?" I pause, folding my lips over my mouth. "Has *anyone* seen the doc?"

Thaddeus goes stiff next to me, halfway between grabbing me to lay on top of him, and his arm is awkward under my back, pushing my hips into a lump in the straw mattress, which only serves to encourage my uncomfortableness. "Painters," he admits.

"And?"

He's quiet again until I backhand his shoulder and collide my knuckles into the thickness of his overlarge biceps.

"If you don't tell me, I'll go to Jane myself."

"The children are all dead."

"What? All!"

"Hush, Marya. You'll wake the children."

My entire being feels frozen and feverish at once. Poor Sally! And the Reverend! How will they recover from such a blow? A mother can bury a babe fresh from the womb without too much pain if she is wise in the ways of life and death, but to lose them all? I fear I might lose my own mind if it were me. It is why I must hold fast to my family so tightly. It is why I cannot lose one more, why I unfairly curse Walter in the depths of night, for beginning the spiral of it all.

It is impossible to fall asleep now, and there is no moon so the room feels like a grave, buried in fear and blackness. I would toss as I lie, but the bed is narrow, and Thaddeus takes up most of it. He does sleep, but never starts to snore.

Just as I think I will finally nod off, catching myself as I do so, there is a deep, wracking cough that splits the night in half, and I leap up from the bed, slapping Thaddeus across the stomach as I do.

Urszula gasps for air and cannot grasp it. As I blindly reach for her, she tears at my arms, her nails grinding into my flesh as I hold onto her as she lifts and strains and tries to scream against the choking of her own throat.

# CHAPTER FIVE

## *Jane*

*January 31, 1883*

It's the deepest part of night—the time when the moon is always eaten up, and the stars are always hidden—when day feels too far away to be real. It's the time when sleep is deepest, when I forget where I live, what I've done, and how I've chosen to exist.

The knock is hard and tight and fast.

It jolts into my brain and hits it against the edges of my skull.

Do I wake?

Is it only a reminder of other knocks?

It bangs again, jarring the window next to the bed.

I jerk upright in the bed, the threadbare blanket spilling across my thighs and exposing the nakedness of Patrick's buttocks in the moonlight. He barely shifts, sunk in deep slumber and the soft breathing of a man happily bedded.

"Patrick!"

My hiss lands on deaf ears, and he only grunts and grabs at the sheets where I lie, as if he wishes to hold me to help him fall into deeper sleep.

I flick his shoulder, then snap my knuckles against his elbow, and he sits up, sniffing hard as he does.

"What is it?"

"Someone wants you!"

I snatch my housecoat, a leftover remnant from my years as a Boston businessman's wife, and trail down the creaking stairs behind my husband, who clambers as fast and loud as an ox. His bare feet slap on the barren boards and bounce on the hallway flooring.

"Paddy!"

He turns in the dark, a shadow against a deeper black. "What, Janie?"

"Your shoes!"

He ignores me and heads straight to the door, opening it just as another knock starts. Behind us, Esther appears, a grey shadow against the deeper dark of the hallway.

"Doc Kinney!" Fred Fawcett, Thomas and Sadie's eldest, stands at the door without a coat or cap in the cold.

"What's the trouble, young Fred?" Patrick questions, already pulling his coat from the hook. I immediately grab his worn and patched leather vest, too, and wonder if I should run up for his socks and pants now or wait to hear what's wrong.

"Mum's asking for the Doc," Freddy says, the words nonchalant and unconcerned, even though he's come to us in the middle of the night.

Patrick suddenly tilts his head at me. "Why not come along to Sadie's birthin'." He gestures to the road, the cracked brown medical bag already gripped in his left hand, the bunchy fingers always red-chapped with wind these days. "You can help, Jane."

I glance into the house. There's no meal on the stove, and the wood is low enough I don't need to watch it. Desire to help my husband wells in me, for all I know—and he knows—I'm unqualified.

"I'll make breakfast, Jane," Esther offers from the gloom. "It'll be ready for you both when you return."

She knows my choice already, and Patrick vaults up the stairs to dress. I offer to have Freddy come in and warm himself, but he glances across at Esther and shakes his head with a nervous tick and fades back into the night-cloaked street.

We dress as quickly as possible in the light of a single candle. Esther already has the stove warm, and the heat curls into the hallway behind us as we leave. It's not a far walk. I can see Sadie and Tom's place from our own front step, but their home is a large corner lot on the edge of Main Street and Second Avenue with an immense yard and relatively tidy white fence, except where Rusty Plackett takes a piss against the paint every few hours when he exits his livery, much to Sadie's extreme frustrations, which can echo up multiple streets at once.

Tom Fawcett has run the bank since Percy Davies's death, and Sadie is one of Patrick's most meticulous and needy patients for everything and anything. At the smallest nick or sniffle in any of her three boys, she's at our door, requesting a remedy. And the Fawcetts pay in cash.

Patrick opens their front door without knocking, and sees Freddy first thing. "Wait a moment, boyo. About how much pain is your mother havin'?"

78

"Oh, something fierce, Doc Kinney," Freddy confides with cheerful relish. "She's wailing and carrying on like the baby is going to tear her apart. So she says, anyway," he finishes, waving his hands at his shoulders in a vision of both slight interest and incomprehension.

I pull on Patrick's arm as he shucks his coat, all my uncertainty about my nursing coming to a high, tight ball under my ribs. "I shouldn't have come. I'll be in the way."

"Do you want to help me, Jane?" he counters.

"Of course I want to help, just I'm not sure if this is where I should be putting all that help."

He chuckles. "Oh, I'll send you off to get us breakfast and bring it back if she's slow, but I'm guessin' Sadie will be quick about it."

Sadie's moans puncture the room from the back bedroom along with short screams, and the tinkle of broken glass. I'm distracted further by the tell-tale stench of food put on the stove but left to burn—likely Sadie went into her pains last night at supper, then, and left the food. At once I take over the kitchen, finally noticing that the two youngest Fawcett children are wrist deep in the molasses barrel in the corner and Freddy looks half-inclined to go join them.

Patrick disappears into the far room, but his voice carries, jovial and calm. "Settle down, Mrs. Fawcett. Tom, if you could send in Mrs. Kinney?" Sadie's moans subside at once. Tom Fawcett enters the kitchen, dressed down to shirtsleeves from his usual banker's suit.

I am more than a little shocked to see him coming from the room. It did not occur to me at all that he would wish to be near his laboring wife. Tom is quiet, and a bit severe, and I never suspected him to be the kind of man who would get involved in the earthier matters of a woman's worries. My husband might—and would—but he is a physician. Tom? I realize I'm staring and rearrange my face into a neutral smile as we pass each other.

I enter Sadie's bedroom in time to hear her gasp. "Doc, I think I just may perish this time."

"Nonsense," Patrick busily lays out his less-frightening tools. "Jane will help you with the last of your petticoats."

There's blood everywhere. It's the first thing I notice, and my hearts stops and my eyesight goes foggy. Memories of my previous pregnancy careen through my mind, and I grasp the bedpost for a moment to steady my ankles. I think Patrick is mistaken—I will be little help at a birth. My dizziness serves one purpose though. Sadie, ever watchful for tidbits she can use for gossip, pauses her dramatic gasping to notice. "Oh Jane! Are you quite alright?

Patrick spins, but I right myself and flash him a small smile.

"I'm just fine."

We pull off her layers. The last two are sticky with blood of various shades of pink, red, and brown. When we're finished and she's finally settled properly, Patrick moves to the bedside.

"See to the children, will you, Jane?" Sadie pleads, her forehead slowly creasing with another contraction.

"Of course."

I go back out, thankful to be away from the blood and memories. Tom has corralled the boys out of the sugar bin and has them bent over the wash pan as he firmly dunks and scrubs each around the ears. Glancing around the kitchen, which is only in moderate disarray, I roll up my sleeves.

"Alright boys. Dinner is overdone, it seems," I peer into the pot and note the half-burned state of the stew. "We'll use whatever molasses you haven't eaten into the pot while Freddy gets us some water from the well bucket."

"Stew for breakfast?" Freddy asks, looking scandalized. "Mother says we must have oats in the morning, every day."

"Well, I'll add some in with the beef and vegetables," I say, feeling out of my element as I search for different utensils and spoons amid Sadie's carefully arranged kitchen.

As I'm a stranger, it seems it takes them a few minutes to absorb my directions, but Freddy complies without comment and a nod from Tom. Soon enough, though, I salvage the stew into something that smells and looks edible.

"Will you want to eat with your sons, then?" I ask the banker.

"Oh. Yes. Of course." He seats himself at once, the English accent more clipped than usual and he glances nervously at the bedroom a few times as I settle him with a heavy helping of the soup. The boys sidle next to him and wait for their own helpings.

"Will Mummy be fine?" asks the youngest.

Tom glances down and pats the boy's head absently, his eyes flicking to the closed door once more. "Of course she will, my boy, of course. Your mother is quite practiced in having babes."

As they eat and I serve them bread to sop up the extra juice, I watch the dark-haired banker speak seriously and carefully with each of his sons in turn. He questions the bit of schooling they have had this week and presses Freddy on his numbers. Many times, his hand drops to the youngest one's hair. As I consider him, I realize Tom is likely close to Patrick's age. The main difference is Tom already has many children.

"How is the bank?" I attempt to make small talk and pass over hard rolls I've found in the larder.

Tom's eyebrows go up. "The same as usual, Mrs. Kinney."

This is the first time I have ever spoken with Tom in relative privacy, and my questions and deep curiosity hook my tongue, unstoppable. "Have people discussed the diphtheria in town much? At the bank? Is there discussion of closing the school yet? Old Henry perhaps maybe might call an emergency meeting, or else risk more sickness."

"That sounds like an accusation." Tom's eyebrows arc up even further.

"It's only worrisome, with some of the little ones not … doing well."

Has he heard about the Painter children's deaths? How could he not, sitting in the bank and hearing from people all day? The tradespeople always get the latest gossip, the choicest bits of news and information. I do not get out enough, nor get enough visitors, to hear of things. And if people talk to Patrick, he never relays it to me.

"I really don't think we ought to discuss this around the children." His reprimand is a sharp jab, and I physically flinch. "It is about their friends, after all."

None of the boys look up, still tucking heartily into their food—likely they had not had supper, making this breakfast at an ungodly early hour a double meal.

Sadie's noises grow suddenly, and Tom stands abruptly, curtly. When he opens the bedroom door, Sadie's voice inside the bedroom is shrill and insistent. "Never again!"

"You always say that, my dear," he soothes, and the door closes firmly. I feel stupid and am abashed at my forthright conversation with the banker. It reminds me how little time I've spent here in Flats Junction, and how I do not know everyone very well—well enough to speak as though I have ideas on how parts of the town ought to be managed.

As the dark wee hours wane, I find myself curling around the small frame of the youngest Fawcett in front of the hearth and starting a game of Cupid's Coming while we wait. Sadie is not quiet. As I hear her yelps and trembling screams, which are sometimes muffled, I think of my own delivery. The small boy, a stillborn come early. I sometimes wonder how he'd look like today. Theodore's square jaw and black, thick hair, or my softer brown? Strong and robust or sickly? Would Henry have understood why I took another man to bed so soon in my widowhood?

I doze off, but wake to soft sounds. It's Patrick, his face slack over mine. "It's time we go."

The little lads are curled in a puppy-like heap around me. Freddy is at my feet, and the two youngest snuggle on either side of my chest.

I sit up. "She did well?"

I know the answer before he gives it, and I don't know how to react. I think of such a thing even before he says the words. What words will suffice when I speak to Sadie? How will she bear a loss? How do any of us women bear such a loss?

"The child is a girl, but not very big," Patrick explains in a deep whisper, surprising me with the news.

So it is not a stillborn, then. I don't understand what he means, though. "Not big? But it's been long enough—"

He helps me to my feet slowly, so I don't rouse the little ones sleeping around me.

The light is murky and brown-black with the banked hearth leaking a weak orange under the embers. A hint of leftover molasses sitting in the pot on the stove tickles my nose as I rise up. My shoes bite into the sides of feet swollen from an uncomfortable position on the floor. "How's Sadie faring?"

"Exhausted, devastated, but fine."

I inhale a deep breath of relief. "And the baby?"

"She won't live long, Janie," he says. "Let's give them some time."

"There's nothing—"

"No." His voice is so terse I clam up and follow him out into the frosty, crunchy winter without another word.

We head home. To our right is the pearl of a cloudy morning just beginning to crack. To our left is an inked navy. The sky is cloudless and the clusters of brilliant white star light still feel close and touchable. My heart aches for Sadie's impending loss. *Loss, loss.* So many children lost this season. 1883 is not an auspicious year at all, and January is not even over yet.

We fumble our way into the dark house, hanging hats on the pegs by instinct instead of sight. Esther has several lanterns lit on the table and in the kitchen against the early hour, and the smell of toasted bread.

"We need a bite to eat," I remind him.

"You didn't eat with the boys?" he admonishes.

"Lost my appetite," I say. "I wonder if she has gone for the milk?"

Esther has gotten the smaller jug of it from the well bucket. She has day-old bread toasted, and looks up at us with hopeful eyes as we each start to help in the kitchen. The hope fades as soon as Patrick shakes his head.

"Stillborn, then," she says quietly. "Sadie will take it hard."

"No—worse, in a way. They'll have just enough time to fall in love with her before she'll fail. It's the cruelest way— one of the cruelest ways—a babe can be lost."

Esther sighs, a long, drawn sound that seems pulled from her soul.

I place out the jam with the bread and pour us all milk. After we all sit, Patrick takes a moment to pray over the meal. He does not do so often, regardless of his Catholicism, but I think today he is saying more than a blessing over the food.

As he helps himself to a large spoon of jam, I watch his hands, now cleaned of blood, and think about my own reaction. Will I never be able to help him at a birth without reliving my own horror? Or will the devastation of my miscarriage eventually fade?

"Tom mentioned you accused Old Henry of not doin' enough to stop the spread of sickness," Patrick says suddenly, slicing through my memories. "Tell me you didn't. Today, of all days."

My mouth drops at the painful worry in his tone, and I lift my chin. "I just was trying to find conversation."

"You're bein' nosy at a wrong time. You know this. You know what's proper."

Tears press, unbidden and hard, against the back of my eyes. I look down at my empty plate and blink hard. Of anyone, Patrick knows how hard I try to be so careful. How I force myself to follow the rules, to hide my questions. That my curious nature is contained, most of the time. That I …

I close my eyes. I shouldn't have pried. I must not make his predicament worse, either, by speaking out as if I have a voice in this town. It's too soon.

When I open my eyes again, there's bread on my plate. Looking up, I catch his gaze, and it is soft again.

"I'm only feeling the weight of my own worries. I shouldn't have suggested you help, Jane. It was too much."

I shake my head. "It will get easier."

He nods and takes a large bit of the bread. For a moment, there's no sound but the crackling of the new wood in the stove and the crunch of his teeth against the bread crust. Esther bites into hers and chews slowly. "You asked about the diphtheria?"

"I asked about closing the school. Won't that … it'll help, won't it?"

"It would," Patrick agrees. "But you'll have to get out to talk to Old Henry and get his Susan to take your side, too."

We eat quietly again. I stand and start heating more slices of bread, as Patrick is tucking into them with gusto. I think on Sadie again and try to overcome my own fears by latching onto something tangible. Knowledge. Questions. Things my first husband detested in my person. Things I've since allowed to surface, with care and slowness.

"Why was the baby too small?"

"There's the Jane I know," he says at once, sitting back and leaning toward the wall. A glimmer of a smile lifts his left cheek. "Askin' the way of it."

"The science makes no sense," I press, finding my footing here. "It was the right time. She's birthed children before. What went wrong?"

"Who knows?" Patrick shrugs and wipes his mouth, then reaches for more jam. "I have a hypothesis or two. Sadie's older. Maybe they waited too long for another. Hard to say, exactly. Time and age don't do a woman any favors, it seems. I can tell you it wasn't the superstitious things you women go on about—eatin' the wrong foods at the wrong time of year. But I don't know."

He surveys the food on the table before giving me an odd, enigmatic look, a trace of an old smile on his long, expressive lips. "Too bad you don't have the potatoes yet. But then, perhaps if you made up the oatmeal for mornin's and we've the milk here." He lifts the tin mug in salute and downs his in one long, wide gulp.

"Are you hankering for potatoes?" I ask, surprised. He rarely makes suggestions on the food, leaving the menu to Esther and me.

"Not especially," he shakes his head. "But they do say it's good for the man who's wantin' babes himself."

I feel a hot flush race across my cheeks, and glance at Esther. She only offers a soft smile and half-shrug, completely at ease with these topics. "Are you—" I close my lips and eyes briefly to gather my surprise. "You're teasing," I admonish, but lightly and with a laugh that feels out of place after the long difficult morning and Sadie's sad news. "Here I thought you are telling me what you should eat for your own virility."

"I'm not teasin'." He shakes his head. "That's the way of the Irish, my girl. I recall as much, growin' up in the boardin' houses. All the women would speak of the remedies for or against havin' another wee babby."

"We have ways, too," Esther says, smiling at us and rising gracefully from the table. The small tin bells on her skirt shower the room with happy jingles. "Ways to keep a child at bay, or ways to help bring a woman's blood, or ways to keep a child in the womb."

"Why aren't people using them?"

"We do. Or at least, I must hope my family still remembers the ways of our ancestors," she says, glancing out the window to the snowy prairie. "I have worked hard to do so, so I might pass it on."

Her wistful words fall into the room and then scatter. Patrick and I exchange a silent glance. Yes, she's saved so much knowledge, so many herbal remedies. But her only living family is Kate.

"Well, I remember my good friend Michael sayin' as how he'd eat potatoes, oats, and milk to get his wife with child from the start. It worked, too. Or at least, he was lucky," Patrick says, overly loud, breaking the mood that hangs over us with Esther's wish.

I give another short laugh, but then the reason behind his memory trickles into my mind. He matches my sudden seriousness by staring into the honey pot for a moment, watching the slow, meandering bubble within the spun-gold yellow find its way to the surface.

"It's only ... even with tonight ... all these comin' babes in Flats Junction has me thinkin' how we'd discussed a family of our own," he says quietly after a moment, his eyes flickering then to Esther and then to me.

Sadness pushes into my shoulders, and I want to sink my head to the table for a moment, allowing his hopes to meld themselves into my very bones. I have wondered such things too—but I have spent so much of my days focused on the actions around me, the need for work and busy hands and a way to shove down my dreams.

This will not do. If he is willing to be open about his heart, I must. I must!

"Do you think it is me—my body—that will not allow for babes?" I ask him, hoping for honesty, or at the very least his professional opinion. But I also fear the answer.

He meets my gaze at once, determined and forceful. "No. At least, after you lost the wee boyo, I didn't see anythin' that would hinder you from bearin' children. I've told you as much before."

"But ..." I pause and realize half of my worries are ones he is not privy to know. Though I've alluded to Henry's poor health in the past, I have not given over the sorrow that had plagued my first marriage. Plunging in without giving myself time to overthink my words, I grip my milk-filled glass tightly. "Suppose it was not only Henry's illness that had hindered me from having children. He and I had been married a good number of years before he passed."

Discussing my fertility, even with my physician husband, feels extremely uncomfortable and foreign. To do so in front of Esther is only less so. I want to clam up and start the dishes if only to keep from talking. I wonder how earthy the chatter is between my friends and their menfolk. Do they sit at their own tables and talk? Do they share their woes and worries in the deep cover of night under the bedclothes?

I sigh and shrug. "I suppose we'll know soon enough. It was only the once, and then it wasn't even Henry's babe. A chance. A failed chance."

Patrick stills as I explain. He grows thoughtful. I know the look and am not entirely surprised when he rises and goes to the office to fetch a medical book, bringing it back and plunking it down between us on the table. "There's not much on the fertility of cancer patients," he says, flipping the pages after cleaning the sticky honey off a finger and ignoring my reference to my fleeting affair in early widowhood. "But I should know somethin' on you. There are papers written of course on maternal health and hemorrhage. A lot on hemorrhage."

"Maybe I'm too old," I say, now that we are in full-fledged analysis of my physical ability to get pregnant.

He dismisses this at once. "Not at all. Sure, the girls might start bearin' around here as soon as fifteen or so, but there's many a lady still havin' a newborn into her forties. Look at Anette, say, who is still able to have children should she wish."

I narrow my eyes at him. "And just how old, exactly, are you, Paddy?"

"Not too old to be a papa," he smiles at me, then bends back over the pages, shifting the lantern closer as he does.

My stomach twists. Since I've known Doctor Kinney, he has always been forward about his plan to fill the house with family and children even if they were not his own. I think sometimes he misses the close, familiar, family-style living of the slums of his childhood in Boston. Perhaps he thinks to recreate that crowded, joyful, insanely colorful life once more. Suppose I cannot give him a family? What then? And I cannot forget my own fears.

Childbirth is said to be a step from the grave, for the child, the mother, or both. There's also all those horrific whispers I've heard in the circle of women who speak of milk leg clotting and needing to cure a gathered breast by lancing the flesh open. What about childbed fever, brought on by some mysterious, unknown ailment linked to birth causing blindness, fever, and then death? Or what if the child is so underweight like Sadie's? I shudder slightly as I think of these things and realize I am grateful too for these months without the worry of childbearing.

"Let's not worry on it," I say, directing attention away from me. "Dishes next."

With Esther to help with cleaning and preparing the next meal, I have far more time than the next woman to leisure—though if I had my way, I'd be busy with the children I know my husband pines to see. Our early morning rising means it's still quite early when I step into Patrick's study. He's tinkering in his surgery across the hall, and Esther is stitching in the kitchen. *I wonder ...* Running a hand along the spines of the books he's lined up carefully to face the window, I wonder if I might learn something about this diphtheria. I wonder if my words will have a different kind of weight. I wonder if mothers and aunts will listen to me better, if I offer advice and medical words to them.

Carefully lifting out the volume *Treatise on the Prevention and Cure of Diseases*, I flip it open to see if there's anything on childhood illnesses. The threadbare cover and cracked binding snaps as I check the pages for any words on coughs and blocked throats. It's difficult reading, and I squint at the wording as I sit down and bend over it.

"Janie?"

I jump in the old wooden chair when Patrick enters the room, still polishing one of his scalpels with a white cotton cloth.

"I'm sorry," I say, standing. "I was only doing some … reading." I cannot even bring myself to say 'research', too stifled by my years of marriage with Henry Weber.

He comes around to see which book I've picked, then shakes his head. "You'll not find anything on childbirthin' in that one."

"I'm looking for the diphtheria."

He sighs slowly, glancing over all the tomes as his shoulders sag slightly. "You won't find much in here, either. Most of what I do know I learned under old Doc Burns in Boston. Esther says her tribe's doctor will take a sinew rope with sandburs dipped in hot tallow on one end, throw it down a throat with a stick, and yank the membrane out of the patient's airway when the tallow melts."

I clutch at my own throat with his words, imagining the terrible burn and pain and sweet relief that would come from such a cure. He chuckles without mirth at my reaction.

"It's not a pretty business, my girl. But you already knew that." He pulls down several other books and stacks them without precision on the desk, offering the top one to me with a flourish. "Start with this one."

I stare after him as he strolls out of the room, and then gaze out to the street, as if expecting someone to scream at me for attempting to read such texts. Yet my thirst to try to learn, to be helpful, to understand more than the way of the kitchen, compels me to open the cover of *Household Medicine, Surgery, Sick-Room Management and Diet for Invalids* and start reading.

But I only get as far as '*Widely as men differ from each other, on almost every subject that either observation may give rise to, or speculation may suggest, they seem to display a tolerable unanimity on the subject of health, and the prolongation of life.'* when another knock reverberates through the house. I leap up, hitting my knees on the bottom of Patrick's desk, and reach the front door just as he does.

The door reveals the tear-stained face of Berit Salomon, her eyes watery with cold and sorrow.

"Please—please come. They won't ask for you, but there's nothing left to do!"

Patrick and I share a short glance. His fingers flex toward the medical bag at our feet in the hall, and I put a hand on the door.

"Won't you come in, Mrs. Salomon?" I say, and she steps in quick and artfully. Her eyes dip around with interest, taking in the rooms and the details, but her mission drives her to plead again.

"Please do go back with me. It's our Urszula. She's been hardly able to breathe since the small hours of the morning, and nothing is enough. Please—save her as you couldn't save my Walter!"

Patrick doesn't move at all, but my entire body cringes with the reminder of that failure—one that was not even Patrick's given how late we were called.

"Will they even let us into the sickroom?" I ask her.

"Marie will. She's a mother. She has to," Berit says, firm and resolved. "And if she doesn't, I'll … I'll move out. See how well they get their stubborn selves fed and their laundry done!" Her voice rises and then cracks with unspent tears. "Just—come now!"

Patrick shrugs on his overcoat with another questioning glance at me, and I know what he wants. I pull on my own cloak and grab a warm bonnet to follow them out, calling to Esther as we step onto the patio into the wind and grey of the morning.

The quick walk across to Soup's Corner and then up to Second Street feels slower than usual, though perhaps it's because I wish we were hurrying even more to avoid the acid cold of the morning's wind or because I am dragging my feet unwittingly, trying to keep away from Marie and Thaddeus's home. I don't want to have another failed patient on Patrick's hands! How will I help him overcome the losses? There are so many! It has only been six days since Walter passed, though it feels half a lifetime with the pace of illness and the difficulties with Kate.

We enter through the back door instead of the front forge, and no one is in the great room, with the kitchen hearth banked and an empty trestle table. But the coughs from the back bedrooms are many and thick, and Patrick heads there at once; Berit and I follow.

The bedroom with the children is obvious as the door is open and Thaddeus stands in the way, his back to us and his arms crossed on his chest.

"Where is Berit?" Marie's voice, tense and heavy, shoots from the gloom. "Maybe another poultice?"

"I'm here," she says, and Thaddeus half-turns. His face darkens in a half-moment, and he turns fully to block the entry.

"Stay out!" he barks. "I've seen what you do! Sawbones as always!"

This time Patrick flinches with the slur, but he stands calmly in the hallway, both hands curled around the shiny leather of the medical bag handle. "I've heard one of the children is quite ill."

"I went for him, Tadeusz," Berit admits, her chin upright and her long neck straight with decision. "There's nothing else I know to do, and Marie's at her wit's end. You know yourself she's getting worse, unlike the boys."

"Who is it?" Marie comes to the door, her hair a wild, untamed dark mess and her eyes sunk in hollows. She stops short at Thaddeus's side. "What is going on?"

Her tone is less angry and more resigned, as if she is nearly relieved. I step forward. "Let us see Urszula, Marie. Maybe there's a chance." *This time.* I don't say the words, but they hang over us all, a curtain of blackness.

She stares at me for a long moment, her eyes flicking to Patrick, too, but a dry, rattling, hoarse cough from the back room spurs her into motion. She wipes her hands on an oily, stained apron and nods once, briefly.

Urszula lays without moving on her single mattress, the bed pulled off the floor by a wooden frame. She doesn't take deep breaths, instead her breathing is short and fast and high in the cavity of her chest.

Patrick moves at once to her bed, and I take initiative to open his bag and pull out the one instrument I know precisely will be needed. After handing him the stethoscope, I back away, nodding at the two adolescent boys huddling under their blankets and doing their best to stifle their coughs as they watch with wide eyes. I wish I could comfort Marie, offering her my hand or a shoulder to grasp as she waits to hear. Thaddeus huffs loudly, re-crossing his arms even tighter and balling his fists. His grey eyes narrow into slits and his gaze flickers between me and the doctor, while Marie only has eyes for Urszula's prone form on the bed.

"It's near blocked," Patrick says to the room. "The esophagus. Windpipe," he corrects himself, remembering at the last minute to switch back to layman's terms. "It has to be opened or she will not be able to take in air."

"What happens then?" Natan pipes.

"She'll die," Patrick says simply.

Natan shivers deeper into his blankets and Kaspar covers his mouth with his sheet.

"So—let's get her to the kitchen. Better light, and the big table will suffice." Patrick picks up his bag and looks up at Thaddeus. "You'll want to carry her—she can't breathe enough even to walk a short way, now."

"What're you going to do?" the blacksmith asks. "You can't be so daft to do what you tried on my father!"

"That's exactly what must be done," Patrick says evenly, though the quiver of his mouth gives away his worry to me. He's afraid he'll have to fight for Urszula's life, knowing it's slipping away in the time it takes to convince the parents.

"It's better this time," I jump into the conversation, ignoring the uncomfortable hit of all the eyes on me. "She's not so far gone—this will save her! Doctor Kinney has done the operation already twice this week."

"Painter kids still died," Marie says, her cheeks tight across her frown. "All of them."

"The Reverend and Sally didn't let me do the procedure," Patrick says gently.

"But Anette and Jacob did," I say. "With their youngest. Only yesterday."

This announcement makes both Marie and Thaddeus wilt a fraction, and Berit inhales loudly. "And it worked?"

"So far," Patrick says. "But as always—it's a cut, a chance. There's a likelihood of infection. And I ... I don't have a foolproof way of cleanin' the skin."

Urszula squeezes out yet another gasp, and Thaddeus turns without another protest to gather her up. He and Marie follow Berit out into the kitchen, and I hear Marie ask about Helena's whereabouts with a higher note of stress to her voice.

"Can you do this again?" I ask Patrick, pulling slightly on his coat sleeve.

"I'll have to," he says, sounding grim. "It's that or she'll surely die. The membrane is infected, and she's already fadin'. It's my callin', Janie. It's the choice I've made."

He strides into the kitchen, and my heart goes with him. I feel a nuisance, an unhelpful wife, one who cannot help with the greatest thing her husband does with his life—a husband who does not scoff and ignore my thirst to learn unwomanly topics, but hands me the books to do so!

Patrick strips off his coat and rolls up his sleeves and I rush to get Urszula as comfortable as I might on the hard wooden table. She moans softly, and Marie grabs her daughter's pale fingers, slick with fever and unwashed sweat.

"Hush, *córka*," she croons, her bumpy scarred hands caressing and gentle. "We're going to fix it. You'll breathe again."

Marie's eyes meet mine with intensity, dark and unreadable. I reach for Urszula's other palm and squeeze it, wondering how much the young girl can feel or understand. "That's right," I say, watching Patrick take out scalpels from the corner of my eye. "It'll be fine soon, and you'll have enough air."

Patrick pours whiskey on his knife and rubs it on Urszula's exposed neck and upper chest. I've only heard him speak of this operation, but other than the unsuccessful attempt on Walter, I have not seen one done that has been complete.

The doctor takes up a tube from his bag and hands it to me, and I realize I'm supposed to help him, whether I wish it or no.

"I must watch for certain arteries and veins," he says lowly. "Bring over another light so I don't nick a nerve, either. Hold her head, Thaddeus, tipping it as far back as you can," he instructs, tilting his own neck to show what he means.

I carry over a lantern and position it near Urszula's shoulder, and then stand, waiting, and morbidly curious. When Patrick makes the longitudinal incision, he does so not on the neck where I thought I remembered he did for Walter, but in the midline of the windpipe. A cracking of cartilage fills the room as the scalpel slices through.

And then a gush of inhaling lungs whooshes into Urszula and the faint blue of her skin seems to disappear at once. Berit turns away, hands over her eyes, as she gives in to weeping. Marie goes white, fingers over her mouth.

"Sit down, woman," Thaddeus says to her, averting his eyes from his daughter's neck. He looks green, too. I want to take his place, but to move Urszula now would be foolhardy—even an inexperienced nurse would know that. I wait for Patrick to ask for the little pipe I'm holding, but instead he shakes his head as bloodied pus and white chunks ooze from the wound.

"Gauze," he mutters, frowning. I go for the medical bag, but he leans over Urszula before I can open it, placing his mouth directly on her neck and making wet sucking sounds.

98

"What—!" Thaddeus's eyes bulge, and his beard quivers as his massive muscles shake with effort to hold still.

"Don't move!" I say, and my voice is loud and more commanding than I've ever been. He freezes, his eyes on my husband, who continues to suckle on the girl's open throat before standing, grabbing a bowl from the sideboard and spitting thickly into it. I glance down at the wound and see most of the mucous and matter have been pulled out. There's still some of the … what must be the membrane causing all the trouble, and Patrick goes back, taking the rest of it into his mouth. Everyone is so stunned we don't move an inch, myself included.

He does it a third time before I find my voice, hoping it's best for me to ask than an irate parent. "Doctor Kinney, certainly there is another way to take out the blood?"

"I'll take the tube now," he says, swigging the whiskey from earlier and spitting that out as well into the used bowl. Inserting the tube carefully, he looks around and finally seems to notice how appalled we are. Straightening, he looks surprised at our reaction, as he shrugs and spreads his hands, palm up. "It's the only way, you understand. A tool—any of my metal tools—they'll do more damage than good – it would destroy her windpipe to have me diggin' in there. It's best I pull it out with my own lungs."

Thaddeus stares at the tube sticking out of Urszula's throat and carefully puts her head down at a normal angle. Her eyelids flutter before the whites of her eyes roll up and she sleeps with a strange whistling breathing.

"There's still cause to worry," the doctor says, wiping his hands. "Without iodine to keep it clean, you'll have to hope the whiskey will do the same and that it won't hurt the healin'. Wash it every hour, you understand?" He looks at Berit and Marie particularly. "If it gets infected, the operation will have been for nothin'."

It doesn't take long for them to shuffle us out of the house after Patrick stitches up the wound now that the airway is clear, as if they think we bring bad luck. I try to catch Marie's eye, but she only cares for Urszula. Thaddeus offers the payment as we walk out, and Patrick takes it and strides down the street with his Stetson on low and his face to the ground.

"Paddy." I grab his sleeve. "She'll be alright?"

"She can breathe now, at least," he says, but the edges of his mouth are flat and grim. "It's the infection, Jane. Without the proper medicines, I'm fightin' a second battle."

As we head toward home, my heart feels wrung and squeezed. I may not be well-studied or wise in the ways of doctoring, but I know how deeply he speaks true.

CHAPTER SIX

# *Kate*

*February 6, 1883*

Bern pours water into the coffee pot and measures the beans carefully.

"You don't need to be so precise, you know," I tell him, pulling my shoes on and tightening the laces with more force than my ankles would prefer. "There's plenty in the store."

"'Til Yves and his gang take the rest," he drawls, dark eyes flashing at me from under thick unruly black hair. "'Til you lose more face."

"I'll be thanking you to not remind me of that," I snap. "Go get more wood."

He doesn't move from the small potbelly stove. We stare at each other a long moment, a taut line of anger, resignation, and knowledge stretching between us. I break it, glancing out at the early morning light, then huff and march out.

Of course, he won't want to be seen near my General Store at so intimate an hour, doing such an intimate chore.

Because of all the men in Flats Junction, only Bern is willing to be with me. And yet unlike all the men in Flats Junction, he wants nothing to do with me.

I yank up the ice-crusted rope of the well, praying the well isn't completely frozen over, but without luck. I pull up nothing but solid ice. Taking the hammer out, I whack at it, and with each swing, I only think of all the times I've found enjoyment with a man's company. Only when I was young did I think attention was for love and affection, and I believed it was true affection until recently. Only when I was young did I believe people might see past my parents' foolishness.

I take the chunks of ice back inside with an armful of old wood and smash the frozen water into an old tin pot. Bern doesn't move from the table as I careen around the tiny kitchen and make the bed with extreme particularness.

Eventually he glances up when my clattering reaches its loudest. "Bad morning?"

I glare at him and shove more wood into the fire.

He only shakes his head and goes back to flipping through the three naughty postcards I leave under the counter by the fabric.

"Don't you have better things to do? Training greenhorns for the spring, and such?" I ask. "I thought that was the whole reason Danny Svendsen kept you in the Dakotas this season instead of sending you south."

Bern slowly places his long legs along the length of my table and continues to flip between his two favorite photographs. "Can't do much training when it's this cold," he says coolly. "Can't do much of anything for a few weeks. 'Sides, a bunch are straight off the Pullman cars, and can't do much with those what are too dumb to understand things."

My hands find my hips and I inhale slow and deep. "I have to open the store shortly, so you best get out. Before anyone sees you."

"Coffee ain't ready, and you know yourself how … precious it is these days, what with the trains broke half the time, and the rest of it you raise the prices beyond what us poor cowmen can pay." He narrows his eyes. "Unless that's the whole plan. Make this place too fancy for the likes of us regular folk?"

"Don't be stupid." I slide into the seat across from him. "Flats Junction needs everyone. It needs more people. It needs a fancier hotel and a few more brothels, and at least one solid dressmaker."

"And you plan to organize and manage it all, don't ya?" He sounds almost exactly like Horeb.

"You saying I can't do such a thing round here?"

"I'm saying it's a tall order, even for you." He gets up, pours the melted water into the coffee pot, and sets it on the stove to boil. "I'm saying you'll have to think bigger if you want folk to think they need to listen to you. That you're nothing until they remember you … your General Store … is everything."

"You think I don't know this?" I hate that he sees me, that he speaks to some of the deepest recesses of my heart. "You think I'm so foolish that I don't know how the minds of these people work, that I am just sitting here all calm and not planning how to rule this town, same as my father?"

Bern stares at me, leaning against the wall by the stove, his arms crossed lightly, the long lean muscles of his torso taut against the worn denim of his shirt. "I don't know what to think of you, Kitty." He grabs his leather coat, lined with old sheep wool, and tugs it on with two thrusts of his arms. His eyes never leave mine. "Just call when you have a notion."

He shuts the back door near silently, so that I almost don't think he's closed it all the way. Not two minutes after he's left, the kettle complains, and I go to take it off the heat and pour myself the brew.

Fool of a man. They all are! I should know.

I take the mug out front and open the lock early, glancing at the tiny watch on my waistband as I do. It's early yet, but with Bern leaving early and the hour still not right, I am not rushed with coordinating this next piece of the plan.

Bern thinks I'm so foolish I don't know what I'm doing? He's a fool himself to think me so ill prepared for the next parts of my life. What does he think we've been doing all this time? Playing? I have a plan, one reaching so far back no one can catch tail of it now. Least of all those who think they know me in any way.

I just make it back to the counter when the bell on the door jingles, but it does so nice and softly so as not to be too obvious to anyone outside the store. I turn and watch her slowly mince round the plow and sacks of flour and rice.

When she reaches the counter, she lifts her chin, same as her mother does, and meets my eyes square.

"I'm ready."

I huff and go back into my rooms, pour her a cup of Bern's coffee, and bring it out. The steam rises thick and grey in the morning, as it's not time yet for me to warm up the place and stoke up the big stove in the corner. Even Gil and Horeb won't come in when the light is still this far off from rising.

"You sure, girl?" I ask, as she sips the hot coffee and grimaces. "I've never been past this town, and neither have you."

She meets my challenge with a defiant stare. "It's that or waste away here. Nothing's left for me but following, and I'm not following."

"You'll still be making your own way. Out East and then again back here."

She's silent for a moment. "Did my catalogue come in?"

"Which one?" I roll my eyes at her worried gasp. "You've got to be less easy to shock, or you'll make it no further than Chicago before you're pulled off and put to use in some madam's parlor."

"It's not going to happen!" she promises, so surely I near believe her until I notice the tremor in her fingers as she reaches for the two thick magazines I slam on the counter between us. "I know what to do, same as here, only with more people around. I'm not weak!"

"Keep saying that to yourself, and you won't be."

I don't mean to mother her, and I don't mean to be affectionate, but I cannot help feeling a kinship grow between myself and this defiant young woman. It's been so long since I've felt true feelings, I'm not sure if what I feel toward her is kindness or simply a strong attachment to the investment I'm making.

Slowly I reach under the counter, feeling behind the iodine bottles and the extra bags of salt and pull out a small sack with two twenty notes from 1880 and a few silver Morgan dollars. It's hard to part with this cash, as I'm still behind from when Yves took so much without pay. But I have to invest in the future of Flats Junction. And I have more, even if I'm loathe to touch it.

"When will you go?" I ask, tenseness filling my belly. It's happening. I'm going to do this. I'm going to build this!

"I thought in March, just as the trains are less likely to break?" She asks it, looking at me with such frankness I have to swallow my knowledge.

"I'll … I'm sure it will be fine. You just let me know which train you'll take to leave, and I'll talk to Franklin. And wire me when you know you're coming back. To be … sure." Sure, not safe. Sure I can keep her safe, if I am smart and careful and beg.

Helena takes the small pouch and puts it in a pocket hidden in the many folds of her dress. When she looks back up, her eyes are glistening.

"I have wanted to do this all my life," she says, her voice hoarse. "My parents don't understand, even though I thought they might. But they don't and … you do. Thank you, Miss Davies. I won't let you down."

She takes the copy of *Peterson's Magazine* for her fashionable eye, which will be put under her father's debt, and the *Dover Stamping & Mfg.* catalogue, which will be put under her mother's, though I'm not sure why she wishes to keep looking at publications in a trade she tells me she despises.

We share a long look and a brief nod, and then she quickly exits the store before a customer can arrive. I sigh with relief and excitement as she disappears around the bend to the north, and make a mark in the back of my ledger where I track the money lost—her sum goes right under the second chunk Yves took.

I chew on the middle of the pencil, my teeth finding the older marks from previous worrying. If I squint, I can just see the shadows of Horeb and Gil as they trudge toward the General and I rouse myself enough to fill the big stove with more wood.

Someone has to take care of Flats Junction. Someone has to think of the future, beyond next year, but ahead, into the century barreling toward us. Someone has to be considered the leader of the town, and Old Henry Brinkley is getting too soft and too easy in his age and his gout. I inhale the sharp smell of the woodsmoke as it catches fire, and stuff more smaller kindling in to hurry along the initial burn.

The fire is brighter than usual, I think, as I stare at it inside the oven. More yellow-gold than red or blue, and white along the edges, as if there is a halo around the heat. What can it mean? Is there truth in flames, that my ancestors sit around and make my judgement even as I deny them and my own skin? I shake the idea off, brushing it back into the forgotten parts of my mind. It's ridiculous. There is nothing but the ideas, the hopes, the path toward control and toward acceptance.

Horeb and Gil enter without a word to me, swinging their coats over the backs of their chairs, and settling into their respective chairs. Gil's chair makes the most noise, but Horeb makes more noise still, groaning and tsking as he sits.

"Well, Kitty, right fine day, isn't it?" he calls, as Gil slowly and carefully lays out the checker pieces on the worn and chipped board.

"It's fine enough," I say, and turn toward my ledger again. I need to do an accounting before the spring comes in and I'll be too busy to take a tally of my items.

It's not long before the store fills up. There's no storm or snow or blizzard, so everyone runs in before the next one hits, to see one another, compare chicken health, and barter their butter for bacon. I march along the back of each counter, unbolting the cloth and pulling down jars of candy and cans of condensed milk. The movement is a relief from my own thoughts, which are too jumbled and difficult to place in order.

As my fingers crawl along calico and weigh fine wheat, I think of my morning arguing with Bern, and of how Jane has yet to be in the store since Urszula Salomon's operation, and how Marie still hasn't returned my copper kettle. I suppose I should give her some stretch of time before I really come down angry on her, given the deaths in that house. But I am envious of their calmness—Jane's comfort in her marriage to Pat, and Marie's cocoon of family. I have neither, and I doubt I ever will. All I have is the General Store, a consolatory gift from my father, and whatever I can build from here. Alone.

For who would truly want to combine their lives with mine?

In the corner of the General, Sally Painter stands with the Reverend, her eyes surrounded by purple, a shade of her former self. Nearby, Julie Bailey, the farrier's wife, forcefully offers her fruit cakes to Father Jonathon, perhaps in the hope that he'll finally put on some weight. There's a two of the greenhorns from Danny Svendsen's ranch. Both have the dark skin of freedmen. One called Paul is a young lad, full of vigor to reach Oregon.

The other goes by Moses Thompson and hails from Pennsylvania originally. He says he was a Pullman porter on the trains after the War between the States. Now they say he wants to make his hand as a cowboy, and given his size and intense stares, he may have a chance should the townfolk not drive him out of Flats Junction first. Then again, they've let the lazy Yang brothers languish on the prairie and no one seems to mind when the Chen brothers help out around with odd jobs, and there's always the indulgent attitude around old Shen Zhao and his pet swine. And everyone still buys their shoes and has the soles fixed by Isaac Horowitz. I suppose, maybe, Flats Junction is as tolerant as the West might be.

Lara O'Donnell, her massive muscles quivering, approaches Sally carefully, but speaks so loud everyone can overhear. "So deeply sorrowed to hear about your children, Mrs. Painter. We're prayin' for them fierce at St. Aloysius."

The Reverend swells. "Don't bother. Don't need any Catholic prayers over my babes."

Sally doesn't move, her eyes planted on Lara's jowls. Her voice is high and soft with pain. "I did everything right, you know. I hung a bag of asafetida around their necks and passed a horse collar over their heads three times to make them all immune to any illness. It didn't work."

"Ah, that's because it only works to serve mashed snails and earthworms," Lara nods. "Barrin' the doc's medicinals."

Sally suddenly spits on the floor, her face a mask of hate. "Quack!"

On the other side of the store, Matthew Winters, Alice Brinkley's enterprising father, talks up his rough-hewn benches as a springtime need for any woman's garden. Alice's mother's sister Doris Tucker sits on the bench near the window, all the while batting her eyes heavily. I can't tell if she's doing it to get a man in General, or to get Tommy

Winters to notice her as he shops with Matthew for leather straps. After all these years, I'm surprised she hasn't given up. Doris's efforts aren't lost on Horeb, who stares at her bosom while losing his first checkers game of the day perfectly to Gil.

I roll my eyes and count up the pieces of candy Nels's children place with care on my counter, lined up according to color if not size. Clara gives me a soft shrug as she comes up behind them.

"Is it enough? I mean, are the chickens able to cover this and our needs?" she asks, her hands fluttering over the candy and the bags of flour, oats, and the like she's already selected. "I can have them put away."

I watch Nels, her husband, hobble around the big rusty plow on his crutches, the lost leg still a phantom I forget until each time I notice him. Shaking my head at her, I ring it up. "It'll all be covered. Don't worry."

She still does, I can see, but is too proud and too thankful to argue. After the Henderssens take their ten children out of the General, it's suddenly quite quiet. I take a deep breath and head back to get more of Bern's coffee when the door swings open so fast and loud the bell doesn't have a chance to jangle.

I pivot only to see Yves stalk in, surrounded by Arnold, Matthias, and Evan, closely followed by Patty, Victoria, and Natty.

As Yves strides toward me, I watch as the morning's customers leak out the front door, until the only folks left are Horeb and Gil.

I pull my shoulders back hard. I must confront Yves, but I cannot let anyone in Flats Junction hear it in case I must give in. The only two bodies needing clearing out of any matter are Horeb and Gil, who are pointedly ignoring the clattering of the posse and playing the cleanest game of checkers to date. I don't think Paul or Moses will spout off, and least-ways, no one will listen to newcomers.

Matthias and Evan drop two heavy bags each near the doorway, and they land with a bump and a thump.

"So, you are pleased with zee supplies we have brought, Miss Kate?" Yves uses his elbows to scoot his upper body closer across the counter. His heavy breathing sprays dill and garlic into my face.

I smile at him. "I'm sure I will be, once I look them over." I flick my eyes to Horeb and Gilroy, in hopes they'll take a hint to get out of the store. They don't, but Arnold does. He twists his belt, and shambles over to the checkerboard.

"Me and Natty want t' play the checkahs. *Now*!"

To Horeb and Gil's credit, neither flinch. But it's Matthias who grabs the collars of both into his massive, meaty fists and pulls them up by threadbare flannel and patched leather. Without a word, he shoves them out the door, held gleefully by Victoria, and despite Horeb's spluttering that they could at least let them finish his turn.

Yves doesn't move or even turn during the entire noisy process. True to his word, Arnold plunks into Gil's chair, but it's Matthias who sits opposite.

I pull back to look straight at Yves, right into his round face and leaking pale eyes just enough to keep from offending the Frenchman, and tap the wood of the counter between us. "The supplies. Whatever you've finally … brought. You cannot charge me double." I want to say "stole". I know they've stolen it—from other stores, from broken trains, from trains they've sabotaged. It grates on me to know how well they are playing the game, when I'm stuck in Flats Junction, battling the role of my skin, my sex, and my position.

*Soon it won't matter. Soon I'll have help.*

Yves blinks, then nods solemnly while wiping his mouth on the back of his right sleeve, which now needs severe cleaning. "But Kate. It ees so very hard to move extra supplies in zee winter."

"Clearly. Since you're weeks late in paying me back from what you … borrowed … in January."

"It ees us or zee train, which is not so reliable. We must be compensated for zee risk."

I frown. Should I accuse him of sabotaging the train every time? It seems excessive to do so. Still … I have to ask. "Tell me plain. Are you the reason the train is less reliable?"

He ignores me. "Free tobacco any time we come into zee town, if we must be paid less for zee supplies. Plus zee … heavy discount on supplies for us."

"That's assuming you get me those supplies in the first place. And pay for them." Frustration zings down to the edges of my fingertips. I clench my hands. "You still owe me funds. If you don't, soon there won't be a General Store for you to … help you with your supplies whenever you need them."

Yves shrugs. "If we don't see zee lawmen, it ees not a problem to get monies."

"Then stay away from the rails," I suggest.

"But Kate," Yves says reasonably, rubbing his fingers together, "broken trains mean money."

"I pay you to move supplies, not *stop* trains!"

"Ahhhhh." Yves pushes back from the counter. "I need a piss." He meanders around the counter and heads through my curtains toward the back door. My heart lurches and near chokes me. He has no need to go through my private quarters to go 'round back! I'd turn on him and demand he come back, but there's the rest of the posse to manage while he's gone, and I don't feel up to the challenge. I never truly do, frankly speaking.

The others are silent with Yves departing, though vulnerability crashes through my limbs. Surely, they wouldn't do anything without him saying so? The only sound is the click of checkers pieces as Arnold pops another black on the squares. A deep sense of helplessness wrings through me. God and heaven, this whole game had better work. They owe me for ruining the train schedules, and I'm sure as hell not going to pay double for any supplies they do bring from Yankton when the trains are running late! They can have free tobacco and coffee for their trouble, since that's expensive and will be worthwhile on their trips. And sugar. Even the white. I can offer that much as payment. What else can I use to sweeten the deal, so they'll think twice about reneging on our situation? Because surely, at some point, Yves will back out ... But I cannot pay double. I won't! I'll go bankrupt, and that's the exact opposite of my plan. I need ... I need another source of income. Another way to be sure I am needed. Important.

Please let Helena leave soon. Let her find what we need, let her be smart and savvy and reliable!

Before all that, though, I need the rails to be more reliable. I need my supply managed in the meantime. If it means playing high stakes with this posse, I will have to take the gamble. Anything to keep my position and the General secure.

The calico curtain behind me flings open and Yves steps through, still buttoning his fly. "So, we will do zee wagons from Yankton to Flats Junction," Yves recites. "Let us hope zee weather does not make this too difficult. And both us and zee trains are not late."

My blood runs a few degrees lower at his words. Weather, indeed! Between trusting this murdering group of people with part of my father's savings, the weather, and the potential loss of any property at all on the prairie, this is one of the most uncontrolled things I've ever done. "If you don't get back with my goods in a month, you'll lose your discount, and no free tobacco."

Yves shrugs, already glancing about the store with keen interest. "We also need food for zee journey, so we not stop at our *usual* stops down and back from Yankton."

Greedy bastard! His immediate possessiveness puts me further on edge, and my teeth grind together. His eyes travel my corsets and hip, and I clamp my thighs together under my skirts in protest, the skin and muscles fitting together like notched wood. They'll never get *that*. I do that on my own terms, and for my own purpose. A quiver of fear skates down my stomach anyway. Sometimes, I suppose it might be nice to have a man on hand.

I think Yves's reputation is disreputable enough to keep anyone from stealing my wagons of goods, though. It is what must be done to get a steady stream of supplies, anyway—I am hedging my bets that one thing—Yves or the train—will get through this winter. Eying up the heavy flesh and broadness of Arnold, Matthias, and Evan, I must believe I've made a good choice. The only issue is Yves drives a hard bargain, his determination so sharp and certain it hurts.

"I think we will start with zee free tobacco now," he says. "And zee whole side of smoked bacon, two bags of flour, one of rice, and zee bag of beans."

"No." I don't have nearly enough to give him some and have leftover for Flats Junction for a month. "Not unless you'll pay. Or bring double next time."

"But you have not paid me double for what we did bring in zee wagon this time!"

This is going nowhere. My head begins to spin.

Arnold wanders over, his black wiry hair taller and bushier than usual today. He smiles, the white striking against the ebony cheekbones, but the smile is cold. "Yves said now."

I lift my chin to show them I'm not weak. Pulling my hair out of the last of the pins, it undulates down my back and Yves's watery eyes follow the length of it as it washes along the bones of my back. It's daring to be so boldly flirtatious but I can't back down. "I don't have enough for you to take what you want now—and certainly not without paying, at least for the last time. When you come back, we speak again. With my goods. You'll be paid the rest of the money then, plus additional goods. I'm keeping track." I tap the ledger.

Arnold sighs and glances behind him, where the rest of the posse gathers. I remember the rumors well enough and am not surprised when Matthias steps up to enforce whatever it is Yves demands, his huge bulk blocking half of the slanted sunlight coming from the front window. It is a cold winter light, though, more white than yellow.

"Get the supplies first. Then the free food." I echo myself, and shake my hair. Yves watches it as it whispers along the base of my spine, and I hide the grin burbling under my skin, though it shrinks when I notice Natty staring at my hips.

Yves reaches to touch the ends of my hair.

"Enough!" I slap away his grubby hand without thinking.

He jerks back. For a moment, there's no movement save the dust floating above everyone's head, twisting in that same cold sunlight.

"Now, do we have an understanding?"

Yves's glare narrows as a wry smile cuts across his face. "Yes, we'll bring zee supplies." He stands up, runs his eyes over my body and moans so softly I barely catch it. "For this winter."

"Yes." Somehow. I have no idea how, especially if they are determined to ruin the rails and try to charge me double— or more—for any supplies they bring. An idea hatches at the same time I spit it out. "If you're later than a month, I pay half of the cost of the goods, not double."

Yves pauses the run of a finger along the rusty plow. "You are threatening us?"

"No. It's just … to be sure we are fair."

"And if we are early, zen what?"

I feel my stomach churn. I shouldn't have spoken. This is getting out of hand! "You just said it'll be difficult. Who cares if you're early?"

"Oh, I think we all will care. Early should be … rewarded." Yves crosses his arms, and the runny eyes travel the rise of my bosom. It's all I can do not to cross my arms. "I will expect … dinner."

"Just dinner?"

116

He cracks a smile, echoed by all the other men except blank Evan and stoic Matthias. Even Victoria and Patty crack a grin. I am so dizzy I may lose my footing. "Oh, *oui*, Kate. Just a nice, full, complete *dinner*."

Before I can argue further, Yves turns around and nods at Arnold, who bends swiftly and grabs a bag of coffee so fast the top splits, and the raw beans skitter into dim corners around the barrels of molasses and salt pork.

My mouth opens and air rushes down my windpipe, but the only sound is a rasp as I try to breathe in and speak at the same time. It does no good. Another nod from Yves, and Evan takes the biggest bag of tobacco. The fuse of fire deep in my belly grows higher than usual, coiling and knotting into a chain of fury. Surely they must see the flush flower across my cheeks. Damn them! My goods. My rules! *Not theirs.*

The town is—should be!—behind me, should Yves not hold his end of the agreement. I am the holder of the food, the flour, the sugar, the coffee. It all rests on me. Flats Junction needs me. The town must need me.

And with their need, my place is safe.

Patty picks up some peppermint candy and Victoria yanks a spool of narrow lace down without a slip, her hands caressing the wood of the bobbin with small, leathery hands.

"*This* is *not* our bargain!" I crank the words out, waving my hands at the additional items.

"It is." Yves doesn't even look back over his shoulder as he leads the posse. I try to count and calculate on the spot as the goods trek out under arms and over shoulders, yellow bile creeping up my throat.

"It's not," I counter, but my voice sounds flat and hollow, and no one listens. It's just as well, I guess, that none of the townspeople can see me at my weakest.

Damn it! This was not the plan! If only ...

If only these terrors lived in Flats Junction year-round. If only I had more to offer them. Then they'd be under my power. They'd depend on me for food and goods, orders and credit. They'd be beholden.

What will people think? How much did Horeb and Gil hear where they shiver out on the porch, waiting to get back in?

Matthias is the last to go, and he takes the most, knocking over two cans of condensed milk as he goes. He doesn't bother to apologize or clean it up, his massive bulk loaded down by the flour under an arm and the barrel of molasses over it. I can understand why his reputation as Yves's muscle is so instant. He fills a room even with his silence, and I am never sure if I should feel menaced in his presence or something else. It's disconcerting and annoying all at once.

I breathe out again when they leave, and Horeb and Gilroy sidle back into their chairs, their eyes downcast but flicking over the store and me constantly. I'm about to defend myself when I realize I don't even know what they've heard. And wouldn't they agree with me anyway if they know what I've done? It's settled at once when Horeb leans over to grab the dented and rusty old tin. Spitting noisily into it after clearing his nose, the green eyes meet mine. I didn't even recognize I was staring, waiting and poised, for their comments.

"Deal with the devils, are you?"

"Not your concern, Horeb."

As he puffs his chest to retort, the door swings open again. I spin, ready to do more battle with Yves, but it's

118

Hardy, a boy who came on a late Fall train and has been living on the charity of Father Jonathon since.

He pushes himself past the worn, pitted oak and glances at Horeb and Gilroy before pinning me with a frank and earnest gaze. It's improper. He's young, and I am his elder. He ought to be showing a bit more respect. A crease twitches between my eyebrows.

"What now?"

"Father sent me," he says carefully. Rehearsed. His tone hides a squeak below the new rumble of male deepness. His skin is flushed pink with worry and cold, and his deep gold hair glints under the lamps.

"Does the church need more credit?" I ask archly, waiting for the charity request.

He shakes his head. "No. Only … only he said to ask about work."

"I'm not hiring."

"Not … not here. Beg pardon, Miss Kate. Only … if you've heard. If anyone needs … help. I can't stay at the church forever, Father says. He says I need to find work. I'm old enough." His chest swells at the last, and I see the giant of the man he'll become when he's grown. Already he's near as tall as me, though gangly yet with newfound height.

"I haven't," I say. "I don't hear of such things."

"Haven't you, Kitty?" Horeb pipes up.

I glare at him. He chooses not to notice and fixes his gaze on young Hardy, where the orphan fidgets near my counter.

"You go on to all the tradesmen and ask," I tell him tersely. "Don't come crawling to me!"

Hardy doesn't flinch. Instead, he looks more determined than I feel, which disconcerts me a bit. I step toward him, towering over his head. He sighs softly and turns to go, just as Helena breezes back in.

"I forgot to ask for—" She stops short and stares up at Hardy. "Who are *you*?"

"Hardy. Miss." He tips his fingers to his forelock in a strange gentlemanly gesture, and Helena has the grace to look flustered.

She turns to me to hide it and clasps her fingers together. "I forgot to ask for the fashion catalogue, just for the ideas."

"As your usual." I push the 1881 *La Mode Française* magazine toward her, and she turns to the ladies' fashions hungrily. As she traces the tip of a worn and dirty finger across the printed edges of a gown, I watch Hardy stare at her as if he's been struck with shock.

Helena ducks her head further as Horeb stands and scratches his ribs, then ambles slowly toward Hardy while keeping his eyes on Helena and me.

"Boys still sick at home?" he calls to Helena.

She hunches her shoulders a bit before giving up. Her eyes meet mine briefly in a silent plead before she turns around. "My brothers are mending," she says carefully. "They'll be back to helping my father soon."

"But in the meantime, he's hard up, ain't he?"

She lifts her chin. "Not your concern."

I like her defiance, and it will help her when she leaves Flats Junction, but it only serves to make Horeb grin wider. He's been in Flats Junction since the beginning, and he's not cowed by anyone—man or woman—and he certainly has no interest in paying attention to the cues Helena shoots his way.

"I'll say, he might want a strapping young man to help, meanwhile, won't he?" Horeb taps Hardy on the shoulder. "I'd wander over to the blacksmith's today, taking this young lady home, don't you think?"

Hardy is rooted to the floorboards. "The blacksmith?"

"It's what I said, didn't I?" Horeb glances behind his shoulder.

"Yup." Gil moves one of his red pieces in plain sight, but Horeb's too busy with his latest idea to care on the cheating.

"I don't need an escort," Helena huffs. "And I'm busy."

She turns pointedly back to the catalogue, and Hardy looks at me with a plead in his blue eyes. I shrug. It's certainly not my trouble to find the boy work in town.

*Isn't it?*

Memories suddenly flash through the back of my mind. Flashes of my father organizing businesses, offering loans with strings, forcing people to bend to his will so Flats Town became Flats Junction, putting us on the map with the railroad.

For the first time in years, I wish Percy was alive. The wishing for such a thing is foreign and heavy and pointed. I don't miss my father with a sharp intensity like others might, but I do know when he might offer some use. He'd know how to piece it all together, to keep any personal risk at arm's length, and the posse in check.

To see the long game.

"I'll talk to Marie."

The promise is mine, and Hardy and Horeb and Helena all stare at me, eyes wide. I don't know why I offer it. It's as if I am possessed with a plan not of my own making. My mouth feels filled with soap as soon as the words escape. But it's too late. And now I will look weaker and more a fool if I don't go about fixing this. Helena will know I'm not to be trusted, and I need her for the next step in my plans.

As much as I hate to admit it aloud, Flats Junction is my father's legacy, and the only thing he's ever left behind that offers me any real strength. I understand it. And I must control it, before it controls me. Before it takes away my power. Before it mutes my voice.

CHAPTER SEVEN

# Marie

*February 7 1883*

There is no more pork, Berit says, and there's only been one train through so food is short—shorter even, according to my husband, because of me.

"I can't keep going to the General and asking for more credit without that damn copper kettle, Marya!" he argues. "Why isn't it done? You won't say, and to be frank it's unlike you."

"I have three weeks backlog," I say, hiding the panic under defiance. "She has to wait her turn same as everyone else."

"You didn't have such a trouble when you took it in early November. She won't give us more than a few pounds of flour at a go now. You've got to finish it!"

"I will!"

"*When?*"

"I ..."

Thaddeus narrows his eyes and his arms cross tightly. "Don't tell me you don't know how. I won't believe it. You don't give yourself enough credit even after all these years. And if you're doing this out of your personal issues with where she comes from—"

"Oh so? And *you* don't make things personal?"

"Marya. Can you fix it?" His question requires an answer. It is hard and worried and fretful. The deep rumble of his voice hitches so slightly no one would notice if they did not know him well.

My heart stutters.

I know the reason for the crack in his voice. I know the reason his eyes glint with a shine that has nothing to do with the cold outside our doors and everything to do with the fact that Urszula lies cold and still in the livery next to Walter, waiting for the first thaw so we can bury them on the crowded family plot.

I know he blames himself for her death, same as I blame myself.

If we'd not called for the doctor, would she still live? Or would she be dead sooner than that? Would we have watched her slowly burn with fever, her skin peppered with red specks, her heart beating so fast in her throat that I could not keep count? Maybe we would have instead watched her turn blue with lack of air, or maybe she would have lived.

I do not know, and cannot tell.

All I know is we must work. We must find the coin for the metal for the future, must fight our way in this world for our remaining children. We cannot just stop.

Death never allows a body to stop. This I know well.

And there seems to always be hope, even as I do not expect it, or believe in it.

Thaddeus stares at me, waiting for my answer to his anger. We are arguing the same topic we've been circling for hours. It won't fix the kettle any faster, and I'm too stubborn to admit what I've done to it. My stomach feels tight and hard, a ball of iron, a knot of grief pulling me down into a pit, where only blood can pull me out. I turn away from my husband and just as I think I will lose myself in the buttery slip of scissors against copper as I make out a new dishpan for Elaine Warren's kitchen at the Golden Nail, the door to the back of the shop swings open.

"Father. Mother." Helena sticks her head into the forge, her eyes red and her face white. "Kate Davies is here."

My shoulders fall and I turn to follow her. Thaddeus is immediately behind me, his boots clunking heavily but his wide hand finds my arm. The squeeze is gentle. It speaks of forgiveness.

How can the sun shine so brightly when a child is dead?

A mother should not have to bury a child. A pretty one, with hair that is glossy like a blackbird's top feathers and big round eyes full of innocence and sweetness. A mama should not have to lay out the thin limbs and blue-tinged fingers of a girl so close to womanhood it was possible to see how the young roundness would quickly blossom. No mother should be forced to listen to the cruel, looming rattle of death as her child's air is slowly cut away, closed off from the chest until it's impossible to think, impossible to hear anything, and nearly impossible to cry.

Kate Davies stands in the middle of the kitchen, looking for all the world that she'd like to be anywhere else.

125

Her hair falls out from under her hat and her cloak is of brilliantly green dyed wool. If it weren't for the obviousness of her heritage, she'd look straight out of a New York fashion plate. I frown slightly at the beauty of the yellow stitching around her cuffs. It's precise and lovely, and I don't remember seeing such details on her winter dress in previous years. What a strange thing to notice. It seems my senses are high with grief.

"What is it?" I ask, jumping in before Thaddeus can grouse. "Are there more supplies?"

"I've come to see about an apprentice."

My mouth drops open. Thaddeus uncrosses his arms. We both stare at her with something close to shock more than surprise. Does she mean for the tinshop or the forge?

"There's a young man needing work. With your boys still recovering, we—I thought it might help you. And it helps him. Father Jonathon can't keep giving out charity for always."

"Why are you asking?"

"Because I didn't think you'd listen to me!" Helena jumps in.

I yank backward, as if she'd pushed me. My daughter knew of this? I am not sure where to look first—Kate's grim face or Helena's shoulders as she bends over the hearth next to Berit, trying to keep her eyes away from mine.

It doesn't make sense, but I can feel the tenseness leak out of Thaddeus as he leans against the fireplace. "For which shop?"

"Yours, Thad," she says. "He's a strapping boy, about Helena's age, I think. He came in yesterday and I promised to help. You need another set of hands or you'll fall behind."

I snort. He's not the only one behind—and not just for lack of help, but for lack of metal. She should know. I shake my head at Thaddeus, but he's already looking beyond everyone's head, his grey eyes half-closed in thought.

"What's it to you?" I ask her, unable to help myself. "Why do you care?"

"Let's just say … the town cannot afford a smithy that fails."

"Now's a poor time to come in and ask," I say with more malice than I plan. "We've just had Urszula die from … her illness."

It wasn't the diphtheria, and as much as I want to blame that, I cannot shake the terrifying vision of Doc Kinney sucking pus from her open throat.

No. It was something else. Something rancid and evil, that ate her skin and infected her whole body. It was a rotting illness.

"Do you think you're the only family who has lost someone from diphtheria?" Kate asks sharply. "Many have died this winter."

"What would you know about this type of loss?" I scoff, then wish I hadn't. An old memory jiggles itself loose, but it's too late.

Kate's face goes white—maybe with anger or sorrow, but her voice is even and hard. "You recall my brother died of it, these years past."

"I—"

"Anyway, did you want the help in the forge or no? There's been no extra help for you since your last apprentice took himself off west. I thought you'd take the kindness."

I want to tell her that I don't want her charity or her kind thoughts. That I don't trust her, but then I'd be admitting to my own deep prejudice, no matter how well-earned I believe it to be after my brothers died at the hands of her kin all those many years ago. Some might even say now that Tom and Al deserved it. That they shouldn't have been pushing so far into Lakota land.

But no matter my own inner turmoil. Thaddeus is already bartering. He's action where I am emotion, and he's best when he has something to take over his mind. "In exchange, will you give us more credit? Guarantee our raw metal comes in?"

"You know I cannot do that," Kate says immediately. "The trains aren't dependable in winter."

"Even worse this year," I mutter.

She flushes suddenly, casting about the room with her quick dark eyes. Then she lifts her face to mine and clenches her jaw with a smile that doesn't go beyond her mouth. "If you take him in, I won't get too antsy on why you're taking so long to return my family heirloom."

The blood rushes out of my skin, and I feel clammy, and can tell Thaddeus is shooting daggers at me. "I'm almost finished."

"But not done."

"It's another mouth to feed," I remind her. "A boy's. They eat much more than a girl."

"I'll add in a bit more flour and some molasses when you come in for supplies," she adds. "Fair?"

I don't like it. Something feels off. Why would Kate take an interest in our family and business needs?

But Thaddeus straightens and nods once. "Send him over."

A flash of triumph flits across her cheeks before she shutters it, and nods back. She spins on her heel and sees herself out before anyone can offer her a hot drink or an extra word, and as soon as the back door shuts, I round on Helena.

"How did you know about this boy, this orphan? Is this where you go every morning, hiding away from us, lying on your whereabouts?"

"No! I just met him yesterday!" she retorts, swinging a spoon toward the door Kate just exited.

Thaddeus's eyes darken.

If I were less frustrated with Helena, I might pity her the tanning he has in mind.

"Where have you been going, then?" I demand. "You have chores to do—"

"I'm not shirking," she says levelly, her eyes cast downward. For a moment, her hands tremble as they smooth the edge of her apron. "And I'm not sneaking off to see a boy."

"Girl, answer your mother!" Thaddeus bellows, stalking behind me. "No daughter of mine should be sneaking about so early, like a woman with a secret, going to the General without an errand! What is in that head of yours?"

She is flushed, rosy, her eyes over-bright. Is she getting a fever as well?

"I just wanted to get coffee yesterday, if there was any in," she says.

"You know very well a train hasn't been in," I say.

"You leave home without a word, and you know better."

Thaddeus reaches for the switch, and I realize it has been many months—no. *Years!* Years since he last moved to take up the whippy birch branch. Last time it was for both boys, for climbing Bone Jump Road in the dead of winter with their cousins with the ridiculous notion to jump off the ancient buffalo leap to see if it made them feeling like flying.

He's hurting hard with Urszula's death, I realize.

Worried on the boys. Needing to lash out.

"You don't mean it, Father," Helena protests, her eyebrows rising. "You just said I am too old."

"I said you are too old to walk about like a child, without responsibility or a note left to your family. *Potępienie! Damnation!* Going out in the dark, before the sun is up! It's the way of the bordello girls, and no daughter of mine will live this way!"

He grabs her by the arm and turns her around. She yelps, but doesn't cry, and lifts her chin as she waits. Her back is a plank of solid will, and I watch the creases of her skirt pause.

Well. I cannot help it—I raise my hand. Thaddeus glances at me, and I recognize the agonized frustration there. She should know better. Did we not teach her properly? *Have we failed?*

*Why was it Urszula who had to die?*

I hate myself for the thought, but it slips through the black cracks of my heart and festers there, making me doubt my own mothering. What mother would think such a thing?

He brings down his arm with the force of a hundred hammer strokes, so hard I fear he'll rip the fabric of her bottom.

It's one stroke only, but it's whip-fast and loud, and she cries out.

Berit watches, her pale blue eyes sad but her mouth closed. I wonder if Thaddeus will continue, the way he used to do.

But she's too old for a real thrashing, and after a moment, Thaddeus tosses aside the switch and fumes back to the forge.

I stare at Helena as she stares back, two red splotches on her cheeks, but her eyes flash. I reach across the space and touch her forearm, squeezing slightly. It did not occur to me that Thaddeus truly was going to punish her, and I hope she knows he simply does not know what to do with himself, with our loss. She turns away from my hand but joins me after she finishes her morning chores helping Berit, bending her head to the tin work I give her when she creeps into the shop. Today she is careful not to complain of the work.

All day the deep yet tight wracking of the coughs Natan and Kaspar battle through the thin walls between my shop and their room. It grates my nerves and yanks at my stomach, which is already tied in knots as it is. At lunch, Thaddeus only glares at Helena, Berit makes soup for the sick children, Helena herself fidgets overmuch, and I am tongue-tied. Why does it feel like everything is falling apart?

I'm frozen. I cannot help. I cannot think.

I only want to escape and disappear behind my copper and tin. It is time to face this, and I'd rather forget and be in the shop.

As I work, I force myself to remember the good things. The roses that will bloom in the spring and the glimmer of metal and the happiness of children still living.

But even with that thought, as I run tinplate through the wiring machine and it turns itself around, the memories of those we have lost pour into my mind.

Urszula was the best of my children for learning the way of the flowers, to plant and make them grow. She had the patience I lack to make fine stews and meats. She is the daughter I yearned for after Helena; Urszula is soft where Helena is hard. She is song and sweetness, honey and sincerity. *Was*. She *was*. I believe she would have been so all her life, and now she is gone, and I will never truly know. I will have to imagine, and I am no good at pretending happy things. We will bury her in the spring. Next to the others in the graveyard, surrounded by worn grey wood fencing and an arch made of saplings. We will put her next to the copper cross of my father and Thaddeus's parents. We will lay her near markers put down for my brothers, whose bodies never came back from the Indian frontier. By the two babes we lost at birth.

Our plot of dead grows faster than our living.

I place a palm against my stomach and close my eyes. No, a woman should not have to spend a moment worrying about her children and whether they will live. It does not seem to do an ounce of good to do so. They die anyway.

The old pain unfurls, a ball long buried, tight and pointed and angry, but I try to shove it down. And if Thaddeus notices during dinner, he decides to keep quiet, which only wounds me further. Death is back in my life. I thought I'd paid my dues. How much more should a woman lose? Who will go next? Natan? Kaspar? Helena? It should be me.

*She's gone, she's gone, she's gone …*

It's so impossible to think Urszula is dead that I do the only thing I can possibly think to do. I must work. It clears my thoughts. I must touch the metal and lose myself in the glimmer of it. My feet move across the big kitchen and into the blacksmith forge, leaving the door open slightly so I might hear if Berit calls for me for the boys.

My scarred old fingers take up a lantern just inside the wide tinshop entry and light a thrush to take to the wick. There are no windows in the smithy, and only a small one in my shop, and it's too cold to open the doors. Against the single flame, the shadows inside the two rooms are flat and bold. Another time, I might think of the romance in these spaces, and how lusty Thaddeus and I have been at times, hiding in the dark against the bulk of an anvil or the flatness of a bench.

But not now. Not tonight. I cannot think past the color of the tin, the rose of the copper. The scribe, sharp and strong, warms inside my palm as I slowly trace a pattern with it, the tip scraping into the softer metal sheet as I measure out a Whitworth cartridge box.

The scribe scratches under the pattern and I shove away the tin sheet and pick up a snips. It slips and renders the cup too small for the base. After a moment, I uncover Kate's damaged kettle, where it hides under burlap under the counter. It is still as broken as ever. I put it over the tinner's anvil stake and stare at the crackling hole along the base and up the side. Just as I pick up the hammer to straighten the dents, my vision blurs. Damnation. I cannot manage it. I cannot stop the sorrow, or the anger, or the pain.

The loss of yet another child, of yet more family, tears into my breathing and chokes the blood from my veins.

What do I do while everything unravels? How can I fix anything? I cannot! I only have the repairs in my shop. I have my wits and the numbers, the copper and the tools. I take up yet another mug.

The coughs from Kaspar and Natan can penetrate through the wood of the tinshop, bouncing inside and rattling in my brain.

My hammer smashes into the piece of tin, and I sigh. But then another thick cough jars in, and I cringe, the crease between my shoulder blades tightening.

*Bang!*

*Cough!*

*Bang, bang, bang!*

*Cough, cough, cough, cough!*

*Smash, smash, smash, SMASH!*

There is no point to hope and wish for something different. I may still see all my children into the ground, no matter their age.

My eyes water as the guilt of my inaction to save my family thunders in my brain. I want to laugh with crazy abandon at the pain of the loss, to cringe inside myself, to pretend it didn't happen, but my younger daughter is gone. There's no changing it. I did nothing. Who is next—

*Cough! Cough! COUGH!*

The hammer falls from my feeble fingers. I need a different tool.

There's no thought or feeling with the first pull of the scribe against skin. Nor even the second. I cannot really see, nor hear, as if I live in a void of darkness, crossing off my sight and stopping up my ears, so I can only exist deep inside myself, where I feel nothing and control everything. The plink and plop of fluid against metal pings softly in the dark tinshop, and I pause halfway through the third slice to stare at the streaks of red on my arm.

Damnation and hell.

What am I doing?

Have I lost my head so quickly? Given up so easily? I cannot. I must not.

"Marya?"

Thaddeus is anything but silent, though he surprises me slightly when he looms out of the black hole of the smithy. I close my right hand over the skin of my left forearm and look up at him.

"What the hell are you doing?" He is frowning deeply, and as his voice goes lower, I know he is actually darkly angry with me.

"Working."

"Goddamn it all to the Devil's hell," he swears. "You're on the edge of a knife again, aren't you?"

"No—"

"*Aren't you?*" He takes the scribe from me wordlessly and tosses it on the bench. It clatters against the tin scraps and bangs into the base of the turning machine's standard. "I have never spoken to you of this in all our years," he waves a hand at my forearm. "But I cannot understand it."

"I do not ask you to."

"But—"

"It is not important." I point toward the bedroom walls. "We must decide about the children."

"What of them?"

"Natan and Kaspar are as ill as Urszula is ... was. What do we do?"

"We wait."

"It's foolishness!"

"I won't discuss it. This is my *choice*!" he shouts suddenly, then lowers his voice at once, glancing at the thin walls of the shop. "Do not ask me to let that doctor in my home. I will not have it. Death is the way of things here."

"I know this." I know it all too well. And I have tried to accept each death, each loss, with logic and practicality. It has worked for me since my marriage, but I feel I have reached the end of my limits.

Thaddeus looks at my arm with despair and sighs. "You must stop. You once promised me that you'd settled."

I won't deny it, nor that I did not speak the truth. It is impossible to completely banish the darkness that will threaten to swallow me. I roll down my sleeve.

"There are other things to discuss," I say instead, offering up the words I do not mean to say so soon. But I must speak so I do not have to hear anything more about my weakness.

"What the fuck is there to discuss besides?" He puts his massive fists on the tinner's bench, and stares at me, his beard haphazard from the blowing winter wind and his shoulders tight and stiff.

"There'll be an addition. Come summer."

The words are too early for so many reasons.

Thaddeus looks utterly strangled for a long moment. "Again?"

I can only nod. The last stillborn had convinced me I was too old, which is the way of things and not a fuss. But here I am again, speaking of a coming child.

He is frozen. Rigid.

Then he softens slightly, and his hands drop to his side. He sighs. "Well, then. That is something else."

CHAPTER EIGHT

# *Kate*

*March 21 1883*

The train hasn't come today. It ruins everything. Yves has to let one through—both here and back. I have to manage that, so I can build my next business in Flats Junction. There cannot be only failures this winter! I step briskly into the train station's office and hesitate before going through to the private back rooms. Behind the door, flesh smashes into bone. The sound skitters through the cracks of the depot. These days, Bess doesn't even bother screaming.

I elbow into the back room and stand to my full height. Franklin's too far gone to notice my entrance, so I grab his shoulder just as he raises his fist again.

"Give me the bottle."

He doesn't hear me, pulls hard, and the stump of his other arm, sharp at the end, jabs his wife in her stomach. She bends over, silencing her yelp.

"Good goddamn morning, *Mister* Jones!" I grab Franklin's suspenders and use the surprise to shove him into a chipped chair. His skull bounces against the wall.

"*Nein*, Kate!" Bess rasps. "He does not mean to, you know dis!"

I stand over Franklin as his eyes squint through the gloom of the early morning. He reeks of bad whiskey, old sweat, and rancid tobacco, his once-broad shoulders hunched forward.

"I said pour me another whisk—hic—key, woman." He looks for Bess, sees me and shrinks, putting his head in his one remaining hand. There are still the scars on the back of his palm, pushing white and red against the pale flesh, from when he used to be a cooper.

Bess's face is a mask, the smooth, solid flesh marked with yellowed and purple bruises, though the new strike is hot and pink. She draws up her ample bosom and attempts to smile at me while hiding her two broken teeth. We are to ignore all of this, as everyone has since '76.

"A-vut are you needing so early, den, Kitty?" she asks, the Austrian accent still as pronounced as ever. She carefully takes the half-empty bottle from the table next to Franklin and places it high on the top of the mantle.

"Didn't hear a whistle. I wanted to see if there were any wires coming down the line about the train, as I've got to pay for someone's ticket."

Franklin stirs slightly, one watery eye peering up. "The train?"

"Train. Your job. About trains."

"My job ..." he mutters, cradling his forehead. "God, do I miss my job!"

"Well, this is your job now, and you need to do it," I say crisply, pushing pins back into the side of my hair. Franklin doesn't stir, so I bend close and put my hand back on his shoulder. Gentle, this time.

He sighs, tries to rise, and trips over the leg of the chair he's sitting in. Bess swoops in to grab him, and he reacts viciously at once. "I can *do* it! I'm the man of the house!" he hisses, his knuckles automatically rising to her cheek, hesitating only as he sees the brand of his earlier slap. His eyes re-focus. "Oh Jesus! Jesus. Bessie. What have I—hic—done?"

He slowly topples over, collapsing over the worn surface of the table, his one arm hanging over the side while he seems to sink, boneless and fluid, into the very grains of the stained wood.

Bess pauses, and I spread my hands. What would she have me do? I don't want to make matters worse for her. She shakes her head, glances at Franklin, and then steps to a small board on the wall. A stack of telegrams is pinched to the wood with a rusted nail. As she does, I crack the only window. Cold, frigid air wafts in, chilling my fingers but clearing out the stale odor of the room at the same time. Franklin sighs but doesn't wake.

At the board, Bess rifles through the boxes and squints at one, then shrugs.

"I still don't do dee reading so good. Franklin ... he try to teach me once, but ..." she trails off and glances over her shoulder at the now snoring lump of her husband.

I close my mind against the memories of that last Crow raid, when the blood spilled in the mud and dust of the prairie. I try to forget the screams of men I'd known all my life as Pat ripped their limbs off. He still says it was to save their lives, but as I look at Bess's soft face, now often so pummeled ... I wonder if she'd be better off if Franklin had died.

Bess hands me the stack of telegrams and goes to clean up the mess in her kitchen. Behind the curtain along the back, the early scrabbling of their children starts up.

The larger train stations in Vermillion and Yankton routinely transmit the status of the trains to all stops along the line. Damn it all, these are hard to read—there! I squint at the sloppy handwriting twice, and grimace.

*Rail cracked a mile outside of Vermillion. Engineer shot by roaming bandits during repairs. Expect long delay.*

Damn it! I need that train! Helena needs it, too! I must speak to Yves. I'm no good cook, but perhaps that meal for all of them will suffice. It's not much by the way of a bribe, but it'll settle the debt I have for him. Maybe come spring, when I organize the Fourth of July festival, he will be appeased with all the food for him and posse.

I put the notes back and give a hasty goodbye to Bess, just as the first of her young ones pops around in rumpled underclothes. She bends over and shakes her man, asking Franklin calmly about his choice for a bed.

Domesticity. It's disgusting in so many instances. Why do men and women try so hard to fit together? They do not. They cannot. Some seem to do so only to survive. Sometimes it's as though they're blinded by some long-lasting passion, rendering them stupid and sluggish in other areas. I should know. I've watched it myself, been stuck in the center of it. It's a rare thing to see a husband and wife pull together as a team. Memories of my mother's family swim up, reminding me how it all can be less violent. That others have found domesticity to their favor. My parents, in their way. My mother's brother. My aunt …

It's the only explanation for Pat to choose Jane. I shake my head as I pause on the edge of the train's platform and stare east, following the ribbon of black track until it kisses the sky. Why else would he choose a dull woman with dowdy hair and muddy eyes, who has no worth except an overlarge bosom? She's careful and proper, even when she dances with him at the harvest festival. And yet he took her spinning many times, I remember, leaving me to fend for myself on the darkened edge of the swirling bodies.

Only Patrick Kinney ever danced with me.

He was supposed to be mine. I don't know if that thought will ever leave me. I stomp on a particularly large hunk of mud and step down, heading back toward the General Store. When he settled in Flats Junction, he was not welcomed by many. Too many recalled Doc Gunnarson. And Pat is so scientific, has so many ideas … but I never questioned him. Not until Jane arrived. He lived with Widow Hawks and Percy along with his great-aunt Bonnie … and me. My bedroom was next door to his, his great-aunt beyond that. I can still recall the way sound carried through the wall, and how his smile sliced through the gloom of the stairs when I'd meet him halfway. He always looked me full in the face, but never for my beauty alone. That, at least, has never changed.

Well, Patrick and Jane are married. There's no point in my seeking the domestic situation that will fall apart, anyway. Bess and Franklin were once in love, young and happy, and whole. I remember that, too.

As I crunch through the hard, frostbitten mud of Depot Row, I grit my teeth against the news about the delayed train.

My bargain with Yves didn't seem so much an issue at first. A loss of goods to be sure. Manageable, certainly. But now? Broken rails and a killed engineer? Both tragedies in their own right. It was never part of the plan. And either way, I'm getting too short on goods for comfort.

"Train not in again?" Bern rides up, then slides down next to me. He's always up early—earlier than any of the other cowboys in the Svendsen bunks on the east end of town. It's as if he never feels the lack of sleep like the rest do.

"You already know there's no train," I say testily.

He raises long, calloused hands. "Just looking for something easy to say, Kate."

"It's a wreck, is what it is," I complain suddenly. "I need that train! All my dry goods are near gone. There's been scarce enough bullets for everyone to get by all winter. Coal is next to impossible to keep in stock. I can't keep up. What am I supposed to do?"

His dark almond-shaped eyes slip at me; the edge of his look traced with appreciation. "You fretting on what people will say about not having goods to be found."

I hiss out of my teeth and reach out to trail a hand on the lower railing of the General's stairs. The wood of the General's railing is sun-soaked and weathered, a soft grey and brittle along the edges. I scrape a nail along the long grains of the board, then squeeze. When I look up, Bern is still there, tall and dark. He studies me with an intensity I know too well. I smile and tilt my head in answer.

"You didn't go out on the land this week."

He shakes his head. "Danny Svendsen asked me to stay back yet. There are some new cowboys who need general winter training on saddle mending and the like. Greenhorns in every way, the lot of them. Cows don't feed themselves, neither."

"Mm."

He reaches across the inches and places a hand on the back of my palm. It's not sensual. It's a reminder. There's ownership in it. I allow him the touch a moment longer and then pull back. "Time to open the General."

"I know it." He waits a beat longer, then sighs and brushes his fingers against the brim of his hat, the deep-set eyes softer and suddenly hesitant. "I'm sure it'll all work out, Kate."

I nod and watch him stride to the livery across the way. He is lean, but the leanness hides his strength, and he pulls his body around the Ofsberger's post office. His shout to Rusty Plackett to open up the livery and stop pissing on Sadie Fawcett's bushes whips around the corners, echoing.

The sun peeks out, tentative and rosy and pale, washing the eastern walls of the Main Inn and the General Store itself with a silver-and-gold light. The wind shifts, shimmying along the packed dirt around the building, and I tug the corners of the cloak around my waist before going inside.

Damn it. No train. How will I get through the next few days? I'm short on all the essentials, plain out on some. I'll have to over-order more of everything if I can get Franklin when he's sober and make sure I can afford the bill. I'll have to raise prices. Ration. Damn again! People will be angry. They'll say I cannot support the town, that I'm incompetent.

It doesn't matter I've had the General for ten years, that I apprenticed myself under old Harry Turner, learning the ways of the ledger and the orders even as he faded into some strange place in his mind, forgetful and child-like. Well, damn it all. I might have to organize a wagon to get to Yankton, though the idea of heading out on the exposed prairie this time of year is a death request. Who can I get to do it? I could use some of my legacy from Percy, though I hate to dig into that barrel.

I start to count under my breath as I climb the stairs and swing open the heavy door, kicking it along the scuffed bottom, where countless gashes sear the wood, to clear my boots. When I reach one hundred and twenty, Horeb's light step sounds on the first step outside.

Before he comes in, I take a deep breath. It never fails to surprise me how the General Store seems to hold onto the musty heaviness. I haven't been able to fully air it out. Sometimes I think I can smell old May Turner's perfume, though she's been dead for years. And occasionally I find a piece of short white hair in the cracks of the boards, as if Harry is still trailing around, listening to gossip. I stare up into the ceiling, where the bolts of calico, wool, and linen slide into the dim dusk above.

Helena loves the idea of silks and satins, brocade and damasks.

By the time I get to the counter, Gilroy Greenman's gravelly voice booms into the space, so when I turn around, he and Horeb are already creaking as they bend into the decrepit chairs at the checkerboard.

"It's them train rails putting Kitty in a bad mood today, isn't it?" Horeb says, his whisper to Gil so loud people out in the street can likely hear it. "I bet they broke again. Those damn wrought iron rails is too soft, ain't they?"

"Too brittle," Thaddeus Salomon booms as he walks in on the conversation.

I look up, feeling surly. "Brought my kettle?"

144

The blacksmith ignores me entirely and marches up to the counter. I pull the ledger close to me and flip to his page before he opens his mouth. He comes to a stop and rocks onto his heels, hooking his thumbs into the copper loops of his sooty apron.

"Need five pounds of coffee beans and fifty pounds of flour. Another mouth to feed," he reminds me pointedly. "He better earn it."

I look down at the list. "Your other goods aren't in yet, so you don't have to worry on more credit if you've cash."

Thaddeus frowns deep, his grey eyes flitting over the numbers, and shakes his great, shaggy black head, the beard bouncing.

"I don't have cash now," the blacksmith says, cold and final. "Hard to build orders when the trains don't come in regular, and my raw stock is still missing."

"We could cancel over half of your food debt if Marie could get me my copper teakettle."

The grey eyes go wide and then squint as he clears his throat and shifts from one long foot to the other. "I'll talk to her."

"You said that weeks ago. She promised she could repair it. She didn't say there'd be issues," I say, too loudly. Two chair creaks come to attention, and I snap around Thaddeus's bulk. "If you two lean any farther in those chairs, you'll hit the floor." I lean back and smile at Thad, who doesn't return it. He never has. "With no train and no extra way to give you credit … it's cash or the kettle now for anything more."

The smith's eyes and nose flare as he looks at me directly, his face tight. "Flour, Kate. I should get back. The new apprentice knows *gówno shit* about keeping a fire hot and the rhythm of the bellows."

I nod and do my duty as shopkeeper, measuring a single cup.

"That's it?" Thaddeus's voice goes up a notch.

I jut my chin to the ledger. "It's all you probably want to afford to take. Also, I only have so much left and other families have money. They come first." I know it's barely enough for a day if handled with care. But they owe me cash and a kettle to boot.

He hesitates, glaring at the black marks under the family name, the lines deepening along the sides of his beard. *"Pieprzyć to. Fuck it."*

When he marches back out, I sigh and dutifully write down his order and what he took today. Maybe now his wife will finish that damn kettle! I wish I could have limited their flour even more, but I cannot be accused of starving anyone, no matter how little they like me.

The sound of horses suddenly bursts out on the street, the pounding massive and rumbly. Who? It can't be the other Svendsen cowboys. Only Bern is ever up this early.

I join Gil and Horeb near the store's large, wavy glass window and push my hands on my hips. It's impossible to stop the hammering in my chest when I notice the massive horse leading the group as they slow by the General.

For a moment, I allow the buried panic to boil up, hot and fast and angry. Then it's gone, and I have the presence of mind to take up the station behind the broad, wide counter. My hand goes to my hair, checking the pins, and I straighten so my bosom is full and wait for Yves.

When he comes in, it's only himself, Matthias, and Arnold. I glance out the big front window and see the rest of the posse sitting on their horses, and hope bounces inside my chest. Perhaps they are just passing through this week. But I must speak to him—I must get Helena out of here.

And I'm too aware of my audience. My eyes flick to Horeb and Gil, and Matthias must see it, because he marches over and physically hauls the two old men out of their chairs.

"Got to use such muscles, don't ya?" Horeb quips. "Can't let them go to waste, can't we?"

Matthias doesn't answer, only closes the door and stands in front of it, eyes focused unnervingly on my face.

I turn to Yves and push a smile onto my cheekbones. "You have to stop."

Yves pauses, where he's fingering the smeared glass case of old brass watches. "Stop?"

"You've got to let the trains through."

"I do. Some of them." He grins, sharp-toothed and leering. "Is the plan no longer to your liking, Miss Kate?"

"I've a young woman I need to get East and back, and I can't have her caught up in your … silliness."

"Is that what you think zee activities are? Zee trains sometimes break, the rails are old, and zee weather is not so fine. You are lucky we bring in supplies for you."

He gestures out the window, and I notice the bulging sacks on the backs of some of the horses. It's still not enough, not for a whole town.

"People are starting to think I cannot manage on my own. They're going to want others to come in and help."

"What an interesting business idea," Yves says, his runny eyes lighting up.

"Look, I'll make you that meal." I don't mean it, and curse myself for saying so aloud.

"Me?"

"All of you," I add. "Just leave the trains alone for a bit."

"And who is saying all the train troubles are only because of Yves?" he reasons. "But I will take the meal."

"For all of you," I repeat, sounding more determined than my wiggling heart feels. I certainly have no interest in being alone with the man. I'm not so foolish as that. Granted, I do not have near enough room anywhere to serve them and sweat breaks out along my back as I wonder how I'll learn to cook fast enough to make them feel served rightly.

"Yes, yes, all of us," he agrees, distracted again by the glimmering watches. "In spring. Once zee trains are … regular."

Two sets of boots hit the porch outside, and there's a muffled squabble before both Bern and that new greenhorn Moses Thompson burst in, shoving the great oak door into Matthias's back. He grunts with the push as he stumbles into the space, his left foot landing with a hard thunk as he catches himself from falling face first into the rusty plow.

"Can't you see everyone in here is busy?" Arnold growls.

Moses pauses, and the two men look each other up and down, measuring. Bern ignores Arnold and Matthias completely and ambles up to the counter, fingers looped in his wide belt.

"Coffee in yet, Kate?" he asks, as if he can ignore the knives bristling on each of the men. My eyes flick to all the shiny metal on each of the outlaws, and try to warn him, but he seems hellbent on trying to protect me. Why? He has never done so before, and certainly not so publicly.

148

"Not sure," I say shortly.

Yves sniffs loudly. "Coffee is in zee short supply, but there is maybe some we are bringing to barter with."

"It's mine to sell," I correct.

Yves just tilts his head mildly. "Is it, then? Why is zat?"

My mouth opens, then closes. Is he testing me? Does he think I will be afraid to stand my ground? He does not know my power, then, for all he's spent many a day drinking and boozing around Flats Junction. Then again, not many know the extent of my schemes and my connections.

"Because you've stolen from me before, and these goods are payment due," I say.

He looks murderous, his eyes bulging and spit forming at the corner of his mouth. "You are accusing Yves of this in front of these men?" He gestures to Moses and Bern.

"I'm saying the truth, is all," I say evenly, watching his hand twitch over his knife. Maybe I will be fast enough to duck behind the counter if he changes his mind about violence. But will Bern be safe? And this new Moses fellow?

I cannot have a reputation for bloody battles in the General! Everyone will be afraid to come in and shop!

Moses suddenly crosses the short distance between himself and Yves, standing at the counter, and grinning at everyone with a genuine ease. How can he be so calm? His smile is even whiter than Arnold's, flashing in even darker skin, and his black eyes find mine.

I don't like the gentleness in them.

"It's only the boys at the cowmen barracks," he says, all conversation as easy as pie. "All twenty of Svendsen's men are hankering for Kate's coffee especially, and the like. Didn't think we needed all the boys to come and check on the coffee, but I'm certain they'll be following us if we don't get back quick like."

Yves makes a soft huff, and my glance slides down to where Moses has grasped Yves's knife hand, his long fingers pinching and twisting Yves's wrist just enough that it cuts off his ability to grab the long knife at his side.

I inhale sharply. "Yves brought coffee, I'm sure—supplies for the General since the train is out ... again. Rails."

Moses nods, but still doesn't release Yves. "We can all head out and bring it in. Do you want help from the boys?"

"My men and I can handle zee bags," Yves says tightly. He nods at Arnold and Matthias, who head out at once. Moses slowly lets Yves go, and the small man glances at me to see if I've noticed. I look away, not sure it's fast enough, and Bern looks confused to the change, as if his plans have not panned out. What could the man have wanted to do to fix the situation?

Moses slowly follows Yves, and seems to completely ignore the hatred slicing the small Frenchman's glares.

Bern inches closer as we watch everyone bring in the sacks of goods. "I didn't know Moses had seen it—them—that he'd followed me."

I open my mouth to answer, but Horeb, Gil, and all of Yves's gang pile into the General, hauling all the goods. There's a clink of metal, and relief rains through me as I realize this time there's going to be bullets to sell.

"Well, now, that is all zee goods," Yves gives me a hard stare. "We will be back in a few weeks for zee dinner you are so kind to be offering us."

"Oh, you must give me more time than that," I say quickly, panic filling my bones. "I need to ... organize the menu. I'll have it ready for you in the spring, as you said. When the food is freshest and the rails are more … regular."

Yves thinks about it for a long minute, so long I can feel my hair slowly slip out of its knots without me even moving. Finally, he jerks his head and stomps out.

I'm about to let fly a long sigh, but even that's interrupted.

"I'll help you," Moses says. "I was once a cook and the like."

"I don't need your help," I snap.

He only looks at me with a mild expression and I think he near rolls his eyes with soft impatience. Who does this man think he is? I barely know him, and he acts as if he understands me, as if my attitude is nothing but a brush on his sleeve.

Bern glances between me and Moses, and I cannot meet his look. What is he thinking? Does he believe I've made a pact with such a man?

Then again, Bern thinks he knows me. No one really does. I used to think I was understood, but time has proven to me that I don't even know myself. I don't know anything other than this burning need and deep ambition to prove my existence every day. It's consuming and eats at me, so there is no peace in my head. Only plans. Plans for my future, so that I will never be seen as someone on the outside. The plans that are complex and sometimes fly away from me, like when they go awry like this foolhardy meal I must make for a posse of outlaws so that they allow me to try my next scheme. But without action such as this, I do not know how I will be content with my lot. I do not know how I will find my own place.

It escapes me, time and again.

CHAPTER NINE

# *Jane*

*March 22 1883*

The tools in the doctor's surgery need another clean, which I will do tomorrow, as today has been a tizzy and the meal is not quite ready for the night's festivities.

As I run out past the surgery and into the chill spring air, the scalpels wink at me from the shelf. I shudder slightly when I recall how often we've used the surgical tools already. Lara O'Donnell had a large growth on her foot, which Patrick burst and then soaked in salt, then whiskey as Kate insists there is still no iodine to be had. My stomach still turns at the memory of the pus oozing out of the slice in Lara's wide, pale skin. Doris Tucker had stopped eating to make Tommy Winters notice her figure in a different light, but when she finally started to take in food again, her belly revolted and she'd been in with a putrid throat and disgorging herself for half a day. That cleaning took another day for me, and I think I can still smell a tinge of the vinegar and lye I overused to scrub the floor.

I've a list for making things a bit prettier, from real curtains to learning how to braid rugs. I could ask Alice, or her in-laws, or even Anette. Certainly Julie Bailey, the farrier's wife, had an opinion. She caught me looking at fabric last week and mentioned curtly that the Doc must be charging a pretty penny if I could afford new calico for such a frivolous thing as curtains and rugs, but she did offer a tip on how thick to cut the strips for braiding. Susan Brinkley, Old Henry's spouse, might have tricks up her sleeve for rugs, too ...

There is a part of me that would very much like to organize a quilting bee or other such events to get some time with the ladies, but I am still not sure of my place. When I was Doctor Kinney's housekeeper, I had a role. But now, as the Doctor's wife, I have a whole new status and social standing and absolutely no idea how to fill it. The properly-bred lady in me holds back my zeal and my ideas. I wonder when I will ever feel right enough to speak up on them.

As I rush to the General, Sally Painter crosses Wagon Street and jams a finger in the soft spot of my throat, forcing me to yank up so fast I almost fall backward into the mud squeezing around my boots. Her face is shadowed in the deep cavity of her winter bonnet, the hollows under her eyes purple.

"There's more sick kids what died last week of the diphtheria!" she says in a raspy voice. "Have you heard?"

My heartbeat throbs where she stuck her finger, and I take a step back. "I—yes I've heard."

"They call the doc?"

"I—possibly. I'm sure some did." How can my voice not shake? "But some may not have."

"My husband was a fool to ask for Doc Kinney's help," Sally says hoarsely. "He killed my children, just like he did yours, Jane. Everyone knows. It's why you left Flats Junction and you're an idiot for coming back. Doc Kinney couldn't save my babes and couldn't save your baby. He's a quack, a child murderer, a *killer*, and—"

"Sally!" Reverend Painter's face must be as red as mine feels when he hurries over from the post office. His belly arrives before he does, and the oil in his dark hair has oozed into the cracks by his ears. But the brown eyes are worried, and he draws up to his commanding height. "There you are."

I'm struck dumb for a moment. Has he heard his wife's accusations?

He wheezes and blusters before he pulls his next words together. "Mrs. Kinney, you know my wife is grieving?"

"I am aware, of course," I assure him. "It's very understandable, and quite awful." Hiding the hammering in my head and trying to sound calm and nurse-like, I nod at Sally. "Do you need anything? Food or—"

She sniffs and leans into the Reverend's bulk. "We need nothing from you or the quack."

Sally bustles off toward the west end of town, wide shoulders and wider hips scurrying under her skirts—perhaps she is finally embarrassed by her words to me—where the newer St. Diana's Lutheran Church rises toward the horizon. Reverend Painter watches her, then sighs and turns a stern eye on me. I can barely meet his gaze. Sally's words keep clattering and careening in my mind. *Quack ... Killer ....*

"You know she was an excellent mother, and feels the loss keenly," he says heavily. And, knowing Sally's overbearing ways with her children, perhaps he's not far off the mark.

"A mother has a right to feel such things," I tell him, slowly inching past.

"As I do. But the Lord giveth, and then taketh away," Reverend Painter says in a darker voice. He clamps his fingers around my wrist and squeezes so tightly I can feel the ligaments smash together, grinding through the brittleness of my bones. "The doctor should be careful." The moment is gone, and he quickly places his hand back inside his deep pockets, rocking back on his heels, acting as if nothing has happened. He tips his hat, once, austere and curt, and follows his wife home.

I keep my head down the rest of the walk to the General, fighting away the sinking anger and shock and pain. Sally's accusations burn. I've so many things to shout back at her, but they are improper. A doctor's wife should never say what I want to say. *Liar! Liar! You're a damn liar!* The next thought chokes me. That had once been me, blaming doctors. It had been me, losing Henry. I had said the same. *Quacks, all of them ....*

How will I tell Patrick what has been said? Do I need to warn him? Half the town is angry with him and reeling from their sick children. He already knows that.

And I must hurry to get the rest of the ingredients! The wide porch of the General is visible along the street and I quicken my steps.

There's much to be done, for Patrick has asked that I serve an especial dinner and I am late to finish it as Esther watches the pots and pans. We burnt the dessert and I need more eggs. There's no time to get to the Brinkley's for more before Moses's arrival, so I am spending precious pennies on Kate's stash. It feels exceedingly awkward to do this—not least because I did not watch my egg use this week as a good housewife ought—but also because I realize I am primping over the meal in a way that seems far too fussy for the West.

The inside of the General is bustling despite the half-empty shelves and I slip past several townsfolk to where the eggs are placed.

I do miss fluffing delicacies using things like white sugar and oysters and apricot jam from the well-stocked larder I had at my disposal at the Chester house in Gloucester. I do wonder how Beth, the young kitchen girl I left ghosting my place as cook, is faring, and I can even twist my heart and think of Andrew Angus the dairyman. Did he find a wife after I left? Since we decided not to marry? And then there is Aunt Mary—our letters are few as it is, and I've had no word from her since I came back to Flats Junction.

"Let me help, Mrs. Kinney."

I stare up at the dusky face behind me, surprised.

The mid-afternoon light slants along his cheek. He grins and tips his fingers to his hairline. "Moses Thompson."

"Oh!" I feel foolish, exceedingly so, for here is my dinner guest meeting me!

"I'll carry the eggs," Moses Thompson says, carefully taking the wire basket from the counter. The handful of eggs roll around with a disjointed rattle, delicately cracking against one another and making me skittish.

Turning to Kate, I count over the coppers, which she takes briskly, snapping the coins in her palm as she opens the ornate register.

"Thank you," she says tightly, and I notice she will not look directly at Moses. The tightness around her eyes warns me that I should not make an issue of this, but her blatant disregard for him rankles me in a way I don't expect. Of all people, Kate should be open and accepting, dishing out the acceptance she's received from the townsfolk! What always seems to tie her tongue? I'm tired of it.

"You know Moses Thompson, don't you, Kate?" I say pointedly, forcing her to sigh and look up from her ledger.

"There are so many new cowboys coming in and out, one is very much like the next." She keeps her dark, angry eyes on mine.

"Pardon me, ma'am. No offense meant." His eyes trained on her, black and fathomless.

Kate's lips curl back in derision, her straight back rigid. "Good day to you both."

"Mrs. Kinney, my offer stands," Moses says calmly.

"That would be very kind of you," I say, a little more formal than necessary.

I lead Moses to our house, a bit tongue-tied. As we go, Bianca Brewer and Doris Tucker cluck their tongue at us. I hear words carried across the road. Echoes of words. *Brown. Quack. Widow Hawks. Killer.* I shiver and keep my eyes down. Does Moses hear them, too?

He holds our screen open for me, and I crack the front door, saying the usual words of welcome as I do. The heaviness of roasting ham hits my nose.

"Esther, I'm back with our guest. Did you check on the oven?" I call through the hall.

"What? I'm cleanin' my kit so you don't need to do—" Patrick steps out of the surgery, wiping his hands in a towel.

157

"Moses! Come in. Let me you show my office while the womenfolk finish the cookin'."

I take the egg basket and continue into the kitchen. After a quick peek at the ham, I decide it's near perfect. Sprinkling a handful of brown sugar across the top, I close the stove door and pull the coffee off the back burner. It will be good and hot for the men.

"What is it, Jane?" Esther asks lowly. Her hand slowly covers mine as I flutter about. "Are you nervous to host a meal? It's fine, and nothing is burnt."

"It's not that." It's agony to keep this huddled inside my chest, and when I meet her gaze, the fear breaks apart inside of me. "It's that children died last week—more of them. I don't even know which ones, and Pat won't say much. I wish he would, so I know what to expect. People are ... they're so angry."

"But none have died this week," she says, sounding sure.

I think back to what Sally said. "I ... I didn't hear. It sounded like ... last week only." Hope wells inside of me. "Oh do you think? Do you suppose? If there are less children sick, none dying ... and you're still here in town, living with us, and they'll see! They'll know you're not to blame for the illness, and neither is Patrick!"

Her smile is soft, but sad. "Children will always get sick, and always die, and parents always want a place to blame. It will happen again."

The same bubbling hope falls flat inside my chest. "Is there anything we can do? For next time?" I move the plates to the table, hiding my face so she doesn't see how devastated I feel.

"Do you think there will be less anger if there is something to be done?" she asks.

"I don't know, but I can't not try. There must be an answer."

She stands so still in my kitchen I have to stop moving, too. Her face is a mask of multiple emotions, so strong and stark and yet hidden from me. It is as if I only know she is feeling things deeply, but I cannot imagine touching her anguish. In the quiet of this moment, the murmur of Patrick and our guest filters into the kitchen like brown butter and sugar.

When she lets out her breath, all the play of thoughts and sorrows drops away from her eyes and forehead, and she seems less grand, as if she has debated spilling her words to me, and has decided against it. I am disappointed, though I do not know what I would have wanted. Would she have told me how it was, to be the one blamed? To say how it feels to always be on the outside, looking in?

For she is right. There is always someone who is blamed for the ills of our days.

"I can teach you the remedies I know for all sicknesses, Jane. It may help. But it won't bring back the dead or heal the rift people feel toward Patrick."

"Or toward you." I blurt.

She pauses, opening the oven door for a slight moment, and then nods once.

Taking the now-hot coffee pot and mugs on a wide tray, I overhear snippets of medical conversation. They've already crossed the hall into the surgery. To think! He's going to bore our guest from the start! Here I have been, thinking it was only me who would hear such things.

When I step in, Moses is peering at the vials in the cabinet.

"Well now, doc, you've a mighty fine room here for your work," he says, respect mingling with approval. He nods, the bob of his broad neck moving the perfectly round curl of his skull. Now that his hat is in his hands, I realize his hair is cropped tightly and the shine of his scalp glimmers slightly in the soft light of the kitchen lamp.

"Thank you," Patrick says amiably, then notices me. "Ah! Coffee."

"In here?" I'm surprised.

"We'll go in the kitchen. It's warmest in there."

I lead the way back in and the men come in comfortably behind me, speaking of nothing more interesting than the weather now, and I block out their deep rumbling chatter as I pour their coffee and move swiftly to the meal, trying to remember the rhythm of making several fine dishes at once, and on a limited stove too. It is a challenge, but one I enjoy. I'm proud of my ability to manage the foodstuffs, anyway, and for my strokes of ingenuity at times. This was one thing I could teach Esther, and I was happy to show her how I made the fine, sweet desserts.

"So you were a Pullman porter, you said?" Patrick is asking, as my ears pick up the conversation. "Were you from the south, then?"

I recall the Pullman cars themselves: sleeper cars pulled by the great black engines on the trips west and east. I myself could not afford them on my journeys to and from the Territories and have heard that while the beds are somewhat comfortable and the accommodations the best that can be found on the railroad, the porters on such cars are almost exclusively of African descent. It has been so for the past fifteen years—ever since the War between the States ended and so many former slaves needed employment. Immediately I assume Moses is a freed slave, though as soon as I think it, I recognize his accent is nothing like the heavy southern one I'd expect.

"No. I'm a freeman. Always have been," he says, the pride in his voice making it deeper and richer for a moment. "My father were one as well. Originally from the Boston city."

"My wife is from Massachusetts too."

"Is that a fact." Moses nods at me. "I'm wondering if we all know the same haunts and streets and the like."

I smile at him, surprised at how easy I speak with him, any shyness gone. "I wonder indeed."

"Anyway." Moses waves a long, graceful hand. "Besides porter, I filled in as a cook. There must have been enough happy eaters 'cause they didn't send me back to being a porter. Only thing I didn't like was the train kitchen being so small. Tight and the like." His eyes sweep over my own kitchen space with approval. "But that was all after. First the big war happened," he says, cutting his thoughts in half with the bareness of his statement. "I went."

Patrick leans forward, his hands clasped together, but stays silent.

The war is a muddled memory of my own. I was a little girl when it happened, and safely ensconced in small little Rockport under my parents' careful protection.

Moses's eyes are half-closed with the recollecting. Some men do not speak of the wars and battles they see. I know Mitch Brinkley's father, Old Henry, has many silenced memories from his time in the Plains Wars for one, but Moses seems inclined to talk, his voice robust and matter-of-fact as he traces backward.

"I joined back in '62, dumb-like, and I were so bad inexperienced, but they trained us pretty well and nice at Meigs. That was where they taught the 54th everything like. And it were … Shaw was a good man." He pauses and gazes on the wall, where the heat of the stove crisps the wood and the chinking a charred bark of grey and black and tan.

"The papers spoke of the casualties at Fort Wagner, and the valor of your regiment," Patrick says gently. "I'm sorry about Colonel Shaw. He sounded a true warrior."

"He was that, in the like," Moses says, warmth and sorrow mingling on his face. Pausing, he looks at Patrick. "You didn't fight?"

"No," Patrick shakes his head. "Though I know many men who did. Many who did not come back. Some did. But not all."

I silently bring over the tinware, careful not to clink it and disrupt the soft sharing of history. Had they decided to do this—to give each other pieces of their past like sweetened morsels of friendship—when they first met? Was there some recognition of their accents and their roots that immediately gave itself over to dissembling? I glance at Esther, and she is as always—gentle and swift—as she takes out the pork.

"And then there was Olustee. Well, and now that was something!" Moses pulls his plate toward his chest and finally starts to pile on bread. "Colonel Hallowell had us under retreat, and the like, but we had to go back and be pulling that train full of wounded, what with the engine all broken down. The boys yanked on that for three miles 'til we arrived at Finnegan to hook up horses to help."

162

"The men pulled the train?" I insert myself, and they both jerk and look up at me, as if remembering I am there even though I have been obviously serving and putting food on the table. This is not exactly the dinner party I was envisioning, but the formalness I'd imagined seems ill-placed now that Moses himself is here in all his calmness.

"We did," he says proudly, the white smile flickering and his hands deftly picking up bread and dripping on the gravy. "We had over six hundred wounded if you have heard," he says quietly, and puts down his knife, his eyes meeting Patrick's. "I were one of them."

"Where were you injured?" Pat asks, his own hands stilled over the dinner, poised and fascinated at once.

"My leg." Standing with carefulness, Moses pulls up his pants, the loose fabric easily sliding over a calf marked with pebbled flesh and the white-pink of deep scarring. Patrick's eyes widen, and then narrow as he tries to see the damage without appearing too interested. The man is not his patient, of course, and scientific curiosity is palatable most times, but not at dinner. I clear my throat lowly and my husband visibly checks himself, leaning back.

"That was a very bad wound."

"It was," Moses nods gravely and sits back down.

"But you survived? You're lucky."

Moses shakes his head, takes a bite of the ham and stuffing and makes an appreciative noise with a small clap of delight as he tastes it.

"That is a very fine pork, Mrs. Kinney," he says once his throat is clear. "I haven't had such good stuffed roast since … well, I'd say since I've had a hand on my own cooking, but that's not true, like. I think it's done better than mine. I've got to practice and the like. Soon enough, I'll be cooking again. I promised."

I smile with pleasure at the compliment and sit myself down to finally serve my own plate, waving Esther to join us.

"Anyway, luck has nothing to do with my living, as it were," Moses says around his food. "I would've lost the leg, if not my life, had the Lord not seen fit to have a good doc in the camp."

Patrick cocks his head to the side, still chewing. "There were some good docs in the war, I give you that. I knew some."

"Well, Doc Stassen was a miracle with the surgery," Moses explains. Patrick goes very still next to me. I can feel the tremor pass through his leg and into mine, and I glance at him. His face is white.

"Who?" he says, his voice hoarse and thick. "Who helped you?"

"Doc Stassen. I don't know his first name were—"

"Georg."

Moses pauses now as well and stares at Patrick with something akin to blank shock. "You knew him?"

Swallowing hard, Patrick nods into his food.

"How do you know him, like? How?"

"He was … I worked under him in the stables at the Tremont House in Boston. Before the war. He taught me all I know of animal husbandry and managin' horses. He was the one who taught me much about bein' a barber surgeon."

I feel I am an outsider staring at the ribbons of understanding passing between them. Suddenly Moses grins.

"Well, that's a small world, as they say."

Still looking amazed, Patrick nods. "I didn't know what had become of him."

164

The emotion he is hiding might not be apparent to Moses, but I can feel the shift in his body and hear it in the small nuances of his broadened Scots-Irish. I wish I could smooth the small crease lining the space between his eyebrows.

"Well, you see now why I reckon I'm glad to see you here in this town, Doc Kinney," Moses smacks his wide lips and wipes his hand along the edge of them to dislodge the last of the oysters and stuffing. "I've a great respect for the profession, and glad to support you in what I can, and the like."

I glance up at this, and my eyes meet Esther's. Though Moses leaves the comment there, my mind jumps.

*What* can possibly be said about my husband in those cowboy bunkhouses that could make this man think Patrick would need his help?

And what kind of help can Moses possibly offer?

*Would anything he does help or hinder?*

I dislike that I should think such a thought. We ought to be grateful for any support, no matter from where it comes. A shiver runs through my arms and down my hands. To stop my mind from shooting down a path of unfounded concerns, I stand and clear my skirts, going to the stove to take in the dessert, Esther taking up the dinner plates and finding bowls.

It's not long after this that he leaves, perhaps feeling the weight of so much said. Perhaps now it must all settle before a friendship can start to fill in the chinks of their discussion. Patrick seems still a little dazed but certainly pleased as we clean up the dishes. As usual, I find his help in the kitchen to be both welcome and disconcerting; for all I know, it is a mark of his childhood and his time with his great aunt Bonnie.

When Esther goes to bed, the lamplight is low in my hand as I head up the stairs after her, settling gloom into my bones, even though we spoke only of a war decades past. Patrick follows a bit heavily, the new thoughts swirling in his mind so loud I can nearly hear them.

As I undress, I flick small glances at him as he echoes me, pulling off his trousers and vest. I still feel the deep pull of desire for him, same as it was when I first realized it for what it was. But it's tempered by something else this night.

*Fear.*

I worry for him. For us. For our future. But I cannot point it out in the way I wish, so I reach for a topic that feels safer, if not less filled with fear.

"Paddy?"

"Mm?"

"Why ... what have you heard lately in town? About the children?"

"Which?" He's wary at once, poised. "Are more sick?"

"No ... no. I only thought ... maybe the diphtheria is done? And the school won't fester with new sick children, and if they all stop dying, maybe people won't be so ... quick to blame ..."

"Who are they blamin' now? It's been only Esther so far as I've heard."

"And us. For bringing her back."

"Kate helped," he points out, thumping into bed. "No one seems to be blamin' her."

"Everyone needs her," I say. "They need her goods, they need her bullets. She's ... important. And people don't forget her father."

Patrick snorts softly and beckons me to join him. "Percy casts a long shadow, that's certain. But this is not the first time I've faced pissed off people in this town, and it likely won't be the last."

But he could make it easier on himself. I want to argue with him—that we should change how we go about. We should try harder to make people like us, and less afraid of him, his tools, and his medicine. He needs to barrel in less and offer more tempered advice. Ease in.

I suppose I'm not fooling anyone. I'm no different than Patrick, really. I don't belong here, and my presence isn't truly helping him in the matter of fitting in better.

He should have married Kate, if he wanted that.

"I'm more worried on somethin' else," he says in the dark. "I'll know more in a month or two, but I always start dreadin' this comin' time of year. It's not always the same, but ... it's impossible to predict."

I turn to face him, curling into the warmth of his side and shoulder. "Is it something worse than diphtheria?"

"Yes."

"Do you want to talk about it?"

"No use keepin' you awake as well as me. You get your rest, Janie."

But it's no use. I lie awake long into the night, my heart thumping low and slow, even after his breathing evens and he drifts off.

What could possibly worry my unflappable husband worse than sick and dying children and babes that are born too early? What would be worse than the fact that we are still on the outsides of it all, unable to puncture into Flats Junction completely? We have little support, and Patrick and I are collecting ourselves quite a menagerie of people who would normally be cast out of proper Eastern society. Between Esther, Moses, and Patrick's own growing unpopularity, I suppose it is no surprise at all that my footing here feels soft and unsteady at best.

## CHAPTER TEN

# *Kate*

*April 29, 1883*

The early train always rattles my jaw just a bit more than I'd like, and it's the worst way to wake up.

This morning I'm up even before the whistle, standing out in the late spring chill with my darkest cloak wrapped around my shoulders and still the breeze fits under my petticoats and makes me shiver once.

Then again, Helena's shivering all over, and I'd bet it's nothing to do with the cold.

"You sure?"

"I said I was ready," she says, clenching her teeth. "Just promise you won't say a word."

"I shouldn't need to. You said you'll write."

"I'll keep you informed," she says formally, her eyes wide and swallowing the bit of light from the dusty old lamp Franklin lit for us outside the depot.

It's not what I meant, but it's not my place to pry.

"I'll keep my tongue. It suits me fine, then, anyway, in case you come back without anything."

"Do you think I'll fail?" She turns toward me and lifts her chin, just the way Marie does when someone doubts her ability to fix a pot or kettle.

"No, I'm just saying I won't speak up."

She huffs, but the bit of defiance seems to settle her nerves, so when the train finally curves into the depot, she looks as ready as any young woman who is heading off into adventure.

"You recall everything we discussed?"

"I have all the plans memorized, and then some," she says, meeting my eyes again, direct and so stormy I feel myself shrink back just a bit.

"Just you recall you'll have to wire me before you plan your train home. Just to ... be sure I know you're coming. Don't surprise me."

She snorts softly and yanks her bonnet down tighter. The ribbons on it are folded in her precise stitching, and she'll pass muster on the train ride like any young lady. If she does what she says she will, then both of us will be set up fine.

"Be safe," I tell her, clasping a hand on her shoulder. "Be well. I will see you soon."

"And I won't be alone when I come back!" she says, almost gay. "I'll have boxes and boxes and more!"

Her face glints with morning dew and youthful expectation, and she fair hops onto the train with her small bag and ticket clasped all in one hand.

I wait on the bench for the train to go, watching Nels and his boys load up crates of live chickens, and two of the

170

Brinkley brothers deliver a wagonload of early cheese for Yankton. In the window of the far car, Helena's pale rose bonnet bobs and fractures in the swirly-whirl of the leaded glass window, a watery painting of her clear self.

As the train eventually pulls out, and the whistle blasts, and the chug of hot air blasts coal smoke and wood chips and dirt into the morning, I raise a hand slightly to do all the proper things of seeing off a person, no matter how much or how little they matter. I think I see her raise her own hand as the engine picks up steam, but I can't be sure.

And then she's off. A speck of black. A last shake of the rails. One more huff of an engine eating up prairie dust and heading East.

How much I envy her!

The jealousy chokes me, near as much as the black smoke. She's free. Free of this town, free of the expectations of her family and even of herself. She's got funds and a fresh, young, unblemished face with rosy cheeks and all the brash confidence needed to barrel through to her end.

My end, too.

I remind myself that Helena owes me. That her freedom isn't without strings. That she's beholden, and I'm her only key back. Without me, my money, and my support, her dreams are dust.

I'm desperately needed.

But that doesn't make me want to stay, all things put plain.

It's all due to my role, my parentage, and the only place I stand a chance to do anything, since if I do nothing, why am I living at all? My whole world is tied and wrapped and snaggled with Flats Junction. It's the only place where I matter, and I'm not even sure I matter all that much. Such a thing grates on my nerves and make me feel like I'll be lost to time if I don't make my mattering deep enough.

Well, I guess Helena's helping with that problem. If she does what she promised, and sticks to our plan, then there's more to tick under my name.

My walk back to the General is slow and pondering. The mud of April is near gone, and I'm feeling the hope of full spring even though I don't feel all that hopeful in the whole look of it all. It's mostly due to the fact that Yves and his posse are fixing to eat whatever I cook them today, and the only place open that's empty and big enough is the derelict tinshop barn behind Marie and Thad's place, which Moses— damn him—managed to get leave from Danny Svendsen to use just this one time.

He said he'd get the old place set up enough to have ready for foodstuffs, but that means hurrying hot food over across town and hoping it's not a ruin by the time it arrives.

I keep wondering what'll happen if Yves decides my fancy meal isn't enough. I'm no cook, though Moses says he is.

And I dislike how I'm depending on *him*! If only Bern had spoken up. Or I'd have taken up some plan with Horeb or Gil! Someone I knew well enough, long enough, good enough. Instead, I'm dealing with Moses, who has taken my lack of words as acceptance. He's so easy about it all, it near stifles me.

There's a low rumbling voice humming inside my room behind the General, so when I open my back door with a jerk, I'm only half surprised to see Moses himself seated comfortably along the long bench of my small table. His hands are wrapped around a mug of coffee and he's sipping dutifully.

"You made coffee?" I say, near growling.

172

"It's hot," he says, comfortable-like.

"Did you need something before the store opens? Couldn't get the cup of sugar from a neighbor?"

The bite in my voice must sting a bit, as finally Moses stirs, folding his capable legs under the table and fixing steady eyes on me. I disapprove their steadiness.

"Now that's hard, Kit," he says easily. Shifting to look up at me from his seat, he gestures with the mug comfortably. "Have a cup before you set on cooking."

"I thought you were doing the cooking."

"I said I'd help."

The hard, angry noise coming out my nose doesn't make him flinch. I fair stomp to the coffee pot and pour it into a mug.

He makes it weaker than I do, with more water than ground beans. I suppose he thinks I've a shortage. And I do—no thanks to Yves—but I don't skimp on a few things here in my own private space.

I take another slow sip. It's not close to how thick I make mine, but I hate realizing how there is something slightly delightful about enjoying a cup of coffee that I did not have to make.

Moses drinks even slower than me but doesn't turn or ask that I sit near or across from him. Maybe he realizes how forward he is, coming over before the day really starts. Was he hoping to catch me still abed? Surprise me with his early start? I press my lips together and then exhale through my nose very, very slow. It seems to help with this morning's unsettledness, chasing the chilly bits of the morning away.

"Have you a menu planned, then, since you're a fine and fancy cook?" I ask his back.

Moses shakes his head, glancing at the faded curtain between my rooms and the General. "I figured that was your choice."

"Fine." I snort suddenly. "What a waste of a Sunday."

The silence rings around the small room, slithering through the sparse corners as we just fill up the space together without speaking. I am not sure what he wants me to say. Does he want me to grovel? Thank him? Does Moses think I'll favor him for help and protection? What kind of *favor* would he expect? And then, I wonder—*does Bern speak of me?*

"Well," I say, pouring the last of the coffee down my throat and feeling the tensions release just a bit in my gut and the lines of my forehead go smooth. "Thank you for the coffee. But food won't cook itself."

Moses stands and puts his cup in the wash bin. He is soft and familiar in my space, moving with a steadiness I find surprising, and I don't like it, but I don't know how to say it. He's too … comfortable. In himself and in this world. I want him to be tight, like me. It's only fair.

I don't like using the expensive foodstuffs on Yves, but I figure it's better than too simple of a meal. I'll make a point of telling him what he could have had if I knew the trains were more regular, this I'm planning. He might've had fresh oysters, just like they do down Deadwood-way. But I'm not putting such an order in and finding out he's waylaid the engineer yet again, leaving them to rot in the spring sun.

In the end, Moses and I stand elbow to elbow next to the tiny potbelly stove, cooking up my corn fritters and the baked and stuffed meatloaf my mother would make for my father, along with his fancy eggplant, though it's a vegetable well out of season, so he's decided to use new potatoes and layer them with his seasoning.

"So we've got the grated breadcrumbs, some new butter, and sweet herbs—"

"What's so sweet?" I ask, testily, pouring my mix of corn kernels, eggs, flour, milk, and baking powder into the long husk shapes on the cast griddle.

"Oregano, thyme, onion, and nutmeg."

"Nutmeg's the only sweet, and you might put in extra."

It's too easy to talk to him, and too comfortable. I slap my mouth shut and finish my fritters, so I might not lose my tongue further. It's just too damnable *easy*.

"You might want to keep away while I serve them," I suggest, watching him beat two egg yolks until they are frothy gold. "Yves won't take kindly to you being there."

"Why not?"

I stare at him. "You're a fool if you don't know."

Moses shakes his head. "I'm Danny Svendsen's ranch hand, worked my way across the country and fought a long war and the like. Yves Gardnier is not a threat, as it were."

He's too careless, but I'm sure it's not my place to press. He's new here, after all. What can I say to convince him of the ways of the West?

When it's mid-morning, I hurry up the footpath between the schoolhouse and the old cooperage to see that everything's as Moses promised. He says he'll watch the stove and the oven, and it's the strangest thing to leave a man in my little space as if he's part of it, as he pours himself cool well-water and near sees me off as if I'm his!

The nerve.

He knows I belong to no man! That's always been clear enough for me. And if I had a choice, I certainly wouldn't be picking him, no matter how easy it is to fix a meal together! It's only a meal. And a meal that might settle my plans with Yves and pave the way for Helena to come home and start her plans, and mine as well.

A meal that should be pleasant and fine and delicious and unlike what they can get from the grease-spattered skillets Toot wields over at The Golden Nail. An old wine from the dust of my high shelf, leftover from my father. Something to rival even the sips of fine whiskey served at the Prime Inn—if Joe is up and willing to have customers, that is. And yes. It's worth the small bottle of port to secure Yves's help in keeping those rails running.

I want to skirt around the outside of the tinshop and the blacksmith's forge, but I know it'll be ten times more awkward if I don't stop in to see Marie if only to wish her good morning now. If I have to say it later, while I'm in the middle of running food to serve these insane outlaws … well, I'd best get it out of the way.

The walkway is quiet as I pick along the dusty ruts, except for Father Jonathon directing Elaine Warren on a particular piece of music for today's Mass. Her overpowering, warbling soprano strangles out of nearby St. Aloysius Church even though the door is closed. The clucking of geese is loud behind the farrier's house.

I've no idea what I'll say to Marie. I don't even know if Moses spoke to them, or if Danny gave them notice that their tinshop will be overrun with myself, Moses, and many unsavory bodies. It's not their building or land, but it's damn near up to their back door.

But when I step up to the cracked door, I see a naked, intimate moment meant for no one's eyes, and certainly not for mine.

Thaddeus has an arm around Marie's thick waist and one giant hand on the faint and newly stretched wealth of her belly. The movement sends a frantic spiral down my gut. *Does anyone know she's expecting yet again?*

He spins his fingers over the edge and then slides his palm under the curve, as if he is testing and supporting the weight of his unborn child. She leans against him, into him, melting to the solidness of his body and he bends down to kiss her all rich and endlessly. It makes my heart ache with what I don't have, and will never feel. I know I should clear my throat to announce my arrival, but I hesitate.

Thaddeus is not one to laugh, especially at himself, and would likely not appreciate the interruption regardless. I move to retreat, but in doing so my foot catches. The shift of stones under my heel gives me away. They pause their kiss, though the blacksmith turns languidly, defiantly, and with obvious irritation.

"What is it?" he asks bluntly, looking disgruntled and annoyed.

"Tadeusz. The door wasn't locked." Marie gives him a significant look with raised eyebrows. "We cannot be upset if a customer comes in."

"It's Sunday, and early at that," he retorts, and glowers at me.

I glower back. He must know how much I don't like interrupting them, either. "Is it too early?" I say belatedly and with heavy insincerity, raising my eyebrows at him specifically.

"Yes!" he bellows.

"No," Marie says at the same time.

They look at one another evenly, and he sighs, glancing down at her belly, strung tight as a drum and oddly out of place.

For a moment, I am jealous of her, too, working as she widens without a care for propriety or pausing to put out her trade. I wonder if I might be so bold as she is—A businesswoman, well-wed and pregnant, yet carrying on as if she's as strong as the seasons. How does she do it, without qualms or questions of herself?

Then again, I have bested her in one thing.

I'd bet she doesn't even yet know it. It *is* early, after all.

"Stay then, if you must." Thaddeus throws his hands up in defeat. He turns to Marie and lowers his voice. "The children are still sleeping, though."

My face flushes with embarrassment under the giant's stare of frustration. I send a short curse to the loud gravel under my feet.

"Well, then." Marie tips her chin toward her shop. "Tadeusz, I'm sure she'll be quick, whatever it is. And next time you might lock the door if you don't wish to be interrupted."

He yanks on his beard, and stomps over to his forge. His arm immediately takes up the handle on the bellows, and pumps it faster and faster along with mumbled Polish, turning the coals as bright as the morning sun.

I move fast, giving him a wide berth, and step into the quieter tinshop against my better judgement. Moses is waiting, after all, and so are the foodstuffs. The day itself won't wait.

178

I suspect Yves, won't, either.

"My ... I didn't mean to bother," I mutter, as I step up to her counter.

Marie shakes her head in her husband's direction, and fetches her fat ledger, bending as much as she can to peer on the shelves below. "So then. You're wanting to know about your copper kettle?"

I'd clear forgotten that this morning, but no sense in letting Marie know it. I turn my frown down further. "Ah. Yes. That, too."

She pauses and slowly straightens. "It's not done."

"I figured as much, as you haven't stopped it off," I say, with too much vinegar in my voice. I clear it. "I was just saying good morning, and ... you know I'll be using the old tinshop this morning."

"Ah." She picks at the edges of the ledger, where the leather frays and pokes tiny tufts of white through the binding. "Thad and I spoke to Danny the other day." She sucks in her mouth once, twice. "That is, Thad spoke to Danny. About one of his cowboys using the shop, and you, too." She pauses, fingering around the seam of the old book. "It's fine, of course. It's Danny's land and his building. He can do with it what he likes."

A loud snort rips from Thaddeus's shop and indicates his eavesdropping. She ignores this. So I do, too, though I want to stomp into his space and spit at him for his pestering.

"Fine, then." I shove off from the counter. The reason for my stop feels too simple and stupid, and only reminds me and her of our strange and strained balance, which neither of us knows how to grasp and twist and fix.

"I don't see why you bother to make Yves feel welcome," Marie blurts out suddenly. "And Widow Hawks, too.

You say you want to grow Flats Junction, you near force an apprentice on us, saying you want to make this place a good and grand stop on the map, and then you go on and make nice with the worst posse in the area!"

"I've my reasons," I tell her evenly. *If only she knew how important they are to her, too.*

"Marya," Thaddeus says lowly, his voice carrying between buildings, a warning in his tone.

She shakes her head in his direction and pins me with her entire body, and I feel stuck and froze by the force of her gaze.

"You aren't making any sense!" she finishes, and crosses her arms tight.

"I'm growing the town, and this is a part of it. I've an agent who is gone East, finding ways to build more business, more storefronts, bigger supplies and choices. There'll be fine dresses of the latest fashion soon enough, with all the delicacies of the cities here. I swear it, today's meal is part of my plan for the future."

She stares and measures me longer than she ever has, and I feel the differences in our years and our lives. Though we are both women in trade and business, we are a sea apart in how our lives have traveled. It feels too much to breach to find a common island.

The tenseness in her shoulders falls away suddenly. "Well, anyway. It's a fine enough spring day for a dinner. I wish you luck, though I've no luck myself in the kitchen," she finishes, marking in her book briefly and then finally meeting my eyes straight on. I force myself to offer a small smile—is she offering a bond of friendship with her remark? It's a soft thing for a woman to admit.

And I'm glad to be free of her eyes and her questions.

Marie follows me out of her shop as I go through Thaddeus's forge. I glance at the back door where the rest of their family is either still sleeping or just starting to stir. "I'm glad your other children recovered from diphtheria," I say. It's an easier thing to offer, other than giving sympathy about her lost daughter.

*And the other one, which I can see already that she has no idea she's lost…*

"It was a longer recovery to health than I would have preferred," Marie says slowly. "I am not sure Natan's cough is completely gone yet. And it's been months." She shrugs, looking unhappy.

Thaddeus has ceased his puttering, staring and daring me to say something more.

"Perhaps next time … if anyone is ill … you could ask Doctor Kinney to stop by," I tell them tentatively, hoping I do not sound forceful on it. Who am I to offer the suggestion, anyway?

Marie's face goes bland, and she puts both hands on her stomach for a moment. It is a protective, fleeting touch.

"We'll be fine," she says simply, with exaggeration on the words. "Death is the way of it here, as hard as it can be."

"Good day," her husband says firmly, taking a step forward. "Thank you for your business." The door shuts and the lock slams home. "Marya," his voice booms. "Come here."

As I stride in silence, I wonder if I'll ever fill my belly with a child. Would my husband be as desirous, or would he be wary of my body's strength? Thoughts spill into my head without warning, hot and intimate and tangling. I may not be as hale and hearty nor anywhere as experienced in birthing as Marie Salomon, but neither am I a weakling.

I march into the old tinshop feeling hot and dusty in the short walk between forge and doorway, and stop short at the sight.

Moses has put long boards on trestles across the old metal shop floor, where hard-packed dirt serves as a stable base. He's found stumps, tables, and benches so there's enough to seat all of Yves's posse, and even pulled in two rusty lamps so there's something on the table besides old, floating dust.

*Why?*

I wonder the word as I hurry back to the General and think the word over and over and over again as Moses helps finish the food and carries three baskets behind me as we head over to the tinshop again.

*Why is he helping?* mingles heavily with *Please let this work!* as I set the table fast and slam mismatched cutlery on the boards. I have just enough, with Arnold and Yves the only ones to get blunt knives besides forks and spoons.

The questions swirl up until Yves and the rest darken the doorway, bringing late spring coolness with them on the edge of the midday sun. I've lit those rusty lamps, but it's still dark and dim inside no matter it's noon, and I wish suddenly I had more lights. I'm not about to go beg for help from Marie or Thaddeus, though. Not now. Not after this morning. Not after they've likely discovered Helena missing.

I cannot think of that, now. And their worry is not my problem or my place.

Yves saunters in and I'm quick to jump in front of him. "You're here, Yves," I point at the setting closest to the doorway. "I've a full set of cutleries out for you."

"Well, now, is zat not the most sweet thing," he croons, and plunks into the high seat I've put there for him. "And it is smelling very nice."

I fill cups and place the fritters on the trestle first. Before I can add the butter, salt, and honey, Natty and Evan grab the basket, each taking two. Patty and Victoria titter on the end of the table without touching anything, near leaning across in order to whisper. I can feel their eyes on me and every move I make. Arnold pulls the basket toward him, and Matthias lifts one out after that.

Yves simply stares at me, not moving.

"You don't like fritters?" I ask him, feeling dread pile up in my stomach. I should have asked! *This isn't going to work!*

"I like them fine, but I am waiting for you to serve them to me," he says pointedly, staring at the food, then slowly up my body.

My entire body cringes, but I reach across Matthias to grab one of the cakes. As I do, Natty reaches without airs and cups my breast. I jerk back, feeling heat and rage build under my skin. Natty only laughs, chewed food speckling the table.

I plop the bread on Yves's plate without ceremony His face crumples ever so little, and I hurry to offer honey and butter.

"You can put both on for me," he says, then leans back in his chair, arms folded and pale eyes boring on my chest.

Bile fills my mouth, making everything smell sour. I quickly slap both on the fritter and back away. Where is Moses? What is taking him so long with the damn country captain chicken?

And I hate that I feel I need him here.

For *protection.*

"We could be used to eating so well," Yves says to the posse, very loudly, as I put the second round of vittles on his plate. No one notices his announcement as they dive into Moses's potatoes and my meat loaf. Arnold nods as he fills his cheeks, eyes closed, and I don't think Natty and Evan have stopped eating long enough to breathe.

"Maybe Miss Kate can be our cook," Victoria calls, a slice of a grin creasing her powdered face. "Maybe it'll give us a reason to stay and put down some roots, eh, Yves?"

Patty giggles. "We can set up shop—have a pleasure house worth noting."

"We've already got The Powdered Rose," I say. Patty only rolls her eyes and starts whispering with Victoria again.

Yves looks thoughtful as he watches Matthias help himself to a second massive helping of the meat loaf. His weepy eyes hood. "It would be good to be done with the fast life. My horse cannot run so very fast so much longer."

"You can always buy another horse," I say, folding my arms and glancing out the nearest window for Moses again.

"But I am liking this idea so much more," Yves says, fingering the butter knife. "It gets very tiring to always be traveling on zee prairie. It would be so delightful to have a legitimate business. A place to settle, as the ladies say." He nods in their direction, but they don't care one whit about his musings.

Only I seem to be tense at the notion he's tossing about, as if it's a simple thing. Maybe he's not serious. Maybe he's only speaking out on such designs to see if they will rattle me. Maybe he's just being sentimental.

Do hardened criminals ever get sentimental?

"But do we want to be living in this here town where there's all kinds of sickness every season?" Arnold drawls. "Seems so sickly it's not a prime choice."

"We've a good doc," I say at once, then slam my mouth together. Why do I keep jumping to defend Pat? It's not my place, and I don't need to do so! A habit. One I must break, damn it!

"Oh, is he, so?" Yves twists to me, a sly smile wiggling across his chin. Spices from the potatoes line his lips, and he doesn't seem to care. I want to gag. "Well, then maybe we are only hearing rumors, and not zee facts."

"The diphtheria has been gone over a month now."

"Leaving many of zee children dead," he reminds me. "But it is not zat. It is the ugly disease, the one that kills without caring if you are well or sickly, young or old, or zee color of your skin and hair. Zat is what Arnold is saying."

A strange wash of panic covers my throat, and I check my skin and the backs of my hands without meaning to do so, searching frantically for a blemish. Yves notices and smirks.

"You are probably just fine, Miss Kate. You are not mixing with those who might bring the sicknesses anymore, are you not?"

He knows about Widow Hawks, and he knows my lineage, but no sense in explaining that I no longer see my mother in any way. She spends her days helping Jane keep house, putting in a garden and generally staying out of sight, leaving me to fend for myself.

The door slides open on rusty hinges, and Moses appears bearing my biggest roasting pan filled to the top with the browned and stewed chicken smothered with Moses's personal southern receipt of perfumed flavors—onion, garlic, and tomatoes, but with pinches of expensive curry, too, from his personal stash, and my precious dried grapes.

He sets the pan right dead center of the table, and the smell chases the sour out of my nose. Natty stares at him, but Evan jumps right in, grabbing half a chicken in one hand and grunting with delight as he tears into it with black and yellow teeth.

But Yves stands up and just stares. Moses turns and stops moving, his hands falling to his sides. I watch Yves slowly finger the long knife still plastered to his side, and I know I'm close enough behind him to grab his wrist, like Moses did the last time we were all in a room. I just don't think I'll have the strength to do it.

"You," Yves says, his voice an octave lower than usual. "Get out."

"Just bringing over food, and the like," Moses says, calm as always. His eyes are black in the shadows, and he moves with grace along the edge of the room, keeping his eyes on Yves. "So Kate can keep on serving you, as it were."

"You stay away," Yves spits at him. "You hear?"

"I live in this town, and work in it," Moses says mildly, reaching the door. "But I see Kate has this in hand." He pushes out and closes the door behind him.

At once, I feel abandoned and angry and uncertain.

How can I want him gone and yet want him here?

Yves slowly sits. He pulls out his knife, points it at me and then the chicken. I get the point, but before I can reach across Natty as fast as I might, Matthias has pulled the pan near, takes a whole side of chicken for himself and then meets my eyes briefly.

186

I don't know how to take his offer and quickly fill Yves's plate in a mountain of curried chicken before anyone else can touch me. Hopefully it's so much that Yves will be too busy to muse and scheme and plot.

Imagine if he lived in Flats Junction all the time? What would become of this place? Would it become like Deadwood—a place of wild outlandishness? Opulent and grimy, fancy and filled with all types of unsavory types? Oodles of coin piling in, dozens getting off the rail cars every day, ready to make a fortune and start a new life in the West …

*I could do much with a place like that.*

But not with Yves helping! I don't need him. I've other plans.

"Maybe we can stay," Yves is saying to Arnold in quieter words, the grease of the chicken staining his collar and cuffs worse off than they were a few moments ago. "If we just get rid of that Negro man, who is bringing zee bad sickness."

"What?" Oh! I need to slap myself! Why do I insert myself into conversations? Is it the shopkeeper's curse, or just because I'm so used to being in the center of most major discussions?

Yves and Arnold give me an appraising sort of look, and it's filled with twenty different feelings. None feel good.

"Only if we are going to make a … *lee-jit-a-meet* go of a solid life of money-making in Flats Junction, we need to make sure no disease carryin' bastards are here," Arnold says slowly, his southern accent even more pronounced.

"Moses didn't bring the diphtheria," I snap. "It comes around every once in a bit."

"Don't all?" Yves says, stabbing another piece of chicken with his long knife, his eyes stuck on my face, then my bosom. "I'm not worrying on the diphtheria, Kitty my sweet."

My nostrils flare, but I bite my tongue as I ask about pie for dessert. Everyone demands it at once, so loudly I'm sure Thaddeus might show up just to make sure the place isn't getting ripped down around our ears. I almost wish he would show up, in all his fire and surliness.

I might even forget how much I embarrassed him this morning, among other things.

But of course Thaddeus doesn't rescue me from this rambunctious posse, grown ever more rowdy and bawdy as Natty produces a large flask full of something so strong it burns away the taste on the back of my tongue from the smell alone.

Everyone drinks heartily except Yves and Matthias, and it's not long before they are rolling about the table and between one another, grabbing at the last of the food and smashing pie into their faces and one another's. If I could melt into the old worn planks of the building, I would. If I could get Yves alone, I could talk to him about the rail again, to confirm he and I are of the same mind. That was the whole point of today, not to bring myself low before him as a serving girl.

My heart stops suddenly. Maybe that *was* the whole point, for him.

Well, I suppose then he's had his way.

I've been put in my place, in his eyes. I only hope it's enough.

As Natty's flask empties, Victoria and Patty sink along the wall and sit in the old dirt of the barn, their voices rising so loud I'm sure Tim and Julie can hear them over by the farrier's.

*I once knew a maiden who lived on the plains,*
*She helped me to herd cattle through slow, steady rains;*
*She stayed with me through long roundup*
*And drank with me from the poor bitter cup.*
*She drank the red liquor that affects a man's soul,*
*She was a fair lady, just white as the snow.*

Well, neither of them are fair or as white snow, covered in dirt, and rusty old muck, but they hold each other and hiccup so strongly I'm fair certain my meal will end up on their skirts.

Natty tries to find another drop inside his flask, pasting an eye up to the hole only to get that last drop right in his eyeball and he falls backward, howling, and hits his head on the ground with a bounce. Evan just sits and watches, as if unimpressed by the food, the liquor, or the antics. Arnold picks his teeth with one eye shut, and watches Natty try to readjust himself from the floor.

"I'll just clear the dishes," I finally say, desperate to get out of the old tinshop.

"You are leaving us so fast?" Yves glances up at me. "You are not amused by zee songs my ladies sing?"

Victoria and Patty hiccup at the same time and break into broken laughter.

My skin crawls as I notice Natty has put his cheek to the floor and tries to pull up my skirts with a hand while the other hand is … stroking his pants in a fashion that makes my throat close up and my eyes burn.

"I've washing up to do," I say, grabbing as many of the plates, forks and cups as I can throw into two baskets. I go so fast I hear the high-pitched crackle of broken china and glass, but I don't care—I don't plan to offer another big meal. "But Yves—you now must keep your word."

"Oh? Which word is that?" he asks, leaning further back and folding his arms over the small paunch of his over-full belly.

"The trains," I say, sounding too desperate even to my own ears. I swallow, and overload another basket as I fly about and keep out of Natty's grasping, drunken fingers. "You have to let the trains through more."

"Oh, I thought it was just the one or two." Yves closes his eyes as he watches Natty make another grab. My hem rips. Arnold chuckles low and slow.

My temper flares. "No!" I snap, and Yves's eyes snap open in response. "You don't do anything to the trains when I ask—and I won't ask more than once more this summer. But … if you leave them alone even more, I can … bring in the fine things. Order in … oysters and more of the curry." I nod at the demolished chicken. "Champagne and caviar. Things that I can't order now, not knowing the train … schedule. It needs to be more regular-like. And then you can … stop in and live a bit in style."

Yves hoods his eyes again, head bobbing back and forth, before he shrugs with both bony shoulders. "I will not trouble zee train you ask on, Kate."

It's not my full request, but it's something, and I can't be sure he'll even stick to his word. Then again … "That's fine, then. What a … legitimate man would do, a promise like that."

He pauses completely at my words, and then slowly pulls his long knife toward him and starts stabbing the wood of the trestle table, watching me as I scurry about and exit.

190

Outside, the spring air is clear and watery and clean. I take in a deep, full breath and scurry around the overgrown rose bushes outside and head toward the General, only for the back door to Marie and Thad's kitchen to bang open and Marie herself charge out, eyes wide.

"Have you seen her?"

"Who?" The lie slips out without trying, sounding sincere because of it.

"Helena!"

"Your eldest? Not lately. Been busy." I nod my head toward the old tinshop, where another crude song fills the breeze.

Marie's shoulders don't lose their tension. "She's … missing. She does that, often enough, gone in the morning for no reason."

I dip my chin slightly, unable to look Marie straight in the eye. But Marie's distracted, looking about without seeing, her scarred hands fluttering in a strange pattern.

"I thought Thaddeus whipping her would be enough," she says quietly, her dark brown eyes looking glassy. "But maybe it did the opposite. Maybe it drove her away."

I shrug. "I can't speak to daughters." As I make my way past the forge and down the street, I only think about how soon I might have to go back and gather the rest of my cutlery and the big roasting pan. They wouldn't have a use for that, would they? They won't steal too much of the meager things I've shared with them? Not after a meal like that. Not after I've made a deal with Yves, all things put.

I ought to be feeling for Marie in her worry and panic. This I know.

But I cannot. If I do, I'll lose myself in the emotions that will curl inside me if I stop to care. If I care, I won't be successful.

As I reach my back door, a clanking reaches my ears, and I spin just in time for the sun to be blotted out by Matthias, who balances all the rest of my wares—the basket of plates and cups, the big chicken pan and the rest of my larger bowls—on his forearms and dangling from wide fingers.

"Oh. It's you," I say, and I know I sound flat. He doesn't move, only looks down at me with something like simplicity. I scurry up and toss everything I'm holding on my table, grateful that Moses has left me alone and isn't sitting and waiting to be overly helpful by washing up the dishes, too. I think I couldn't stand it if he did.

I spin to take the rest from Matthias, but his footsteps on the stairs make them creak extra loud and squeaky, so I spin and keep hold of a single cast iron skillet. I've seen Fortuna wave a big one around many a time when she's chasing Dell Johnston away from The Powdered Rose and figure I can copy her technique when it comes to keeping men at bay.

Matthias drops his load next to mine on the table but turns around at the door, blocking the late afternoon's gilt sunlight so my room feels grey and brown instead of gold.

We stare at each other as fear makes my palms sweat and I'm suddenly conscious of the hair falling down my back and the stains of oil on my apron.

He makes a soft sound, like a grunt or a sigh, before touching his fingers to his eyebrow.

"You're welcome," I say stiffly, remembering at the last that of all Yves's posse, the stories say this one at least once was not blinded by heritage. "I'm glad you enjoyed it."

"Very goot," he says, and his voice sounds low and rusted, catching on the vowels even as the accent is smoothed over with American roundness.

My eyes widen. I didn't think he spoke—everyone says he doesn't speak!

My mouth drops open, but before I can return anything, he clambers down the stairs without grace, all bullish and clumsy, and strides back north without looking back, and I'm left with an ungodly amount of dishes and filth to fill my Sunday night.

CHAPTER ELEVEN

# Marie

*April 29, 1883*

The sun sets all streaky with gold and pink and deep red, with bruising purple and navy creeping ever closer. It's a lovely sunset, filled with all the colors of the coming summer, and promise of a lush garden full of fat leaves and swaying corn.

But! An entire day without Helena!

This is worse than her morning disappearances and late morning returns. She's staying away all the hours! Why? To teach Thaddeus and me that she's older, that she doesn't have to follow our rules?

Foolish girl! Her antics only infuriate Thaddeus and make me want to strangle her!

My heart pounds inside my lungs and bangs around inside my rib cage. To think this morning I was so casual, so able to enjoy Thaddeus's arms and lusty embrace, to revel in

194

the fact that our living children continue to be healthy and well, all memory of Natan's and Kaspar's coughs fading as fast as the late afternoon light.

Where can she be? What has she done today? How can she keep us worrying?

The bang in the forge is extra loud, now that we've added Hardy to our home. He sleeps in the old loft above the kitchen, where Thaddeus and I used to bed before we built onto the home, when funds were richer and the work came fast and the metal was plenty. Not like now, when we must take on a hungry apprentice just for an extra meager share of food from Kate to help … grow the town. And we cannot get credit because of this *gówno shit* of a copper kettle staring at me on the tinner's bench.

Maybe we should have told Danny that Kate could use the old tinshop without a mutter from us if only she will leave me be on the kettle and start to give us back decent credit. It's not our fault if she's running her business so close to the line that she cannot be generous!

But the tinshop isn't ours to make demands. Nor can we make demands of Danny, given I refused his offer of marriage only to turn around and agree to wed Thaddeus all those years ago.

So instead, I'll stare at the kettle and will myself to figure on how to fix it one last time, and fight the terror yanking me in every direction.

*Where is Helena?*

Berit says she never saw her wake, meaning she was up at an exceedingly early hour and gone. I forgot to check her trunk, to see if anything is missing. I drop my hammer, happy for another reason not to attempt Kate's repair.

As I push through the kitchen, Berit glances up with hopeful eyes. I shake my head and her slim, proud shoulders sink. I open the door to the side hall and head toward the children's rooms while terror builds in my throat.

She wouldn't run away, would she? She hasn't enough funds to make it all the way to Vermillion let alone far enough west to matter. She's not old enough to be out on her own at all! She'll die! She'll be taken for! She'll …

I close my eyes as I sink to my knees and fumble at the latches. We have always told the children that these boxes are for their especial needs—the only small bit of privacy we can offer.

*Please let things be as they ought! Let her things be here!*

As the brass clicks and I swing open the small chest, my eyes take in the boxes and trinkets with relief. She didn't pack up and leave us, then—she's somewhere in Flats …

Though her best bonnet is missing, the one with the perfectly rolled ribbon and tiny rose thread.

What could it mean? Is she being courted by someone we don't know?! Dressing up and meeting for a frolic and does not care about whiling away the Sunday, leaving us to make excuses for her at late Mass today?

But … her extra socks, too. *Gone* …

I pause again as old newspaper catches my eye. Before I can think, I'm pulling it out, realizing it's not a newspaper but a full catalogue, tattered with pages cut and ripped clean away, but it's clear what it is.

*Dover Stamping & Mfg.* it reads across the top, in block letters with touches of filigree. The pages are littered with black and white renderings, sketches, and graphs of

196

pre-made tinplate parts. Descriptions of what this Eastern stamping company can do with a sheet of tin in a matter of seconds sends my already tingling nerves over the next wave of despair.

There's a step behind me, and I whirl and shake the magazine in the air in Thaddeus's face as he peers into the room.

"What do you think she's doing with such a thing? Where did she get it?" I shake it under his nose.

He pulls it from my trembling fingers and frowns darkly as he pages through the same photographs and prices I just saw myself.

"Why would she have something like this? She knows already we cannot pay for new tinplate, let alone some of these wares! She knows business is already hard! Is she mad, to dream of such a change in our circumstances?" As my ire rises, the child in my belly throws out a foot into my backbones with vigor. I wince.

Hardy, Kaspar, and Natan poke their heads into the hallway, as if drawn by the shouting, as boys are wont to be. As I rub my stomach, Hardy pushes to be nearer me, a hand hovering over my shoulder.

"Mrs. Marie. You alright? Is it the baby? I mean … should I get—"

"No, no!" I wave away his concern, surprised a young man would be so quick to try to aid an ailing woman. Where did Kate find him? "Don't get Berit, it's nothing."

"I meant Doc Kinney," Hardy explains, still looming and wavering.

I'm not pleased the conversation has shifted, and I feel my entire body turn to black pocked holes inside. The sorrow and darkness spill into me, and I shove off his concern. "Damn it, no. Never the Doc, anyway. You two!" I wave the catalogue at Kaspar and Natan. "You have to explain what the hell this—" I wave the thin pamphlet. "This *blasphemy* is in my house!"

"We haven't seen it," Natan says with all youthful earnestness. Kaspar nods vigorously, eyes round and eyebrows high under his black bangs.

I am running out of words and steam and vigor, and fight against the deep horror mincing into my reality. I spin at Hardy as Thaddeus stands like a mountain, silently paging through.

"And you? Did you know of this?"

Ripping the papers out of Thaddeus's grip, I march into the kitchen and smooth out the front cover of the Dover Stamping company catalogue on the kitchen table. Berit turns around.

"What is it?"

"Something of Helena's." I squint and take a closer look by the single lantern at the address out in New Hampshire. Will people pay to order tinware and the like from so far East when they can come to me? I doubt it greatly. Surely some fancy expensive machine in a factory cannot compare. We'll be safe. My world, my business will be safe. And yet …

"It's not a bad idea, Mother," Natan mentions, reading upside down as he sits next to the other boys across from me. "All the tricky work taken care of by their stamping press—if the math works out, it could actually help you with shop work."

How? The catalogue boasts of patterned toilet wares and washer buckets and a hundred other items. I smooth down the bottom corner where the paper has already wrinkled. I want to glance through it more myself and read the heavy-inked inscriptions and explanations. *I wonder—* No! I cannot entertain anything new, any more change.

"We'll do no such thing with this. It's for the fire," I decide. Thaddeus hums a soft approval over my shoulder at my decision, and our two boys protest in various ways.

"No!"

"Mother—"

"Who else knows of this catalogue?" I press.

"Probably Nancy. When the post came in with it," Berit says as she places plates and cups on the table with soft bangs and pings.

I groan softly, and Hardy begins to rise again. "Sit down, boy, it's not the babe. And too early to worry on even if it were. *Potępienie, damnation*! If Nancy has seen this, everyone will know of it. They'll come asking to see it. They'll want to order from it! And then where will we be?"

"If you'd just look—"

"Natan, you must not argue—"

"Listen to your mother!" Thaddeus growls. "It's a trouble, not a new amusement!"

Natan and Kasper wilt in their seats.

"I don't … I don't think Nancy saw it. Maybe." Hardy's voice is soft after Thaddeus's booming shout.

"What makes you say that?" I say testily, flipping through the pages once more.

"I … I saw this. Once. It was at the General Store. Maybe … maybe Miss Davies sent for it, and Nancy didn't see it?" Hardy seems to shrink inside himself as he offers the information, and that's no small feat as he's bigger than both our boys in shoulder and chest.

My head spins slightly and the skin wrapped around my chest feels too tight. I shift the edge of my corset and steady my hands as I walk to the hearth with the offending paper.

"Well, then. She's trying to put me out of business! So much for her promises!" It almost makes me choke on my own spittle. I crumple the cover, moving to burn the slim volume of images and information and figures.

One last, long flip through the pages … it is a fine dream, to have a tinshop that could offer such beautiful wares—things I cannot make by hand no matter how well I practice.

As I glance through, I notice notes in the wide margin of one page, which boasts more white space than others. It's not print, it's ink.

And it's Helena's penmanship.

*Mother and Father—Please do not fret or feel sorrow. I've gone off to see about the business, to help in my way, before I settle into my own. I couldn't ask permission, as I know you would have refused and forbidden it. You'll be glad I've gone, you'll see. With fondness and love, Helena B. Salomon*

I turn to Thaddeus with my heart sitting on my tongue, and he moves faster than usual to grasp the paper back. Turning back to stare at the flames in the hearth, I cannot hear the shuffling of the boys behind me, or the clank of Berit bringing out pork pie. Thaddeus's body tenses next to me, bristling and bitter.

When I take it back from his limp hand, I finger the soft frayed edge of the ripped magazine, and the word, spoken quietly, hoarsely, through the thick grey of hearth-smoke, hits my mind and collapses my thoughts.

What had Kate said only this morning?

*"I've an agent who is gone East, finding ways to build more business, more storefronts, bigger supplies and choices. There'll be fine dresses of the latest fashion soon enough, with all the delicacies of the cities here. I swear it ..."*

No.

She wouldn't.

She can't.

I fling the magazine on the ground. Natan, Kaspar, Hardy, and Berit all jump slightly at the slap of the paper packet on the floorboards. My eyes rise to Hardy's, and his shoulders rise to his reddening ears.

"Goddamn you," I say, and my voice is oddly flat. It comes from the black fury always buried in my gut, careening out in a violence that raises my voice with each word. "How dare you! How?! My God! *Pieprzyć cię! Fuck you!* Oh my God!" My hands cover my ears and I close my eyes. When I open them, Hardy is standing, frozen, his blue eyes wide and shot with strips of blood. "Helena—you—how did you—with Kate Davies! And you didn't tell us?! You've kept it a secret!"

"I didn't know what it meant, when I saw it! I didn't understand, not then! I swear it!" His voice squeaks at the end, but Natan is too struck with fright to tease. Hardy clears his voice and tries again. "Truly, Mrs. Marie, I only know it was ... they were ... it was something Helena wanted special! And ... Miss Davies wants to build up her store so she don't need Yves or something. I don't know, I wasn't really paying attention, I only know because it was Helena what had the papers, and I ... when I first saw Helena I only ..." He trails off and looks terrified of me. As he ought.

Helena. Who wants nothing to do with my tinshop. Who wants to make her own way, as hard-headed as the idea may be.

Ice folds itself down my spine, even with the uneven wavering of the hearth behind me. Thaddeus is absolutely silent behind me. I can sense him, solid and still, a rock of his own power.

"She sent her—she knows nothing of the world! Nothing!" I hiss, turning to look up at my husband. "Alone! Gone! She stole Helena from me! What can a girl do—how can she possibly—What is Kate thinking?!"

The anger and fear turn on themselves in my body, devouring one another over and over until I think I might faint with the headiness of it all. My knees sway slightly, and I try to catch a full breath, except it hitches painfully with each gulp of air.

Hardy looks pained, his shoulders quiver. "I don't like it neither, Missus Marie. I swear I would have offered to go, as I know the riding of the rails. She said she was wanting a journey someday, that's all. That's all she was saying. I said I'd help if she wanted. And she said if we both would go, it would be worse if we both left, or people would be saying we'd run off and got hitched." He dips his head down, staring at the patched, scuffed leather of his boots. "And then she run off today and left me behind anyways. So I guess no one will think we done got hitched."

"It would be better than her going alone!" I shout. "God knows what has happened! She's likely … gone! For good! Get out of my sight! I want you out of my house! You kept this from us, knowing why she left—my God—"

"Into the forge, boys," Thaddeus says quietly, but his voice rumbles and shakes through the boards of the house, and there's no arguing with him. "Dinner won't be ready just yet."

Hardy hunches his frame and steps out of the kitchen in four quick strides, with Natan and Kaspar chasing his shadow. Our sons glance at us with wide eyes but hold their tongues after a quick glance at their father.

Berit has been rooted to the same spot in the kitchen since I started to lose my senses. Her eyes are bright. "Oh, our poor Helena ..."

I clench my fists so tight I know my short, broken nails are likely going to break skin, and turn to Thaddeus. My limbs are zipping with a strange, disjoined sensation, as though I have beads of strength running up and down my skin. I prickle and then go hot, and I ache to be in the cool darkness of my tinshop, where the metal is white and gold and sharp. Thaddeus seems to sense my desire to flee, and puts an iron hand on my upper arm, holding me in place.

"Go check on the livestock, mother," Thaddeus says, keeping his gaze locked on my face.

Berit does his bidding, likely because he gave her the title he rarely uses except when he is quite serious or very happy.

Finally, I am alone with Thaddeus, and I think I truly might faint from it all.

"Kate Davies ..." I breathe, trying to calm the swirl in my heart. "She sent our daughter—*paid* our daughter—to go off alone. Like Helena is some whore, and Kate paid the way! With all the dangers! I don't care the reasoning behind any of it. How could she? How dare she?"

"Helena is young and impressionable. Anyone with eyes can see that," Thaddeus says, his voice strained and strung deeper than I've ever heard. "Kate isn't stupid."

203

"She sent our daughter off to be ruined. It is inconceivable. It is reckless. Selfish! I cannot—Helena could be dead! Ruined! She—"

"There is nothing to be done, Marya," Thaddeus interrupts, his shoulders square and his jaw turning to stone.

"*Nothing?*"

"Not until we hear from Helena herself. The girl knows her letters, and if she needed help, she would write."

"Not if she's beyond that. Not if she cannot—"

"We cannot go chasing after her."

"We could demand Kate bring her back! She must! A child is not a ... a piece of cookware, meant to be borrowed and able to be repaired!"

"Helena is old enough to be wed. At times ... we must know when it is time to look ahead. You know this. Helena made her choice. So then." He inhales loudly, and then turns on his heel toward the forge, following the boys back out to the fire and soot and coal.

I stare after him, screaming to my core at his dismissal. It's only at the last moment that I see the tremor in his shoulders and the dip of his neck that I know how much he's hurting, too. When the door to the forge slams closed, I look up and stare at the flat boards of the ceiling and will my tears to stay inside my eyeballs.

In our life, there are things that are precious, and a daughter is one of them. I know how deeply my connection was with my own mother, and I had always looked forward to that for myself.

*My daughters!*

My feet move slowly along the hallway, and I sink into the quiet of my bedroom. The padding of the quilt, set with orange and red and green in the pattern of Poland are muted in the slow fading of the light as the evening pulls onward.

*And where is Helena sleeping tonight?*

A poke in my thigh makes me shift and dig into the pocket of my apron. It is nothing but a triangle of tin, leftover from some project or another. I lay it flat on my scarred palm, staring at the pure cut of the shape, the stubble of rust bubbling along an edge. If only it were all this simple. The math, the preciseness, the exact rules of my trade. Why can that not be how it all is?

The trace of the line is almost loving when it carves a thin, straight cut through the edge of my palm and into the softness of my wrist. The slice is a relief, the red blood a mirror of the other, older, white lines. I sigh softly as the tin edges under the flesh, and with the second, absent cut, the tears finally go, flowing as silently as the web of ruby on my hand.

I bury my bloody fist into the dark fabric of my skirts, bending over the edge of the bed, weeping as silently as I might so I do not bother Berit in the next room, and take great gulps of air to try to catch up my sobs.

*My daughters!*

How was I not enough of a mother for Helena?! So unloving that she would leave, choose such a dangerous path?

How could I let Urszula get so ill?

My daughters, my daughters! I am so sorry! *Bardzo przepraszam! So sorry!*

I was not enough! *Nie jestem wystarczający! I am not enough!*

The familiar thrum of my heartbeat, held within the roughness of my hand, bumps louder and louder inside my head until I bend over across my thighs, holding my head in my uninjured fingers, and my calves bump the trunk at the end of the bed once more.

The violence tearing through my heart sharpens and quenches suddenly, as it always does. I sit up straight, pressing on the slices to slow the bleeding.

Well, then.

I will not go against my husband's wishes and stir trouble or point fingers about Helena's rash choices and the opportunity handed to her by a cold-hearted woman, but I can still speak in my own way.

My daughters have been torn from me, but it is not *all* my fault.

I wait another few hours, when it is dusky dark, and the dinner is served. Thaddeus does not question me when I say I must step into the tinshop. When I set out across Second Street, the cool spring night closes around my skin and a wind tugs at the edge of my skirts. One of the dogs at Jim Bailey's barks, and the answer from our cow is low and warm and throaty.

The stars peek through scattered clouds, and enough lanterns sit in windows that I can see my way clear enough.

The light in her kitchen is yellow and muted, but no matter. I don't care if she's home or not.

I have nothing to say to her.

The old cracked lasts of my boots creak slightly as I take the three steps up to her back door. Delicately, slowly, I perch the metal on the top stair, then go back down at once.

The destroyed kettle tips slightly, and the destruction of it is palpable even in the dimness of night. The dull old copper and deep dents and ripped seam are waiting for Kate, stout and immobile, robbed of life and glow for all time.

CHAPTER TWELVE

# *Jane*

*June 10, 1883*

I wipe a sleeve across my brow, and the fabric comes away dark and creased with sweat. The June light is bright and the last of the snow is an old memory already. I plug the hoe back into the dirt and chip away at the mix of clay, dust, and mud as I prepare another row for bean seeds so we might have a late harvest come fall. It will be good to have the backyard in order once more, good to know I will have months of harvest if I plant things in just the right way.

Beyond the limits of my garden, the prairie seems relieved with new growth, and is bursting with thigh-high grass. The promise of hot, brilliant flowers shivers on the tips of some plants, so different from the early pale colors and instead fair ripe with crimson and yellow and darkest pink. I am always pleased with my view but never more than now, in the first flush of summer. We have survived a winter and a spring, though with far more illness than Patrick expected. It is not only unfortunate for the people of Flats Junction—both those who called on us and those who didn't—but also quite difficult for our pocketbook.

With the start of the warm season, Patrick is called for more issues with livestock than people. Sometimes I think he prefers the shift, as it harkens back to his very first work in medicine, which was not with people but with small animals and horses. The veterinary work is crucial to his practice here, and never more so than now. The staunchly supportive Danny Svendsen, with his brilliant gold hair and serious blue eyes, uses Patrick as almost an insurance, checking over his animals often for disease, birthing issues, and stoutness for the summer of grazing. To be competitive, the Brinkleys do the same, and Patrick is also called out regularly to the Zalenski farm with their mix of cows and sheep, and of course there's the occasional visits to the General he makes for orders and medicines. I try not to think about things whenever he sees Kate, even as I rarely see him for supper these days.

The cash we receive from both rancher and farmer helps keep us in foodstuff bought from the General until I coax seeds to root in the garden once more. The pleasure of planting is made more palatable by Esther's presence. She comes to help me weed and place the rows of hopeful crops, and though her silences are the same as they ever were, I find her nearness just as soothing. It sometimes seems as though Kate and I have traded partners.

Her mother for my husband.

"You should think of building yourself a new place," I tell her, as we sift through the soft earth in the warm dirt nearest the house. My apron is completely full of dust, and

208

I glance a bit covetously at her long leather dress, worn soft and pliable by the years of use and wear.

"Is that so?" she says without much enthusiasm or commitment.

I pause, feeling the crumbs of dirt trickle out of the creases in my hands. Does she think Kate will allow her to stay in Flats Junction indefinitely? Does she not feel the rancor of her daughter through the distance, for all Esther keeps well away?

There must be a plan, though I have been unable to think of one.

I sink lower into my knees, the fold of them caught between the layers of petticoats. Perhaps she doesn't understand. Perhaps she only is happy to be near Kate, as she has always been, never mind the angry words or stilted quiet between them. And who am I to force her to leave? To create a house if she doesn't want one?

It's only ... with her here, any lawman who comes to Flats Junction on a whim will see her living with us, and we will be yanked apart and torn from home. Without Esther's half-breed daughter to lay some claim on her, speaking up for Esther so she does not have to move to a reservation ... it falls on Patrick and me. I do not know if we are strong enough, with enough support from the community, to protect Esther. She should understand this, but it is too bold to say my thoughts aloud.

"Well, Patrick and I only wondered if you wanted a place of your own again," I explain. "No ... need to rush off and build one."

She smiles very slightly and kneels again further away, her old ligaments moving with a natural, graceful fluidity.

"And what would I put in this new place? What furniture and clothing? What pieces of an old life?"

She's perfectly, calmly correct. The truth of that pounds into me at once, and I feel foolish and hard-hearted to have not realized it. Everything, save the handful of clothes and the deer hide she'd been wearing that day, had burned in the fire that had destroyed her small home on the edge of town. That and the single tin box she'd found under the crispy stove, charred and falling apart but holding a few precious mementos.

"I'm sorry," I say quietly. "I—we only want to try ... piece back your life—It seems the right thing ... so you can feel like you belong, again." A dagger of embarrassed shame carves across my stomach.

"Like one feels with family?" she counters. "I have that in Kate ... you." Her fingers curl into mine. "Things cannot go back to what they were. Percy, my relatives, friends ... it always changes. Even my houses. I have had so many, even since living in Flats Junction. From my first home to this one."

I know the place she mentions. An ostentatious, brilliantly painted two-story home now used by an enterprising young couple who rents it out as an 'inn' on the first floor and surreptitiously runs yet another—and unnamed—brothel on the top.

"Percy's place. Ours," she says. "Though he at first built it for the wife he expected to follow him when he was moving west for gold."

I don't know my Flats Junction history perfectly, and she sees my confusion and settles herself comfortably into a knee-stance, one I know well. I inherently understand the cadence of her storytelling, and move into a comfortable seat on the ground, feeling the hardness of the unturned earth under my bottom.

"You know I married him, Jane?" she says, repeating gossip I've heard years ago. I nod and she continues, speaking slowly and without actually looking at me. Tracing back decades, she lists out Percival Davies's birth to a Welsh father and English mother in the hills of North Carolina in 1830 and how the gold promise in California sent him rushing westerly at the prime age of nineteen.

"He never made it further than here," she gestures around, her strong, capable hand including all of Flats Junction. "It wasn't much back then but he saw potential to do well and use a trade he had learned briefly from his family. So he built the house for his Bets—the wife he'd just married before he left in '49—and waited. She never came, and then he met me."

A smile, as rare as anything, slips across her face, and at once her beauty mirrors Kate's.

"He said the year was 1852 when he met me, though I was not counting in the way of your people. My own birthing had happened in Šúykawakhą hípáȟpa wi—the month when ponies shed." She pauses briefly, as if to remind herself to speak in English as she reminisces. "Well, so we loved. And he married me in the way of my people though he had only one horse, which my father and brothers and brothers-in-law thought entirely inadequate." She laughs softly, but with memory and not sadness. "They did not understand he was becoming the most powerful man in this town, that he'd turned his business into the bank. And when he showed them the types of pelts he could afford from the East and the dresses he had made for me, and the rifles … well, then we married."

"He was already married!" I sputter, the surprise of the story making me speak out of turn.

"His marriage to Bets gave him esteem in my family's view. It is common for the Lakota to take many wives, Jane. I did not mind sharing him in that way, and truthfully it was as though I was his only wife. Bets stayed away until her death. So we lived in the cake-house. It is where Kate was born a few years later. And our son many years after that," she plunges her hands back into the earth, breaking up the sod and crushing the stubborn clumps of clay with determination.

"Why did you leave it? You ended up marrying Percy in ... in our ways, didn't you?" I ask, hoping to get as much out of her while she's inclined to be talkative, especially about herself and her past.

"But the house was not mine, even in his death. There were other reasons at the time, too. And truly, Jane, do you think they would have let me stay in the nicest home in town without Percy?"

*Who is 'they'?*

She continues slowly. "Sometimes, I think I will not find a place of true happiness again. Not with my people. And not here."

We leave it there, though my mind still turns over the story, guilt building. Someone—*they*—who don't like Indians in town? Well, that's nearly half of Flats Junction. And she doesn't think she will be happy here? Did we wrong her by bringing her back? My lungs tighten.

When she goes in to start the midday meal, the sun slants across the hides of her shoulders and paints them a deep butter, supple and shiny, just like Patrick's often-patched leather vest. The sway of the ragged fringe along the edge of the garment tangles a bit as she walks, pushing the faded flowered calico skirts around her leather soles. She is still as straight as she's ever been. I'm so struck with the way she blends into the soft lines of the garden dirt, and how the muted colors of her body fade into the soft fluffs of spring green and old wood, that I fail to notice the shadow flowing along the edge of the fence.

When the shadow hits my sight, it's too late to ignore the horse or his rider.

"Good—hello." My voice is too soft and citified. "How are you?" The last is stronger, and I straighten my spine as I speak.

Bern stares at me from the saddle, and his horse lowers his nose to nibble at my carefully planted trailing nasturtiums. The animal goes straight the blooms, and I jerk forward to swat my hand, wanting to keep some flowers so I might have seeds for next year's planting.

Bern yanks up his horse's head, but not too harshly, still caring for his ride as he always has—so very, particularly careful.

"Your husband is at the General again."

"He keeps hoping to get in a stock of iodine."

There was some late winter, but too late for so many. I shade my eyes so I might gaze up at Bern without struggle, and he tilts his brim lower so I still cannot see him properly.

"Strange, ain't it, that they spend so much time together."

They don't—not really. Not that I am aware of, I think, but I won't give Bern the satisfaction. "It's only … she's the only place to get dry goods. You know that."

"And you know womenfolk should do the bulk of the shopping."

"But he's a doctor. So it's different."

"So it ain't done, Jane."

He turns around his horse and bumps along toward the Svendsen bunkhouse, the sun blazing across his shirt and his back as straight as the church steeple.

*What is he playing at? Should I doubt my own husband?*

I shake off the question. He's only jealous. Only hurting. Only wishing I'd said yes to him, not Patrick.

Well, disturbances won't fix the meal or the laundry, and since Esther is already halfway to getting the food ready, it's up to me to pull the wash.

I go upstairs and into Esther's room, taking her extra calico skirt and the two shirts, leaving the deer and buffalo hides. As I lean in, I get a whiff of the smoke that hangs, tantalizing and bitter on the skins. It is familiar and green, and suddenly I realize it is the smell of the sweetgrass, imbedded in the flesh of the garments from years in Esther's small house on the edge of town. I recall some days how the one long room had filled with the fat, grey smoke of sage, but often there was sweetgrass too, and it had stayed with my undergarments for weeks when I'd lived with her, long before I married Patrick.

Thankfully, there are no immediate holes to mend in anyone's clothing, though some pieces look dangerously worn. Next time, I will have to sew.

The talc stinks today, and I wonder if my nose is particularly sensitive after smelling the sweetgrass. Hauling the extra bucket over, I soak everything briefly, hopeful I can get out most stains quickly, and then start to rub everything with the paste, feeling the talc eat into my skin and soak into the sleeves of my dress even though I have rolled the sleeves to my elbows. Why is bending over such a difficult thing?

My stomach is not so large yet. In fact, it is still as flat as ever.

"You are nearly indecent, you know."

I jerk up. Mrs. Molhurst glares over the elderberry bushes, which are hanging heavy with tiny, bubbling dark fruit.

"Excuse me?"

"Having that woman live with you, as if it's natural and normal. People talk, you see, and I can see with my own eyes. She's living with you like she's relations."

"Maybe she is like relations!" I harp back, feeling snappy and strung tight.

Her mouth hangs open, brown, crooked teeth showing in the back. Then she sucks in her lips and cheeks and narrows her eyes. "You think people forget. They don't."

"I don't either. No one has yet to admit to burning her house to the ground."

Mrs. Molhurst leans over the bushes, her thin neck stretching from bony shoulders and she glances further into the garden where the prairie slips into my yard. "Mm. And you think you'll get out so easy, with all the sickness in town? People know, people watch. The doc has best be careful and having that woman stay with you is not helping."

She speaks to my own worries and fears, but my loyalty is not to her. "So you best stay away, then, in case the sickness is catching. I might speak too loud, and she might answer, and you'll get so sick you'll die!"

I shouldn't goad her, but I can't help it. Someone needs the brunt of my frustration and my emotional uneasiness, and it cannot be Esther or Patrick.

Her front teeth come out and she sucks through them. The pound of hooves on the street interrupts her next barb, and we both watch the storm of cattle winding its way from the south to the north end of town. It is an anomaly. Most of the time, the cattle are driven around the town, but today the men are coming on East Avenue, though I am not sure why. The longhorns jostle for room, horns raking and scratching and swiping as they go by, stamping on that same prairie grass that hinges on my lawn. The lowing, the pounding, the cloud of dust is disconcerting and overwhelming, and I cough hard and feel the anxiety and frustration zoom. My laundry!

When cowboys come by, shouting, yelling and yipping, I can barely see for the grime clotting the air. By the time the last steer go through, and the dust starts to fade, Mrs. Molhurst is gone and hidden in her house and I'm stuck with a cake of dirt in every crease of my skirt and settling on my hair. Wishing I could scream aloud for all the frustration bubbling in my gut, I move back to the washbin and stare at the water, which is now brown and muddy, and at the handful of shirts out to dry, which are dry, certainly, and all covered in dust.

It means starting fresh and the agony of that makes me want to give in and settle on the dirt of the ground. My body aches to stop, throbbing at the idea of pulling water again for all I consider myself seasoned to the territories. Is it the child in my belly? Is it the fact that all the time I spent over the laundry is lost? I should have … I pause. I should have *what*? Yell over at Tate and Hank and Bern and Moses and the rest—told them to go another way? Thrown my laundry into the house where it would sit, wet and dripping but still cleaner than now? Scream at Mrs. Molhurst that her distraction kept me from acting at all?

Sighing with defeat, I dump the laundry out and start to fill it back up, trying to hurry so I can get the first stage done before Patrick is home and we can eat.

But I only get as far as another fresh tub of water before I see him walking up the road toward our porch. By the angle of his jaw and the way he holds his medical bag, my skin tightens and my teeth feel dry against my lips.

*Something is wrong.*

I meet him in the kitchen, and I stoke the fire and start the coffee again while Esther puts out the day-old bread. I remove the lid to the bean pot and give it a stir, hoping they are not going to taste burned.

Patrick sits heavily, folds his hands and stares across the table. "I'm sorry I must harp on this, Esther, but remind me again me how it started."

*It?*

She hesitates for a moment, her eyes down on the wood grain. "I can barely remember, Pat," she says softly. "And it all happened so fast."

"I need to know, and you didn't have me with you at first."

I close the bean lid and turn. They're speaking riddles. I fight the annoyance in my chest but cross my arms. I've never seen Patrick's complexion like this since he leaned over me during the miscarriage. He's worried.

Frightened.

It's no good when a man is afraid and even worse with my husband, the self-assured and confident physician. Exasperated, yes. Frustrated, certainly. As I saw him with the diphtheria this past winter, handling the ignorance of parents, and the endless wait for medical supplies ... but now. This is different.

Esther seems to find some inner source of memory and she pulls up her spine.

The boiling coffee breaks my concentration for a moment. I yank the tin pot off the stove, throw in a few odd eggshells, and fill three mugs with steaming black liquid. I bring them to the table and sit next to Patrick.

Finally, Esther inhales. "But you're sure that's it?" she asks in a strained voice. "You're sure?"

He sighs, a huge mighty gush, and lays his palms open. "As sure as I can be. I just don't ... we know so little."

I cannot handle the riddle. "What is going on?" My gaze swings between the two. "Is there threat of some sort of epidemic?" Not again. Please God, not again. We only just managed to get rid of the diphtheria! What could possibly be worse?

Patrick's mouth goes tight and quivers with indecision, the way it does when he wishes to simply spew a hundred theories or say something laying on his heart.

I want to drape my arm around his shoulders, but now is not the time. The worry is palpable in the entire kitchen, more stifling than the oven's heat, wrapping around my chest and squeezing.

"Old Henry stopped by this mornin' and passed on a call to see the son of one of the new families out on the outside of town. Mid-age boy, close to adulthood," he says finally, drawing up to sit straight. "But ... it's not just any type of sickness. Based upon the rash, I think it's worse. I'm thinkin' it's black measles."

*Black measles.*

The two words have meant little to me, even as I've heard them whispered here and there. The red measles, of course, is a scourge all fear no matter whether one lives on the coast or in a territory.

"It's to be a measles epidemic?" It's a terrifying thing. An exhausting notion.

"You mean *black* measles," he corrects at once.

"It's different, then?" I ask, my voice scratchy.

"Jane, don't fret. I'll explain," he says, his tone calmer than I expect, given the pastiness of his skin. "In terms of the disease itself, how it starts and jumps, it's ... difficult to understand. To find. But it's not different because the patient displays lots of tiny red spots—at least, before they bleed and turn black inside."

"Why are you asking Esther?"

Patrick exchanges a glance with her, and she sighs and places her hands, palms down and flat, against the worn wood of our kitchen table.

"My Percy came down with it in ..."

"1879," Patrick supplies quietly.

"Yes. In ...'79, as you say. He died within a week of getting sick." She says it so simply, as if it happened to someone else. As if it was not the man she'd loved for decades, who had thrown away all propriety, who had been at her side as they built Flats from the bare earth of the prairie using nothing but their wills.

"Do you know what the symptoms are?" I ask, absently rubbing a hand over a sore spot on my hip under the table, where my ligaments feel soft and stretched.

He runs a hand through his rough hair and sighs. "I've read a bit. Enough," he says, as if admitting his lack of knowledge will help. "Panum's *Observations Made During the Epidemic of Measles on the Faroe Islands in 1846* durin' my apprenticeship, but I don't have it memorized."

"Can you send east for it, from your friend—Doctor MacHugh? Maybe the paper will help," I offer, hoping it will snap him out of his morose pose.

"I have no idea. I wouldn't be much of a physician if I wasn't honest."

I meet Esther's bright eyes, and she simply tilts her head, recognizing the same thing I do in the doctor's naked words. Suddenly she stands, and walks out the back kitchen door, as silent as ever.

"It's too much for her," I say. "The memories."

"Likely." He sighs and reaches for my hand. "It's goin' to be worse than the diphtheria, Janie. I wouldn't be fair if I didn't warn you."

"Does it mean a ... different sort of operation?" I cannot imagine one worse than what he did on Urszula Salomon and others. Enough lived that I believe in his plan, his surgeries. But so many died. It feels too much a gamble.

Maybe I still doubt all doctors, as he once said I did.

But not Patrick. I must trust him—least of all as a husband.

He stands and picks up his coffee. "I'll be in the study, tryin' to find the old books."

As soon as he's out of the room, Esther walks in, smelling like fresh prairie grass and dust. She carries a basket filled with an odd assortment of leaves, blooms, and weeds. "Where's Patrick?"

"The study."

I stand, but can't help pulling some of the flowers out of the basket as I do. "Where are these from?"

Widow Hawks rummages in the depths of the wicker. "There's the yarrow from the near prairie." She pulls out a feathery plant with round, globular ends that look like it was considering blooming in the near future had she not plucked it. Some of the tight white-green tops break off and scatter across my pitted table. "Try a tea to help with the bleeding. How the spots of the measles bleed."

"How does it work?" My wild curiosity picks up, unwitting and strong and my fingers tickle the wilted greens. "I'm not familiar with too many myself, other than such things as peppermint and lavender."

"This one you will call fireweed, which also will stop a bleed." She picks up a violent purple-pink flower. "Or stem a stomach-ache."

"Does Patrick like to use such … local remedies?" I pause as I pull out fresh herbs and flowers with her, wondering if this is only her way of dealing with the return of an illness. "Does any of it work?"

Widow Hawks ignores my questions, continuing to pull out fresh herbs and murmuring as she does. If I believed in such things, I'd call her a witch woman of some kind, and I repress the urge to turn away from her. Instead, I think of the black measles, and wonder if there's anything truly in these old medicines and lost ways of her people.

221

"If I could find the others ..." she mutters, and places more yarrow in the pile. "Then maybe I could teach you, as you asked."

"Teach her what?"

We jerk and jump at his abrupt return, and my hands, already stained pale, lemony green, pause over the tops of yet another plant. I feel caught, and his eyes are shadowed in a frown—a strange thing to see on my mild husband.

"I've only asked about her medicines. I'd wanted to know before this." No use in hiding this truth from him, and I've promised myself to be open this marriage, to explain all the quirks of my character in the belief he will take them in stride. "Maybe one will work."

He wanders up to the table, tucking a thick book under an arm. "This is all very well," he says, as he examines a hunk of crusty willow bark. "But do you think these will work this time?"

"Have you used this on people before?" At once, I wish I had remembered to cut my tongue.

The air in the room goes stale and still and grey. Esther stares at the weeds slowly curling along the wood planks before us. "They didn't help," she says, the words sinking into the silence of the kitchen. "But I didn't try them all."

I reach for her, grabbing her fingers and squeezing once, twice. She shakes her head and straightens past her obvious sorrow. "I will think to recall other remedies for such an ailment. My people do not seem to suffer the same way. It is the one type of measles we do not catch from the White men."

"That's hardly a comfort!" I burst out. "This news of a boy dying of the disease is not going to go away. And just because no one else has caught it yet, doesn't mean it's gone! People are on edge about any unknown sickness, and we need something foolproof to help them this time."

I don't voice the next bit, hanging on the edge of my tongue.

Patrick cannot manage another full failure.

He must be shown to be competent. He must get some success and gain some support. I am powerless, it seems, to help him. A woman's way is generally quiet and gentle, put to work on the side and yet able to move tremendous burdens. It is a dance, and a silent one, but until I'm given my chance, I won't be able to help him.

He runs a hand over his dense hair. "The truth of it is that I don't know if I can recognize and diagnose what I'm seein', and that's if *I am called in time*!" He stands and begins to pace. "Both cases were quite similar, Percy's and this boy." He ticked off the symptoms using his fingers. "Head and body aches, cough, sneezin', chills, sour stomach and so on. Overnight, a fever kicks in and climbs higher." The doctor seems mournful as his shoulders fall. He starts to list off symptoms of the disease I did not even know. "I noticed the blue fingers, toes, and tongue. That, coupled with the high fever and rash, the red spots were enough to convince me it was the black measles." He glances up at Esther, then me. "What's puzzlin' is no one else was sick in the house." He lifts a shoulder. "But that does not mean the infection itself will not spread."

The pacing makes me nervous. I understand most of his words, but it still sounds as though the illness ends with death.

The doctor looks frustrated and worn, his back taut and pulled tight. "I appreciate you tryin' to help, Esther,

223

truly, but if the herbs didn't work on Percy back in '79, I don't know the purpose of keepin' them on hand. It's not *science*, you see. It's not researched."

He turns and returns to his study. The thunk of a heavy book on his desk bounces through the hallway.

My arm reaches to sweep the weeds off to the side. "If he says."

Esther blocks my arm with hers and when our skin touches, there is a shock, like that of lightning. I pull back at once, gooseflesh spiraling along my arms.

"I believe it is worth a try if others get ill," she says with determination, the steel in her voice and arm enough to make me pay attention. "I did not have all of these herbs when Percy took to his bed. It was too late into the season for some of them."

I sit slowly, almost gingerly. "What do we say to Patrick, though? I ... I would like to learn what you know, but ... people don't ask for me. And they rarely call Patrick in enough time. Even less so ... now."

"Learn for yourself, as you have always preferred," Esther says gently, picking up another hunk of greens. "Your husband is not the guardian of your mind."

She's right, and I close my hand over the stalks of grass, inhaling the familiar scent. "Sweetgrass."

CHAPTER THIRTEEN

# Kate

*June 27, 1883*

"Summer onions?"

I glance over at the loosely woven basket, where Clara Henderssen left her morning crop. The long, shiny greens are already wilting, but still dark and green and cool in the corner by the bushels of early potatoes and some floppy pale green lettuces, a late crop and showing it.

"That's all I have," I tell Orla Grady, who is so new in town she doesn't know where I keep the fresh goods apart from the dry yet. I try to smile encouragingly at her, but frankly it's next to impossible to be myself completely.

Damn Moses and his liquid eyes, staring at me from behind the thick upright plank, though he pretends to finger the newest saddle. What does he want from me?

And Bern, perched behind Gil at the checkers board, watching me and Moses as if trying to unlock a clue.

I want them both gone, but neither are taking any hints, no matter how subtle I'm trying to be in front of all my customers. The gardens are not quite in, so I'm still inordinately busy, and the rails are down again, though Yves has been staying at the Prime Inn, so I know it's not him, and he's assured me the same as well, as if I couldn't figure it out on my own. Damn the soft wrought iron! And damn that I must keep up the loose agreement with Yves. It means I still have to use him throughout the summer to bring in wagonloads of dry goods from Vermillion and Yankton, and I cringe when I think of how much food and goods his posse takes as part of their payment.

Nodding at Moses curtly, I move around him to get some of the last root vegetables for Orla and take down her man's information with care. It's a fresh page, with new ink, and I only make a tiny blot while Toot asks about trading lanterns, and Trust Willy is paging through a six-month old *Chicago Times* newspaper nearby.

"This one!" he crows, pointing, expecting me to exclaim at the sketch advertising a new Wagner cast-iron stove-top sandwich toaster. I glance over, the distraction rising by the moment, a fizzling energy popping through my limbs. The General is both a goodness and a curse at times like this.

"It's nice," I tell him.

"You barely looked!" he huffs.

Horeb shouts to be heard over the din. "Did you hear the one about the lady whose skirts were so short—"

"Yup."

"I ain't even said it yet!" Horeb fairly shouts over the noise in the store, trying to capture an audience. So far, Gilroy seems to be the only one answering.

Elaine Warren, with new oil in her hair, stomps over with her arms full of canned peaches. She looks annoyed, though I'm not sure if it's the prices, her prickly mother-in-law's demand for the fruit, or Horeb's gleaming, appreciative eye on her breasts. I wonder what will be up for dessert at the Golden Nail tonight with those delicacies, and wish I had the reason and ability to stop over and eat, but a single woman eating alone anywhere is like to ask for trouble. And I'm certainly not about to pick obvious favorites, as my eyes swing once more between Bern and Moses.

Julie Bailey, the farrier's wife, is examining a bag of tiny bronze nails, likely for her husband Tim, and I sidestep broad, strong Lara O'Donnell as she pushes several of her nine children along the edge of the General's walls on the hunt for the biggest bag of flour I have left.

"For the picnic on the fourth," she announces loudly to me—to everyone—as she sees my questioning glance over the mountain of peach tins. Only Mary Winters forgets to avert her eyes at the statement, and within a blink, Lara begins to strong-arm Mary into making the potatoes for the next saint day picnic at St. Aloysius.

"I'll get to you next, Jane, but I'm afraid if you're here for coffee I'm completely out," I tell her curtly, when Pat's wife inches through the door, looking fascinated by the crowd. With the early train not coming through, I have had to wait on Yves for another damn delivery. The next train will be here.

He promised …

The door creaks and slams and everyone glances around and takes stock of who has come or gone. It's Moses who's left.

"It's likely him who's brought the black measles this year." The whisper is loud enough to carry, but hoarse enough that I only know it was a man who said it. The crowd in the General mutters and shifts as one body, and I feel myself carried with it briefly. "Or our own doc."

Jane swings around wildly, looking for who spoke, her face white. I myself cannot place the voice, but I don't suppose it matters, now that the words are out and scattering like new-plucked feathers.

"Do you think?" Toot whispers loudly back, but so raspy and obviously sarcastic, the mood darkens and goes softer at the same time.

"Well, the diphtheria started around when he showed up, not the black measles." Sally Painter pushes, her face pinched.

"But it's black measles, Sally," Lara reminds her.

"I meant the diphtheria, myself. Widow Hawks came back and—" Mary snaps her fingers hard and sharp.

"I said the black measles, what killed that boy on the far homestead," Toot says, even louder than her last whisper.

Nothing is making sense, and I catch Bern smirking before he whips his head around to stare out my big window.

"There's only been two more taken ill. Other side of town."

"Not near the Brinkley farm! We'd have heard!"

"Did that Moses feller come near your farm?"

"Or was it that boy the Salomons took in? What was his name?"

"Hardy." This is a deep, rumbly sort of voice, but everyone knows it's Thunder, the old grizzled hand at the Svendsen ranch. He doesn't look up from the leather scraps he's sorting in the rag bin, but there is a splotch of pink on the tips of his cheekbones. Thunder hardly ever speaks in public, and I'm duly impressed, as is everyone else. His tone also brokers no doubt that Hardy is to be left out of the discussion.

I tilt my head at him, then catch Bern's direct gaze. He shrugs, and I shrug back, and then Bern uncurls his strong legs and stretches, obvious and widely.

"Well, I suppose I'll head on back to the bunkhouse. Though if I catch the black measles, what with sharing a space with … *him* … then, I guess you'll all know."

He slowly swaggers out of the General, leaving a wake of wide eyes and open mouths behind him.

"Danny Svendsen shouldn't keep Negros," Lara says quietly to Sally, and for once the Catholic and the Lutheran agree, as Sally nods.

"There are others what look like him, over near Soups Corner and the Yang families never get sick."

"That's only as they're foreign, too."

I should speak up and tell them how ridiculous they all sound. Though to be sure, I have no idea what is going on with all this illness. It's like the town's cursed.

A small voice pipes up in my head: *It's like as soon as Yves showed up and staying around town to help you, everyone started getting sick*. I swallow. Then again, who am I to tell people exactly what to think?

After a few coughs and scuffles of feet, the commerce starts up again with hiccups and pauses, as if waiting to hear if more speculation will stir. It doesn't. Jane approaches as Elaine and Toot leave, with Trusty Willy sputtering behind them, his shiny head sparkling with sweat. When she puts the small potatoes on the counter, specks of dirt fall off, and I flick at the pebbles impatiently.

"That's all?" I ask. She glances at her hands, then at me, trying to make her brown eyes match my black ones.

"Credit, please," she says softly. "Pat hasn't had much luck lately."

I want to deny her. The urge is so strong I have to chew past the words that contradict my preference. If it was just Jane, I would. I'd tell her the credit wasn't possible this time. I'd … well, I'd make her hurt. Somehow. She's done it so many times to me and doesn't even know all of it! But I cannot do it to Patrick. I simply cannot. I nod once, hard and fast.

"Credit is tight, too," I say anyway, the warning low. My eyes bore holes on the ledger until I sense her gathering her tiny potatoes and leaving.

"Trouble with the sawbones, is it?" Horeb tries to bait her as she leaves, but Jane bites her tongue and pushes out without answering. Horeb twists to Gilroy, deflated momentarily, until he shimmies his skinny behind in the sagging chair and leans forward.

"Did I ever tell you about the priest I once knew—"

"Heaven help us!" Lara thunders, clapping her hands over her nearest child's ears. "Horeb Harvey, I swear on all that's holy—"

"Now that's the point of it, ain't it, Missus O'Donnell?" Horeb asks, but his cackles are drowned by the suddenly loud argument of Julie and Tim over how many nails they really need for their experiment on cloven hooves. It sounds like a failed idea before it even starts, but I sell them the ten nails anyway.

The door keeps on opening and closing, and I lose track of the minutes as I flit around the shelves and answer the hundreds of questions.

I've always liked the busy-bee hive of the store. It's like a pulse, and I'm at the middle. It's where I feel most alive.

It's where I can forget any troubles.

When I nip in the back room for a quick bite and cold coffee, my biggest trouble is at the stove, calmly stirring something in my small skillet. I skid to a stop, my right boot hitting the high point of the floorboard just inside the room.

"What are you doing here?"

She glances at me, then sprinkles more things into the iron pan. "Can a mother not make a midday meal for her daughter?"

"I thought that was your job over at Jane and Patrick's." I feel hot under my blouse. How much did she hear in the General—both the accusations, and my refusal to speak to defend her?

"Sometimes it's good to leave two people in love alone."

Heat fills my cheeks. "*What* are you putting into that?"

"Dried sage and some late yarrow—"

"Disgusting. You know how I hate native spices. It makes me ill."

"Your father always loved my cooking."

"Percy had questionable taste."

Her head goes to the side. "You know, the *Lakhota* food doesn't really disagree with your belly, Katherine. You just believe it does—you ate plenty of it as a young girl."

I shove down the memories of fragrant food on the table, of her humming over the wide stove in the huge, airy, luxurious house. And the thoughts spill at once to when Patrick and his Aunt Bonnie arrived, and the toughness of her Irish bread, the roll of his laughter in the parlor with

Percy, his gentleness … and how eager he was to meet Widow Hawks's people.

*If only …*

"Well, it doesn't matter, as I won't have anyone to cook for—no matter the recipe—and you can be sure it's plain old American food if I did!" Suddenly, the severity of my anger, the rushing quickness of it through my chest and into my head, is enough to make me feel faint. I think I might collapse with the weight of it. I haven't felt this sick with rage at one of my parents since my father explained the nature of my birth. "You can stop cooking and get out!"

She looks directly at my face, unblinking and stoic, with something like a lost, sad smile tracing the edges of her dark eyes though the pull of her shoulders is one of resignation. "Your father would have done whatever you wished, you know. If you'd asked him to make a marriage, he would have—with anyone you chose, if he was willing."

"There's the issue, then," I say, as I reach around her for the coffee and slam it into my throat.

White. The thing I am in part, what my father gave me. And yet not white, thanks to his love for the woman standing in my house. Not white and yet white. Both things and neither thing.

"It's too bad Percy isn't here, to actually help me beyond what he owed me in the first place," I tell her, the bitterness lacing my voice with a gravel that almost hurts. "If only he could have lived and done something hard, something that mattered. Instead of wasting all his influence on what he wanted for Flats Junction, he might have used that influence to be part of my life, to actually help me when I need it."

232

"I am part of your life," Widow Hawks says softly, with tenderness, so my eyes squeeze shut at the sugar in the comment. "I will always be so."

My eyes pry open, and I throw back my shoulders so I might return to the counter and the customers. "That's not a comfort. In fact, it's the last thing I want. And you know it."

Another hour shortens, and stretches and shortens again. I watch the road for Yves, catching myself doing so enough times that I'm sure I look as though I'm a lover waiting on her man.

For all I cannot trust him, I have to believe he'll do what he says, leave the rails alone, and as soon as I hear from Helena, I can tell her it's safe to come back.

The afternoon is hot and scorching, though it's only June, the bright sunlight reminds me it's time to start planning the July Fourth festivities. No one does anything to help, of course. It's as if they expect me to handle it all without any direct assistance and offer no response except to complain if things aren't how they hoped. It's nearly more than a woman can manage, and sometimes I despise doing anything at all!

But I need to do such things.

Don't I?

I can feel the disregard of the town, buried deep under the layers of kindness and niceties. It crawls across my skin every once in a while. No one says anything, but I'm sure I can feel it if I stop moving long enough. If I were white through and through, would it be different? Would the men have courted me, and my father's wealth and influence have reflected differently on my future?

Would I have rosy cheeks that blush when I am upset or flirtatious?

Would I still be tall?

He'd given me the General Store, but surely he was only doing that out of pity. Or because he knew he owed me more than just a simple inheritance?

The evening stretches, and still no sign of Yves. I'm not sure if it makes me happy or nervous. Where are they? Did they head further east, past Vermillion and into Yankton to bring back more supplies than I expected, using the wagons he'd promised and not robbing trains along the way simply to get free goods to trade with me?

The memory of nearly tripping over my father's old copper kettle scorches my mind briefly, and I tug at my hair pins, hoping the pain of jabbing them into my skull will cancel the hurt. Marie Salomon couldn't have made herself any clearer …

She knows, then. She knows what I've done.

Maybe when Helena returns, Marie will see how much happier Helena is to be a seamstress.

If, that is, Helena makes it back.

She's written me twice and cabled once, and I've arranged as best I can.

Surely, she will make it back. I can see it all, how the months will stretch fine and wealthy and smart with what we'll build.

I head back to my quarters for a bite to eat, dreading it, but surprisingly the back room is empty; the dishes are lined up neatly along the wall and shelf, the stove banked, and the rugs straight along the floorboards. Something about the perfection bothers me, so I drag my toe along the edges of the raggedy floor coverings so they are all slightly off. Rolling my shoulders, I debate making coffee again myself, but decide against it.

It's so much to balance. I want to control Yves, but I cannot. I want to have some say over the rail and the trade in town better than I do now, and I cannot. It will take weeks to get answers in regards to that piece of my plan. And I want to have … I want to be finished with my whole charade. And I want to stop straddling both worlds. It's impossible, I know, but it's still tiring.

*If only …*

The only way I will survive is this way I'm carving out for myself. To do anything else is to write the lines of my own death. I could leave, I suppose, as Jane did once. I could disappear to the East, and see the sea. If I had a way to make a living, to be safe and secure and satisfied, I would go. Maybe. And what would I be? I'm too dusky to be hidden in plain sight, and the skin across my cheeks pulls in the way everyone knows to be … unlike the rest. Damn my father. And damn my mother.

Pushing out through the back door, I fill my chest with the air of the town, tasting the dust and the warmth of the sun-ripe weeds along the side of the General and glance up and down Davies Avenue and the chipped siding of the Main Inn. Alan Lampton is kissing Harriet Lindsey in plain sight beyond it. If I squint, I can just make out the bright yellow bloomers one of the kept girls hangs out of the window of my father's old house when she's available for 'business.' All this sex. I let the sun and the skitter of nerves skate down my back with the thought. Carnal thoughts pour into my forehead, weighing me down with the images.

A vision of Jane, sweating in her childbed, runs through my mind. Or what of Grete Fawcett, and her overly fertile marriage to Larry? Just remembering some of the comments

Berit's lusty daughters make is enough to make sweat run between my breasts. "If he loved me, he wouldn't have gotten me big with another baby," Grete says every time. Larry always just reminds her that it takes two. And someone— typically Anette, Grete's sister—usually mentions the fun it is to do so. Lovely for them all, of course. They all are married and seem well content with their men. They were courted. Desired.

Wanted.

Most of the women here have children, inviting their men back under the sheets and between their legs. Even some of Fortuna's girls at The Powdered Rose have had babes, or at least fallen for one at some point. No man will want to have their children cursed with my nose or coloring. And truthfully, I don't know how I would help any child of mine in this world, where they would still have to straddle both sides.

The bell rings, and I sigh and walk back into my back room and then step through to the store. The soft falling of dusk heralds Gilroy and Horeb's departure for either Matthew Winters's mess or one of the inns for a meal. They go without telling me good-bye, which is usual. They haven't said hello or good-bye to me in years, ever since Percy died.

I debate starting my own supper, and wonder again where Widow Hawks has gone. In the leftover, wide silence of an empty mercantile, I inhale again. At first, all the gossip of Flats Junction fills my empty mind: the rumors of the same disease that killed my father, the speculation on where the sickness starts, and who might die next. A stab of something hard and unfamiliar pierces the space under my ribs.

When I inhale again and close my eyes, all those troubles and questions slip off of my skin, flaking away and disappearing into the heavy dust of the floor, falling into the wide cracks between the planks. The silence cloaks my shoulders, and my hands float freely at my sides. I can feel my feet touching the floorboards, but my body is feather-light. Moments like these can be turned to crystal, to be brought out in dark nights when I am alone and need to feel some sort of power, however fleeting it may be, or when I am so worn and tired by the unending work that I think I will never be free of it and might scream with the crushing trap of my existence.

The clip of a horse rouses me from my half-dream. Black shapes pick through the southern brush toward town, hats pulled low on heads, and there is a mutter of a male voice. Yves? Without his posse? My heart jumps. I should grab a lantern, but there's no time to fill the wicks with light from the stove.

"Kate." A shape pauses at the threshold. In the deep twilight, I cannot see his face, but I know the voice near as well as my own.

"Good evening, Bern," I say without pause, reacting to his height and his darkness.

"The store is still open?" he asks curiously. "It's always closed by the time I come out from getting victuals."

"I just haven't locked yet."

"Ah." He glances up the dirt-packed Main Street behind him, a crumpled shadow cutting across the land and scrub of the prairie.

"No one should worry." I bend around him and wave gaily at the other cowboys leaving Matthew Winters's place, full bellied and belching loudly. "There's nothing amiss lately, as you know."

"No. Not lately," he says blandly, glancing around the store.

My blood feels icy. "What was that stunt, today? Tempting fate? Suppose someone knew it was you, starting rumors about people ... and what if you're wrong?"

"I'm only repeating what others say," he says, sounding mildly annoyed. "It's to help you, you know. I said I would."

"You're trying to drive Widow Hawks out of town? This is your plan? It's not the right one. We've talked about how to manage my ... future. It's the right notion—what else would you have me do?"

"I can think of a few things, though they're not kind," he says lowly, and a shivery coldness climbs up from the base of my spine up my back, quenching any heat from the day.

A thump of boots on the stairs makes my bones bump back into themselves.

"I'll close up now," I tell him, feeling a need to hurry. I don't want any other men in my store at this hour. "So, you need something?"

His dark eyes go flat and the smooth skin on his cheeks seems to tighten, but the oak door groans even as it's obvious Bern wants no interruptions between us.

"Kate!" Moses arrives as if he is inhaling fresh spring sunshine, the chocolate of his voice curling around the room. "How are things, as it were? I was sorry to leave earlier without saying good-bye and the like." He is a darker shadow against the candy pink and lavender of the sunset, soft and pale on the horizon. The swipe of his smile is a flash of blue-white in the hazy gloaming.

"You're both kind to worry so much." I remember, at the last moment, to straighten my back and raise my chest.

Bern glances down at my bosom, the lines framing his mouth deepening briefly. The fidget of his wrists flicks around the denim of his shirt, frayed and fluffy, and then he lifts his face to mine.

"I suppose I'll just bid you good-night then, Kate," he says. My shoulders lift as his slump, and he slips a furtive glance toward Moses. "We both will?"

Am I relieved? Or disappointed?

Moses fingers his hat, and his eyebrows lift toward Bern. "Yes, we will both say goodnight to Miss Kate, like." His tone is final, but it is oddly protective.

Bern's scowl flips within itself and turns almost ugly, which is odd on his smooth, unblemished forehead. He seems to take the dismissal, and my lack of immediate words, to heart, and he stalks out without saying farewell. His coldness is worse than the shivers in my backbone, and I want to chase after him, though it's something I've never done to a man before and I don't know what I'd say if I followed him to his horse.

Moses doesn't turn, and waits for the door to grate behind him.

"Bern Masson doesn't like your mother, as it be," he says quietly.

Ah, so he had overheard enough. I wonder how thick that glass and my walls truly are. Or I guess Bern wasn't talking all too quiet-like.

"What of it?" I cross my arms. "That's not my problem."

"He doesn't like me," he adds.

I fail to see how this conversation matters. "Weren't you and Bern both leaving?" I point out. "You here without a chaperone doesn't seem right, either."

Moses takes a step toward me, and the evening settles further into itself, couching us in secrets. I can smell the horse and grass and old sun on his leather chaps, and sense him move even closer. I decide right then I won't take a single step back. If I want to control something, I can at least control this. Whatever it is.

"When has the lovely Kate Davies ever been worried on a chaperone, as it were? I'm trying to say it as it be, like. Bern Masson don't like people like us."

My hand raises at once, even if it's too dark now to aim and hit the mark. The power of reaction and anger slithers through my fingers. I can feel the tingling of it at the tips of my hands.

Why do I stop?

I can, if I squint, make out the edge of Moses's cheek and the angle of his jaw and the width of his left shoulder.

If I can see this much of him, surely he can see my raised palm, but he doesn't flinch or twitch. He's as still as the grave.

Maybe it's the quiet in him calling to me. Or it's the fact that I don't want to miss and feel the fool. I'm grateful he can't see the heat flooding my neck, writhing up to my ears. Once again, I worry. Does Bern talk? Or does Moses mean his words innocently and as a compliment to my strength?

My hand lowers as I consider all of this. I wish he would leave. Bern must know Moses is still in the gloaming with me. Perhaps he's even trying to see in through the foggy, smeared front windows. The thought makes me additionally nervous. Moses is right about Bern, in some ways. He doesn't like Widow Hawks or the doctor's accent or Moses's chocolate skin. I know this as surely as I know Bern has no qualms where I'm concerned—at least, in one place.

Like the others, he'll never marry me.

The silence between Moses and me stretches thin and brittle. He breathes softly, and in that moment I almost wish he would fall for my beauty and catch me up. Just for once to have a man do so.

*Enough! No!* I am worth something else. I deserve what Jane has. *I am not an outsider!*

"Why did you help me?"

It's not what I mean to ask. I want to make him leave, to show Bern I am not sitting in the dark, kissing this man like some wanton wild girl.

"Just now? You don't want to be alone with Bern, then?" he sounds satisfied, as if he'd guessed a secret.

"Ha! I've known Bern for years—he's not near as much a threat as you, being a stranger. I mean—you cooked for me. With me. For Yves. Why?"

"You needed help. I wanted to help."

It's not a decent answer, but he stands there, as if he thinks it is. I rouse myself from this evening stupor and step around Moses to wrench open the door, raising my voice in case Bern is watching. "My needs are none of your business," I tell him. He follows me, and the late tendrils of the old sunset dance across his forehead and the scalp visible through his shorn hair.

But instead of leaving me, quiet and subdued as I expect, Moses squares off on the porch of the General Store, hat in hand and the scent of dust and warm grass circling us. I face west, and he looks east now, so he is a tall, long shadow.

"I'm trying to do the right thing, Miss Kate," he insists. "You're talking all cozy like with Bern, and he's not thinking kindly on your kind."

I smack him hard. My palm stings and burns with the connection, and it jars my shoulder. Moses jerks backward and then kicks out a hand to brace himself against the beam of the store's porch support.

"*My* kind?" I hiss. "I don't *have* a kind, as you put it."

He straightens fluidly, as if my slap never happened. "You know what I mean, as it were. You understand me. I'm just saying it as it is, and you should watch what's said on you, like. You understand." This last is said firmly, confidently, and then he's gone, taking the stairs two at a time.

Goddamn the man. How dare he lump me with everyone else in Flats Junction who's different! Of belonging to anything!

I slam the oak door behind me and bolt it before leaning heavily against the fat, old wood. If I were a woman who weeps, I'd give in now, but there's no point in tears. That, at least, I know I get from my mother.

The worst of it is, Moses is right. I do understand him. And I don't like it at all.

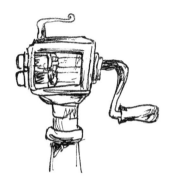

CHAPTER FOURTEEN

# Marie

*July 1, 1883*

The numbers are stark and simple and slanted on the page. My own writing, going back to the mid 1860s, filed and categorized and sometimes a bit messy along the edges, but my own hand, showing the numbers.

I don't have enough tinplate to get me through the rest of the year.

I'm certain we could get some, if the trains were regular, and Kate actually put in the order when we asked.

Everything I've built is now balanced on the edge of a blade, as the saying goes.

The irony of that.

Thaddeus sighs loudly from his forge, the crinkle of pages peppered by questions from one of the three boys, who are trying to put their learning to real life figures. He at least has help – even if he is short on raw iron stock. I stand alone in the middle of the tinshop, hearing the echoes of my girls and feeling as though my belly will burst open with this child.

How can the trains never bring in stock? How can so many have been broken this spring? How do we come back from this? Can I take orders early, with the promise to do them whenever I next get the raw materials to do my trade?

Panic and fear and a yellowy liquid swim in my mouth that makes my jaw feel extra tight.

I've lost my girls.

I cannot afford to lose my shop!

It's all I have of my legacy ...

Of my family ...

*Stop it!* I shake out my hands. It's not so forlorn and lost. There's still a chance the next train will finally bring in the tinplate. Kate won't hold it away from us. She may be hard on funds herself to cover the upfront cost, but she said herself she wants what's best for Flats Junction. She wants to see it grow. Isn't that why we are hosting Hardy, teaching him the trade, bolstering the blacksmithing?

In fact ... I ought to speak to her on this. It's better than worrying over my numbers and dwindling tin plate.

I walk through my shop and into Thaddeus's. His grey eyes harden as he takes in my slow, wider walk.

"Where are you going?"

"The General. See if we know about our metal orders. They're too long in coming."

Thaddeus looks like he wants to argue, but lets it go, and I know he too is anxious. Summer is here and Kate had said it would be in during the spring.

What is she playing at?

If anything, it's me who should hate the look of her. Her, who stole away my ambitious, overly eager daughter! Her, who didn't ask before she filled Helena's head with plans for the city, dreams about building up the tinshop to be something massive, something so grand I cannot see it or consider it.

As I walk south toward the General, I find myself counting my steps, the old black leather creaking. It's as though I need a distraction, as if I cannot face my world and what it has become—another scrabbling for money, another desperate attempt to cobble together a family that will not leave me!

By the time I climb the General's stairs, my heartbeat feels extra fast, and I'm sweating in the July heat, the calico doing nothing to stem off the baking sunlight. It doesn't help that the General is packed, people doing rapid trade between what they have on their farm, and what they want to buy.

When I get up to the counter, past the press of Helga Wagner's wide hips and the stench of her husband Klaus's ongoing gas, and catch Kate's eye, my breath is so rapid I think I might fall over. I grip the counter tight and will Kate to meet my eyes.

Can she?

Does she dare?

She knows that I know. She knows I want to scream at her.

She knows I cannot.

Her brown eyes meet my matching ones, briefly, as she rings up the fancy barley Joe Greenman has bought for his backdoor still. I watch as he takes the bag of precious kernels, and find my voice in my shock that a good sweet thing like imported barley can make it to Flats Junction, but not my own order!

"Kate," I say. She tilts her head to me as she writes in her ledger. I press into the counter and cling to it, my finger pads gripping only because they are so rigid with scars. "We need to know—Thad and I—we need our metal. We need the iron and the tin."

"I told you," she says, testy. "I cannot control the trains."

"Can't you?"

She suddenly looks uncertain. "What? Who says differently? That is ... how could I have any control over the rails?"

"I only need to know when our order will be in. We've waited too long, Kate."

"I can't help you, Marie."

"Can't you?" I feel desperation marry fury, and I reach across the counter and grip her wrist hard. My fingers and hands are nothing but sinew and muscle, long strengthened by years working metal and machines. She flinches as I squeeze. "Don't you have influence? Aren't you so important? Can't you get anything anyone needs? That's why you're here. That's what you imply."

"Let go," she says, so quiet no one can possibly hear.

I squeeze harder, knowing there will be a bruise and not caring. "You said you wanted to help Flats Junction. You said you wanted to make it bigger. Better. It will fail without a metal shop, or a blacksmith. Fail."

"I know that," she snarls slightly. "You think I can magically find your raw materials, pay for it so you can keep on living on credit, and survive?"

"Is that it?" I press. "You've run this place aground and cannot put up the cash for our order? Can't get the trains to bring it?"

246

"No." But she looks desperate and uncomfortable in her bright orange and blue frock, and I give her wrist an extra pinch, feeling the bones shift under my thumb and forefinger.

She can't help but yelp, and that's enough for me. I let her go, and she's too proud to rub her skin in front of me. Instead, she lifts her chin, and our eyes flash and burn as they meet fully.

"Whatever you think, I have had no intention of keeping your order unfilled. I did not … I could not anticipate how … the trains … would run."

"And my daughter," I hiss. "Will she at least make it back to Flats Junction, or have you made sure she also will be lost in the travels? She doesn't write, doesn't send word."

Kate's face freezes. Maybe she's surprised I dare bring it up, and in public, too. But no-one is really listening. It's too busy and too frantic in the store, too loud.

"I have no way to tell you how … I'm sure—"

"Kate! Hurry up! I've got to get back to the office—if there's really going to be a train again, there'll be passels of mail!" Nancy Ofsberger shouts from the other side of the counter. "And that bolt of blue cotton won't climb down by itself!"

Kate turns, relief etched across the lines of her mouth, but I lunge forward again, my belly hitting the hard wood of the counter and causing a searing pain to rip itself across the top of my womb.

I grit my teeth as I grasp her forearm once again. Hard and vice-like. "She could be dead, for all you know!"

Kate yanks herself out of my grip and marches away, head high. I breathe harder and near gasp in a full gulp of hot, dusty air as I exit the General in a flurry of caught skirts and elbows.

I hurry home as the ache in my stomach rakes down into my thighs. I have to stop alongside the old cooperage across the street from Thaddeus's forge, holding my side and bending in half.

The pain comes again, yanking my flesh into pieces. My bones are cracking and melting, and I put my head down on the hot wood of the building, panting. For a long moment, it feels as though darkness will shade the edges of my vision. I have had many children, and know the early signs of labor, but this is stark and white and hot. I am not prepared. It feels too soon, and the mathematics of my cycle suddenly allude me.

*It is the sorrow of losing Urszula. That is what this is.*
I know it is not, and the truths pile in.
*It is the babe. Something is wrong.*
Surely not. How can a woman know such things?
*It is Helena. It is the feeling of her coming death.*
Suppose we never hear from her again?
*Stop. It is not the end. You still have children to live for.*
*A child to be born …*

Two pairs of arms lift me up, slow and steady and sure. I know it's Hardy and Thaddeus by their differing heights. and the sooty dust feathering from their clothing. As I am taken across the shop floor, the familiar gush of hot, sticky fluid spills through my skirts, sopping my stockings and staining the dark earth under me, which eats up my blood as though it wants to devour all of me, burying me into the bottom of the world.

CHAPTER FIFTEEN

# *Jane*

*July 2, 1883*

I lean against the doorframe to Patrick's office, holding a lantern with a new candle, and watch him with concern and worry and fear.

Five more cases of black measles appeared this week, though most people don't yet know it: three males—seventeen, twenty-two, and seventy; and two girls—two and fourteen. Only one of the young boys survived.

The doctor is exhausted and sleeps little between checking on patients and perusing through medical treatises and books on the causes, symptoms, and treatments for various infectious diseases.

I help him when I can sneak away from house chores. When he is not at home, I speak to Esther and she brings me different summer flowers and plants, walking me through what she remembers. I have a small sketchbook where I

249

attempt to make notes and draw out the slightest differences between herbs, and though he has never told me to stop learning I constantly worry what Patrick will think when he discovers what I'm researching.

What man has ever preferred a wife who is too curious?

I stand up and touch his shoulder. "Why don't you take a break and eat in the kitchen with me, today?"

He turns, takes the lamp, and throws a weak smile under red-rimmed, bloodshot eyes. "I'd like that, if it's ready." He pauses, squints, and turns back to the books, spurred on by churning ideas, and I leave him be and go to the kitchen to help Esther finish the cooking.

In the kitchen, I carve three slices off the ham hanging in the larder and make us sandwiches with my fresh bread and grainy mustard. Esther slices the morning bread and gets the butter from the bucket in the well.

I loathe seeing my husband work so hard without rest. Today will be no different. After he visits the Woodman homestead, he may sleep between bouts of reading. He's frustrated at not being able to discover any connection between any of the cases, save that everyone has the same black spots and symptoms. I put out plates and set them down harder than I mean.

This damned disease is so random: old and young, healthy and sickly. People around town are terrified, and, in all honesty, so am I. It could get to any of us.

I sip from my coffee and call down the hall for my husband to come to the table. No one really knows how hard he is working for everyone. Whenever he leaves the house, he's both reviled and sought, depending on the preferences, tolerances, and beliefs of the patient's family. I too feel the heat and shame, hear snippets of disparaging whispers, as my identity is so firmly wrapped with his. In this, at least, we can share the burden and many times, between sleep, cleaning his tools, and more reading, we spend our time recounting of the day's frustrations, as if speaking of them will wash them away.

He trudges into the kitchen, plops into his chair, and glares at the sandwich as if he's never had one before. "What is it?"

"Ham."

He sits and flings letters on the table between us. "Can you take these to Nancy later?"

"Of course. Now, eat." I sift through my memory to count how many letters he's written over the last three weeks. Perhaps twenty-five, maybe thirty. He's reaching out to different doctors, including military, across the Dakota and Montana territories, Iowa, Nebraska, and Minnesota seeking any and all information about black measles. Not one reply has been received. The silence from his pleas for help is deafening.

A rapid knock echoes into the kitchen. Patrick flashes a wry smile, sets down his food, and heads to the door. I follow close behind as Esther continues to slather bread with butter.

"Yes?" Patrick opens the door, revealing Hardy, the new blacksmith apprentice.

The boy fidgets, the blue eyes unable to meet ours through the dimness of the screen. "I ..." His voice cracks at once, with the falling cadence of a boy on the brink of manhood. Clearing it, he finally meets our stares and looks slightly defiant. "We need you quick. Please. It's Mrs. Marie."

Patrick absolutely freezes for one, solid moment. He blinks, his eyebrows raised. "Did she send for me? Or did Thaddeus?"

The boy shakes his head, looking both furtive and defiant at once, which translates to some sort of odd strength across his broad features. In the early afternoon, his hair is butter-white, and wavy to the point of fuzz along the tips. A softness along his lip shows promise of a heavy beard, but his eyes are anything but soft.

"No—neither did. But you gotta come, Doc Kinney," he says, his face painted with anguish.

Patrick glances my way, shrugs, and reaches for his Stetson and medical bag. "Let's be off. I don't want to keep them waitin'."

"Wait—what about food? You must eat something, Pat!" I call to his back.

"Have Esther push it to the sideboard or somethin' and come along, Jane," he says from the road. "You might help me, whatever it is."

I fly to his bidding, wondering if he seeks reassurance with my presence or if he actually believes I might assist.

How will we possibly get in the door this time? Twice now, our appearance in the Salomon home has resulted in death. What will make this time any better? And with Patrick's late record of dying babies ...

"What is it?" Esther asks, her hands poised above the bread and butter.

"Marie Salomon. I'll be going, too."

She puts her hands down slowly, a careful movement that suddenly pulls me up straight.

*She hates it here.*

The thought tears into my flesh as if iron hooks were doing the work. We shouldn't have done it. We shouldn't have begged her to return under the false promise of reuniting her with Kate. I shouldn't have forced Kate's hand, asking her to come along to the Fort to fetch her mother. I shouldn't have torn this woman from her family, hoping I was family enough.

"Jane!" Patrick yells from the front yard, loud enough that surely Mrs. Molhurst will poke her head out to watch us hurry down the street.

I reach across the table and clasp Esther's arm. "I'm so sorry."

Her eyes are unreadable. "Go."

I pick up my skirts, only slightly embarrassed by the view of my booted ankles, and jog out after the doctor, feeling foolish and dumb and ever so stupid.

*How can I fix what we have done?*

There's no time to speculate, as Patrick keeps a hard pace, pelting toward the smithy.

"Go! Go!" Peng Yang yells at me, waving furiously as we pelt past Soup's Corner. *Go* is one of the handful of English words he knows, and he uses it every time I pass. Yen, his brother, is supposedly younger, but I have a hard time telling them apart under their concave hats. Peng forgets to hold up his half of the great iron cauldron in his enthusiastic greeting, and Yen starts to shriek at him as the remaining contents start to spill over the side. Peng tries to grip it, but he's too late. The soup sloshes onto the mud, and there's a deep grunt and squeal from Alan's farm.

I can't tell how many there are behind the fence, but undulating backs of the hogs boil along the fence as they scramble toward the fragrant soup stream heading their way.

I sidestep the egg and onion concoction and scurry onto Second Street as Patrick and Hardy's strides take them many yards ahead of me. They don't even turn around when the pigs start to shriek with glee.

Harriet sticks her mousy head out the door of the pig-man's home and screams for Alan. "They're going to break through! Alan!"

Her lover streaks out of the house, still doing up his pants and spinning a rope around, two activities that don't work together even without rushing. "Hi-yay! C'mon girls, settle on down! *Suuuuu—*"

Alan's rope tangles just as he trips over his sagging trousers, falling to his knees in the churned puddles and slop of the pig farm's yard. Harriet yelps again, but Alan's intent on the pigs, who are now attempting to climb over the fence, their flattened snouts quivering and their tiny front legs pawing ceaselessly at the half-rotted wood of their fencing.

When I glance behind me to see the way it's ended, Peng and Yen are dancing back and forth, their long glossy braids keeping time with their leaps, and their voices higher than usual. Their wives peek out from the small shacks and cry out in Chinese, though I don't know if they're asking their husbands to help Alan or to come in to re-make the soup for the evening.

Alan struggles to stand as each leg slides in the opposite direction, catches his boots, and reaches his animals, smacking each one on the snout. The soup reaches the fence line, and all the sows begin to lap it up, grunting with happiness.

Alan grins at me, even though he's mostly covered in pig manure and old rotting slops.

"You're lucky!" he calls to me. "They would've stampeded ya if they got out, Mrs. Kinney!"

254

"Don't I know it!" My heart is in my throat, and I stride as fast as I can toward the blacksmith shop, thankful Alan has the grace not to poke me about my yelling at his pigs.

"Doc's way ahead of you," Tim Bailey mentions to me in his slow, deep voice as I rush past the farrier.

Reaching the blacksmith's forge, I curve around the worn wooden corner and mince around the burning fires. Most look banked, but it's clear someone has been working until recently. I push against the back door, feeling as though I am violating the sacred space of the Salomon family, as I have never entered their private rooms without Patrick. As I take an uncertain step in, forgetting about my muddy boots, an atmosphere of hushed, thick agony stifles and crawls over my skin.

Patrick stands at the table, his medical bag perched on the edge, facing Thaddeus, who guards the closed door behind him.

Hardy looks nervous and stands along the wall next to Kaspar and Natan, but he clears his throat. "I wouldn't have gone. Truly. But I overheard Mrs. Salomon say she don't know why the babe won't come, and can't stop none of the bleeding, and everyone was starting to go all worried, so I went to fetch the doc. Docs are good, truly, they are, sir!"

"Hardy. I can see why you did this, *honning honey*." Berit says, turning from her kettle with a spoon raised.

"Berit—" Thaddeus shakes his head, his towering body magnified by his abruptness and his anger.

Berit stands straighter in front of the hearth and points the spoon at her step-son, her voice low and quiet, perhaps for the sake of the children in the room. "He was worried."

The blacksmith is rooted and rough and fuming. He chews on his lip, the grey eyes swiveling between Patrick, me, and the rest of the bodies in the room.

He rounds on us suddenly, the emotions running through him in a shivering, trembling mess before he makes a brusque slice with his hand. "You may as well go in since you're here," he growls. "But don't touch her. Not unless I say you might. *Pierdolić!*" He stalks through the door without another word.

Patrick waves me forward and we follow quickly. I find my palms to be sticky, and worry I'll have to help him with his instruments. If I ... can remember what to do.

*Oh mercy! I don't know if I'll remember!*

The small bedroom is stuffy and smells of new sweat and the strange, metallic tang of birthing blood.

"Marya—*moje serce.* The doctor is here," Thaddeus says, his voice softer and gentler than I would ever expect of him.

Marie's red, glossy face twists into a confused frown. "Wh—" Her head falls back into the damp bedding. Her body shakes and squirms as she cries out in pained agony. "No doc, you said. We said."

Thaddeus catches his step, his dusky skin draining of color. He kneels down next to the bed, gripping her shoulder hard as if to coax her upward by his own sheer strength, bending over her, the silvers of grey in their scalps touching. "Marya. *Bądź silny.*"

Marie's belly is full of child; it's oddly distended and swollen. But it is the brilliant red blood that is the most shocking. I peel the blankets back further to her feet, and Patrick sets down his bag.

Without pause, Patrick touches her stomach, gently pushing against the taunt skin.

Thaddeus jerks back upright. "No!" His right arm slams against Patrick's chest forcing him to step back. "I told you not to touch her!"

"Damn it, man." Patrick says in clipped frustration as he turns to face Thaddeus. "Do you want my help or not?" He throws his arms out. "My hands are as important as my eyes to diagnose a patient. I—"

"No." Thaddeus forces himself between the bed and the doctor. "I don't trust you. You'll cut her open. Like my father and daughter. You cannot touch her!"

"I won't cut unless I must," Patrick says with conviction.

"Get out!" Thaddeus's eyes go wide and wild. His gigantic body tenses, quivering as he points at the door.

"If I don't treat her, she could die. My oath is—I won't leave her, now that I'm here."

"*Out or I'll throw you out!*" Thaddeus takes a flat, hard step toward Patrick, the physical height of him only adding to the intensity of his anger.

I stand and fall back against the wall as my gaze swings between Marie and the two angry men. I'm paralyzed and helpless, searching for words to stop the shouting.

"You'll have to force me out. I took a vow." My husband's shoulders twitch. It is the only sign of his anxiety.

"To hell with your vow."

Marie gasps behind us, and Patrick ducks suddenly around the bigger man's shoulder and presses a hand once more to the lower shelf of Marie's stomach. "I know what's happenin'."

Thaddeus appears stunned by Patrick's audacity, as am I. He presses on her stomach with sure, strong fingers, searching and playing across her skin.

Marie cries out, her face twisted and the cords of her neck bundled and high.

"Out!" Thaddeus rips Patrick hard to pull him up, and then whips his fist across the doctor's cheekbone, the dull thunk of bone hitting flesh thudding into the pit of my gut, and bile rises, curdled and acrid, up my throat.

My scream rivals Marie's. A stomach convulsion sends the burning bile upward into my throat.

Patrick staggers. A welt rises, brilliant and red, and he involuntarily puts his fingers to the throbbing spot. A fine trickle of blood drains from his nose. I instinctively pull out my handkerchief and press it to his face, still reeling.

Thaddeus ignores me and balls his fist. "I said get *out*!"

Without thinking, I reach across the bed and encircle my hand around Thaddeus's. "Stop! Please … stop!"

He jerks then stills, breathing heavily, as if even in his agitation he recognizes that he will not be violent toward a woman. The violence stays there, though, zooming through his veins. I can feel it bumping under the pad of my thumb.

"Thaddeus, please," I plead, releasing him. "Let Doctor Kinney try something." I wave a hand over Marie. "She's suffering."

Thaddeus stares at me, his forehead crumpling slowly. "I won't have him cutting her."

Patrick glances at my handkerchief, where his blood makes circles, folds it, and jams it into his pocket. "I promise if I must use a knife, I will ask you first." He steps forward and pulls the covers back again, heedless of his blackening eye. "I need to touch her to confirm my suspicions. I think the baby is breech at the very least."

"*Moja miłość,* let him look." Marie's voice is quavering and yet determined, as her hand claws for Thaddeus. "The pain—never like this. There's nothing … let him see." Her eyes squeeze shut against another contraction as her strong, scarred hands smash the bedding, the creases of the sheets digging into her fingers. The fear in her voice nearly cripples me, just as the rose and pink blood stains blind me, dragging me into my own memories.

"We're out of time." Patrick is stalwart and stoic, and the calmness of his voice succeeds for now. "I will only look, first."

Thaddeus pauses a moment later, and then storms out with obvious reluctance.

Patrick glances at me and jerks his chin. "Go out after him. Keep him calm."

Gripping the door frame briefly for strength, I go out to the hallway between the bedrooms. Can I do this nursing duty? Will I be strong enough?

Thaddeus can pace the hall in four huge steps, and he does so unceasingly, glaring at the closed bedroom door.

"Marie will want you to stay near and stay calm," I tell him, but my words do not seem to settle him, and instead he rips his hands through his scalp, and then his beard.

"Stay near? Where else would I go?" he grinds out. "I cannot believe that—that *quack* is seeing to her!"

My good intentions flee. "My husband is not a fake!"

"Oh no? He's so brilliant then that people are dying of black measles left and right, and likely as he can't take a saw to cut off their disease!"

"That's hardly fair," I say.

"Fair?! My family dies whenever he is here! He's going to kill her!" he fumes, and for a moment, I am truly frightened by his rage. A sharp, deep cry from the next room stops his rampaging. In a heavy, inarticulate moment, he collapses onto the one bench, and crunches his eyes into massive palms.

I hesitate to touch him, to comfort. I feel if I put fingertips on his shoulder, he could explode at any moment and blast me into the wall. His obvious distress almost makes me forgive him for striking the doctor. I speak first. "My husband will help her, truly. He has managed worse."

He scoffs, the noise absorbed into the floorboards.

"He will do everything he can to stop the bleeding. I know he will," I try again. I speak a truth for all this man does not believe me. "His only hope is always to help, to save. I promise you, a wife's word. He only wishes to heal."

A warbling scream slices through the walls again, and my throat closes.

Thaddeus looks up, and his lips curl across flat teeth. "He must heal her. He must. She is the mother of my children ... the only one ... press tin and copper ... *moja miłosc* ... How will I—"

The door swings open and Pat's hands are stained scarlet and ruby.

"What is it? How is she?" Thaddeus shoots up from the hard seat and grabs Patrick by the shoulders. "What must you do?"

My husband does not fight the man, allowing the smith to physically shake him.

I hold back a cry. Now is not the time to intervene on behalf of Patrick. He must face this man on his own, or there will be no going back. I understand this, and it is breathless and frightening and hopeful at once.

"The babe is twisted, and more—I can try to help her deliver, or I can open her stomach, though the risk for infection is far greater then. If I do nothin', she will bleed out and the child will die, too. But we must decide now."

"Cut her open! I knew it!" The blacksmith shoves Patrick aside and disappears into the bedroom.

In the moment of silence in the dim, unlit hallway, Patrick glances at me and draws in a deep breath of frustration. His mouth tightens, and I know what he thinks. Time is running out. Though he says nothing now, I know he is remembering another time, another hemorrhage. Mine, when I did not yet belong to him. A child not his, brought to me in an unexpected, fleeting passion untied to a marriage.

And under this, in the tightening of his mouth, I see his fear.

I think of the question in my womb and know I cannot tell him yet. At least not while Marie Salomon lies in her bed, still soaked in blood.

## CHAPTER SIXTEEN

# *Marie*

*July 2, 1883*

When Thaddeus opens the door of our bedroom, he looks conquered. I am asking him to do what he has always sworn would not happen since Helena was born. I should feel guilty, but ...

Almost.

I am almost guilty. It has been too many hours in bed, too many pains in my side, too many pulses of blood. Too many ...

"She asks you to help," he says into the hallway. "And if you cannot save her or the babe the usual way, to cut the child out." His lips seem frozen, but he forces the words out anyway in deference to my whispered preference.

Fear wars with pain, and I hold onto the sounds in the room, even as I close my eyes.

"Will you stay with her?" The doc's request surprises me, and jerks my body in the middle of another aching pull.

"What? Me?" Thaddeus sounds disgusted.

"Good God man, you want to be with your wife, don't you?" The doctor says it with intensity, as if challenging Thaddeus to defy him. It is a prickly place, for it forces my husband to both agree to be part of the process and give approval to it. It asks him to take up a woman's role and play the comforter in childbirth.

It is too much to ask. He will deny the doctor ...

I gasp, hard and loud, doubling over and into myself. When I open my eyes again, Thaddeus is beside me, a black form hulking at the side of the bed. Jane's shadow hovers behind the Doctor, grey and patchy. Doctor Kinney turns to her, and his voice carries in the tight space.

"You recall the instruments?"

"Mostly." Her answer isn't reassuring in the least, but I feel a deep sense of comfort knowing Jane will stay. I need her to stay, if only to remind me that it's not Doc Gunnarsen here.

The doctor puts the sheet back over my legs for modesty, then opens his bag. At the head of the bed, Thaddeus has his two gigantic hands sandwiched over mine, and he refuses to look at the doctor or Jane, or at the silver forceps, or the blood. His face is turned completely to me, the sweat beading his face and collarbone matches mine. Doc's carefulness delays things further, and I want to scream. He cleans the instruments again, and douses his hands, his stethoscope, and his tweezers with liberal amounts of what reminds me of my etching acid, the scent like pine and vinegar and coal. He takes up a small glass vial and pulls a thin needle out.

"Let's try a tiny spot of morphine," he says, nearly crooning to me but firm, so unlike the whiskey-fumbling of

Doc Gunnarsen. "It'll do nothin' but help you relax, a wee bit, so the baby will not be so tightly wound in your womb."

"A needle!" Thaddeus turns, but he's too late. I've already nodded at the doctor, who plunges it at once in the white of my outer thigh, the pinch over before I can speak.

As soon as that is finished, he hands Jane the syringe. Her hands tremble, and her mouth sews itself shut. I recall, briefly and too late, what my birthing must be like for her. I recall standing at the grave of her stillborn son, the way the grass rocked, the way she looked confused and lost and uncertain ...

The room is close. Too close. Tart sweat and fear mingle with blood and fluid. There must not be enough air in the space for the four of us, and yet we still keep breathing, combining with my stuttering gasps. It is dreamlike. The odd, thick, muddy earthiness of my mind is slow and sluggish. And, tiredly, I can only stave off the pain when it comes. It stabs my back, and shoots down to my knees, and wrestles with the muscles of my arms. I'm locked to the bed with it.

Behind the doctor's dark head, Jane hands him instruments as he asks. His forearms are slick, and the bubbles of perspiration soon stream down his neck and behind his ear. His hands—strong, thickly knuckled, bunched hands—are steady, and the fingers he places on my flesh are spread and sure. They remind me of Thaddeus's hands, and the notion is calming. I can almost take a full breath in. It goes out with a stutter, shaking the bedframe.

"It'll be a breech delivery," the doctor says, muttering, but the words are the first ones he's spoken in a long moment, and they feel stark and strange. "It must be, or risk further issue." He glances up, as if measuring me. "It's good you've had many babies, Marie, as this comes easier then."

The roiling in my belly is both an itch and a pull, pain and strangely sensual. Thaddeus stares at the doctor, grey eyes narrowed, as if daring the man so he can punch him again. The feel of the babe slipping out slowly, as my worn womb begins to contract, is backward. The poke of the small limbs, the pressure of the head as it catches my bones, and the turn of the shoulders makes me near faint. I think I might do so, suddenly, and I inhale quickly, trying to draw in air. My vision goes foggy and grey and distorted. The world spins, the room closes in, and I arch my back without thinking.

For a moment, all goes dark.

And then I am awake again, the emptiness of my body a strange, sudden, cold shock.

The doctor breathes out loudly. The relief sagging my husband is palpable and chilling at once, and the doctor hands Jane the slippery babe. I strain up, but it's too much and I fall back. Boy? Girl?

*Alive?*

I hear no cry, and tears push against the corners of my eyes. The doctor has had poor luck delivering children, this I know. Sally's baby ... Sadie's ... now mine.

I am losing my family.

They are leaving me again.

*I cannot ...*

"Clear his mouth," the doctor says shortly to Jane. His eyes are glued to my legs, but I don't feel he does it to be lewd. There is no stinking breath on my neck, no clammy hands, and there isn't a whiff of whisky. There is only the doctor's clinical concern.

Wait.

*He?*

"It's a boy? Alive?" I whisper. "*Udać się ... please.*"

Jane finds my eyes, and she smiles, all warm and trembling and joyful. "A son." She brings him to my side, wipes and rubs the limbs, and in a second, he squalls!

Jane gently pushes down his flailing and swaddles him. When she hands him to me, the wrappings are unwieldy, tied by unpracticed hand. I tighten a corner as the tiny muscles swat and swirl madly, twirling and jerking in surprise before settling into my arms, melting back toward my flesh as if content. The familiar love and surge of fear marries within my chest. So much joy with a little one, even this late in my life. Such a wavering possibility he will thrive. There is no knowing. Just like Urszula—no! I won't think of her now. Not this moment—this is for the baby. I squeeze him slightly, as if I can keep him safe by my strength alone.

Doctor Kinney pulls the ruined sweat-soaked sheet to cover my legs and settles back to a comfortable crouch at the foot of the bed.

"We'll wait and watch a bit, you know," he says conversationally. "But the worst is past. You did very well, Marie."

"The doc hasn't said if you're clear." Thaddeus fixes Doc Kinney with a glare and a glower. "And is she?"

The doctor nods. "I think so."

"Hm." For all the doctor has just proven how he can do his job without a knife or saw, my husband doesn't sound convinced.

Carefully, Thaddeus reaches for the boy, taking the baby delicately into his paws before cushioning him into the vast muscles of his chest. "So ...?" He looks up at me, and for the first time since Helena left, his face is clear and nearly content, revealing the handsome man he is. And then, to my shock, he forgets himself and smiles, fleeting and brilliant, before bending over and coiling into the baby, the huge hand covering the boy's head completely. I am breathless, and my heart feels as though it will creak with the weight of the emotions flying through me, fast and hard and white.

It is something a woman is taught, of course: manage the children given, and do not fuss over it. A husband will take what he is due, and the babies that come from such unions are the duty of the wife, no matter how difficult it may be. And childbirth itself—well, that is a death knell for half the women who do it—more so if one lives far from a physician. Or refuses to call for one. I am grateful, suddenly, for Hardy's meddling.

At the first whimper, Thaddeus hands him back to me quickly, as if the babe will catch fire. I catch him up with one arm, as the doctor is holding my wrist and checking a small watch he's pulled from his vest pocket. Jane picks at the traces of blood on her hands and fingers a slice along her thumb, where she must have cut herself on the doctor's tools.

Slowly standing, stretching the soreness out of his legs, the doctor rubs the tops of his hips, forgetting that his hands are still not completely clean. He pauses, then looks down at his fingers speculatively.

"Marie is as well as she can be," Doc Kinney says finally. "But … we should let the baby rest, and the mother as well." He clears his throat loudly. "I'll check on you tomorrow, if I may?"

Why not? He's already done this much. "Of course, Doctor Kinney." As I give the permission, Thaddeus stiffens next to me.

"And no gettin' up for a bit. Let the sheets be, they're ruined as it is. Give yourself over the night." He glances out the small, narrow window that lets in the southern light, where dusk has given way to pure dark. How long has he been here? Minutes? Hours? "Tomorrow, only move to the chair while the beddin' is changed. Then back in. You understand?"

There is a small noise outside in the hallway, and Jane opens the door. Hardy stands at the threshold with Kaspar and Natan, all sets of eyes as wide as they've ever been. I clutch the baby to me, and make sure my legs are covered. How long have they been there, listening or fidgeting? Thaddeus seems to be mulling the same question, his hands clenching and unclenching silently. I hope he will not blame our apprentice now for anything else, especially as it was his quick thinking that may have saved me and our baby.

The boy's bright eyes swivel between us, bloodied and weary as we are, and he steps forward. "Will Mrs. Marie be alright then?"

The doctor takes pity on him. "She'll be fine. It was only—"

"That's enough!" my husband interrupts tightly. "This is your mistress you're asking about, boy. You don't need the details." Thaddeus grabs the lad by the shoulder and physically turns him back toward the door, running Hardy into Kaspar and Natan in a jumble of too-long legs and arms. "You all go on and tell your grandmother how all's well."

Thaddeus turns to the doctor abruptly. "What is the cost for these services, then?" he asks gruffly.

The doctor considers, and then looks up at the man squarely. "Would five dollars be satisfactory?"

Thaddeus's eyebrows go up. I think he is appalled at the cost, but he chokes a harsh, incredulous sound instead. "That's all? For the life of my wife and son, you only ask so little?"

"It is the cost of a delivery, difficult, successful, or no."

My husband swings his head to look at Jane, but she only shrugs. I am impressed that she holds her tongue where money is concerned. Then again, she is well-bred. And she isn't Polish.

Grunting, Thaddeus folds his arms, then shakes them out again uncertainly. "Very well," he says finally. "Though if you are coming to check on her, I would expect there to be some payment for that service?"

The doctor nods once, then dives into more medical talk. I try to pay attention, but my mind feels soft and boiled. "I want to surely be able to come and visit until she's feelin' better. But you must also come get me if she spikes a fever. I've done all I can to keep infection away, but it is a sneaky thing, and still might come as she heals. You understand the infection, your daughter—."

"Quiet!"

"The doctor was only trying to explain—" Jane interjected.

"I know what he meant, Mrs. Kinney, but I'll not have reminders of Urszula's death today."

The two men leave to collect the cash, and I can hear Thaddeus stomping all the way through the kitchen to the tin over the hearth. I pull down the neckline of my dress to start nursing. Jane watches me, her eyes bright, her hands twisting at her sides. I've never been one to extend easy welcome or courtesy, and my throat is dry and my limbs exhausted

269

from the hours of pain and hours of laboring. I'm saved from womanly chatter when Doctor Kinney calls for her to go.

"Good night," Jane says at the door, her eyes on my face. "I ... I'm so happy that ... this time ... we were able to help." She smiles at me when she reaches the bedroom door.

It is a deep smile and speaks to me not only of this shared moment, but also of the losses we both have endured, the miscarriages we hold between us, silent and half-forgotten in the busyness of each day and week, but there anyway in the quiet pauses of a task or the passing of the cemetery. It is the kind of smile that only another woman understands, and through the last of my fatigue, I recognize the friendship stretching between us, as new as the babe I hold.

CHAPTER SEVENTEEN

# *Kate*

*July 3, 1883*

I cannot sleep this morning. There's much to be done. A festival to prepare, food to organize, tables to set up, and prizes to be sorted.

And Yves and the posse. They'll be back today, along with a train running full steam.

So he said.

So I promised Helena.

I sit up so fast I'm light in the head. Next to me, Bern's hand is insistent and firm, sliding along the edge of my waist and cupping my bottom, hidden under the folds of my chemise. I pull away from him, feeling warmth, hot and purple, float up toward my cheeks.

"You want to stay for breakfast, I'm sure?" It is a highly intimate question even at the best of moments and my heart rears at once in objection after I ask it. But it's an old question, asked so many times over the years, that it *must* be asked. The strings attached to the asking—and not asking—are too thick and intertwined now.

He doesn't bother to answer and rolls over, pinning me back down to the bed, a muffled groan stifled in the pillow, as if for him there's no place he'd rather be than here.

The rustle of the dry corn husks is different when there are two bodies on the bed, and the ropes below us squeak and groan. Bern smells of horse and leather, grass and grease. He never has a whiff of whiskey on him, and his hands are rough and coarse along the edges of his thumbs. The skin of his neck is smooth, as is his chin. Bern has never had to shave as long as I've known him. And the hair, always a tad too long, is as straight as my own, slipping through my fingers as I grasp him, where he suckles my neck and collarbone.

The sex is always fast, yet never hurried, as if he desires me so greatly, but cannot wait to be finished with the task. I used to think there was passion between us, but it is not that. Passion would mean change, I think, as time goes. I would expect our joining to soften or slow, to become familiar and easier. I would expect to feel something other than regret and loss during the act if I truly had passion for Bern. Instead, it is something else that binds us, though I have never been brave enough to put a name to it. I don't know if he can, either.

Sometimes, it is all only painful. At times I can find enjoyment, and when that happens, I allow myself the idea that maybe Bern cares. I have allowed few men between my hips. One I even desired, adored … and at least one of them adored me, I believed, even if it was a short while. Bern is the only one who comes to me, though, and our arrangement is a currency. It reaffirms our link, my plans. It gives him the power he craves in the act itself, even as it affords me power in the future. I hate all of this, but I need it, too. How much can a woman truly do without the support of the menfolk? It is foolish to believe I am on an island without them.

And no one can ever know how deeply he has wormed his way into my life. How much he knows, and how much I must trust him.

"Bern, why do we do this?"

The words bring his head up from my shoulder, where he catches his breath. My stomach is sticky with his seed, and my legs are cool.

"Do?"

"Yes. This." I have never asked before in the years we've created this strange tie. I should not allow my musings to come out, I know. But it's too late, and my heart is racing now more than it did when he took me.

He pulls himself up, peeling his skin from mine. In the dark, the rustle of his clothing is loud and raspy. "It's the least you can do, for what you ask of me."

"The protection you once said you'd give me?" I ask, hiding the scorn buried deep.

"Maybe that," he agrees. "But it's also more than that, now. You know it."

He cannot be speaking of affection. "But what can you possibly get out of it?" I wonder, the surprise eating at my voice. "Is my bed worth so much to you?"

The silence between us is almost painful, and I feel the fool. What man will admit to his desires so baldly and with boldness? Bern is no different. And he is less a man than others I know.

"You saying you wanna stop?" He stands up inside the quiet, and the clang of the metal on his belt and suspenders is loud and tinkling. Outside, the first cockerel crows near Nels and Clara's chicken farm.

"No."

I do, though. I simply don't know how. I tingle before freezing inside, the blood curdling in my head and the veins of my arms. I wipe off my skin and begin to yank my bodice and petticoats from the nearby hooks.

"I said I'd help you. I been helping you. From the start, as you asked," he says. "I light the fires as you want and I keep my silence. It's you and them outlaws what's causing you real trouble, now. Not me."

It feels like he's doused me with hot water when he talks of our deeds so plain. I shake off the uneasiness. The tenderness of the morning has fled, leaving me only with hard schemes.

"And why'd you have to go and get Widow Hawks?" he suddenly complains. "You undid what you wanted done. And then you go on and bring her back!"

"I didn't expect the doctor and his new wife to go fetch her," I say, ice and anger smashing together in my tone, the old emotions blowing up into my lungs. "I didn't realize they meant to truly do it. And I figured if I didn't … go with them … it would look poorly."

"Damn quack." He pulls on his socks so fast, the stitching rips on one.

"You're only saying that because Jane chose him over you."

"And you'd miss me, would you?" His eyes are blank. "If I'd wed her, I'd have maybe stopped coming here. You'd be alone."

I push away the feelings storming around inside my gut at our conversation. I shouldn't have started it. "So that's what this is for you. Like having a wife, but not a wife. Is that it?"

He slides into his boots and straightens to his full height, looking down at me, where I scrabble in the bedclothes.

"Why you asking now, Kate, a day before the fourth and all the festivities around it?"

"I'm asking because you just came from between my legs, and a woman has a right to ask questions now and again."

"Does she?" His eyes trail down the dampness in the sheets. "I thought your payment was my help and my tongue. I've kept your council these past four years. D'you want me to come clean?"

He won't, and we both know it's an empty threat. He'd be hanged. Same as me. He heads to the door, hurrying now, so it's less likely any will see him leave. When he opens it, he turns back and pierces me with his slanted eyes.

"I want the same as you, Kate. Flats Junction, clean of anything and anyone unwanted. However that happens, whatever it takes. It's my home, where I'll live my years and likely die. I want the place cleared of troublemakers before I do."

He shuts the door with extreme care, and I can hardly hear the soles of his boots as he gets away cat-like and quick.

Shaking my nerves, feeling unsettled by his bald revelations, I brush back my hair and put on my freshest apron.

There's not enough coffee left now even for me to take some off to the side. Yves with his wagons and the train with the rest of the goods—and Helena herself—will all come in just in time for the July Fourth celebrations tomorrow.

Everyone will be in high spirits. Everyone will be thinking of how nice it is here. How they want to make their lives here, and build their families. And ... in case they do not understand how impossible that would be without me ... well, with all the plans in place, no one will forget how much they need me.

I watch the posse come over the far eastern hills, going slower than usual given the two massive wagons they have with them this time—one driven by Victoria and the other by Patty. I'll have to pay for some of these fine things they bring, but Yves will be able to settle his debt with me just as I will be able to sell everything quick over the holiday and make up the months of debt in my ledger, no thanks to Yves himself.

But he's trying. I'll give him that.

As they near, I shade my eyes while the sun rises with a new paleness that casts everything in peach and pink and grey. Yves arrives at the hitching post with his oversized Clydesdale puffing hard. He leaps down faster than I expect of a man his age, and glowers at the rest of his posse as they follow.

Arnold's next off his mount. Matthias and Evan arrive and turn to wait for the wagons, with Natty bringing up the rear and the two women's riding horses.

Yves and Arnold pound their feet extra hard on the floorboards as they come up to me. I fold my arms under my chest and smile at them brightly.

"You've brought everything and then some, it would seem," I say.

Yves snorts. "And your precious train will be here soon."

As he says it, a long, slow whistle yodels across the prairie, muted only by the tall grasses on the edge of town.

276

"It carries more than you ever could even if each of you drove a wagon," I say. "And you can't put a price on the life of a young woman, either."

"There was a time I did," Yves sneers.

"Ah, but a businessman must make some … allowances," I tell him, trying not to make too much an issue of our height difference.

"Pay him no mind. He's just ornery as an old sow," Arnold says, leaning against the railing. "Wanted to tickle the train just a small bit, but he was … advised against."

"What?"

I shouldn't be shocked Yves had considered reneging his promise to keep this train untouched, but it's even more surprising that he didn't do it! My mouth falls open, but I'm not even sure what I'm asking.

Arnold rolls his eyes and juts his chin toward the wagons as they clatter in along the rhythm of the oncoming train.

"He was told … no."

Yves spits a gob from his mouth and then out one of his nostrils. "Son of a pig." If I didn't know better, he sounds almost impressed.

I glance between Yves and Arnold. "Did you kill this man, who would say no to Yves?"

"Can't." Arnold's mouth twitches. He nods again toward the rest of the posse. "He's too big. And Yves figured …"

Matthias hikes up the stairs, two huge bags of coffee beans on each shoulder. He clambers past the three of us, and I push open the door of the General. At the last moment, his eyes flick up and meet mine. The strange recognition there means nothing to me.

When I turn back to Yves and Arnold, they're staring at me and at the door. Arnold's eyes narrow.

"Never heard him talk," Yves spits again. "Never. Didn't think he could. All I know is what they said in Vermillion the day he joined with our little group of citizens. Matthias has not spoken since zee day his Cheyenne wife was killed outside of Yankton oh so many years ago."

The way Arnold and Yves stare at me make me feel naked. It's worse as Matthias trudges back out to get more sacks, not looking at anyone. They stare at me as if I've cast a spell on the man, as if I've somehow loosened his tongue.

"You're saying Matthias forced you to leave the train alone?"

The whistle shrieks as the train rumbles close. My fingers feel twitchy—I'll soon need to go and meet Helena and see how she fared. But there's no chance I'm leaving the store unlocked with Yves and his whole gang walking in and out.

"He just said ... no. And didn't get out of the way," Arnold drawls. "And then the girls started on about how you've said you can give us a place, so we'd best stand by our word this time."

"Right. Surely." I have no clear notion how I'll do this, but it's important. I can tell just by how Yves quivers every time I use the word *legitimate*. I watch the train squeal to a stop at the depot, and make a hasty decision, turning and locking the door as I speak. "Look—I must meet that train. The special one that I told you all about—the one with the lady stuffs that I have been looking forward to bringing to Flats Junction for months. You all go have something to eat at Matt Winters's or the Golden Nail, and I'll meet you back here in an hour to finish unloading and going over the inventory."

Yves swells when I include him and puffs out when I say *inventory*. His eyes gleam. "It is like we are zee partners, is it not, Miss Kate?"

"I suppose."

The simplicity of my words are suddenly not enough. Not at all. Arnold grabs my arm, pushing his thumb into the soft spot inside my elbow so fast and hard I know at once it'll leave a mark. Yves steps in front of me, blocking the stairs. The rest of the gang pauses below and gathers on the stairs below me.

I'm utterly, completely trapped.

My legs feel like rods, sweat pours between my breasts, and I feel like my scalp is pricked with a million needles. The world suddenly feels stark and swollen and airless.

"You *suppose* we are zee partners? Or we *are*?" Yves asks, his voice soft, and his fingers tickling the top of his longer knife. "My English is not so poor that I do not understand the difference, you see. And here I have been thinking all year that we are zee partners."

"What more do you wish of me?" I ask, keeping my voice light, trying not to wince as Arnold increases the pressure on my elbow. "You've taken—paid—received a steep discount on goods, paid in stolen goods, and have been able to keep up your ... preferences with the trains near all year without a word from me to the authorities. You've even had a homecooked meal. I don't see the fuss."

"But you said I would be legitimate, here in Flats Junction. And now you are bringing in fine lady stuffs, and starting another trade? Without asking Yves? For this I was to leave the train alone, so you could pour your money into something else?"

The panic starts to swirl in my stomach, the acid eating up my throat, coupled with the soreness between my legs from yet another trade today.

I'm so sick and tired of all this bartering, just to stay on top of my world, my plans, my life!

If only my parents hadn't met.

If only I'd been born within the rules.

*If only …*

"You cannot be serious," I say.

Yves cocks his head and frowns. Arnold twists my elbow and a pained whine pulls out of me before I can stop it.

"I'm very serious, Miss Kate," Arnold replies for Yves, smiling too much. My gaze darts down to the others in the gang. Natty is grinning eagerly; Evan stares off into the distance; Patty and Victoria have mildly amused smirks, and Matthias—Matthias, who spoke to me, and for me … is holding his knives in both hands, waiting for Arnold or Yves to tell him what to do.

My heartbeat throbs in my neck, and I pull thoughts from the depths of my throat, where they sit choked and stiff. "You want to be considered a … a man of society, Yves. You must act like one!"

"It is not me who is acting so … ungentlemanly," Yves says. "Just Arnold."

Arnold chuckles, low and salty, and pulls my elbow up and round my back, and white spots appear in the corner of my vision.

"What are you asking of me?"

"A business. Just like you are doing with the lady stuffs. Unless you want Patty and Victoria to manage that for you?"

Victoria's and Patty's smiles widen, showing split and yellowed teeth under their grimy hats and painted lips.

"I didn't mean for you—Yves—to start a dressmaking shop! Why would you?" I ask, sounding strangled and desperate to my own ears. "You ... you're to have something else. Something bigger."

Yves wrinkles his nose. "Why should I trust your word, that zee bigger business will be mine?"

"I trusted you, all this year."

"That does not mean I must do the same."

I want to struggle in Arnold's grasp, and curse the earliness of the hour—if only someone was here to help! Damn Bern, leaving so early! What of his protection ...

"You—you'll have the old cooperage."

Yves pauses picking at the corner of his nails. "The old cooper building?"

"Yes." It's been derelict for years, ever since Patrick sawed off Franklin's arm. Surely ... surely Sadie will put in a good word for me with Tom at the bank—she'll make the deed exchange move quickly, especially as I will be paying rent for her summer garden.

I hope ...

Isn't that how business is done? It's even more fair than when my father would have run Flats Junction. The realization of this sparks my next words.

"I've been trying to build up this town for years, Yves. The town needs a place where they can trade their farm produce. Eggs for onions, potatoes for peas."

He frowns. "This is what is needed? This is zee business for us?"

"You wanted to be a merchant. I'll make all my customers do that trade with you—set it up how you like, leave whoever you wish in charge."

It is a piss-poor business, but Yves has spent all these years doing nothing but stealing and terrorizing trains and wagons. If he gets smart and starts importing other things or recognizes the work is seasonal ... But I cannot imagine he will understand the push and pull of numbers and ledgers, nor want the regular hours. I have to hope this is so ...

And it's better than nothing.

"Is this not what you are already doing, Miss Kate?" he asks warily, and my hopes sink a little. So he understands some of commerce then.

"All the big towns have more than one store," I tell him, and he knows it's a truth. "How else will Flats Junction grow if there are not two stores?"

Yves nods slightly at Arnold, who releases my arm at once. I stop myself from rubbing the sore spot at once and will my wobbly ankles to toughen up.

"I'll see you later, then," I tell him. "We'll settle up shortly. Go on and get some grub."

My smile is tight and plastered as I work through the gang and step fast toward the waiting engine. With shaking arms and trembling knees, I try to walk as calm and slow to the depot, feeling the eyes of the posse between my shoulder blades.

What in hell have I gotten myself into?

I'll have to use more of my inheritance than I planned— between starting the seamstress shop, paying for Yves's goods and the orders on this train, and now this other plan ... well, there will be little cash needed to start Yves's little shop.

There's some comfort in that. And likely Helena has not used up all the funds to buy sundries and silks.

As I step up onto the platform, both Franklin and Bess are hauling out boxes and barrels with Helena, looking for all the world like they know what they're about.

More boxes come off the train, stacked for me to send for later today. I can tell several are heavy and weighted in the middle. Marie will have cause to celebrate twice over today. Helena back—and her precious tinplate, too.

"Is that everything?" I ask Helena as she looks up. "It's more than I thought you'd get."

"I'm good with funds, as I've always be taught," she huffs.

Helena looks exactly the same as when she left—same dress and same bonnet, same shoes and the same rosy cheeks. But it's something else. A way of her shoulders? The direct slant of her eyes in mine? The tone of her voice?

She continues to pull more boxes out, muscles pressing against the calico of her dress, ordering Franklin about as if he is her servant.

"Two more like this," she says, her gaze brushing on each case, visibly counting as her mouth moves without sound. "And then I've five large ones the porter said he'd bring from the other car once the janitor opens it."

Sure enough, as she says it, two men in uniform come from the far car, carrying and dragging boxes with them. They make an odd clanging noise as they bump along, and Helena cringes as they dump the crates at her feet.

She opens her small bag and offers each a coin, the suave genteel movement so citified that Bess stops shifting barrels to watch.

And then, finally, Helena turns to look at me with a wide smile. I find I want to match it, but it's too early and there's too many pieces floating around me these next days to truly feel any kind of soft emotion.

"It's done."

My eyebrows shoot up. "You did it? As we discussed?"

"It was easy. It was mostly women who held the patterns, and we've promised to correspond so that I might stay in touch."

"And ... they were happy to share what they knew?"

"Once they saw my stitching, certainly. It was all the introduction I needed," she tosses her head with a satisfied shake. "And some of it comes from knowing how to walk among people, no matter where one might find oneself."

Oh, it's airs she's got, now.

Marie will be livid.

A grin tugs itself on the corner of my mouth at the idea.

"We'll store everything over in my back rooms, until I speak to Sadie Fawcett about using her summer kitchen. She never uses it, and it'll have good lighting."

"You haven't spoken to her about setting up?" she asks.

"No. I didn't want people talking too early." *In case she didn't come back ...* "Besides, I figured you'd want to set it the way you prefer."

The answer seems to mollify her slightly. It's true—I didn't want to move things along too early. I help her load up Franklin's rickety wagon as the train peels itself from Flats Junction and heads further west, and we curl around the outskirts of town toward the General.

"I'll get Sadie during tomorrow's festivals, or the next day. She'll be glad for the distraction," I say. I'm blathering.

What I really want to know is how Helena found the cities. Was Chicago as big as they say? Did anyone give her trouble at the stops? Does she miss the bustle or glad to be home in the quiet stupor of Flats Junction?

Does she think I might do well if I went there?

But I'm not asking a young girl these things. She'll think me daft and I'll sound overeager. We trudge up the stairs together and start shoving things anywhere they'll fit in my room, but as I grab the big one nearest me, Helena pulls in a breath just as the items clatter and ping inside the box.

"What fine fabric sounds like a bunch of tin bells?" I ask, pulling on the wooden cover. "What did you buy with my money, Helena Salomon?"

A final tug has the cover popping up and all I can see in the sawdust is the glint of silver in the morning's early sun.

Helena grabs the cover from me and places it back on. "It's tinplate items. For my mother."

"I just ordered tinplate for her. Which she'll owe for, too!" I retort, yanking open the box again and poking a finger inside the packaging. "I thought you said you didn't tell her you were going east!"

"I didn't!" Helena says. "She didn't order these. I picked them up."

"With what funds?"

"Yours, of course."

If she were my kin, I'd smack her a solid one for her impudence and cheek! "Mine! I told you only to buy what was needed to set up a full-fledged seamstress business! It's not your place to use my money to buy things for your own family!"

Helena puts her hands on her hips. "It's the price of the journey."

"I paid for that!"

"It's the price of the risk I took. For you."

"Your payment is what I have already offered—work as a seamstress, as you've always wanted. A way to see and bring the high fashion here to Flats Junction. A business you want."

"But it all benefits you, too," Helena says stoutly, planting her feet further apart and sticking her hips forward. "I require payment outside of a business beholden to you. And I chose this." She whacks her hand on the biggest box.

"You ... she won't like it," I retort, betrayal the first emotion sinking into my words. I'd ... well, I'd trusted her. "I'll bet she won't even use the stuff!"

For the first time since she's stepped off the train, Helena looks a bit nervous. "She'd be stupid not to grow with the times."

"I thought you didn't want to be a tinsmith," I say, gripping a delicately formed teapot spout in a fist and squeezing, feeling the tin give way slightly under my palm.

"I don't. But that doesn't mean I want my family to lose ... to fail ... just because I'm getting everything ..."

She clamps her mouth shut and glares at me. "Well, it's done. It's my payment for the work I did for you. The shop is for both of us. It's fair and you know it."

I shouldn't have sent such a headstrong girl to the cities. She's learned too much, and it's only served to make her smart mouth and her stubbornness stronger.

And yet ... I cannot help but be pleased I picked a young woman who understands it. Who sees my ambition and how hers matches it. One who could manage—and even thrive—in the world I flung her into, for my own means.

286

She's backhandedly blackmailed me, and I find all my arguments against this are dust in my mouth.

"Fine then. Take these off to your mother," I say, flinging the piece back into the crate. "What use do I have for the junk, now that you've brought it here."

I turn and march into my back rooms with another small barrel of fabric, sweat beading under my arms and on my brow as I do, and not before I see her fair dance up the street with the smaller box. Slamming my door, I sink onto my forearms at the table and cradle my head, which throbs and pounds and feels filled with nails.

There's no time to shirk, and no time to tremble. So much to be done, so much to plan, so much to smooth over and make well.

It is the worst time to appear weak.

I pull myself up and smooth my skirts, shaking my hands at the wrists to stave off the trembles and yank open the door to finish hauling in the fabric, stashing them near the door, where I know they will be safe.

CHAPTER EIGHTEEN

# Jane

*July 3, 1883*

Picking my way through the ruts in the late afternoon, I rub my hand across the edge of my waistband and wish I could somehow take out the threads and wear looser clothing, except then I will certainly be met with some hostility in patient's homes.

I'm only glad that Orla let me see her children, all of whom are suffering from a rather awful case of chiggers. She says they'd only been in the high grasses near the forest once this past week, but the bugs are digging into the soft, innocent flesh of each of her brood, and I can only offer small advice. Little Alma has the worst case. At least the family has taken to boiling most of their water. And I gave Orla some of the tea Esther recommended—she seems keen to use it, though if it were to be known that a Lakota woman made it, I wonder if she'd be less so. It's good to get out of the kitchen, to help Patrick with patients now and again. It's my role, one I'm finally sliding into without too much friction. Especially with newcomers like Orla—ones who perhaps have yet to hear the ugly rumors about Patrick and me and Esther …

The clod and clop of hooves coming from the north make me stop as I wait for them to cross before I reach home and the coolness of the hall.

The cowboys that pass me come from the Svendsen ranch, and I wait, tired and hot and more than a little cranky, as the July sun bakes the earth.

As I stand in the heat, one of the horses pauses, and I look up when the shadow blocks the light.

Bern stares down at me, his eyes intense. "Jane."

I want to tell him that he has no leave to call me that, anymore. We're not courting, and I'm the doctor's wife! But the sounds stick as he starts to slowly grin at me.

It's a cold sort of smile, slithering along his mouth and never reaching his dark eyes.

"What? And now you're too good even to say hello, as neighbors should?" he taunts.

"Good afternoon, then," I say carefully, and bob a small bit at the knee. This makes him snort and inhale his laughter, so it comes out sounding hard and harsh and spiteful.

"Good day!"

Moses rides up next to us—he must have doubled back—and salutes me with the brim of his hat. Bern shoots him a look filled with so much dislike, it feels like a punch to my gut. Moses either doesn't notice or doesn't care, as he twists in his saddle.

"You'll be at the festivities tomorrow, then, Mrs. Kinney?" he asks pleasantly, leaning on the pommel. "Bern here tells me there's plenty races and the like."

"Yes—there are."

"That'll be just the ticket—we'll race for the prizes, won't we?" Moses says to Bern, who clicks his tongue at his horse and trots away without a word.

Moses tilts his head at me, shrugs slightly, as if to say he is unsurprised, and follows.

I put a hand unwittingly to my stomach, and then my throat. As I cross to the house, I meet Mrs. Molhurst's beady eyes under her wide hat as she stares at me from her porch, broom in one hand and not a bit of sweeping happening.

I ignore her glare, cross the short front yard and then pause when I notice who is in my husband's study—the open window giving a clear view from the porch.

Thaddeus Salomon is in the office!

What now?

This close, I hear every word trip out the front door screen and office window as if I was in the room with them.

"... it's only just in the journals, Thaddeus. I don't want to risk it."

"So instead I risk her?"

"Look, a salpingectomy is new science. I shouldn't have mentioned it—I didn't think you'd want me to attempt it, to be honest. Not after ... everythin' else."

"*Niech cię!*" Thaddeus's voice is a muted roar, and even without meaning to pry, I cannot help but hear him clearly in the yard now. "I'm asking you for help, man. Finally— *finally*! And you cannot offer me anything?"

"It's too new, only months ago it was done in Scotland—I can't—not in good faith. The likelihood of infection and death is too great, I promise you."

"Aren't you the sawbones? I know, I've seen—even when it won't work, you do it anyway! You like taking up a knife!"

"Not if I don't have to—surely—you know I do it only when I must."

"I know thanks to you Nels had to give up his farm, and Franklin stews in his anger at the depot instead of being content in his own cooperage."

"Those men would have lost their limbs no matter what doc was here. And if not, they would have died. You must know this! Jesus, Mary and Joseph, Thaddeus! What more can I say? It's done, and they lived. Sometimes surgery works, and other times it doesn't! Urszula would have likely lived, had the iodine been available—the surgery didn't kill her. Surely you understand how it is!"

There's a pause, and then Thaddeus's voice comes quieter, but still audible. "I know it."

A longer pause. I think to make for the front door screen when Patrick's voice comes, muted and firm. "I'm glad to hear it. But I can't—not in good conscience—do what you ask of me."

There is a loud thump from inside the house. I wonder if the smith has smacked Patrick again, and imagine my husband slumped over his desk with a purpling, bulging eye or jaw. But before I can rush into the house, they speak once more.

"Is there nothing else, then?" Thaddeus's voice is still low and mellifluous. But it is not so very angry. Instead, he sounds oddly defeated.

"There's one thing, but it's not perfect. And ... it's illegal. We'd have to talk to Nancy."

I don't want to hear another word of this odd plan my husband is hatching with the surly town smith, making some sort of devilish pact with a man who hit him not two days ago at Marie's bedside! Purposefully, I make an intense amount of racket as I enter the house.

"Patrick? And ... Thaddeus." I poke my head around the corner, and smile briefly at the big man who has crashed into the uncomfortable, straight-backed chair opposite the desk, and looks outrageously out of place.

My appearance catapults him to his feet and he grips his hat so tightly the hard leather starts to crease.

"Mrs ... Jane," Thaddeus says belatedly, looking at the floor instead of my eyes. If I didn't know better, I'd say he was blushing! What on earth?

Meeting Patrick's gaze, I raise my eyebrows, and say off-handedly, "Is Esther home?"

"No," he shakes his head. "Though ... might you go into the garden for a bit, Jane? I think we'd do for some beans tonight for supper."

His obvious suggestion isn't lost on me or Thaddeus, but I play the dutiful submissive wife and head outside through the back door, ideas swirling and swooping about what, exactly, is going on in the office.

Patrick's right—there are plenty of beans good for picking. I glance at my apron, smudged with invisible remains of carbolic acid and even some crusty blood. It needs a wash, just like my other two, so I'll have to do a laundry sooner than I want. I've taken to wearing a new apron as many times a week I can manage due to Patrick's insistent fastidiousness about bacteria, and it's rubbed off on me too, it seems.

Flipping my apron over to the clean side, I sink to the ground and begin to pull at the green poles, tugging under the fluffy leaves for the pods. The sun, even in late afternoon, hits my neck where the bonnet rides up under my hair and sends a line of sweat along my collar.

The stamp of boots clatters from the front of the house, and Thaddeus's voice rings out, though it is muffled and undiscernible. A few moments later, I sense more than see Patrick come around back to look for me.

"Find some?" he asks humorously.

I look up and smile, the laugh in my eyes tempered by the questions I have for him. "What exactly is going on with you two?"

"How much could you hear from outside?" he counters, and at my surprised start he chuckles. "Even though Thad couldn't see you, I could."

"Only a bit about risking some impossible-to-pronounce procedure. And doing something illegal."

"Would you think badly of me if I promoted illegal activities?" he asks carefully.

I push back onto my legs and settle myself more comfortably on the ground, flicking away one of the checkered beetles skittling across the garden floor. Rolling the beans in my lap, I look out over the grass. The town is growing, and there are more shanties popping up far along the horizon, though the prairie still creeps along everyone's borders; a confident, stealthy march of grass that starts to take over the yard if one doesn't keep it tramped down. It still looks like waves and water to me some days. If I let the sound of the thrushes and stalks of thick, fat grass wash over me, it nearly sounds like the ocean, too.

Would I think much differently of Patrick if he suddenly started to do something illegal? Is helping the hurdy-gurdy girls at the Powdered Rose illegal, given their soiled reputation? He does—giving them morphine and mercury for their boils and bottom blisters, and once Eva Rose needed a safe abortion. He did that, too, at her request and he tended to her carefully so she recovered well. He does not ask about certain gunshot wounds, even when it's obvious a wife shot a husband and missed. Does he do something wrong when he guesses at a treatment, without being fully certain? I don't know. All I know is that whatever he does, he generally does it to help people. I must assume that is the case, once more.

"I wouldn't think poorly of you at all," I finally answer him, glad I am speaking truthfully when I do. "Though I expect as your wife and helpmeet that you'll tell me what exactly you're planning."

Suddenly he grins, a wide, crinkly smile that cracks his face into fissures of barely controlled mirth and happiness.

"What is so funny?"

Patrick gets to his haunches beside me, a hand on the dirt bracing his frame and the other covering his forehead as he laughs so hard I think he'll still topple into the bean poles.

"Paddy!" I flick him on the shoulder lightly. "I can't join you if you don't let me in on the joke!"

"I'm sorry, Jane, truly," he says, gasping for air, and then finally taking a seat next to me in a jumbled plop. "It's only ironic."

"That Thaddeus Salomon is here asking for your medical assistance?"

294

"Yes, that. And what he asks."

"The surgery?"

Sobering slightly, Patrick dusts off his knee absently, and pulls a bean out of my lap. "Yes. That too. I won't do it, and he knows it."

"Why not? You're a good doc, Pat. Do you need me to say it every day so you believe me?" I sigh, and go back to plucking down beans. I should make enough for Kate too, perhaps, just in case she needs food tonight as well. It'd be yet another peace offering. Perhaps one of these times she'll finally collapse and be kind to me again.

"He wants me to keep Marie safe. No more babies. No more pregnancies."

"There's a way to manage that," I say dryly, lifting an eyebrow.

Patrick nods, the last bit of laughter teasing across his brow. "Of course there is, Jane. But Marie could be havin' children for another ten years. Could you imagine abstainin' from the sheets for the rest of our days? Now?"

"But we're newlyweds," I dismiss, tossing more beans in my apron. He takes another, crunching on it loudly, and then reaches in to help me.

"I doubt I'll want to stop touchin' you even twenty years from now. And they've been married … oh, since the mid '60's I think. Before my time. They still … desire each other. It's a fortunate thing for them. There are so few true and love matches."

"But what then? You can do something to keep Marie from conceiving?"

He sighs. "I could. A Scottish surgeon did a successful salpingectomy several months ago. The woman lived and has no need to worry of havin' more children."

"You might want to enlighten me on what a sal ... salpingotomy is," I tell him a little testily.

He drops the beans into the green puddle on my apron and then moves the vegetables slightly to the side. Gently he puts his hand on my womb, and my heart races. Can he feel? Can he tell? It's so early ...

"It means openin' you here, Jane," he says softly. "And taking out the tubes a babe travels so a woman cannot become fertile anymore. Ever again. But it's a very delicate surgery, and very dangerous. The chance of recovery, for all Doctor Tait's success, is very slim. The infection alone ..." He shakes his head and pulls away his hand.

"Well, there are other ways to try and prevent pregnancy, though I haven't tried them myself," he finishes, meeting my eyes and looking a little wicked.

"Such as?" The old interest in all things medical surges into my blood. Imagine! A way to protect a woman when she can no longer manage another pregnancy! Such a thing could mean life, for so many women. "Do you have books on this?"

"Books? They'd have been burned before they were published!" he scoffs. "But ... let's see ... there is the rhythm method, of course. And ... then there's the rubber condom. And that, my love, is the illegal part."

"Rubbers aren't really illegal."

"No, but they've restricted uses," he says lowly. "And the Comstock law of '73 means the post office can confiscate ones that come in the mail. So we've got to talk to Nancy ... it shouldn't matter here—we're not technically part of the Union yet, though I believe the law includes the territories. But protection is safer—especially for the girls at Fortuna's Powdered Rose. And it's ... ah, well, it's not exactly the

Catholic way, as my old auntie would say. But it's a good way to keep a woman alive."

"What does Thaddeus say to all this?" I pick up the edges of my apron, cradling the beans and trying very hard not to burst out with my early hopes of my own womb. All this talk of death and childbirth makes my nerves fizzle.

"He brought it up," Patrick reminds. "And it was … it shows how much he loves her, that he will come to see me about somethin' so private."

It means more than that too—and we both know it. I give him a look laden with meaning, and he returns it. It's too soon to put much stock into Thaddeus's request. He could still be reeling from near losing his beloved wife, and he may still decide he doesn't like doctors or medicine or science as Marie recovers.

We enter the kitchen together, but at once, tramping footsteps fill the hall. Glancing down the short hall, I am not surprised to see Esther coming in for the evening meal, which is not anywhere near ready yet. But it's Thaddeus, coming behind her, squinting suspiciously and ducking his head automatically as he comes in, who is utterly unexpected. He's covered in soot. Had he gone back to the forge, thought fast, and returned just to tell Patrick he'd already made up his mind about contraceptives? What an odd man he is.

"Esther—and Thaddeus," I state the obvious. "Come in." Slapping my mouth together, I move toward the beans and start to pop off their ends for the cooking pot.

"I am not staying long," Thaddeus thunders, trying to hush his overloud voice to the indoors and failing miserably. "I only came to say that I will speak to Nancy myself when she opens the post tomorrow." He sounds defiant now, and woodenly keeps his arms at his sides, though his eyes continually flick to Esther. She unpacks another basket on the kitchen table, slowly and carefully aligning different plants in a row.

"If you wish," Patrick nods. "Will I send east for you, then?"

Thaddeus hesitates, frowns, and eats his bottom lip, still watching Esther's lean, strong hands as she strokes the long, slippery leaves of sweetgrass and the small flowers tickling the ends. He shakes his arms out and nods once. "That would be good of you, doc. So then."

He marches out, leaving the slight whiff of coal smoke and fire in his wake.

"More remedies, Esther?" I ask, curious about the new bundles on my table. I shift over the bowl of beans, supper half-forgotten in my interest, and Patrick comes around too, fingering the bold, prickly purple coneflower blooms.

"I had to wait until they flowered," Esther starts without preamble. "But it's time we looked at these."

"You're still goin' on about these?" Patrick sounds affronted. "It's not proper science, Jane. No point in it."

"It's not hurting anything," I say. "And it gives something for Esther and me to do—to see if we can't help, anyway."

He frowns and puts his hands on his hips. "It can harm. We don't need people thinking we're peddlin' Indian charms for healin'. I can barely get people to let me in when they've children dyin'—worst thing to do is to tell them to use remedies that I can't explain."

He shakes his head and heads back into the hallway, and I wait until I hear the door to his office shut before turning to Esther. We stare at one another before I shrug slightly.

"He didn't say to stop."

She smiles at me without showing her teeth, warmth lighting her eyes. "True, Jane. So here it is. I know the cone-flower is used for many things—almost any ailment—by many of the tribes. It is not the important one, though. I only recall what my own mother did with the leaves and petals, and while it may bring relief to any of the people already ill with black measles, it is not helpful before. But drinking much of it from the start of feeling poor? It may stop the illness—it is a powerful medicine."

She then sifts through the long stalks of the sweetgrass as I continue preparing the beans, keeping one eye on the greenery.

As her hands lift up the long dark-green stalks, rolling the edges and breaking open the strips, the strong smell of vanilla and earth lift into the kitchen. "I have wondered why this black measles does not affect my people, at least not as readily as it does for yours. I even do not have memories of the disease before ... Percy died." She pauses and swallows hard. "Perhaps it is like the smallpox," she says finally. "We died of it in great numbers, but so many of the whites did not. And the sweetgrass is something we do that you do not. We use it often for weaving, of course, and our food is stored in it. But it is a prayer plant."

"You want us to pray with it?" Patrick makes us both jump. I had not realized he was back, but he is, standing at the doorjamb, leaning on it with his arms crossed. He still looks annoyed, but by the line of his mouth I can tell he's more curious than he wants to be. I try not to tease him with a look.

He shakes his head at Esther. "The Catholics won't agree to it. They'll call it blasphemy. And I call it hardly scientific."

"Let her speak," I interrupt him, and his eyebrows go high. "Why not? You always said you'd let me, that you wouldn't hinder my learning."

"I meant with my books."

"Books start somewhere. You said yourself this morning that some things can't be put into books. It's good to discover things like this, I think."

"Now I know how Mr. Weber must have felt," he says, irritation filling his accent.

I jerk as if he'd poked me in the side, and suddenly my eyes feel sodden. Tears leak at the corner of each, and I duck my head down to the beans, trying very hard not to sniff.

"It is burned," Esther says quickly, glancing at me and then Patrick. "Braided and dried, it burns with a low, black flame for a very long time. Most of my people have it lit in their homes—or we did. And it is used by many as a perfume. It keeps away the bad spirits and brings only the good to the sweet smell of the smoke. It may be that is all that is needed."

"We dance about in a circle and light a huge fire with sweetgrass?" Patrick mutters, but he's still listening, frowning, his looming dissatisfaction eating into the corners of the room.

Esther looks up at him seriously. "Nothing that dramatic. No—burn it. Fan it over you. Lay the smoke on your eyes, ears, and heart. Your whole body. It may keep the black measles away from you—your house."

This is the most native thing she's ever done or said in my presence. I can't help but be drawn in, filled with trust of her, her history, the certainty in her movements. Would that not be something, to have a cure? To know how to stave off the disease that randomly appears and kills? The disease making everyone nervous this summer, just as the diphtheria did in winter?

Without glancing at Patrick, I pick up the bundle, inhaling the faint, spicy scent of the greenery. What will it smell like when it's dry and burning? It's completely against any type of medicinal training Patrick has, and is close to the snake oil concoctions I remember sold along the eastern seaboard. And it's nothing like any of the doctors back east would have recommended for Henry's cancer. None of them would use folk medicine.

My husband sighs, shrugs, and walks out. In a moment, there's a clink in his surgery—and I realize he has not thoroughly cleaned his tools since helping Marie give birth.

The memory of it clouds my vision, and I feel as if my world is on the edge of something insane and relentless, when all I want is to find something solid to land the day. Everything feels like it is uneasy and uneven beneath my feet.

The oven door squeals, and I turn to see Esther poking a long braid of the grass into the coals. In a moment, plumes of smoke entwine over the tin exhaust pipe and circle her arms, snaking up into the house.

"There," she says, satisfied. "The smell of *wačaŋǧa*. It is just like my youth, the smell of tipi and the call to the spirits."

I inhale and strangely do feel a bit of peace drop into me, for all the questions still swirling in my mind.

Esther turns and looks at me directly, her eyes a little shiny. "It might work. This grass already brings good fortune, Jane. Today is the first time Thaddeus Salomon has ever met my eyes."

CHAPTER NINETEEN

# Marie

*July 3, 1883*

I wake when I think I hear Helena calling my name. Stirring, and shifting the child next to me, I sit up and call out—both the bedroom and hall doors are open—hoping Berit can tell me what is going on.

"Berit? Who—"

And then it's Helena herself, bursting into the room looking exactly as I remember, without a scar or a rip in her clothing, bubbling and bursting and huffing with running in her skirts.

"Mother! You've had the baby!" She rushes to my side and scoops up little Gerik, who only sighs and nestles into his blankets, a full tummy and birthing exhaustion still keeping him content enough. "He's lovely!"

I sit up further, tucking my legs up and wishing I'd changed the bloody sheets by now regardless of what the doctor said, and pulling her down to me so I can crush her to my aching breasts. She smells like travel—old dust and sweat and a faint perfume that rings of a faraway city. But she's still my Helena, and her eyes are brighter and happier than ever. It is as if she needed to run from us to be glad to see us.

"Daughter!" I say, my voice hoarse. "You can never leave again!"

"Oh, I won't!" she says. "And I'll tell everyone all about it!"

"Where is your father? Does he know you're back?"

"The boys said he went back to Doc Kinney's again." She pauses snuggling with Gerik and cocks her head. "You and Father like the doc now? After everything?"

"Again?" I'm stuck on the word. "I didn't even know he'd gone." Likely to see about what can be done for payment in the future—we are too short on cash for Doc Kinney to make regular visits. "He will be pleased you're home to stay."

"And he won't whip me for leaving?" she asks, lifting one brow.

Who is this brilliant girl—woman? How can she have changed and blossomed so fast, near overnight it feels? Relief to have her back, safe and unharmed, swims through me, and tears spring up and trickle to my chin. She looks up and purses her lips.

"Don't get emotional, Mother. It's unnatural for you."

So she believes, never seeing the truth of them. I jab at my skin, and blink hard. "I've just birthed a babe and my eldest has come home. I'm allowed a tear or two."

There's clattering out in the kitchen. Thaddeus strides in, followed closely by our sons and Hardy. He looks more flustered than I've ever seen him, hair sticking up everywhere, and his eyes rake over Helena and me urgently, softening only when they rest on the babe.

"She's back," he says, talking to me directly.

"And so are you. Twice now you've been to the doc's in one day, so I hear." He opens his mouth, but I smile and tease before he can grouse. "If I didn't know better, Tadeusz, I'd think you were sick and hiding it from me."

"I'm not ailing, woman," he says gruffly. He glances at the three boys. "Forge won't keep itself lit. Get back in there."

Kaspar and Natan scuttle off, grinning like fools. Hardy spares another long look at Helena, who notices enough that her cheeks flush pinker. My eyes feel like they'll fall out with how much I'm catching in these quick moments. Children—growing up!

Thaddeus clears his throat. I wonder how much he's noticed, too, but all he says is practical. "Well, then. Helena. Your mother is to stay in bed a bit. Off to the kitchen with you."

"Tadeusz. She's just returned! She doesn't need to tend a meal right away," I say.

"She's under my roof again. She can work."

"I won't be staying long," she says easily, all breeze and fine manners, and I'm shocked at her tone. It's flippant and solid and concise.

"So! You're leaving again?" Thaddeus asks, looking more shocked than I feel.

"K—that is, I'm to live over at the Fawcetts. Their summer kitchen will be where I sew the latest fashions and fix the hats with ostrich feathers and spend my days, creating the most wonderful dresses anyone has seen in years!"

304

"A working girl!"

Helena just looks at him. I am suddenly, fiercely proud of her. She's become more than me. Stronger than me. How? When? I want to know everything of her journey, all that she's seen, and tell her what has happened in our small slice of the world, but there's no time, because she's holding her ground as she stares up at Thaddeus, and his frown gets darker by the second.

"A businesswoman. Same as mother."

Thaddeus stares at her, his mouth open under the wiry beard. I clear my throat, and shake my head at him. He has said herself she's getting older—old enough—and now he must swallow his words. Will he remember to do so? And he cannot argue with her on this—he is the one who told me I might be a mother and a tinsmith, a wife and a tradesman.

He cannot contradict himself so deeply. And I know he won't.

With painful slowness, he rotates on his heel and walks out. As soon as he's gone, Helena spins to me and carefully sets her baby brother back on the bed. Her eyes run along the dark blood still smearing the linen, but she ignores it with all the well-bred fineness of a city lady.

"Mother—I won't be far—"

"We know Kate Davies helped you," I say quickly. "You'll have to tell us all of it."

She's suddenly flush with anger, mercury-fast. "She said she wouldn't tell!"

"Never mind that. So you're truly fixing to take up the trade?" I wait to feel the disappointment, but it's buried under too much relief. If she means to live across town, I can manage it. I know I can. "You've said you might, that it's what you wanted to do. However did you manage to convince Kate to fund it?"

"I did more than that." She dashes out and comes back with a large box. Metallic clinking fills the room and she sets it on the floor next to the bed with gusto. "I got her to fund this!"

She opens up the box and the glittery tin fills the room with soft moonlight silver. I gasp and swing my legs over the side of the bed. I can feel blood weep between my legs and onto the rags as I do, but it's impossible to stay abed when I see the riches nestled in the sawdust.

"You ... did you go all the way to Dover for this?" I reach and cradle an ornate teapot handle, already tracing out a new pattern for a new kettle, one that Lara and Elaine and Sadie will ache to own ...

"I know you thought it foolishness," she starts, careful now with her words, and her eyes meek and low. "I know you don't want to keep changing things ... but you must, Mother! Or everything you have made for us will die. This is just one of many boxes—and we can get more if you need. I've made connections and know the right people in Chicago—you will be the finest tinsmith with the best offerings in the whole territory!"

My scarred fingers trail over the intricate lines, and then I reach for another and another until my lap spills with tin parts, all pressed and fanciful—things I could never make in my shop. Beautiful, modern, wonderful pieces, ready to be attached to the fine seams and long lines of so many other things—and I will have enough tinplate now that the trains are running. Likely my order is finally in.

Everything will be alright. Nothing will swallow me, or my family, or my shop.

I close my eyes and clutch the metal to me, and when I open them, Helena stands before me with clasped hands and a face full of hope.

"I … I hope it is enough."

"Enough?" The echo of the word tears at my heart. "You will always be enough, daughter."

"But I … went away. I was going to write the letter, I had even practiced what I'd write, but then I never left a note, and I just … left without word. And made you worry. And now I'm moving to Sadie's and won't be staying here. I just wanted to give you something … is it enough?"

I reach across the short distance and pull her hand to mine. "Well, then. So it is. It is generous and a very fine thing you have done for me."

She takes a deep breath. "Good! Good! Then I'll get the boys to help move the rest of the boxes into the tinshop. And I'll go help *Babcia*." She smiles, a bit nervous.

"Helena."

She pauses at the door and looks back at me, and I smile through the fog of fatigue suddenly swelling around me once again.

"I'm very proud of you, *córka*."

Her smile is wide and filled with excitement. She makes to leave, but then turns around again. "I have watched you all these years, Mother. You've suffered and tried and worked and failed and then tried again. I wanted to be strong like you, to build something like you did. Just with … less difficulty. A trade that will not push against me, or keep me outside society, as yours does. But I only have to look at you to know what to do, no matter how trying things might get."

She smiles again, and leaves me be, to nestle with a warmed heart and a deep, beautiful delight. It is so deep that it bites into the black hole of my spirit, tearing into it, and cracking into it, so the darkness is less, and likely will always be so.

The morning drifts to dinnertime, and the clatter of a plate and knife rouse me from my stupor. But it is not Berit or even Helena bringing my meal. It's Jane Kinney.

"Oh!" I yank my small shawl over my shoulders, though the heat of July keeps the rooms hot and close. "Where ... is the doctor here?"

Jane shakes her head. "He's been called out and I thought I might check on you first." She sets the plate on the other side of the bed, but her gaze lingers on Gerik and I reach for the bread and nod at her.

Carefully, with near reverence, she picks him up, her elbows sticking up in all the wrong places as she tries to fit him against her body.

"He won't break so easily, Jane," I say. "Just tuck him into your waist."

Her head comes up fast and her eyes widen, then she offers a small smile. "The doctor once told me the same thing when I was helping Alice and Mitch Brinkley with their first."

"He's right." I rip into the bread and realize how hungry I truly am as I do.

"Your Helena is back."

"She is." I don't know how much to say, or what is gossip, or what Helena would prefer I keep quiet. I've never been one for the gossip—usually I'm being told it without prompting as I work in the shop. I grasp for something—anything—and fall into something shared. "How ... how are things with the new sickness? The black measles? Is it bad?"

She sighs. "People are afraid." Gerik makes a small sound and she checks him nervously. Seeing him sleep on, she meets my eyes. "I'm afraid, too. Pat—Doctor Kinney has no notion on how to cure it, and the only thing is what Esth—" Her lips slam closed.

"There's nothing to be done?" I push away at the fear creeping back into my bones. I'd only just rid myself of worries—I do not want to invite more. "Well, then. We must hope he figures it out."

Jane's eyes widen, and she clutches Gerik a bit tighter, her eyes suddenly bright. He wakes with her squeeze and lets out a high whimper. I put the last of the bread on the plate and reach for him.

"He'll be hungry."

She stands and shoves her hands in the folds of her skirt, looking about at the bedding and not at my breast. "I ... you'll want to get out of these sheets today yet, Marie. Clean linen for everything. How is the bleeding?"

She's all medicine and nurse now, a far cry from the Boston widow who arrived in early 1881. Her eyes sweep over the room and land on my face.

"It's not terrible."

"More soup. Beer if you have it. Stay off your feet until the doctor can come and see you."

"I've never laid abed after a birth before," I say. "Feels strange to be so ... lazy."

"You've never delivered breech before either, have you?" she counters. "Best give yourself time to heal than have to start all over again later." Her arms flutter slightly.

"Besides, Flats Junction wouldn't be the same if you were to … be unwell."

She means *die*. I can see it fumble on the edge of her mouth. But the sincerity of her words hits me in the chest, where I feel raw and open to all emotions. My rough fingers play on the basketweave of Gerik's swaddle, plucking at the ball of cotton stuck on the edge of the hem. When I look up at her, she's watching me with such desperation, I blurt my first thoughts.

"What is it you want, Jane?"

I expect her to say she wants a child, but she hesitates only a moment before answering.

"I want to feel like I belong here."

My shoulders go soft and my bones feel liquid. It is a tender thing she offers, and I shake my head at her slightly. "We all want that."

"You have a place. Your family. Everyone does—even Kate." Bitterness and frustration lance her voice. "The doctor and I … we struggle every day to figure where we stand."

"Everyone here can likely remember the day they stepped into this town," I say. "Or their parents can do so. The one with the deepest roots is Kate herself. And even she frets on her place, I'd warrant."

Jane's cheekbones relax, and the tenseness drops out of her in waves. "Do you think? We all feel the same?"

"I'd wager." I slip my chemise down further and switch Gerik's suckling. Jane watches this time without fluster. She seems … more at ease, somehow.

As if my words are the right ones.

Well, then. That would be something. Perhaps I'm finally finding my own footing.

CHAPTER TWENTY

# *Kate*

*July 4, 1883*

Under my direction, the town square once again bursts with color and shouts, dogs and horses, children and skirts. The tables sag with goods, and the smells combine as spices, herbs, and juicy cooked sausages swirl into the bright summer air. Alice Brinkley moves over her cheese wheel to make room for the pot of Berit Salomon's dumplings.

"You're looking very well," I tell Alice, glancing down at the toddler in the sling around her torso. He's currently calm, but his eyes are wide. "Though you might have to tie a string on him when he's wanting to run."

"Oh, you're quite right, Kate! How do you know such things about children?" she asks, not even pausing to see how I take her comment. "And did you see, Elaine Warren actually baked this year!" She brims with the gossip, only to be interrupted when Sadie arrives.

"No, no, Toot Warren made the potato pies," Sadie says, tipping toward Alice. "Not Elaine. Apparently, they had a bet over which of them made it best, and had Trusty Willy do a pie contest at the Nail last week. The men voted Toot's."

"Well, that's no surprise," Alice says.

Sadie's mouth thins, and she glances at her own contribution. I wait for her to speak of her own pastries, but instead she lands on the tomato tarte. "Bess Jones used some of her fancy plants to make a design this year."

We marvel at the decorative pastry. If Bess has anything left to salvage, it's her tomatoes, and she did not hold back with the pink, purple, red, green, yellow and orange swirls on the top of her huge square dough, the recipe as old as her Austrian ancestry.

"Er … *cén áit? Where?*"

We all turn around, but John Brinkley isn't talking to us. He's struggling with a huge barrel of last year's pickles and speaking to his red-headed wife who is shepherding their four children, short the two who passed the other week from the black measles. They all wear the black armbands but seem determined to make a go of a good time.

Cora points John to the end of the second table and he sloshes off, brine leaking between the slats of the wood and soaking the entire front of his shirt and pants. Noticing Alice, Sadie and me, she shrugs, a small smile playing the corners of her mouth. "He's tryin' to learn th' Gaelic for me, don't mind th' poor man."

She hustles her youngest one off while the two oldest sneak off to join their friends playing with the leftover wheels Jarle Henderssen brought out.

Alice and Sadie turn back to the pies, but Sadie shakes her head as Cora follows John, "That pickle barrel is leaking so badly. Dag's work."

"You know old Orville does a fine job sometimes," Alice adds.

"He does floors and cabinets." Jane inserts herself into the conversation in her smooth Eastern accent, fluidly sliding her pies in line. "He built Doctor Kinney new shelves for his surgery."

"If you ask nicely, he can do a bucket with tighter seams, so I've been told," Alice says, shifting so Jane can join us.

Sadie smiles at the doctor's wife, but her eyes are tight in the corners, and she seems to run out of air, the lack of chatter stark and painful. She turns her back on Jane and pins Alice. "Don't say such things about Orville's buckets around Dag, he'll blow your ears off with curses," she says, finally giving in to the gossip.

"But his wife will scorch his food if she hears him." Alice laughs.

"Are David and Caroline coming into town in a month?" I ask Sadie. If Tom's brother comes in, he'll want ammunition, and I've plenty to spare now that Yves brought in extra yesterday. The sale will do me good, with the lost monies toward all my endeavors.

Sadie makes a face at mention of her brother-in-law. "Good heavens, likely. Unfortunately. Wanting to stay with us."

"You've room," Alice says, jiggling her baby.

"It's not that. It's Caroline and their brood. They haven't been properly teaching those children English, and they all run around shouting in that heathen language." Sadie speaks matter-of-factly against her adopted nieces and neph-ews, sniffing.

Nancy Ofsberger plants wide feet in front of our group. "Did you *know*, Danny Svendsen's low-life, gold-hunt-ing, no-good, brothel-owning brother just sent in a letter from California-way?" No one answers. "And it be a *fat* one! D'you suppose he's found gold? I say he's filtering dirty whore money through the ranch."

"Was the letter for Danny?"

"Old Oddvar."

Jane and Alice link arms as they walk with Nancy toward the lemonade, and I step back so I can speak with Sadie quietly.

"I've to speak with you," I say low and quick. Her tired eyes meet mine, and I realize how thin she has become in the months after losing her tiny daughter. I try not to stare and meet her gaze head on. "It's about your summer kitchen. I'd like to rent it."

The notion is unexpected and she cocks her head. "For what?"

"I've brought in heaps of silks and lace, brocades, satins and so many buttons you couldn't count them in a day," I say, watching her face slowly fill with wonderment and a hint of excitement. Sadie's always had a soft spot for beauty, and I rush. "Helena Salomon will be opening up a full dressmaker's shop, complete with new patterns from out east, and she needs a place to live and sew."

Sadie clasps both of my arms tightly with both hands. "Do you mean it, Kate?"

"Of course. It's all set, I've the dry goods at my place. We just need a spot to set up."

314

"The latest fashions! In my own backyard!" she breathes, and a tiny sparkle lights up her eyes. "Oh, Kate! You needn't pay Thomas and me any rent for such a thing—finally! A seamstress! Might she take my measurements first? Do you have any blue silk?"

I haven't even opened the boxes, but I nod anyway, and Sadie actually squeals in a girly way.

"Consider it done. She can start in tomorrow—oh! I must make sure it's clean! And we can fill up a mattress for now, for her, it'll be fine 'til Fall. Let me go find Thomas!"

She bustles off with more purpose to her step than I've seen in weeks, and I am relieved one thing has gone off without an ounce of trouble for once.

I pass by the refreshment table, where people dip into the barrel filled with sweetened water. A smaller bucket is supposed to have lemonade made by Trusty Willy's fruit press and a few of my expensive lemons, brought by Yves as well, though everyone thanks me for them, as they think the lemons are my especial treat. A small taste of it confirms it is only lightly sugared and spiked with a fair amount of whiskey. The warmth of the liquor tingles on my tongue.

Veronika Zalenski hobbles in on the arm of old Simon to deliver a beautiful dish of pudding, expected and admired by stately Marta Brinkley and wide Bianca Brewer, who says she can make a similar one.

"I would not be to tasting anything Bianca is making no matter how she is bragging of it," Veronika sniffs to Simon as she moves off, loud enough for Bianca to hear. "To see the many times she's to be cleaning that privy of the Main Inn, there is being no possible ways her hands are being clean."

*"Leck mich am Arsch! Kiss my ass!"* Bianca shouts, her giant bottom wiggling as she shakes her fist at Veronika's back. Horeb, Thunder, Lawrence Fawcett, and Bianca's own husband Robert all pause in passing to watch her hips jiggle.

Father Jonathon and Reverend Painter stand by the edge of the dessert table. Reverend Painter does not look as though he needs a single additional sweet to add to his girth, though on the other side of the table, Julie Bailey the farrier's wife is forcefully offering her fruit cakes to Father Jonathon, in the hope that he'll finally put on some weight.

Turning back around, I notice Wang Chen is in from his small farm, joining the other Chinese around the Yang family's huge soup cauldron, but staring appreciatively at me. I roll my eyes at him and snort. He barely comes up to my shoulder—but he apparently does not consider our height difference to be a trouble.

"Ten cents says Fortuna will nail Dell on the head before noon!" Horeb shouts from the shade of the General's porch as I head up the stairs.

"I got my money on Dell this year!" Alan Lampton yells back, shouldering the pig he's brought. Harriet Lindsey is on the other end of the iron stake, hoisting the cooked animal between her strong shoulder blades. Horeb takes the bait and yells down more expensive odds, but Alan refuses them and moves along.

"What about you, Kitty?" Horeb finds my eye as I cross the front of the General, and glints with glee, rubbing his hands together. "Care to take a bet on whether the owner of the Powdered Pig or the Powdered Rose is triumphant this year?"

Gilroy answers before I can. "Stupid bets."

"I ain't asked you your opinion, Gil," Horeb snaps, flicking his fingers at Gilroy's staunch bulk.

"Still stupid."

"It's good money!" Horeb argues, spinning in his creaking rocking chair.

I squint east across Main Street, where the prostitutes of the Powdered Rose this year string the windows with tattered satin sashes instead of their ribbons. The colors are mostly a garish pink and yellow and deep green which gives Dell Johnston an additional reason to rip down what he can reach any time he dashes past on the pretense of visiting Rusty at the livery. Dell's tall and wiry, and his drink-heavy gut doesn't seem to hinder his ability to get out of Fortuna's way. The madam of the Powdered Rose has had many issues with Dell since she first moved from Deadwood, not the first that he purposefully renamed his saloon after her establishment just to annoy her. Fortuna has never needed a strongman to guard her girls from what I can tell, mainly because for all her broad, buxom roundness she's fast with a skillet.

As I watch, Dell detaches from the shadow of the livery buttoning his fly and tears down a particularly low-slung strip of fabric from the brothel's upper-story window. Fortuna is waiting for him around the corner of the building, though, and a few of the men shout out a warning to Dell. Still, he misses his ear getting cracked open when Fortuna slips on a patch of mud.

Dell grabs her up about the waist, ignoring the flailing iron skillet and putting her right on her pearl-buttoned boots. For a moment longer than needed, he holds her close and tight against him, her soft giant bosom folding into his height and her arm drops slowly. There's a bright whistle from all the Brinkley brothers, and Dell smacks a wet one on her mouth, releases her, grins smartly at all the onlookers, and yanks another satin sash down around their heads. In the ensuing laughter and the coarse curses Fortuna yells at Dell's retreating back, I give in and chuckle slightly, allowing the worries to roll off my skin and out of the back of my neck.

Turning to Horeb, I challenge his bet. "Perhaps five cents on how long before Dell and Fortuna tie the knot?"

Horeb looks scandalized, but Gilroy leans forward. "Five on how long *and* which church."

"Oh, you won't bet on any of my ideas, but Kitty comes and you'll take a wager, is it?" Horeb rounds on Gilroy, his skinny back cracking as he twists.

"By the month or by the week?" Jarle Henderssen, the wheelwright, jumps in. "And if we keep to five cents?"

"No, no, ten on the pair of it—church and the month." Horeb dives back into the betting, and I wander away just as Jarle's father and grandfather meander over, and old George Ofsberger as well. It sounds as if it will be a popular wager. Feeling silly that I even engaged in such an idea, I sidle away. I've much to do today, and it's not just keeping the festivities on track.

Isaac Horowitz the shoemaker passes me and nods but gives Alan Lampton wide berth even in the fray of a town on full holiday. There are so many more people this year than last, given the number of homesteaders new in. I can't believe how much Flats Junction has grown.

Would Percy ... would Father be happy?

Would he think it my doing, or only, simply, happenstance?

The races are the same as always, except Moses wins everything he tries, even though it's the first year he rides the obstacle course. While he looks exotic and dark and dashing on his large animal, the other racers have blank faces as he takes each prize. This year, most of Danny's ranch hands don't enter. I see them under the shade of the crooked elm tree of the Post Office across the street watching Moses win, along with Patrick, who is already sweating under the collar. Hank sleeps over his food, but Noah and Manny swap horribly off-color jokes about Catholics as loud as possible, trying to get a rise out of Pat. Thunder, big and grizzled, actually laughs gruffly at one of the sallies, which surprises me until I notice the jug passing between hands. That the doctor is drinking rather early in the day does not truly shock me, though maybe he'll curb himself now that he is married.

Several of the army officers from Fort Randall cajole the local musicians to strike up some tunes well before dusk, and the unmistakable twang makes me spin mid-arranging of the next round of food. Someone has a jaw harp, and the song picks up amid cheers.

> Well I went to California in the year of seventy-six,
> When I landed there, I was in a ter'ble fix.
> Didn't have no money for vittles for to buy.
> And the only thing for me was to root hog or die.

The talk swirling around me turns to town gossip, speculation about certain Army individuals from Fort Randall, concerns about the year's crops, the lack of rain, the extra rabbits eating the spring plantings, and confusion about

319

the Chinese Exclusion Act. Speculation also wanders about Dell and Fortuna's earlier surprise kiss, Mary Brinkley-Andersen's large roses, and what Trusty Willy will likely order next from the East.

"Do you need a hand, as it were?"

I don't have to turn around to know who asks. "No."

Moses steps up next to me and moves the one empty board nearer the rest of the dinner spread. "There's to be more vittles coming, and the like?" he asks.

"Usually there's more once it gets full dark."

He surveys the makeshift tables, and nods, then half-turns and watches the dance, and I follow his stare. It's now in full swing, and I want to pretend I don't see Patrick and Jane dancing comfortably and close. I squint at them through the lantern lights. He is certainly enjoying the liquor, but he's not anywhere near as far gone as usual. The music seems to sink itself into the pebbles of our feet, skittering the stones and pulling me toward the floor, but I dig my heels into the earth and grit my teeth.

> *I once knew a maiden who lived on the plains,*
> *She helped me to herd cattle through slow, steady rains;*
> *She stayed with me through long roundup*
> *And drank with me from the poor bitter cup.*
> *She drank the red liquor that affects a man's soul,*
> *She was a fair lady, just white as the snow.*

The song, like most of them, has nothing to do with me, but I like to listen, just the same. I don't know if it's because I like this one, with the notion of a woman with such power, or because it is a good tune overall.

"Did you want to dance?"

My entire body freezes on the spot, and my hands feel tingly. A deep wrench in my gut makes me cough, and Moses clears his throat.

"I asked—"

"I heard you."

He stares at me, unreadable and solid, then sighs long and slow before picking his way back to the dance floor, pulling a jaw harp out of his pocket as he goes, and I realize he's the new player.

"Will the fireworks start soon?" Bern asks, slipping up to me and gazing up at the new, inky night sky.

"Yes." I glance over to the edge of Wagon Street, where the peddler is still gesturing to his wares. The fireworks are vital to the night's success. I'm so glad a peddler came through in time. It's not every year we have them.

"Mm." Bern's fingers find the lowest curve of my back, a gesture hidden by the shadows and dancing of lantern lights. The touch is protective and possessive at once. I stop moving, letting him choose the next path, wondering if he will finally do something more.

"Will you dance tonight?" I ask, unable to stand silent.

He does a good two-step and waltz. I know, for I've seen him do it. Bern ignores the question, and I overlook the twinge seeping into my stomach, settling deeper into the powdered, dry mud under my boots. Only one man has ever been brave enough to dance with me in public before tonight, and that man now holds Jane.

And I've denied the other.

The next song threads a needle in my heart, even though no one is singing it. It doesn't matter. I know the words.

*Remember the arrows he shot from his bow;*
*Remember your chiefs by his hatchet laid low;*
*Why so slow? Do you wait till I shrink from my pain?*
*No! The son of Alknomook shall never complain.*
*Remember the wood where in ambush we lay,*
*And the scalps which we bore from your nation away;*
*Now the flame rises fast, you exult in my pain,*
*But the son of Alknomook shall never complain.*

It is a taunt and a question. Moses opens his eyes as he moves to another verse, and they swallow the light. The melody rings around my head, but when his gaze narrows to me, I look away and note the peddler—someone new this year, thankfully, who goes by the name of Melvin Waters—is finally stacking the fireworks I've purchased along toward the rail tracks where the area is marked. It is a new location, and the wind is down. It will work just fine. I wonder where he'll park his wagon.

"Is it all the same?" Bern asks behind me, his voice low and hidden against the ruckus. "Everything you need will be safe?"

I nod once, but dread prickles along my skin. Maybe it's too much. Maybe I'm trying too hard. Things have settled far better than I expected. Helena's returned with the cloth, Sadie will let her set up shop, and suddenly I've Yves's business to manage, too. In a handful of days, I've managed to pull myself even higher, and more people will know I'm a reckonable force. Maybe it's enough, for now. Maybe it's worth the funds I've lost—to support Hardy as the blacksmith, to let Helena have her expense and Marie her tinshop wares. It will build Flats Junction, all of it, just as I say I wish. And I do mean it.

Maybe it truly will be a place for the maps. A city on the plains. A masterpiece.

Maybe it's all happening better than I'd planned ...

*Maybe ...*

I glance around and notice Widow Hawks standing on the edge of the oily lanterns, waiting for the fireworks. She is the woman I have pushed against beyond the defiance of my youth. She is everything I reject.

She is the reason I must remind everyone how much they need me, over and over and over. They'll never really forget, no matter what I do.

But to go to such lengths.

Biting my lip, I turn to speak to Bern, but he's not there, melted off into the night, and heat floods into my marrow and bone and skin. Am I too late to find him? What had he planned? I glance up and search for a shadow, a hint, but there's nothing.

Only blackness and starlight, and the threat of the fireworks.

With a strangely bumping heart, I climb up the General's stairs. I must be seen when they are off, as I am every year we have them. I slip behind Gil, Toot, Horeb, Rusty, and Dell. The old steps groan and sag as Fortuna marches up the stairs to join us. Dell's eyes are not on the fireworks but on the gigantic breadth of Fortuna's bosom. He makes room for her without thinking, and Horeb immediately stops watching for the fireworks in favor of the close view of Fortuna's cleavage. I sense movement next to me, but it is only Toot's skinny fingers brushing absently on Gil's back. He doesn't seem to notice.

And then rockets screech upward and explode, filling that night air with bright colors, to waves of cheers and clapping, whoops and hollers. Showers of sparks and tiny embers rain down like falling stars onto the structures and onlookers. A thickening cloak of smoke, flavored of burnt coal and rotten eggs, churns through the area, burning eyes and throats.

I stare hard at Melvin, watching his fumbling. Is he in the right place? He jumps and cowers with each boom and blow above, shoving dirty fingers into his ears. The brilliant colors in the sky blind us all, and the night is hazy and choking. I can no longer see the real stars themselves.

Some of the older Henderssen, Brinkley, and Zalenski children lie on their backs as their younger siblings run and dance around them. Everyone seems to be having a wonderful time.

I do this, every year.

They look to me to set up the festivities. I hold it in front of the General. I find the peddler and manage the prizes for the race.

And yet.

As I watch people around me enjoying each other, I feel cold and lonely. If I look down, I will see the crown of Moses's head, where he leans up against the porch, and I suppose I could lean into him the way he leans into the wood, but where would that put me? In the same place I am now, surely.

For a moment, I envy Helena Salomon and her escape from it all, however brief it was. *I gave her freedom.*

The shadows and lantern glows of all the homes and businesses shift again, and more shapes quiver on the edge of the smoke. It's Yves and the posse, participating as well as they might. Yves has spent the night bragging on how he's setting up shop, and most everyone looks more appalled and upset than happy about another store.

I wonder if he'll force people to buy from him? I wonder if he'll get angry and make them? Or if he'll get bored with sitting in one place and give up and finally go away.

Maybe I can help him with the last ...

I resolutely look up at the tiny mini fires raining from the heavens. I'll deal with him later. Maybe I can even ask Bern to ...

Under the heat of the smoke and the fluffy greyness of old ash, I sniff suspiciously, then turn my face to figure on the wind. Moses shuffles, his boots dragging in the ragged dirt by the General, and I glance down at him sharply. Does he smell it, now? Acid and wood and powder? My body tenses, as if debating if I should run or call out.

When I hear the first scream, it is much farther away from the General Store, and I jerk, pushing past the spectators on the porch, tearing past Moses, who tangles his fingers briefly in my skirts. Now that I am not under the porch's protection, the sizzle of the remaining fireworks drips on my shoulders, and I smell burning hair. Is it mine?

The shouts pick up. A wave of them, rolling forward.

"What is it?" I call out against the rising yells. Half the faces turn to me, strangely lit with soft flickering, and the lanterns and shadow make them all unfamiliar. The others are looking away, east, beyond the rows of darkened houses and old shacks and the long livery. Inside, the horses bicker against their enclosures, hemmed in and knowing it.

I glance up at my precious General Store, and the sight near stops my eyes and ears, even though I should not be surprised. It sears into my eyes, branded into my fiber.

The roof of the mercantile is lit, the blaze licking hungry and urgent and confident, picking up speed even as I watch.

My life is on fire.

It should be what I expect, but it is one thing to think of such a thought on its own, and another to see it in truth.

The call to action catches on my lips, and I cannot move. I am both fascinated and appalled at the fierceness of the fire, the surety of it. Within moments it has covered the main roof, and everyone under the porch flees. There is a blur of hats and skirts and suspenders, but not before one of the porch timbers crashes down. I cannot tell in the gloom if it catches anyone as they flee, but it is all happening so fast. Too fast. Every fiber and tendon within me stretches, pulling tight and sticking. I am rooted just as power seems to speed through my limbs.

They must help. They must save me. They must know I am the lifeblood of this town!

Finally my eyes and ears begin to work again, and I hear the calls of my neighbors and the town folk separate, turning into two voices, and I cannot understand it. Why are some of them ignoring this?

Pain stabs my stomach, and I spin, knowing I look for Patrick, expecting to see him arrive to help me and mine. He is always here, always dependable. Surely nothing could be as shocking as this—

When I see the doctor's dark head bobbing at the head of a small group tearing away from the General Store, I think if I were a weeping woman, I might cry.

He is leaving me? Now? How dare he! It's Jane's doing, surely. She might say I don't need the help, that I—

All thought flees again when I see the ball of orange growing beyond Sadie and Tom's place, and I know Patrick is not leaving me on his own accord. His is mind is on his books and his laboratory.

The General is not the only thing on fire.

CHAPTER TWENTY-ONE

# *Jane*

*July 4, 1883*

I run.

Run and run and run.

I am heedless of the smoke that plumes about the air, forgetting the ball of my hidden belly and my layers of skirts. There is a roaring ahead and behind us. Patrick leads the group, shouting at everyone, though I cannot tell what he says. The smell is first and then the screams. Is it women? Horses? Children? What is that keening?

Harriet Lindsey yanks at my arm, near tripping me. "Jane! We have to save the General!"

"No! Our house, too!" I shout, my voice sounding rough against the smoke.

"What?" The pale half of her face in fire glow looks appalled. "Is it spreading?"

"I don't—" I'm ripped from her as another group of men stampede past, heading toward the General with buckets of sand and water. When they clear the way, I round the corner of Sadie's house and stop short.

Our house is not completely on fire, but the entire porch is covered in brilliant, hot white yellow of the flames curling up from the porch. It is impossible. What is the meaning of this? Why only our house? How? Why?

I dash around the small crowd in the front of our place, and grab the smaller bucket of old laundry water from earlier in the day from the yard, coughing as I go. A chunk of the water pours over my bodice and down my skirt, skating along the dust of the hard-packed garden trail. Four men, black shadows and blurs, skid past me on the way to our well out back, shouting hoarsely.

My thoughts whirl. Which way did Patrick go? Who is even here?

My heart chokes me.

Or is it the smoke?

Where do I go first?

The house—the house—*our house!*

Patrick is suddenly behind me pulling water up from the well with the townsfolk who care to help, but the dark figure at the porch is not who I expect at all. Mrs. Molhurst, is here too, dumping the contents of her dinner pot and her tea kettle on the fire.

Her bit of water isn't nearly enough, and the fire is insidious, as if it is able to burst completely back to life by itself from the half-hidden coals and edges of the wood. Already most of the porch is eaten away and the blaze reaches for the door with hungry hands. Black chunks of sooty logs fall. The lab and the office are closest to the door, and are filled with paper and books, chemicals and acid. It will go up in a boom if the fire goes much further! I try to see if there are flickering lights from the depths of the house, but the smoke is blinding and grey.

Fire . . . fire! *Fire!*

I can feel the blaze, an orange ball, a bonfire of horrible, terrible proportions, rising up and scorching my skin. It is eating the store, eating our home, eating the livelihood of Kate, searing Flats Junction. It's impossible to think in a linear fashion, and my head aches with the pummeling fear.

We must save the house!

And the General ...

Blindly, feeling wooden and burning myself, I step forward and try to pour the contents of the washbin into the heat, but the basin is unwieldy and I stumble and it slips. Mrs. Molhurst is next to me at once, her skinny arms as strong as my own youthful ones, and together we pull and heave the soapy water onto the house, getting a good amount on the fire.

But not all of it.

"Refill!" she screeches—to me or to everyone—then falls to her knees for fists of dirt from the road, which she starts to fling wildly at the beams. Each pale, frivolous handful seems to do nothing at all, though I know inherently she means to smother the fire.

Should I help her? Go for more water? Should I—

Whirling around, I nearly collide with Patrick, Tommy Winters, Rusty Plackett, and Tim Bailey, who barely notice that they cover Mrs. Molhurst and me with more well water as they swerve around. As they pour the contents of the big laundry tub on the porch, Tommy's foot sinks through the stoop heavily as he steps forward, and Rusty trips as they heave, his face sliding into contact with red-hot and angry wood coals. His scream careens through my mind, a knife tearing down my backbone. Patrick whirls, his eyes wild, and land on me. I shiver, but my hands are already in motion, the wet fabric of my skirts raising to Rusty's face.

He is rocking, moaning, and I am too short to reach the burns. Pulling on my waistband blindly, I tear down the outer garment, bunching it, and then cramming it onto his blistering cheek and pointing to the other side of the street.

"Hold that there! And get out of the way!" I command, but my voice is hoarse and tickles the back of my tongue. Rusty holds the calico at once, his eyes watering and his breathing shallow. He needs more water—his face should be submerged as much as possible.

My thoughts spin and I grab the small washbin, running back again toward the well, tripping over my skirts and falling on my knee into the squash patch. One of the fruits smashes under me, and somehow even with the grey ash coating my mouth, I can still smell the quick green of the zucchini.

Patrick and Tommy are yanking up more water, their hands raw against the sodden rope of the well bucket.

Patrick pours part of the well bucket's contents into my smaller bin and the rest in the huge wash tub. It's only half-full, but Tim and Tommy pull it up between them and head back to the front yard. I follow, behind them, and Patrick races ahead of us with the well bucket now full of dirt from the garden. Mrs. Molhurst hasn't stopped throwing fists of earth at the steps and Rusty has sat in the middle of the road, shocked and pale amid the roar of orange and red and the dust of smoke in the heavens.

"Damned if this blaze is going to get anywhere else but here," Mrs. Molhurst says tightly as I brush past her.

*Where is Esther?*

The tears streaming down my face have more to do with the acrid heat than sorrow or pain. I run my smaller bin to Rusty and shove his face down into it.

"Hold your face on the water," I tell him. "Keep it submerged as much as you might." As I brush his hair back, my eyes are stuck on the flaming, impossible torch that has become the General. It lights the whole town with an unnatural, eerie rose-red, splashing cherry and gold on the vulnerable planks of each building around it.

A shout goes up—the roof of the post office next to the store has caught—but by now there are enough people streaming around the bigger blaze and throwing chunks of dirt and whatever water is on hand that the small fire snuffs out quickly. Nancy's stout figure stands on the edge of the post's property, and by the way her head is thrown back, I can imagine her shouts and cusses.

But our house. Is our house safe?

*Let it be safe …*

There is a muddy river from the center of the porch where the water hits the piles of dirt that Mrs. Molhurst has piled on the smoldering chunks of wood. Tommy, Patrick, and Tim are wheezing, the big wash tub overturned at their feet, the leather of their boots fuzzy with wetness. The fire is hardly sizzling, and suddenly Patrick jumps up to the embers. A cry catches on my lips. What in all of damnation is he doing?

His dark head bobs out mere moments later, his doctor's satchel swinging from his bunchy fingers. *Of course ...*

When Patrick bends to see Rusty's face, I have to look away. The sores are already bubbled and wide. It looks appalling.

"Well, now, you'll certainly be dashin' after this with some manly scars," Patrick says mildly, turning Rusty's cheek into the glow of the store's blaze. "Could be worse, though."

Tim and Tommy exit our home, where they've been checking for sparks. One flinches, the other blanches, and then they heave a breath.

"Doc—we'll go off to help the General," Tommy says, his flamboyant moustache singed on the edges now, but his eyes are bright with action. Tim is already on his way, and I suddenly wonder where his Julie is at, and their children. Safe, I hope.

"Good, good," Patrick says. "I'll be there shortly myself."

The doctor gets Rusty to his feet and slings the man's arm around his shoulders. "I'll take him home." He juts his chin at the livery across East Avenue. "Then ..." His eyes sweep over the black of our porch, and relief drops into me slowly.

The house is, for the most part, relatively unharmed. But now what?

"You go on, Doc, to the General. Be sure no one's hurt," Mrs. Molhurst says tightly. "I'll watch this so it doesn't start up again." Her long, knobby hands curl into fist on her hips and she glares at the ruin of our porch as if daring it to reignite.

Patrick nods, and I catch his eye, gleaming bright and blue. Oddly, he is in his element in the catastrophe, where I feel like my insides are pulled out and left to bleed. How can he be so calm and so in control? I suppose I should continue to offer some semblance of being a proper doctor's wife, and be in control of something, too.

"I'll grab your saddlebags," I offer as he starts off. "Is the inside floor sound enough?"

"Be careful," he instructs over his shoulder.

I gingerly walk around to the kitchen, inching through it to the hall and instinctively crouch when I pass under the surgery door lintel. The heat of the wood on the far wall and on the floor eats through the soles of my shoes, making the bottom of my feet itch. Patrick's saddlebags are in his surgery, filled with extra bandages and speculas. They are heavy and my arms quake briefly as I hoist them.

When I exit, Mrs. Molhurst is still standing in the yard, her eyes narrowed in her already narrow face, as if daring the flames to start back up again.

"Mrs. Molhurst. How can I thank you? Your help—"

She jerks her arm out, dismissing me. "Well, I didn't want this coming toward *my* place."

My feet feel as though they are wearing straight lasts that are new. I can't walk straight, and the smoke closer to the General makes it nearly impossible to breathe properly. My sodden skirts slap and chafe against my legs, and I suddenly realize Rusty still has my overskirt and I'm heading into the fray in my petticoats.

But this is no time to worry on properness. The relief of saving our house is overshadowed once again by the shock of the yellow fire eating at the General. The front of the store is gone, the porch a ruin, the glass windows shattered, and the roof twinkling with little tiny embers.

Dear God. How will Kate manage?

It feels like everyone in Flats Junction is in the street. Four hundred bodies—men, women, children and even dogs—cram into the space between the General and the train depot, but wide berth is given to the men and women fighting the fire. Four lines of people run haphazard dashes between wells, handing buckets to and fro with a speed that is both surprising and reassuring.

The fire on our porch is nothing compared to this. We were a small candle compared to the blaze here. My heart is thumping, then plummeting, burying into my stomach, pulpy and tight. I feel sick and light-headed and stop walking so I don't fall.

I search the crowd for Patrick, but night is on hand completely and the moon cannot pierce the fog of ash and the blinding glow of molten coals. Each body is a shadow, a black, rustling, muttering piece of the crowd. At the edge of the crowd, watching silently on their horses, are the figures of Yves's posse, motionless, a fence against the yawning distance of the land beyond. I squint, and only count six people—where is the seventh?

Words clatter across my brain. They are an echo, a shout, a thunder.

*What do we do? Who do we blame?*

It is the same, all over again: fire in the night, pointed fingers, the anger and hidden hate and violence. I push a hand into my chest where my heart won't stop pounding.

The blaze is beaten back, hammered and smothered and heckled. The clump of hard hooves shakes the ground about me, bouncing small pebbles. Once again the Brinkley men arrive with a wagon of sod and sand and animal dung.

Shovels are brought, and at least one person cries out from being accidentally whacked as people scramble to find tools to help. Where is Patrick? I cannot find him, and the saddlebags wear against my shoulders, rubbing against the soft flesh on the back of my neck.

Who would want to ruin Kate so soundly?

I cannot stop the refrain, the questions, the aching curiosity.

*Who—how—why?*

I push my way through the bodies, silhouetted by the General's flames, barely recognizing faces as I go, though I see them just the same: Clara Henderssen and Nels on his crutch, several of their children careening through the crowd; Anette and her brood; a flash of Berit's white face. There is Sadie, her cheeks washed in tears, and the hard-faced Painters. Father Jonathon is praying along the edge of the fray. Franklin—suddenly like a whole man again, his broad face filled with satisfaction—hustles together all the extra spare buckets and forms more lines of people.

"Watch it! The Chinamen are comin' 'round, there!" Mikey O'Donnell shouts.

I stop and step aside when Peng and Yan Yang, out of breath and sweaty, shuffle by carrying their entire cauldron of soup swaying between two wooden poles. Their wives chase them, scolding or encouraging, I have no idea. When they try to pour it, a hulking man picks up the base with ease and raises the massive iron piece into the air and dumps the soup onto the coals. The figure straightens and the fire glints against lighter hair and a beardless face. One of the posse …? I turn and keep looking for Patrick, uncertain if I should start healing burns and scrapes myself without him.

Most of the menfolk are near the blackening skeleton of the General's front porch. Jacob Zalenski and Moses, young Henry Brinkley, and Trusty Willy, Dell, and even Nancy. There is young Alek Zalenski hauling more dirt, and even all four Wu men help. One of the Brinkley brothers backs away, his clothes smoldering, and nearly steps on my feet. I jump back, and Nancy screams as her dress starts on fire. David Fawcett dumps water on her and she steams at once. Isaac Horowitz beats the building with a huge piece of leather from his cobblery, while old Morten has decided to handle the blaze by pissing in a half-drunken stupor on a corner of the building.

Even though I am sure my heart has stopped working, and I'm falling through a crack in the earth, I fist my skirts and move amid the crackling heat and swarming people, dread and denial twinning in my stomach.

And then I finally see the figures crouched on the edge of the swathe of bodies, hunkered over the prone forms laid out on the ground next to The Powdered Rose across the street.

A small crowd huddles next to the bodies—at least a half-dozen are prone, most moaning and tossing. Two sit up, holding heads and arms. One little girl is crying horrible and hard, her eyes purple in the greasy light of the fire. Next to Thomas Fawcett is old Gilroy, and I am not sure what ails him until a deep cough runs through the stout, wide body. And there are others, too. A redhead I know only as Lugh, Noah Burns, and Jorge Andersen. I heave a deep breath and tap a shoulder.

"Where's the doctor?"

No one answers me. Horeb and Danny Svendsen push past, carrying another between them—this time it's Dag, his eyes bloodshot and his chest heaving with smoke.

"Another one!" Danny rasps loudly, and I finally see my husband as he stands, nods at the new arrival but heads to Tom Fawcett's side instead.

I wrestle to where Patrick pours whiskey straight on his scalpel and pull out bandages for him, careful to put them on the leather of the saddle instead of the ground. My foot shifts and another groan meets it. I glance over my shoulder and try to keep in my dinner.

Kaspar Salomon lays on his side, his face like whitewash and his right arm swollen and mottled black and yellow. The sourness of bile pinches my cheeks, but I turn back to Patrick.

"So many."

"They'll all likely be fine," he says. "It's mostly inhalin' a bit of smoke."

"But—have you seen Kaspar Salomon's—"

He nods. "A bad burn—a timber fell on his arm. It could have been worse. He's not burned clear to the bone." Sweat pours in rivers down his cheeks and soaking his collar, and he wordlessly reaches for the bandages I've prepared and shines his scalpel on it.

"If Sadie comes over, tell her to stay clear. I mean it!" he tells me tensely. "I've got to look on Tom now or it'll be too late."

He peels away the hair on Tom's head, revealing a gash the length of a finger and it's bleeding outrageously.

As the flames devouring the General disappear, more lanterns and lamps come out so the glow transfers from blazing to dim, and the punctured, flickering small flames are spots compared to the yellow and gold and red burned into my eyes.

"Jesus, Mary, and Joseph!" Patrick swears. "I can't see a thing. Jane—find me—"

"Here you go, Doc Kinney."

A lantern swings over us with the doors open and blasts the ground with ochre. It's Berit, and she puts the lantern as close to Tom Fawcett's head as she can, though I can hear the gag she barely holds back.

"Is it bad?" she mutters. "Should I find Sadie?"

"Leave her be. Dammit—Jane." His fingers are crusted in blood and the ground next to him is as well. It is soaking into his pants and the dust is black with it.

"You gonna cut off his ear, doc?" someone drawls.

"Shut off it, Manny, can't you see the man's working?"

"Doc Kinney—Doc—please—my Tom—"

"Well at least you don't need an ear to count money."

"He ain't cutting off his ear."

"Sadie, come here to me and Jacob, we'll keep you near, come here."

"Is he dead?"

The words blend together as I count the moments between breaths as I hold Tom's head completely still between my knees, trying to think only scientific thoughts as Patrick's fingers quickly move across the skin, cleaning it with the last bit of the iodine we'd kept for emergencies, just like this one.

A shadow crosses, and I look up. Kate is here, walking among the injured, her face tight and hard and smooth. As I gaze out at the sorry group, I realize Hardy, the blacksmith's apprentice, moves along the line, offering water as if nothing unusual.

"Jane! I need you to hold Tom's wound together so I can stitch. The bone appears completely solid."

"Of course, Patrick." I have no idea what he means, but I put my fingers on Tom's skin and smash the two sides of his wound closed, hardly able to look at what I'm doing. But that was part of the deal—coming here—and I mustn't get prim now. I had said I wanted to be a nurse.

Patrick has the presence of mind to look up blindly. "Sadie—where's Sadie?"

"I'm here—here I am! I'm right here! Tom!" She pushes through, past Anette and Jacob and goes to Tom's other side, fairly shoving Gilroy out of the way. Gilroy himself is looking managed, Toot's skinny arms wrapped around his neck. He sits a few inches further back, but watches Patrick as avidly as the rest.

"So Tom'll be alright, Sadie," Patrick says calmly. His voice is clear and bouncing, even in the ebb and flow of the chaos around the town square.

"You can save him?" It's Kate, surprisingly, who asks. She stares at Patrick's hands as he prepares the thread.

Patrick doesn't waver. "He'll have a bad headache tomorrow, but he'll live and be right as rain in a few weeks."

"You shaved off half his head!" Sadie says belatedly.

"His hair," Patrick corrects.

"Could've been his ear, Sadie," someone guffaws.

"Or his head. He didn't chop off his head."

"Doc ain't chopping of heads, so. That's plain stupid, Jim."

Sadie croons to Tom, though he obviously cannot hear her. And Patrick, bracing and calm as always, starts to explain his process slowly and firmly. At first I think it is for Tom, but then I realize it is for Sadie, and for everyone else in Flats Junction slowly inching forward to watch and listen. Perhaps some more good will come of this.

Perhaps it will help.

Perhaps they will listen, when he speaks to them of surgeries and medicine, how to heal and how to live.

Perhaps they will see he has a skill, and a care, and is only here to save them.

As he once saved me.

"And then you want to tie it, like so, so the scar is not very thick and the hair will grow back as nicely as possible. And the bleedin' out has kept him from havin' too big a bump. See how the skin is swollen, but there's no egg? He'll be feelin' this one, as though he'd had a day of whiskey on an empty belly."

"Just like you at the whiskey, eh, doc?" Nels calls out, but he's teasing, and several people start to laugh. The tension sweeps away from everyone as a group, even though my nerves are tingling and my fingers are sticky with Tom's blood.

"Like that," Patrick agrees amiably, and there's another rumble of approval at his self-deprecation.

I can't tell now if the mood is lightened or if people are venting to their personal thoughts on Doctor Kinney.

All I know is I am in the thick of it, bound to him and the opinions of everyone I live with, whether they be good or bad.

# CHAPTER TWENTY-TWO

## *Kate*

*July 4, 1883*

Yves and his posse mill about the edges of the town, stalking, waiting, shifting. Their presence is both power and menace. I wonder if Yves thinks I'm worthless now, or if he will understand how necessary I am when the town rallies behind me. They must, of course, or I'm ruined.

And so would be Flats Junction.

"Anyone know who started the fire?" Old Henry Brinkley, limping on swollen feet, pushes through his sons, leaning on his wife Susan. He fills his chest with air and bellows the question louder.

I look around at the wide eyes and raised eyebrows, trying to read the lines across foreheads without looking obvious. What is everyone thinking? Are they worried about the General? About their goods? About me?

I cannot stop the questions rattling in my head tonight. They suffocate me.

No one seems to notice the battles under my eyelids and inside my mind. Instead, the focus is either on the doctor's hands or Old Henry's drawl.

"Who started the fire? How's about *what*? Them damn firecrackers was raining on ev'rything!" Tim Bailey yells out. "Kate shouldn't bring them no more!"

"They weren't hot enough to start a blaze," Alan Lampton says.

"Sure they was. They was fire, ain't they?"

"Not as far as the doc's place. You tellin' me to believe the fireworks reached so far? That's plumb stupid to think so," Lara says, her vocals overpowering all.

"We need to think on whether it was arson, too." Old Henry breaks in, his deep voice ringing like a bell from the bull-like chest and overriding the speculation. I feel myself shrink inside my own skin. "Question is, what really happened?" He glances at me briefly, the usual blue twinkle in his glance gone completely.

I try to arrange my face to be bland and straight and calm but doing so requires me to square my shoulders and look defiant, and that stance seems beyond me in this minute.

"My Mikey and I cannot afford some arsonist loose in town. Our lumberyard is vulnerable!" Lara shouts, her eyes bulging as big as her bosom.

Elaine pushes herself to the front. "And I'll be damned if I lose the Golden Nail!"

"And the Powdered Rose!" Fortuna calls. "Where would my girls and I go?"

"Top of the Prime Inn!" someone yells.

342

"You shut your face, Dell!" Fortuna turns purple.

"I'm right here, woman," Dell says, directly behind her. "And I stand with her." He inclines his head at Fortuna. "No way am I livin' in a town with an arsonist. I'd as soon as head somewhere else."

"Well, *some*body did it! Them fireworks ain't touchin' both the General and the damn doc's place!"

My heart is lead. I feel Old Henry's eyes flicker to me over and over.

What do I say? How do I stop them from overthinking this?

Why ... why did the doctor's house have to be part of this? It ruins everything ...

"What about that Moses feller? The big black 'un," Tate O'Brian drawls, then hiccups before swinging back a small crock. The raw whiskey drips down the side of his chin as he pulls it down. "He ain't even 'round helpin'!"

"I'm right here, and I was helping, as it were." Moses steps from the crowd, looking as if he'd been inside the fire for all the soot covering him.

"*You* ain't helpin' neither, Tate!" Hank Martin says, then recedes under his hat, looking shocked he actually spoke out against one of the older Svendsen cowboys.

Tate aims the side of the clay whiskey jug at Hank's head but the arc goes wild and Tate ends up off balance, careening into Old Henry, who staggers, stepping on Susan's skirt and Thaddeus's ankle. Thaddeus grunts and pushes Tate back, then folds his arms and glares.

Old Thunder grabs Hank and Tate by the collar as they swing at each other and shakes them hard. They wither, shooting daggers at everyone.

"Still say it's trouble," Tate mutters loudly. "Next time might be the bunkhouse."

"Yeah!" Noah shouts. "We cowboys could be dead next!"

"I don't want anyone killing my babies! I have already lost Tom!"

"Tom ain't dead, Sadie."

"Shut-up Rusty! What do you know about having a family, you brainless, piss-poor—"

"I still say we find what done it!"

Old Henry pulls himself up again and Susan takes his arm more firmly around hers. He nods at her, the steel-colored head straightening to find the gaze of many. There's a mutter and a grumble, and Old Henry turns to me.

This attention. It is what I wanted, to be this needed. To have this voice.

But now that it is my turn, I struggle to find it.

"If it was the fireworks, we can't go lynching a man," Old Henry says severely. "But with the two separate fires, and the others in years before … we have to believe it's something more."

"The fire hurts everyone." It's my voice, and Old Henry and Susan turn as one at the sound of it. I clear it. "Without the General Store, Flats Junction dies. No one should have to leave and start over. We have lives here. It must be rebuilt."

Old Henry's face is stern but speculative, and I feel odd for speaking so boldly in public.

I don't know if my voice matters.

"It's always fire with these damn Indians!" Tate spits.

I wonder if he means to lump me with Widow Hawks, and the memory of her house going up in flames. *Where is*

344

*she?* Does he link the two fires? Will anyone else? Fear clings to the edges of my stomach like sour wine, and I clear my throat. "Whoever—whatever—the cause of the fire, I thank everyone for their help to keep it from spreading."

"But what happens next time, when it's more houses?" It's a yell from the back.

"Or the lumberyard!"

"Or my saloon!"

"I'll head to Injun land afore I let my post office burn down around me!"

"Then zee ... mayor ... should hang somebody." Yves takes a place next to me, standing so close it makes me shudder despite the hot July night. Behind him, the rest of his gang hunkers closer, looming, blocking. "But if there is not really a mayor, I can do zee work."

I'd take a step away from his nearness, but it'll anger him, and I am rapidly losing the thread of the chatter. My schemes balance on the edge of a hatchet.

"Old Henry is our acting mayor," I say loudly, and Yves glares at me. I can only hope I'm safe enough in the eyes of the town. "Or—we listen to him."

Old Henry's gaze darts between me, Yves, the gang and all of Flats Junction. "I've never been elected, Kate," he says slowly, looking worried. "I shouldn't act as sheriff, too."

"So we need a lawman?" Yves sounds even more gleeful.

"We only need to find who did this," I insist, then bite my tongue when Old Henry looks even more upset.

"Then you know it's arson?" he asks, and his voice carries enough that everyone hushes.

I'm caught.

All the eyes bore into my forehead, grazing over the inches of my face, my hair, my clothes. I feel stung and branded with their expectations. They think I know.

They will ... will they believe me, no matter what I say?

Is my power in this town strong enough for that?

I cannot believe it.

"It was the firecrackers, I'm a-telling you all!" Horeb calls out, but no one is listening.

"Arson, then, Kate?" Old Henry leans in toward me as the talk filters the heavy air, and his voice goes soft and low and deep. "You do want justice?"

I close my eyes, and then nod. Once.

It is enough. The instant muted uproar is only tempered by the shock.

The power of it surges through my veins and pours into my fingers. It makes them tremble, rocketing against my thigh.

"Arson!" The word filters through the crowd, gaining momentum as it races. "We're never safe!"

"Someone will have to answer for it!" Old Henry juts his chin toward Kaspar, where Thaddeus now kneels, staring at the extensive burn on his son's arm.

"Without the General," Henry continues, relentless, "folks'll have to work with Yves or David Fawcett to bring in supplies from Vermillion and Yankton for a bit, and no one will like it. And it'll be pricy. Can't have that during the winter, and when the trains don't come in ... or the rails break ..."

"I know all this!" I feel frantic and worried, uncertain. I had no idea I'd be cornered so fast, and so publicly. "It will be fine. I'll keep supplies in town!"

"I'll be doing zat," Yves says, looking particularly smug. "I have been doing just zee ting for Miss Kate."

"And how exactly is using Yves Gardnier going to help us all?" Joe Greenman asks, coming up behind the large Brinkley clan with a glance to his father and Toot on the ground.

I look for a rock in the middle of the chaos, but find none. Patrick has his head down, and Jane seems harried. Once, she meets my eyes and there is a blackness in them that sticks in my throat. And then I remember the other fire, the one that burned my mother's house to the ground. The one that drove the wedge between Patrick and me ...

The unending smoke continues to overwhelm everything else; my thoughts, my vision, my ears, my tongue ... my life.

"Yves has ... proven himself to be trustworthy." The compliment is like acid on the insides of my cheeks, tight and bitter and stinging. "He's helped me when the rails break."

"I heard it's only the rails 'round here. Maybe someone is breaking the rails deliberate like." Mikey O'Donnell says pointedly. "But he's bringin' you supplies by wagon and the prices keep going up." Grumbles of agreement bubble across the gathering. Mikey raises his voice. "I—we don't need my lumber any more expensive than it is. I say no to Yves and yes to finding this damn arsonist!"

"You are saying zat we can be so powerful, as you say, zat zee rails are so soft?" Yves scoffs, and a mist of spittle glues itself to my exposed forearms.

"Soft my ass," Mikey says as he bristles, his heavy shoulders heaving and people move away to give him space. "I got that in a letter from my brother-in-law who's a

Territorial Marshall out of Westreville. In fact, he's supposed to be through here in the next coupla days. You can ask him."

Matthias shifts slightly. I want to laugh. Is the posse protecting me? Glancing up at the charred frame of the General's storefront, I feel less protected than I've ever been.

"Yves is setting up a store—you'll shop there until the General is rebuilt! Everything will be fine!"

There. Let them see the alternative.

Yves or me.

They'll come crawling back. They'll build my store.

And Yves himself is too caught up on the idea of legitimacy. He turns to me, grinning so wide I can see his black molars. "So! You are true! It is like we are zee partners for good!"

I open my mouth to deny it, but Old Henry barges in. "Then who is to blame for this?" He spins his wrist behind us at the black porch of the General. "It's too many fires, and no one will be safe until we figure this out!" He glances at me, and then at Yves, and pulls himself up, slowly. "It's my job to see the town safe."

"You all act like the law don't apply." Trusty Willy shouts. "Maybe Yves and his boys—and girls—started this!"

Yves turns to ice next to me.

"Naw—it's them outsiders. Ever since more's been settlin' in, we're getting all the types, even the bad kind."

"*Who* is bad kind?" Wang Chen shouts. He folds his arms as the entirety of the Chinese townfolk gather behind him. They are not many, but they bristle with long-hidden frustration, bubbling with it. Boiling. "Not us! You kill the bad man, and we will help!"

"It was the Injuns!"

"Aw, they ain't even here!"

"The Horowitz's!"

"Damnit, Isaac's too damn old to go runnin' startin' fires! 'Sides, I like his shoes!"

"It's fires and diseases all year—maybe it's this town what's cursed! Someone's tryin' to tell us to git the hell out!"

I suddenly feel like a spider who has forgotten how to spin, and instead finds itself tangled at the very center of the web, unable to be free. My breath is bound. It squeezes itself around my chest, so every time I inhale, it stutters through my bones, catching on my ribs, and sticking under them. I can't seem to grasp at my own plans. They fall around me in pieces, suddenly unclear and unwieldy.

"I still say we find the bugger what did this and make him pay! Tonight!" Franklin shouts.

My tongue is dry and stuck to my teeth and it feels like they bleed when I raise my voice to a shout. "The arsonist—should pay!" I say.

*Who? Who is it? Who pays?*

The words hit me like rocks, and I feel buried.

"We'll kill 'em! All!"

"Who was it? Anyone see anything?"

"Could 'ave been you, Rob Brewer! I didn't see you nowhere—"

"I was 'round back!"

"Doin' what!? Startin' fires?"

"Kissin' my wife!"

"Kissing?" Bianca hoots. "He was up my skirts and—"

"It could have been you, Trusty Willy, tryin' to gain—"

"Could've been any—"

"I ain't stayin' in no town with a fire-bug!"

"No, me neither!"

"I say we have a militia! Guard everythin' til we find the fucker—"

"Start hangin' til someone talks!"

"What the hell plan is that! I 'spose it's *you*, Joe Green-man, what's the arsonist then?"

"Someone get some rope!"

"Old Henry! Hold court! Right now! Every manfolk what looks shifty goes on trial!"

The words swell and crest, and swell again.

*They're going to kill! They're going to leave!* I will preside over a ghost town! Everything I've built, all the plans and the figuring and hopes—everything I need to … The fear and anger swirls inside my chest. It grows hotter and fiercer as everyone eyes the other, as talk swirls and a surge of anger near flattens me.

And around my own fury grows the black wall of hate, growing and tipped with red, whipped to frenzy by the words of each man and woman screaming for blood.

I'm aware of my hopes and plans, of my failings, and the knife at Yves's hip, the weight of hundreds of eyes, and the guilt of all those injured, like young Kaspar.

It went out of hand, so fast. Too fast.

No one was supposed to get injured.

And the doctor's house was never part of the plan.

I open my eyes and feel my finger rise, and point.

Straight toward the passel of cowboys, straight to Moses.

Straight beyond.

Where Bern stands, soot-weary and sweating, his hair stuck to his ears and his leathers covered in charred wood.

Everyone turns as one to look at him, and I can feel the bloodlust rise within the bones of every hot-blooded person in Flats Junction. The heat of it is stronger than the fire, hotter than the summer.

It is the fury of loss.

With a muted roar, drunken slurs, and guttural shouts, there's a grab and grasp at Bern before he can even make a sound. I want to turn away, but it would only make me appear weak again, and I cannot show that I feel any remorse.

Even if I feel it.

Even if I know I'll likely never have a man in my bed again, for all he never liked it, that he came to me out of spite and disdain and disgust.

Even if I know he is not the only one to blame.

It happens so fast, then, that I could not stop the tide if I tried.

It's a drag and a scream, a whisper of rope and a creak of wood. It's the snaggle of a knot and the boom of a deep voice to hoist it.

It's the hate and the fear and the relief of blame, all rolled together, mashed with whiskey and dance, fire and death.

It is my legacy, if I believed I had the ability to make one.

CHAPTER TWENTY-THREE

# Marie

*July 5, 1883*

I know burns, and they can be dangerous. Sometimes deadly. Thaddeus and I have many scars, but ours are small compared to Kaspar's arm.

I know burns.

I'm not too worried about the red blotches with bleeding edges. It's the larger ones that are white and black and flat. Thaddeus says he will be able to use his arm again.

That is, if he lives through the agony of it.

What will become of him?

Of all my children, Kaspar is the least deserving of his injuries.

*Urszula did not deserve to die.* The thought comes, unbidden and ugly, and I shove it away, clutching little Gerik to my shoulder as I stare over Kaspar's bedside. Is his skin fevered? Should I know if his wounds are infected?

"Is he well?" Kaspar rasps suddenly, his eyes flying open.

"Who? Who is well?" I jerk hard, and Thaddeus sits up from the chair he's been slouching over.

"Hardy. He's the one who pulled me—he didn't get hurt?"

"Hardy?" I glance about the room, as if expecting the apprentice to appear in the gloom. Thaddeus frowns at me and shakes his head. "No, no, he's fine. You're the one who's hurt, my dear boy."

"Oh. That's right."

How can he be so calm? I place my hand over the huge bandages of his right arm, and Kaspar follows my fingers, his eyes going wide. The dark lashes gather tears almost at once, but I don't know if it's pain or something else.

"You were burned at the fire. You don't remember?"

He huffs. "I remember, *Mamo*." He glances at his father. "Is the General saved?"

Thaddeus coughs. "*Tak. Yes.* Just the porch and front window are ruined, mostly. It's salvageable."

"That's good, then." Kaspar leans back into the pillows.

Has he even felt the pain of his injury? Kaspar is not quite so devoted to the craft as Natan, but he still is prideful of his strength and his trade. What will he do if it doesn't heal right? Suppose he is a cripple, just like Franklin Jones?

"Do you feel fine?" I ask, and his eyes flutter open again.

"I'm right enough, just tired," he says, and fades into the pillow, twitching and wincing as he sinks in. When will the pain come? How long before the doctor's medicines fail?

I finally let myself out of the room. I am tired, too. Thaddeus follows me, and then stalks the length of the kitchen. "The doc stopped by earlier."

"Oh yes? You didn't send him in for Kaspar."

"There was no need. The boy was sleeping." Thaddeus finally stops in front of the fire.

Berit looks up from her needlework but leaves us to our discussion. She has been quiet since the fires, her head bent lower and the joy wiped from her wrinkled face. Helena stirs the pot at the hearth, the wooden spoon banging softly against the sides of it.

"So what did the doc want?" I ask, shifting Gerik, and he presses his damp face into my neck, sated yet from his recent feed.

"To figure on what support he has for raising the General out of its ashes. Says we need it, or else it's dealing with Yves from now on."

"And he wants your word?"

Thaddeus shrugs. He pulls out a hefty log from the pile and inspects the bark, absently picking off the larger pieces of it and tossing them into the fire. "I'd be of a mind to do it for the doc, for all he saved you." He sighs and lays two more logs into the fire, sending a spray of sparks up the chimney. Helena puffs her disapproval. "I will not abide more loss."

"You've said yourself death is the way of it here," I remind him, unnerved by his emotional words, unwilling to let the ball of anger and sorrow rise up my throat. "And Kaspar lives."

Death is the way of things.

*Ah. But what about a hanging?*

Bern Masson was no one to me, a face and a name. But he was lynched without a trial or a word. No one gave him a chance.

It was done, so they tell me, on the word of one woman.

What would it be, to have such power? What would one trade to have it?

"It's wishful thinking to think Kaspar'll heal quick, Marya," Thaddeus growls, breaking into my appalled thoughts, and sounding more like himself. "Without his help, we'll have less steady income for a time—Hardy's not even close to Kaspar's skill. I can't put money toward rebuilding the General Store even if the doc asks it. And you—you need to get back to work. Finish all the orders you can."

"Doctor Kinney will struggle to get everyone behind the idea of the General," I tell him. "You're important in town, whether you own it or not. Everyone will follow you."

"I don't know. It's all *gówno shit*. It'd be putting support behind Kate Davies when she's been tight with us on credit."

"You don't need to remind me."

Hardy and Natan walk in from the forge, black to their elbows, and glance around for breakfast. My eyes narrow when I look at the apprentice boy. He's still a stranger, but I am grateful for provenance now more than ever that we should have an apprentice, as it makes Kaspar's injury more manageable.

The worries slam into my gut, but now is not the time to give into the craving in my head, pounding away with the throb of my blood. I pull Gerik tighter, and he grunts and squeaks. Berit gets up, and begins to make breakfast quietly, and I try to help with one hand. I miss Kaspar's willing arms for Gerik, and sigh as I shift the bump of the boy's bum into my other elbow. Natan slides over next to his father as Hardy picks a seat directly across from Helena.

The bread is like dust and glue, and the overnight oats quiver on my plate. Berit has lost her touch today. When I look up at her, though, her eyes look red around the edges, and I wonder how much of the night she lays staring at the wide boards of the wall. Likely she worries over Kaspar like me, but without the exhaustion of the baby to offer fatigue to escape it in the dead of evening. I reach out to grab her hand, the chaffed skin of hers rubbing with the grooves of mine. The crinkle in her brow seems to soften slightly, and a glimmer of her old self lifts the corners of her mouth before she presses my palm.

Thaddeus folds his large frame to the bench and reaches for his plate. He chews carefully, and then looks up at me.

"I have given up much to build my trade here," he says slowly. "I don't want to see it lost if Flats Junction fails. I'll help re-build the doctor's house. Not the General."

There is silence in the kitchen, and my foot aches. I realize I'm pressing against the floorboards, and a knot in the plank has wormed hard under the leather of my shoe last.

"People will talk. They'll say you're siding with him on all things. That we support the doctor and Jane, and think they're doing the right of things. Especially with this black measles going around. Whatever medicine he pushes, he will think you will support that, too."

"You weren't there last night, *moja miłość*. He saved so many. Everyone was impressed. They said anyone would be lucky to have such a doctor, that he was … so many good things. It is like he never chopped off limbs in the first place."

I shake my head. "It won't last. They'll say we're wrong to choose him. The next case of black measles will shut them up. They'll stop coming to us if they think we are friends."

Helena's head comes up and the glint in her eye gives me enough warning to know she'll be contrary. "But you're the only tinsmith for miles, Mother. And the only one with the pressed goods. You can do what you wish, now."

She says it with pride, and I cannot help but feel the same as I look at her and swallow her words with some strange satisfaction. She's right. She's made it so.

"So we'll say we are for the doctor … for now?" I look at Thaddeus. "People will talk and think we change our minds like the wind in our old age."

"I know. Do you wish me to say otherwise?"

"No."

"Well, then."

I rearrange the newborn in my lap, and feel the exhaustion of the night weigh down on my ears and my shoulders. "How will Kaspar manage it? We know burns." I glance up at Thaddeus "But something like this … it will make him go mad."

"Jane said there are teas and medicines that can be used."

"Last night?"

"As I was bringing him home."

"But the doc can't guarantee it will heal well," I say. "Teas? Herbs? Who can believe such a thing can be real medicine? What doctor would say so?"

"I should hope by now you have some trust in his trade."

I hadn't even heard her. The step outside the open back door, letting in the steamy early morning, so fresh the dew is thick and the sunlight still pale pink.

Kate Davies steps into our kitchen unasked, her face blank and her bright, fashionable clothes drowning in soot and ash and black.

"I'm so sorry," she suddenly says, and it's the most broken sound I've ever heard from her, even when I knew her as a young child, going to learn her letters and running home past my tinshop, torn and chased by the others in her school.

Why is she here? What has she to apologize?

I stand and hand the baby to Berit. She takes him absently, cradling his fragile neck in her long fingers.

"If you've come to say so about Helena, it's settled," I say evenly.

Kate spares Helena a look, and it is a gentle one, full of respect and understanding, and it makes me realize I know so little of this woman and my own daughter. I'm always too wrapped up in my feelings and thoughts, lost in my mind and in my metalwork, as if I cling to it and forget all else.

This is how something else can grow and I cannot see it.

Helena smiles slightly at Kate, as if offering support, and I swing my head between the two women as Kate fumbles in her dirty dress, searching for the pocket in the folds. Her eyes are rimmed with purple and sleeplessness, and her hair has completely fallen out.

"I know Helena can manage herself," she says, the old wryness creeping back into her tone. "And I'm glad to hear we can be well on that account."

She finally reaches inside her skirt, and pulls out a large brown bottle, rolling the glass between her palms. My eyes catch the light as it glints off the curved surface, but I'm unable to read the label as she twirls it carefully.

"But this is not for Helena."

Thaddeus clears his throat slightly, and my spine cracks with brittleness. I know what he wants me to do. What I must say.

"I am … your father's kettle …" Anything else catches on my tongue and stings my gums. My teeth feel both sticky and loose, and I realize I cannot apologize as it will be flat.

Kate pauses. Her eyes pierce mine, a pinprick of pain flashing from her to me. And then she nods, once.

Carefully, as if afraid we will scatter, Kate approaches our breakfast, and slowly presses the bottle to the worn, etched wood of the table. It settles with a full, dull, thunk.

She straightens, smiles tentatively, and exits as soundlessly as she came.

When the watery morning light filters through the door again, I can finally see the label, written in blocked print on cream paper.

*Iodine.*

CHAPTER TWENTY-FOUR

*July 5, 1883*

Patrick sits down on the ground and sighs. The lanterns around us flicker and the lights inside them twitch and quiver, and we don't need them anymore, anyway, now that the sun is slowly edging up. I want to rub the heels of my palms into my eyes, but everything is saturated with tears and sweat, mixed with soot, mud, and incessant, mucky blood.

I want to leave the town now, and never come back.

Never had I expected to see a hanging, to see a man's eyes roll and his face turn black and his body release their fluids ...

*Stop! Don't think of such things! Think instead of your world, your life!*

And then I immediately turn cold when I think of our crisped porch.

*Why? Was it truly Bern?*

Did my rejection of him cut so deeply? Did he feel so slighted that I would not wed him?

*Or was someone else?*

Perhaps it was done as a warning? Was it a patient who has not forgiven Patrick for a remedy gone wrong? I cannot believe Bern would be so angry ... but then, I did not know him. Not well enough. And now ... will I never know? And who would tell me, if they knew?

Behind us, the General Store's porch smolders like a disgruntled dragon, but ahead of us is something far worse: a burned entry to our own sanctuary.

We walk home in silence and trepidation as the morning wakes, and the sun peeks through.

I cannot stay awake the whole day. It is impossible.

Mrs. Molhurst sits on her front stoop, staring at our house. How are her old bones still awake? I feel as though I've just done battle. Is this how Patrick suffers every time he comes home from a long day?

Mrs. Molhurst takes one look at me and shakes her head. "You should not have run off in your condition, Mrs. Kinney."

I start, shocked she has finally given me a title and that her voice is tempered with something close to kindness.

He stops completely beside me. It's impossible to look at him. I slip into the proper, ignoring his shock.

"There were many injured," I raise my bloody hands, and then stare at the damaged porch, the memory of it crashing around me again. What will we do now? Fix it, I suppose. What else is there to do?

"You're lucky it were only a bit of a flaming brand on the stairs," she says, echoing my thought. Her beady eyes narrow. "Saw Tom Fawcett brought home on a stretcher. He going to die?"

"No—no." Patrick finds his voice. "Just hit on the head pretty hard. He'll be alright."

"You've visitors, by the by." Mrs. Molhurst juts her chin outward. "Behind you."

Now? Who? I cannot manage entertaining or making a meal over the stove. I feel utterly defenseless.

I spin, and my nerves spike. It's Kate, holding nothing but a small barrel under her arm.

"I need a place to stay. A day or so. Until I know the fire's out and the roof will hold over the back of the General." Her words are clipped. There is no asking. She is demanding.

But I hear the shame in her voice too, and the frustration at needing to even ask for a bed.

"Of course, Kate. Of course," Patrick says at once. "Though … it's not too much of a safe haven here, I'm afraid." He gestures behind us to the destroyed porch.

Kate glances at it and then at the ground. Her lack of acknowledgement of our own misfortune flares inside of me, a twisted, hot anger. And then I am ashamed. Last night she lost so much more.

But her head comes up, and her eyes are unreadable. "Your house. It's burned—it's not—it shouldn't be you, too. No one hates you this much."

"We'll need to go around the back of the kitchen," Patrick says. "I don't trust the porch boards."

The doctor walks next to me, and I cannot read him. Is he reeling with Mrs. Molhurst's revelation? Is he angry? He makes no motion toward me and instead wordlessly enters the kitchen.

I step over the threshold and inhale the smoke that has sunk into the fiber of the wood. The whole house smells like fire: acrid, hot and dark. And under it is the vanilla-green of the sweetgrass, faithfully burned each day.

I can feel Kate behind me and hear her huffing as she carries the barrel of her property in. When Patrick pulls a light out of the stove and stuffs it into the big kitchen lanterns, my first instinct is to run to him and squeeze his middle and sob into his vest.

But Kate is behind me.

And Esther is sitting at the kitchen table. *Safe!*

I give in. My knees and thighs are too exhausted to stay upright, and I grope my way to the bench. The wood feels cold after the heat of the night's blazes, even through my damp layers. Patrick catches my elbow as I ease down, concern rippling across his brow. Behind us, Kate drops the barrel with a vicious thump.

"Mother."

Esther's head jerks up at the title. Her eyes are black, surrounded by bruised circles, and the deep creases of her face are carved with a knife. Anything I could possibly think is at once overshadowed. I have never, nor did I ever expect to hear Kate call Esther by her proper title again. The immediate jealousy ripping through me is unbearable; doubly so because it is unfair and unfounded. It does not matter that I have shared two houses, countless meals, tears, and blood baths with the widow. She is not my mother or my kin. Esther belongs to Kate, and Kate to Esther, and any illusions I have to that notion are made strikingly, outlandishly clear by that one single word.

"*Ciŋkši. Daughter.*" Esther's voice cracks, and her hands splay on the table, wide and worn.

363

"Have you been here the whole time?" Patrick wonders, and I can't tell if he's angry, shocked, or aghast. "Just … watchin' the fire come up into the house?"

She shakes her head slowly, her eyes still on Kate. "No. I was up on the old buffalo jump once the fireworks started. It's the best place to see them, but no one knows that. Besides, sometimes it's best I am out of sight."

"It didn't help, though, did it?" Kate sneers suddenly. "My General still burned."

Patrick rounds on her. "Do you mean to say you're blamin' the fire on Esther? She didn't start the blaze, Kitty!"

"It doesn't matter," she says stoutly, suddenly looking wild and unhinged. "No one wants an Indian in town."

"You're an Indian," I remind her, realizing only after I say it that it's the worst thing I could possibly offer her.

Her eyes go to ice and her fists curl. "Damn you, Jane," she says.

"Kate!" Patrick barks. "That is my wife!"

Rising unsteadily, feeling the reassuring twist of the babe in my womb, I turn to face her. "You are, Kate, and there's no denying it. How do you know it was your mother who was the target of this violence? Why else start fire to the General? It's nothing to do with Esther! Someone wants *you* gone—*you* ruined."

"I'm not ruined," she says quickly, and then flushes and stares at the floor, chewing on the inside of her cheeks.

"What?"

She kicks the barrel at her feet with a hard tap of her boot. "Well, the money isn't going to get stolen anyway. Others … I need it."

I want to slap her. It's the first reaction I have, and yet I'm too tired to do it.

"There's only the one bed," Patrick says evenly. "You and your mother will have to share."

Kate glares at him suddenly, a look filled with hurt and disappointment and frustration, and it's too much.

"Damn *you*, Kate!" I say, my voice as hard as my heart suddenly. "You won't stay here if you can't make room for Esther. You can sleep outside tonight!"

Her mouth goes slack and Patrick looks appalled.

My fists mash into my skirts, and I pull on the fabric to keep my fingers from shaking or from picking up a fork and flinging it.

"You owe it to me," she says, and her voice is like knives. "*You owe me.*"

"For what?" My voice burns my throat, harsh and thick, and it's no use. The fork is suddenly in my palm, and then shooting toward the opposite wall. The clatter as it hits is flat and tinny. "For *what?*—other than—"

"Marrying him!" Kate points, her own finger shivering. "For seducing the only man who ever looked at me, whoever cared to court me—"

"You mean to despise me forever, then?" I ask, taking a step closer. "Our friendship is gone, and you'll never forgive me?"

Patrick is frozen next to the lantern and Esther looks cut from stone.

Kate fumbles with the edges of her blouse, casting about the room for someone to agree with her, but we are each stuck in our own circle, framed within the argument long overdue. "Were we ever friends?" she asks.

The question burns. "I thought we were."

"I don't want your notion of friendship," she lashes. "Not if it means stealing a woman's man. Taking away her only chance at love."

"I didn't love you, Kate," Patrick says in a steady, clam tone. "Not like that. Not in the way—"

Though I appreciate the words they only add to the fire between her and me.

She puts her hands over her ears and shuts her eyes briefly. "So it's doubly cruel, then? You mean to say you played me false? What was I, some distraction? A way to make Jane jealous?"

"No," his voice falters, "not as you think. You were—"

"Your first lover!" she shouts. Her cheeks are red, and her eyes are sunken. The air in the room disappears.

I feel as though I'm drowning. It is as though I have turned, and instead of finding the ocean or the prairie, my face has smashed into the solidness of a wall.

*What did she say?*

It is impossible, and yet so very, very obvious.

Patrick's face has gone slack, and for the first time he looks old. The lines along his mouth and eyebrows are deep folds, the day-old stubble is haggard and rough, and his entire body seems to lose its very heartbeat.

Kate looks between us while triumph and pain war on her face. "It's true," she says again. "Patrick had me well before you ever came to town, Jane. And even though it's been years ... I'm still the first one. We pledged. You remember, Pat? You said I was the woman you'd—"

"Enough!" he says tersely, his hand waving once, then dropping down, as if the weight of it is too much for his shoulders. "It was long ago."

My fingers find the edge of the table, but my elbow can barely keep me from sliding onto the floor. The other hand trails over the small curve of my womb, just visible when the fabric is pulled, and Patrick's eyes follow the movement. I rest my hand there, defiant. Let him know, then, the way of it. Kate hasn't noticed, though. She is still staring at the doctor, as if willing him to refute her. Next to me, Esther grips the tabletop so hard her knuckles are fully white against the nutmeg of her skin.

"Long ago, but it was ... it wasn't supposed to be like this," she grinds out. "Jane came and ruined the possibilities."

"I told him to court you, Kate," I remind her slowly, feeling responsible, guilty, and yet angry at the same time, a strange, outlandish combination that bites and stings and aches. "I didn't know it would all end this way. I didn't know how ... how you felt about one another."

It is the worst of it. I'd so carefully allowed myself to explore my own personality after coming West. To be curious. To be loved and to love, after my first chilly marriage and the brief affair that followed ... it was my greatest luxury. To know it may not be what it seems is both vindicating and destructive.

Am I once again with child by a man who won't keep me?

The room is spinning, so I sit carefully next to Esther. The one lantern seems to ebb and pop, and my vision goes foggy on the edges as the morning creeps into the kitchen.

"I'm married now, Kate," Patrick says slowly, and his voice seems far away. "We had differences. Too many that mattered."

"My skin?" she hisses.

"You know it's not that," he says, suddenly furious. "It's never been that."

"Oh, is that so?" She tosses her hair, completely down and out of pins. It is a black river down her back, and still as glossy as a bird's wing. "Could have fooled me."

"So Kate," I interrupt, unable to sit still, unable to care. "Are you going to stay here, under the roof of your old lover and with your mother, or will you take the garden?" I hope to close the discussion, unable to listen to what feels to be the start of a lover's old quarrel. The acid in my tone is enough to scorch the rest of the walls.

Her lips go white against the dark skin, and in a moment there is a fast, heavy glimmer of tears in the black eyes. Whirling, she marches up the stairs, the stomps reverberating so heavily that the lantern jumps on the kitchen table.

Esther stands too. "I will share a bed with my daughter tonight, but I think I will leave then. You almost lost your house, Pat. I won't put you and Jane and your children in danger."

How can she just ignore the fact that Kate and Patrick have shattered my world? How can she be so calm at all times? I want to press myself to her bosom for comfort as I once did, but it's more impossible now than ever before.

"You're not leavin'," Patrick protests. "I won't have it."

"You stay for us," I say. "We asked you to come to Flats Junction, pulled you away from your kin to be in this town. You stay as our family, and damn what others might think!"

And finally … *finally* I can say the words without an ounce of fear as I do. For the first time, I completely mean it. I don't care if people shun me because I'd feed Esther and give her a place to live. I don't care how proper it is, or how uncomfortable it might make some of the ladies. Esther is my mother here. She is the family I've formed. And though I know Kate is Esther's flesh and blood and her last tie to Percy, I love Esther fiercely and deeply and fully as if she was mine as well.

She doesn't say more, and I have no idea what she's decided, but when she rises I move to embrace her and she lets me before she, too, disappears up the stairs.

I turn to look at Patrick, but he's peering into Kate's barrel. His prying is out of character, but then I see the blood still crusted under his nails and drying on his knees, and the smell of the burned porch drifts into my nose and I think perhaps everyone is allowed to be a little unusual for a bit. He's certainly doing his best not to look at me, and frankly I don't know what I'll say to him in this moment.

How do we recover from these hours, and these revelations?

*I don't know if I can speak to him.*

I'd much rather take the biggest cast iron skillet and smash it about, destroying the pottery bowls and flattening every tin cup. It would feel better to tear apart my clothes, to burn the bucket of the well, to rip the drapes off the windows. If there were a moment for me to do some sort of violence, I would, but as it is, I'm simply rooted.

Have I lost my own fire?

"It's a small fortune in here," he says into Kate's barrel, so softly it's nearly a whisper. "No wonder Kate's not entirely broken up about the General. She's not poor, at least. And her own back rooms are safe at the General. The fire didn't go near as far."

He sighs and heads down the hallway. Following Patrick into the surgery, I start to pour water over my hands and scrub while he pulls out the bloodied instruments.

"We'll clean everything now," I say, sticking to the mundane, surprised I bother to speak. Anything professional or clinical will save us from the boiling emotions hanging just below the surface of any word.

He nods, his head down. "Doesn't do to let them rust. We can't afford new ones. It won't take long, and then we can go up and change into fresh clothes …" He's lost in the care of the tools.

I pull off my soiled top petticoat and wonder how I'll get the bloodstains out of my sleeves. Well, there's laundry tomorrow I suppose, and there will be more to do in terms of fixing the house. I must think of these small things or lose the control I've pulled together.

The burned porch sears into my mind in a way that is too big to fully comprehend. Who would do it? Was it done to scare us? To hurt? I don't understand it and wonder if I will feel safe at all tonight.

Likely not.

Likely not for a long time.

I bring Patrick the extra kitchen lantern and watch him scour the tools with salt and a bit of carbolic acid, and then I dry them.

"First the black measles, then the fires. It's never dull," he says, almost rueful.

I grab at the words. "There haven't been any new cases."

"I know," he says, and sighs deeply. "But it'll be back. I have a feelin' there's a cycle, just I haven't been able to crack it. I'll figure on it, and with you here to help, we'll settle on somethin'. We have to."

When he's finished with the instruments, he washes up too, and looks at his pants with a soft huff.

"I'm sorry they're so banged up, Jane," he says. "It's more work for you."

"I don't care right now."

He glances at me sharply, hearing the note of panic under my voice.

I can't hide it, and I'm shaking so much I don't think I can manage the stairs up to the bedroom.

"Jesus, Mary, and Joseph," he says roughly. When he reaches for my arm, I jerk away, and a flash of something hard flares in his eyes. "It's not right, the way you've heard—"

"You were *lovers*?" I repeat, daring him to deny it. "When? For how long? I thought you said … you told me you were nervous for our wedding! You *liar*!"

His temper leaps. "And you've always been so truthful to me? You cannot point at the black kettle without includin' the black pot."

"Damn you!" My voice rises, and my hand goes, too. The fury punches through the fibers of my arm, just like when I take a skillet to a mouse's crunchy body. I aim to hurt. The sound of the slap is raw and deep and meaty. "I told you I loved you," I say, resignation filling my bones along with the fatigue, my hand dropping. "You were the only one." How is it a memory feels like a betrayal?

"I *was*?" he presses, ignoring the bloom of my hand-print along his jaw. "You'll give up so easily? I couldn't have expected that of you. Not my curious wife, with the mind that wants answers. Hear me out, at least."

I want to listen, to believe him. It is only the enormity of climbing the stairs that keeps me from walking away. If I don't go up to the bedroom, where else will I go? "You want me to believe what you say?"

"I've never lied about Kate," he says. "I just simply never told you. Same as you. You never told me the truths of your own trysts."

"But you knew it all well before you married me," I point out, finally meeting his blue eyes and then flinching from the earnestness in them.

"Be as it may," he sighs, then leans his knuckles on the laboratory's surgery bed. "It didn't seem relevant to what I felt ... after you ..." He pauses and glances up at my face, then his shoulders slump and his voice quiets further. "It was when I lived with her parents. Percy and Esther would go at times to see the Sioux when they came to town. Kate and I ... we had moments between us, and there were times, much later, when those moments got the best of me. I'm not denyin' it, and I won't say I didn't think the world of her then. I was young. And untried. But time ... well, I didn't have much to offer her at the first, and then her father passed and I thought she'd want to work at buildin' up the General. My auntie was ill and took time I might have used for courtin'. And then you came, and other things came to light. My tolerance, and her lack of it. Your mind matching mine. It was easy to understand, I didn't even need science or logic. I'm home with *you*, Jane. I still am."

I stare at him and try to take in a breath, but it wavers as it comes in. "And that's all."

"It's all there is, in short."

"You pledged to her."

"In the way a young man does in the throes of passion."

"You played her false, then."

He closes his eyes and stands up straight. "Not on purpose. I have always felt a kinship with Kate, Jane. I still do. I tried to court her, to overlook our different philosophies. I cannot. What do you want me to say? It was six years ago."

"Six years," I echo, then turn away, so he doesn't see the well of tears pressing into the corners of my eyes. I lean on the door jamb as I make my way to the narrow stairs. He still needs to put away the rest of his instruments, but he is quick and my pace is slow, so I am just to the top of the stairs when he comes up behind me.

"Jane."

"It's enough you've told me," I whisper at him. "I perhaps just don't want to think of you in the bed of any other woman."

"Aye, I don't blame you that, but Jane—"

"We've more to worry on now," I say, just to put him at bay, bending my head toward the dim grey morning light in our bedroom. "I need to get out of my sodden layers."

"Jane!"

"What? Hush! They need a few hours of sleep, and you'll keep them awake!" I nod toward the closed door of the spare room.

He grabs and kisses me at the exact same time, slamming the bedroom door. The motion is a whirlwind and a flurry of gripping fingers and gasps. The kiss is hard and fast and strong, and when he stops he bends and presses his forehead to mine. Through the fabric of my skirts and blouse, I can sense the tremble that runs through his arms. Or is it me trembling?

"What was that for?" I want to stay angry and frustrated and hurt, but it's hard to do so after a kiss like that.

"What do you think?" he manages, his voice going lower than usual and hoarse.

"Well I—"

"You're carryin' my child! Good God, woman. How can I not be happy with such news?"

His words catch me completely, radiating out of my ribs and through my skin. He takes my momentary silence in stride, kissing me again briefly and then giving me a small shake.

"How long have you known?"

"Not long," I confess. I am bewildered and uncertain of my footing, shocked we can be discussing this news after the other revelations and tragedy. It is disjointed and disconcerting.

"But why didn't you tell me from the first?"

"Well, I wanted to be sure." That, at least, is the truth.

"I am a doctor. How else to be sure than to ask me?"

"I ..." There is no good reason for keeping my health to myself, other than I didn't have what I thought to be the proper words. What could I say, if I had the chance to try the announcement again? Damn Emma Molhurst and her wicked observations. I still don't have the words.

"Jane, there's no reason for us to keep secrets. Not now," he says, his voice reasonable but a little gruff.

"No secrets," I agree, feeling the rough rawness of his latest secret tear into my heart. Will there ever be any more left to keep after today? We have been broken, burned, and tested, the both of us. To imagine more pain between us seems inconceivable. We will come out alright.

We must.

His unshakable confidence is a comfort in itself, and I allow myself to pretend, if only for a moment, that there was no fire on our porch, that he is not reviled by half the town, that we can work miracles.

If I cannot trust in the man who wears my skin, who is the other half of my life, why did I bind myself to him?

There is strength in who we are, together. It will only take time to learn it.

And for now, time is what I have to give.

## CHAPTER TWENTY-FIVE

# *Kate*

*August 24, 1883*

The heat is unbearable. I'd forgotten the weight of it after the winter, just like I always do. It is heavy and shallow, and makes my breath feel short and tight against the ashboard and double sewing of my stays.

Late summer is dry and brittle and the hardness of the road is only good for completely drying out the horse, pig and ox dung mixing with the mud.

The rings of hammers in the late afternoon echo and slam into one another as half the town rallies behind the fixing of my General and Patrick's house.

There are those who refuse to work on the General, for all they pitch in to help with the doctor's place. I've heard enough snippets and can piece together what is gossip and what is truth. And if that is not enough, it's clear what people think based on who works where and where money comes from. I would have thought it obvious how important the General Store is. How much *I* am needed. How much my power can extend.

I refuse to think how I have used it so far …

Yves and his posse have taken to half-running the town, which sets my teeth on edge and makes the back of my mouth feel sour. He sells the goods he brought to Flats Junction for me. His posse pulled everything sellable out of the store as soon as Mikey said the boards were sound enough to hold a man's weight.

And as much as I complained, no one backed me again.

They're going to Yves for the goods until the General is restored and safe, and I know my partnership with him and the posse is tight and delicate and as fine as a thread.

When I look at the yellowed walls of the tent they've raised outside the old cooperage, my whole body feels like puddling. Sadie got the deed to me, as sure fast as she promised, and now is spending far too much time helping Helena set up the dressmaking store. But it's money spent—always money spent, and nothing coming into my coffers yet.

Please all that's revered that I've placed my bets just right. That my plans will still work.

I want to fall into hysterics and lash at everyone. Yves doesn't seem to care of my issues. And why would he? He gets what he wants and how. He continues to promise to repay me later. Always later. This said with the glint of the knives in his belt. It's not exactly how I'd hoped to use the posse this summer. They were supposed to keep me in power. Not continue to ruin me.

Nothing is exactly as it should be.

But I can't deny that the future finally looks clearer than ever it's been, which is saying something at least.

I used to think Percy Davies would make a deal with the devil himself to make his schemes work, but I'm starting to think my father was the devil, and everyone jigged to his tune. I don't know if I've quite figured out the dance.

And I sure don't want to be the devil.

I stalk outside to see the progress on the General, trying to feel hopeful as I do. Even though there are many able-bodied men sawing and sanding and hammering, it's not like a barn raising, with the whole town pulling together at once to finish in a day.

No, instead I'm given snippets of time and small hiccups of cash. The doctor's place is fixing up faster than mine, and that grinds on me sometimes fiercer than I like.

Clara Henderssen wanders up to the construction and peers through the sawdust. I wave at her and she lights up. "Any coffee beans yet, by chance?" she calls out.

"Soon. Train hasn't brought my order yet," I say.

"Oh." She sinks a bit. "I suppose I'll check with Yves's shop."

She has to, I know, but I wish she wouldn't. He doesn't need encouragement. Yet I need him, now, as strange as it be.

"No coffee, is it? May as well do up a sign, Kitty," Horeb yells from his creaking perch on a half-charred beam in the front yard.

"Who reads?" That's Gilroy, shifting in his own seat.

"It'd be a favor to me," Horeb reasons, "so as I don't have to hear the same conversation here all day of the folk coming in for the beans."

The General is crumbling. I think of this as I survey the damage, taking in the damp rotting of the old porch boards and the acid of old smoke still hanging in the air. There is much work to do to fix the place back up.

I hadn't expected so much damage. And Jane's house. That was never to be part of it.

When I think such things, I can almost shake the guilt about him …

I can almost forget how he looked, hanging …

Crunching through the debris to the front of the yard, I survey the ongoing board game. Horeb and Gilroy staunchly pretend they are still under the shade of the General's porch. Now they both wear broad hats against the sun, but they've carved out a flat space between them and have stones for their checkers.

"Goddamn it, Gil, you're cheating again!" Horeb howls as they rock back and forth.

"Ain't!"

"You are! I seen you move that stone over when I was spitting. You cheated!"

"Ain't."

"You goddamn—what do you need, Kitty?" Horeb stops his prepared litany of cursing when he finally notices I've walked nearer. "Need us to clear out the extra menfolk for you?"

"Extra menfolk?"

Horeb's pointy chin angles toward the General, and I turn to gaze up to the porch roof. The black mountain on the top unwinds and climbs down. Who? And then the sun reflects the gold of Matthias Hummel's scalp. What the hell is he doing here? Has Yves sent him again? They were just picking through my goods this morning!

Moses walks across the half-finished porch and lays down a plank. I frown at them all, feeling as though a cloud is constantly over my brow. This is what I wanted. Help. Recognition. So why does all the attention make my skin itch?

When I turn back to Horeb, he's smirking so hard I'm sure his cheeks are sore. "Plenty of young'uns here to help you, Kitty. Take your pick."

"Take my—"

"Where you wantin' extra lumber?" Mikey O'Donnell near catches my shoulder with his load as he spins, and I jerk backward, my heel catching on the pile of charred planks, twisting my knee uncomfortably as I land in one of the larger piles of black ash and crumbling wood.

"Woah, Kitty!" Horeb leans forward as if to help, but his eyes are at my legs and he angles his head as if hoping for a glimpse of my knee. Gil starts to get up, but his hacking cough stops him short, and he bends over heavily.

"You are goot?"

The late yellow sunlight is blocked as shadows crowd over me, and I stare up at the stoic lines of Matthias's face. Behind him, Wang Chen bobs on the edges of his toes, trying to see over Matthias's broad back.

Mikey lays his lumber down carefully, inching toward me with his hands up. "Sorry, Kate," he says.

"It's just fine," I tell him as Matthias takes my elbow and hauls me to my feet, near lifting me off them in the process. I don't want to know how blackened my backside is and refuse to even look in Horeb's direction as I face all the men milling about, waiting for ... anything ... from me. Each seems to have his own hopes, expectations, and desires. Each of them offers something and nothing, but there is a strangeness in my chest cavity when I look at them all together. I cannot put a name to the feeling.

"You hurt, as it were?" Moses asks.

"I'm just fine," I repeat, waving my hands at each of them. Mikey looks relieved, and immediately heads back to Lara and his lumberyard. Wang backs up, nearly running into old little Shen as he hops onto his massive pig and whacks her like a horse. The wizened man's cackling fades as he jabbers off toward Soup's Corner. In a moment, there's more scuffing and a peck of a hammer from the Kinney's house. Against the gold of the western sun, I can make out who is working on their roof: Thaddeus and Mitch, Hardy and Tim and Patrick himself.

My own roof is shaping up. Tommy Winters hands up nails to Wang when he climbs back up, and Noah takes a saw to some of the new lumber.

Moses moves to help Noah with the saws though every move he makes seems to speak to me in a language I push against. Matthias fills up more space than any man has a right to, and I'm glad when he joins the others on the roof.

It may not be all what I had expected, but maybe it's better. I'll do my best to make it better.

Flats Junction hangs in the belly of a truce. I can feel it. Like all things, a truce is only temporary, but it is a rest all the same.

And there is a chance, during that quiet, that the real roots can be forged, and it will last until it becomes an understanding. And from there, perhaps contentment. And while contentment is fleeting, it is worth reaching and grasping and holding close.

And then I know, suddenly, what the feeling is inside my lungs. It is comfort. A sense of belonging. Of being.

Acceptance.

It is a glow, deep inside, and I suppose it could be called joy. It's an unusual feeling, and I try to grasp at it, holding it tightly so I might always feel weightless and free like I do right now.

But it is not so real a thing. Freedom from the reality of this world is not for me and those like me. I'm two things, and somehow that makes me nothing at all.

And so the surety and solidness fade, ebbing away with each breath I take, riding toward the empty land over the grasses of the prairie where it sighs and whispers and flees.

*The End*

# Historical Note

In the early 1880s, especially in the west, doctors were still not always considered to be the be-all and end-all of advice, and were certainly not considered a necessary staple when it came to injuries and illness and childbirth. The modern notion of sanitation and disease was still not an acceptable practice in all corners of America, and doctors would have often been ignored in preference for home remedies or because of the cost to bring in a physician. Having a doctor present during labor was more likely in the event there were no midwives available, but it would have still been considered by some to be unnecessary, expensive and, in some cases, the husbands themselves did not always put stock in their wives needing help.

However, childbirth was indeed one of the biggest killers of women in the west, and the many horrors that could happen after giving birth—starting in a woman's teens and sometimes going all the way into her forties—were whispered amongst each other. Jane's worry of breast abscesses, hemorrhages, venial clotting and prolapsed uteruses were common, as was milk, or "childbed" fever, which usually resulted in death.

Diphtheria's inoculation was not available yet—1883 was the year the bacterium causing it was identified, but it would not be well-known immediately and a vaccine not available for decades. The techniques Doc Kinney describes as Native methods for dealing with the disease, as well as his own attempt to cure Urszula, are all documented.

All the medicines and tools Doctor Patrick Kinney uses in *Outcast 1883* are period appropriate, though 1883 was almost a decade before the medical community learned the difference between regular German measles and black measles. In fact, while today we have a vaccination for the typical measles virus, black measles is still around, with cases randomly reported around America. Without doxycycline treatment in the first few days, a patient has a 20 – 30% chance of death. Before antibiotics, doctors would expect a 75% fatality rate. During Jane and Patrick's time, the cause for black measles was not yet known, which created all the more mystery why one person could get it, and no one else would become ill—the disease did not act like typical, airborne measles. Why? There's only one way to get black measles. You must be bitten by an infected tick. Tick-borne illness was not yet discovered. Today, however, we know black measles by another name: Rocky Mountain Spotted Fever.

While *Outcast 1883* only touches on black measles, it will become a greater piece of the puzzle in Flats Junction as the years roll forward.

The tools and methods Marie uses in her tin and copper shop are all period and trade correct, as are the items available for sale in Kate's General Store.

Some of the other quirks are indeed true to the time, such as the Irish folk remedy for male virility, the battles fought by Moses's regiments in the Civil War and the fact that most Pullman cars had exclusively Black porters. And while most of the characters in this book are fictional, the world in which they lived, the prejudices, intolerances, celebrations, and hard-won respect, are as real today as they were in 1883.

With joy—Sara Dahmen
*during a pandemic*, Wisconsin

# Author's Note and Thanks

The irony of some of the themes in *Outcast 1883* is not lost on me. I wrote the very first draft of this novel in summer of 2017, years before the coronavirus disease (COVID-19) pandemic hit the world. I felt a bit of a fortune teller. But one person cannot predict such a wild thing. I debated changing the entire book. Would it be too soon? Too on the nose? The world has changed so drastically—and not just in the sense that we are shouldering that pandemic. Social justice has upended much of how we talk about certain topics. Should I start over? Change everything?

But I believe there is value looking back, and if we're able to really look, we can see the repetition of patterns, and how they don't really change. Things ebb and flow, but so many issues we feel in today's modern world are echoes of the same words from centuries past. If we are reminded enough, in many ways, maybe we will be able to change—whether that is how we see and support one another as humans or how we battle something like disease or our economies.

In the end, I just like writing to entertain. I hope this has entertained a little.

And such entertainment would not be possible without my intrepid publishing house. Ben Coles, thank you for letting me be part of the Promontory family and going along for all my very wild rides, including this one. Thank you, Craig Anderson, for reading and re-reading this manuscript and helping me build it from "the weakest thing you've written" to "the best thing you've written". I must thank master tin-smith Bob Bartelme, who always answers my questions about cramp seams on copper sheet metal, Summer White Eagle for reading the manuscript early on and supporting me and all of Flats Junction, and to my manager, Noah, for guiding me around all the insanity in the intellectual property world.

I'm grateful for all my beloved friends and family—those who are blood and those who I have chosen—who have waited years for the next novel.

And I must also thank my wonderful husband for reminding me that writing is an actual day job, for picking up the kids from school so I can zoom thousands of words a day to hit deadlines, and for looking at me with love in his eyes even after twenty years together. Now *that* ... that is enough!

# Bibliography

American Chemical Society. (2015). *Mosquito-repelling chemicals identified in traditional sweetgrass* [Press release]. Retrieved from https://www.eurekalert.org/pub_releases/2015-08/acs-mci071615.php

Bealer, Alex W. *The Tools that Built America*. Bonanza Books, New York; 1976

Gilmore, Melvin Randolph. *Uses of Plants by the Indians of the Missouri River Region*, in Thirty-Third Annual Report of the Bureau of American Ethnology to the Secretary of the Smithsonian Institution 1911 – 1912. Government Printing Office, Washington DC; 1919

Halpern, Monica. *Railroad Fever: Building the Transcontinental Railroad 1830 – 1870*. National Geographic Society, Washington DC; 2004

Hertzler, Arthur. *The Horse and Buggy Doctor*. Harper & Brothers, New York; 1938

Johmann, Carol A., and Elizabeth J. Rieth. *Going West!: Journey On A Wagon Train to Settle a Frontier Town*. Williamson Publishing, Charlotte VT; 2000

Jones, Constance. *Trailblazers: The Men and Women Who Forged the West*. MetroBooks, New York; 1995

Josephson, Judith Pinkerton. *Growing Up in Pioneer America 1800 – 1890*. Lerner Publications Company, Minneapolis; 2002

Kauffman, Henry J. *American Copper & Brass*. Masthof Press, Morgantown, PA; 1995

Luchetti, Cathy. *Children of the West: Family Life on the Frontier*. W.W. Norton & Company, New York; 2001

Moger, Susan. *Pioneers*. Scholastic Professional Books, New York; 2001

Nevin, Alfred. *The Presbyterian Encyclopedia*. Presbyterian Encyclopedia Publishing Company, Philadelphia PA;1884

Pickover, Clifford A. *The Medical Book: From Witch Doctors to Robot Surgeons; 250 Milestones in the History of Medicine*. Sterling Publishing, New York; 2012

Sioux, Tracee. *Immigrants and Westward Expansion*. Rosen Publishing Group Inc., New York; 2004

Sloane, Eric. *The Seasons of America Past*. Dover Publications, Inc., Mineola NY; 2005

Steele, Volney. *Bleed, Blister and Purge: A History of Medicine on the American Frontier*. Mountain Press Publishing Company, Missoula, MT; 2005

White Hat, Albert Sr. *Reading and Writing the Lakota Language*. The University of Utah Press, Salt Lake City UT; 1999

Wilbur, C. Keith. *Antique Medical Instruments*. Shiffer Publishing Ltd., West Chester, PA; 1987

# Language Glossary

**POLISH**

*Babcia – grandmother*

*bądź silny – be strong*

*Bardzo przepraszam! – So sorry!*

*córka – daughter*

*gówno – shit*

*kurczaki – chickens*

*Mamo – Mom*

*moja miłość – my love*

*moje serce – my heart*

*Nie jestem wystarczający! – I am not enough!*

*niebezpieczny – dangerous*

*Niech cię - Let you*

*piekło! – Oh hell!*

*pieprzyć cię! – fuck you!*

*pieprzyć to – fuck it*

*Pierdolić – Fuck!*

*Potępienie! Damnation!*

*Psiakrew, nie! – Hell, no!*

*skurwysyn – bastards*

*tak – yes*

*udać się – go*

**NORWEGIAN**

*Honning – honey*

**LAKOTA**

*Šúŋkawakȟą hįpáȟpa wi – the month when ponies shed*

*Wačháŋǧa – sweetgrass*

*Čhiŋkši – daughter*

**FRENCH**

*ma chérie – my dear*

*oui – yes*

**GERMAN**

*Leck mich am Arsch! – Kiss my ass!"*

*Nein – no*

**GAELIC**

*cén áit? – where?*

# The Flats Junction Series

*Tinsmith 1865*
*Medicineman 1876*
*Widow 1881*
*Outcast 1883*
*Trader 1884*
*Stranger 1886*

For more information,
visit www.flatsjunction.com.

To connect with Sara,
visit www.saradahmen.com.
Find her on Twitter at @saradahmenbooks,
on Facebook, or Instagram at @housecopper.

To learn about Sara's cookware line
inspired by her research for Flats Junction,
visit www.housecopper.com.

Printed in the USA
CPSIA information can be obtained
at www.ICGtesting.com
LVHW062316220524
781161LV00042B/1607